STAR TREK

BOLDLY GO

written by
Mike Johnson

art by
Tony Shasteen

issue #6 written with
Ryan Parrott

issue #6 art by
Chris Mooneyham

Special thanks to Risa Kessler and John Van Citters of CBS Consumer Products for their invaluable assistance.

For international rights, contact **licensing@idwpublishing.com**

ISBN:978-1-63140-923-3

20 19 18 17 1 2 3 4

IDW®
www.IDWPUBLISHING.com

Ted Adams, CEO & Publisher • **Greg Goldstein**, President & COO • **Robbie Robbins**, EVP/Sr. Graphic Artist • **Chris Ryall**, Chief Creative Officer • **David Hedgecock**, Editor-in-Chief • **Laurie Windrow**, Senior Vice President of Sales & Marketing • **Matthew Ruzicka**, CPA, Chief Financial Officer • **Lorelei Bunjes**, VP of Digital Services • **Jerry Bennington**, VP of New Product Development

Facebook: **facebook.com/idwpublishing** • Twitter: **@idwpublishing** • YouTube: **youtube.com/idwpublishing**
Tumblr: **tumblr.idwpublishing.com** • Instagram: **instagram.com/idwpublishing**

Originally published as STAR TREK: BOLDLY GO issues #1–6.

colors by
Davide Mastrolonardo

issue #6 colors by
J.D. Mettler

letters by
AndWorld Design

series edits by
**Sarah Gaydos
& Chris Cerasi**

collection edits by
**Justin Eisinger
& Alonzo Simon**

collection design by
Shawn Lee

cover by
George Caltsoudas

publisher
Ted Adams

star trek created by
Gene Roddenberry

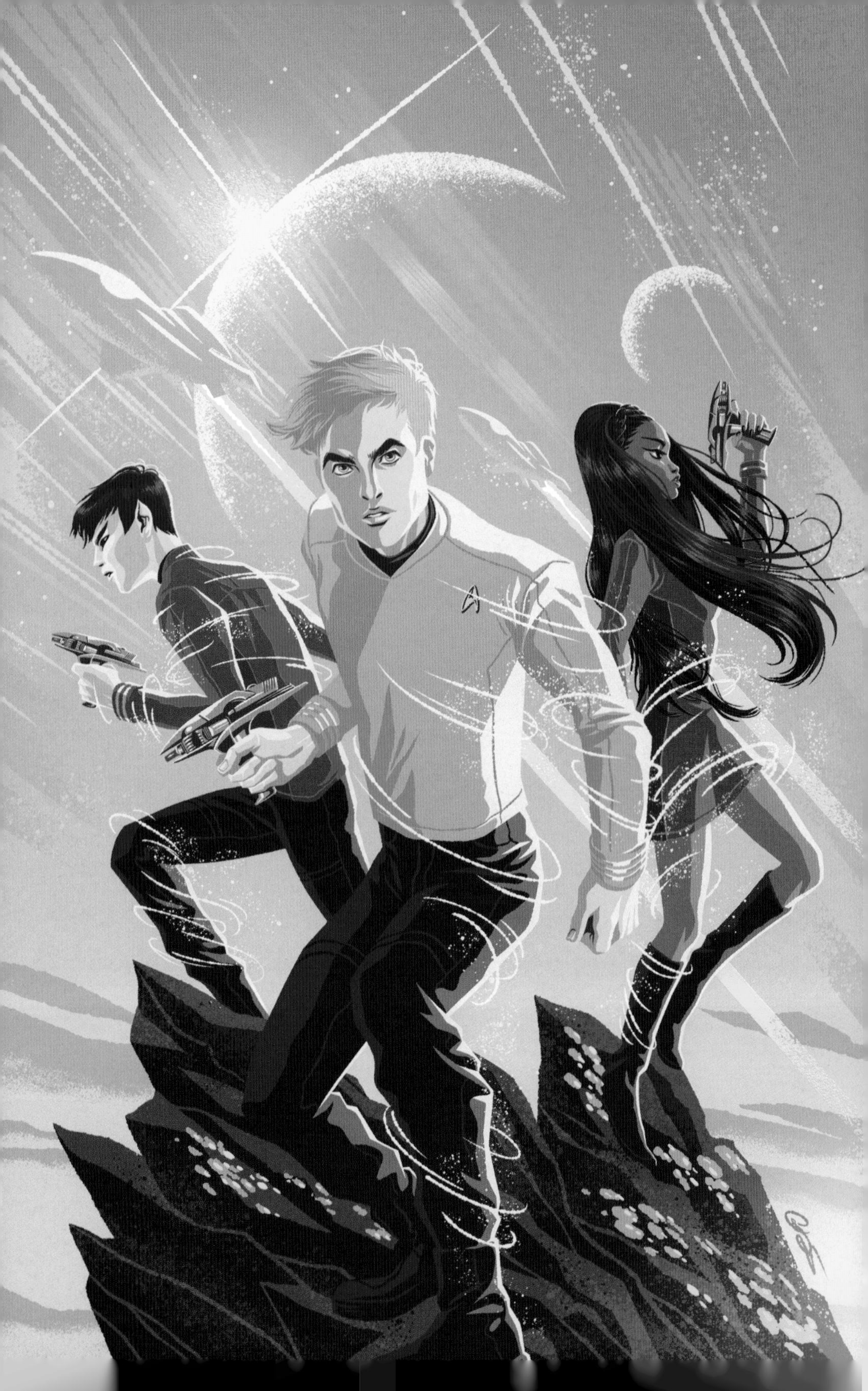

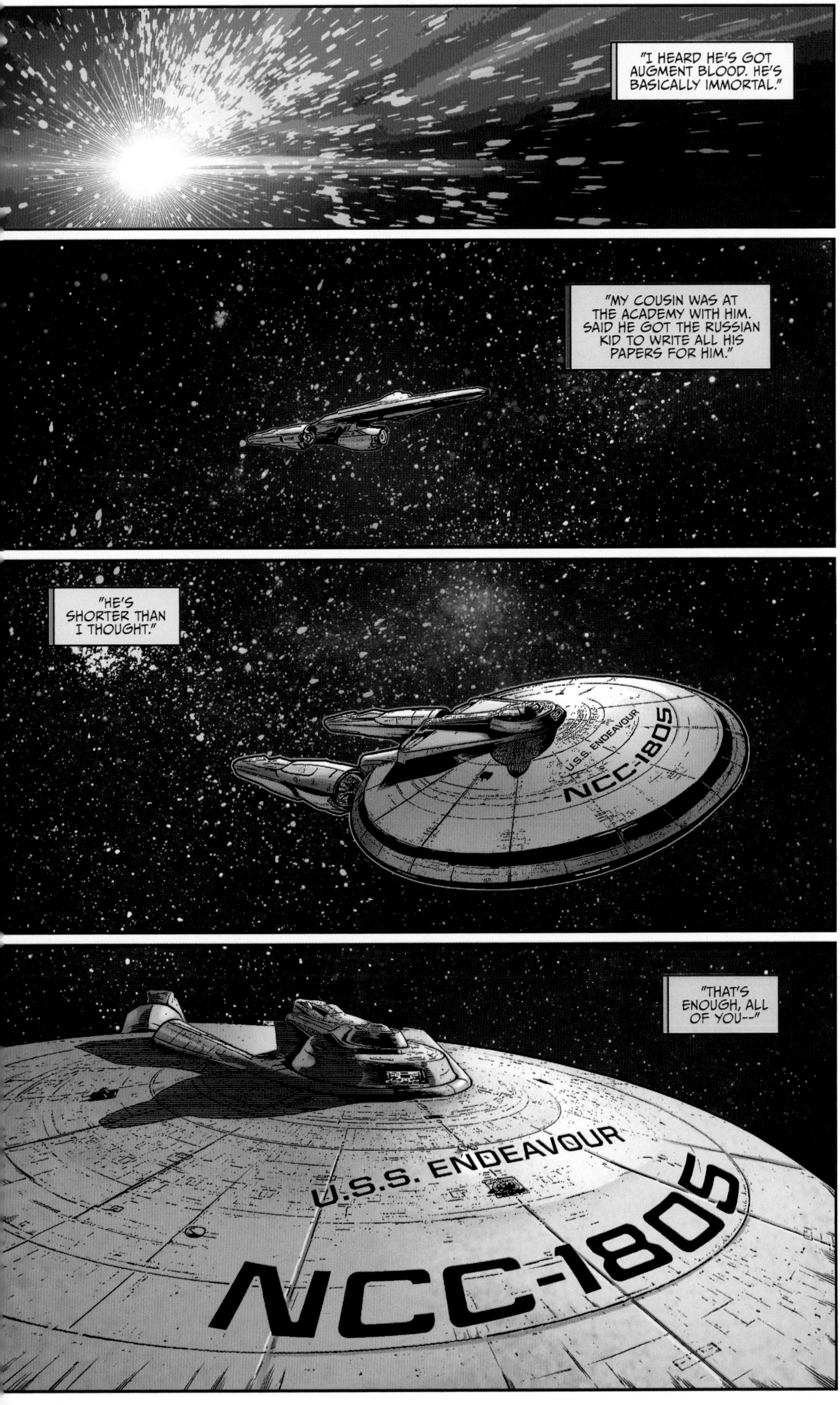
"I HEARD HE'S GOT AUGMENT BLOOD. HE'S BASICALLY IMMORTAL."
"MY COUSIN WAS AT THE ACADEMY WITH HIM. SAID HE GOT THE RUSSIAN KID TO WRITE ALL HIS PAPERS FOR HIM."
"HE'S SHORTER THAN I THOUGHT."
U.S.S. ENDEAVOUR
NCC-1805
"THAT'S ENOUGH, ALL OF YOU--"
U.S.S. ENDEAVOUR
NCC-1805

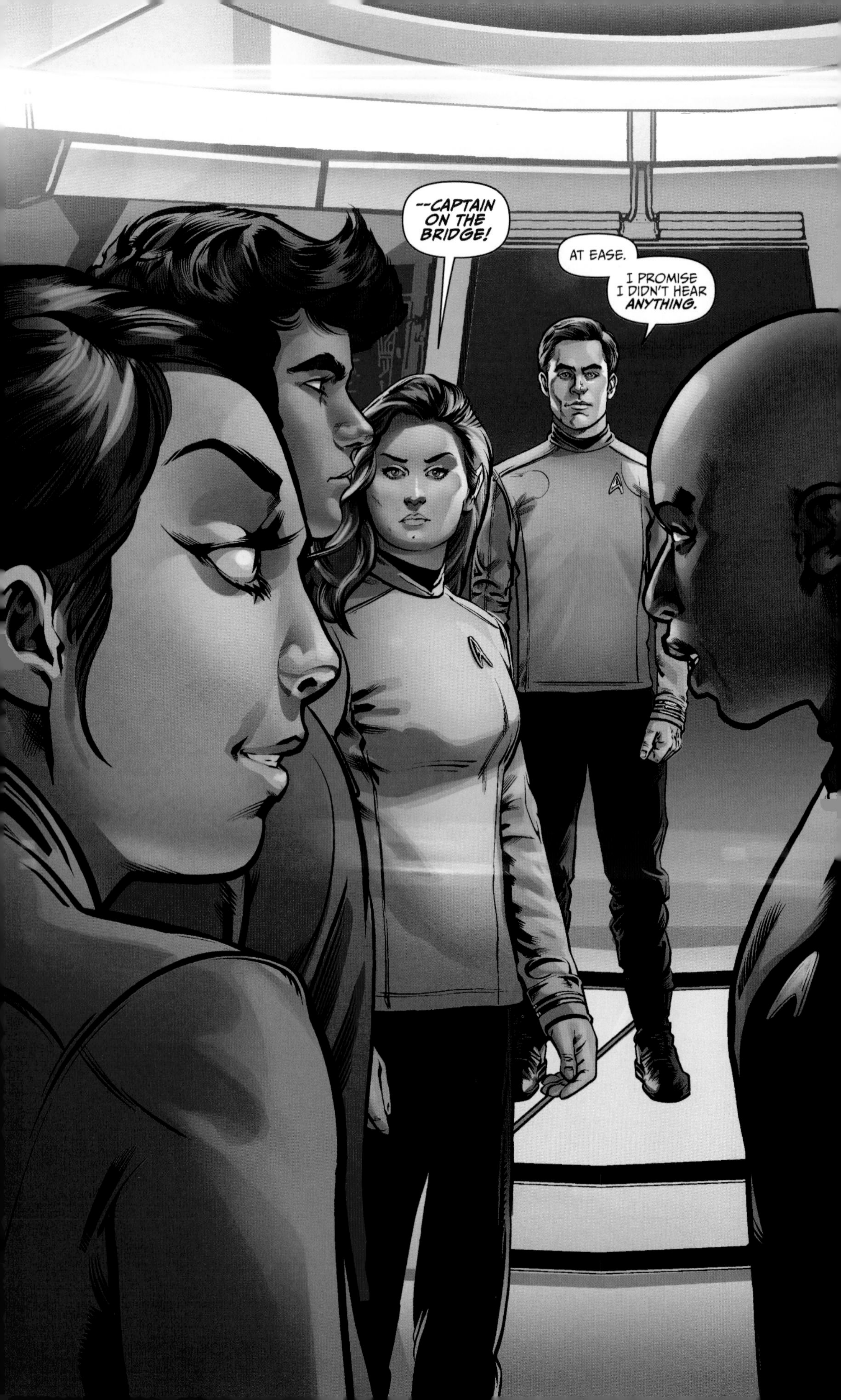
--CAPTAIN ON THE BRIDGE!
AT EASE.
I PROMISE I DIDN'T HEAR ANYTHING.

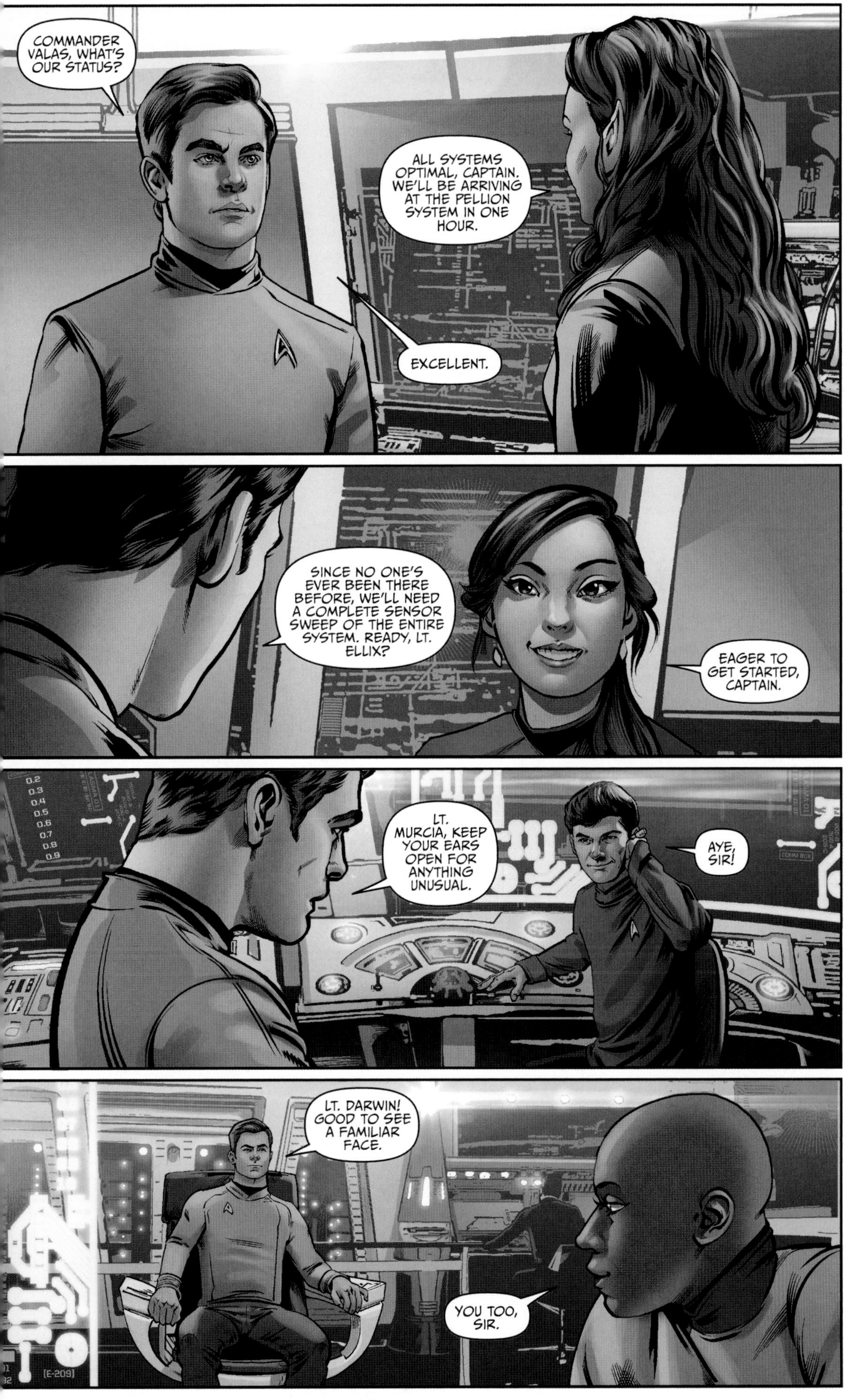
COMMANDER VALAS, WHAT'S OUR STATUS?
ALL SYSTEMS OPTIMAL, CAPTAIN. WE'LL BE ARRIVING AT THE PELLION SYSTEM IN ONE HOUR.
EXCELLENT.
SINCE NO ONE'S EVER BEEN THERE BEFORE, WE'LL NEED A COMPLETE SENSOR SWEEP OF THE ENTIRE SYSTEM. READY, LT. ELLIX?
EAGER TO GET STARTED, CAPTAIN.
LT. MURCIA, KEEP YOUR EARS OPEN FOR ANYTHING UNUSUAL.
AYE, SIR!
LT. DARWIN! GOOD TO SEE A FAMILIAR FACE.
YOU TOO, SIR.

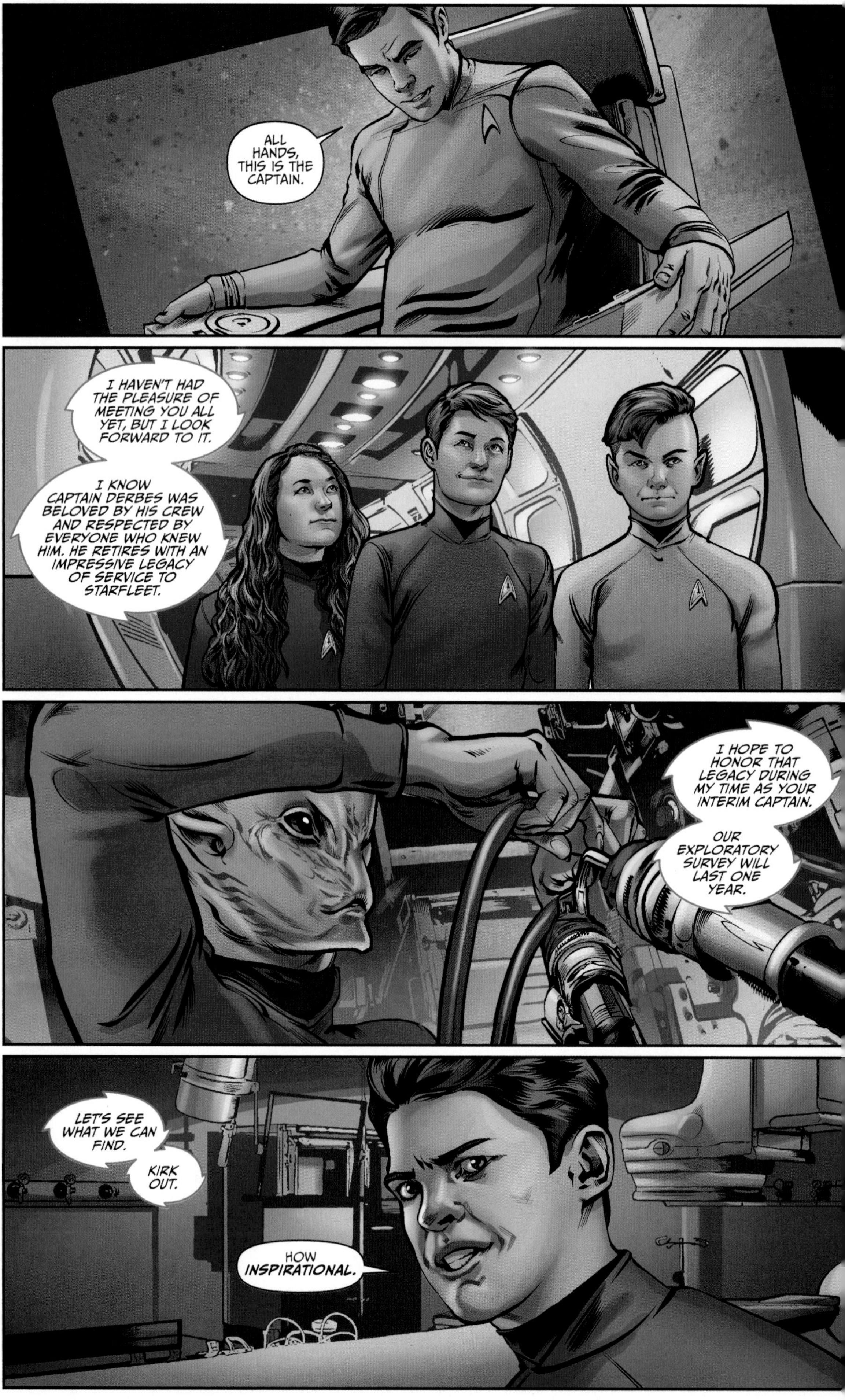
ALL HANDS, THIS IS THE CAPTAIN.
I HAVEN'T HAD THE PLEASURE OF MEETING YOU ALL YET, BUT I LOOK FORWARD TO IT.
I KNOW CAPTAIN DERBES WAS BELOVED BY HIS CREW AND RESPECTED BY EVERYONE WHO KNEW HIM. HE RETIRES WITH AN IMPRESSIVE LEGACY OF SERVICE TO STARFLEET.
I HOPE TO HONOR THAT LEGACY DURING MY TIME AS YOUR INTERIM CAPTAIN.
OUR EXPLORATORY SURVEY WILL LAST ONE YEAR.
LET'S SEE WHAT WE CAN FIND.
KIRK OUT.
HOW INSPIRATIONAL.

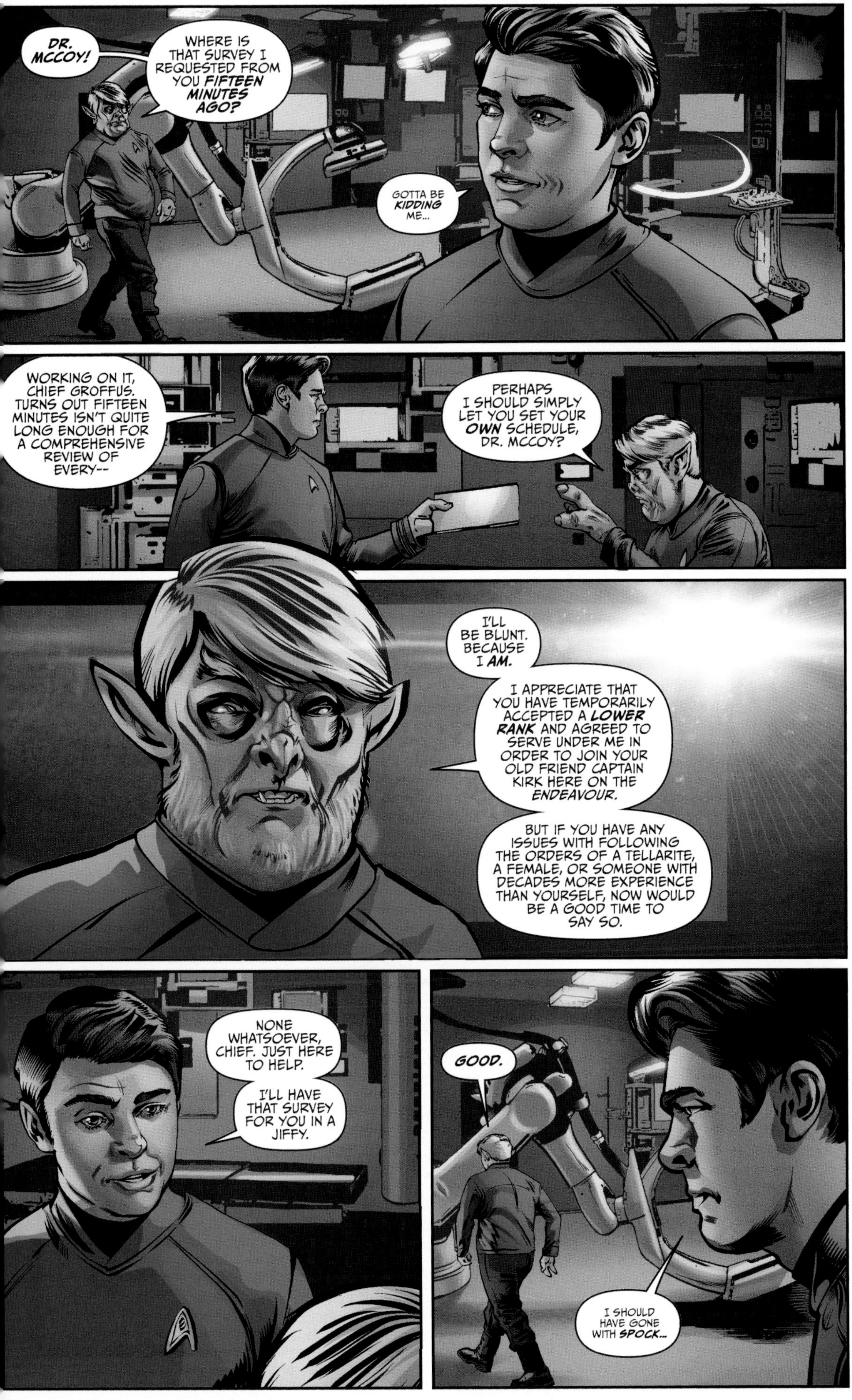
DR. MCCOY!
WHERE IS THAT SURVEY I REQUESTED FROM YOU FIFTEEN MINUTES AGO?
GOTTA BE KIDDING ME...
WORKING ON IT, CHIEF GROFFUS. TURNS OUT FIFTEEN MINUTES ISN'T QUITE LONG ENOUGH FOR A COMPREHENSIVE REVIEW OF EVERY--
PERHAPS I SHOULD SIMPLY LET YOU SET YOUR OWN SCHEDULE, DR. MCCOY?
I'LL BE BLUNT. BECAUSE I AM.
I APPRECIATE THAT YOU HAVE TEMPORARILY ACCEPTED A LOWER RANK AND AGREED TO SERVE UNDER ME IN ORDER TO JOIN YOUR OLD FRIEND CAPTAIN KIRK HERE ON THE ENDEAVOUR.
BUT IF YOU HAVE ANY ISSUES WITH FOLLOWING THE ORDERS OF A TELLARITE, A FEMALE, OR SOMEONE WITH DECADES MORE EXPERIENCE THAN YOURSELF, NOW WOULD BE A GOOD TIME TO SAY SO.
NONE WHATSOEVER, CHIEF. JUST HERE TO HELP.
I'LL HAVE THAT SURVEY FOR YOU IN A JIFFY.
GOOD.
I SHOULD HAVE GONE WITH SPOCK...

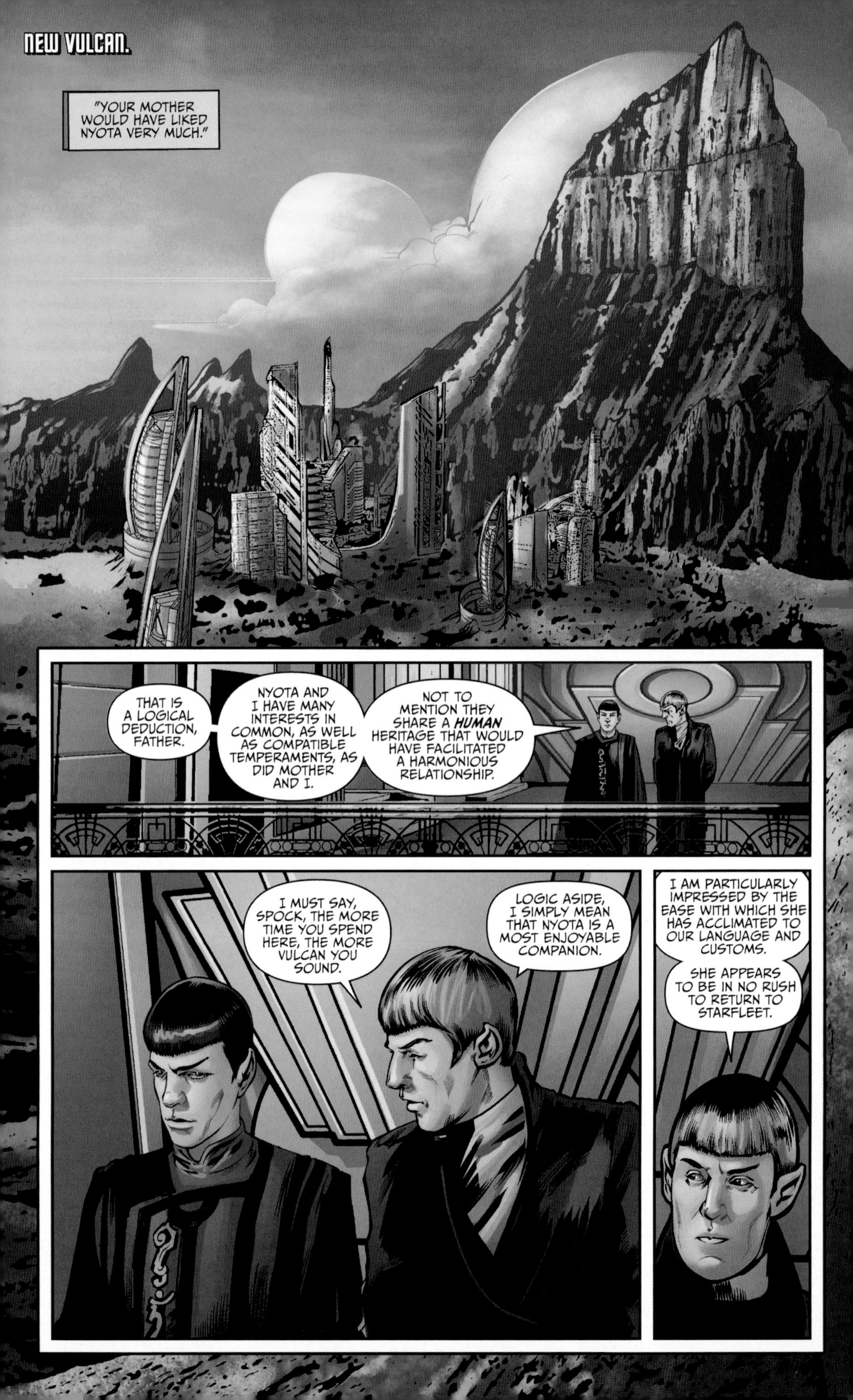
NEW VULCAN.
"YOUR MOTHER WOULD HAVE LIKED NYOTA VERY MUCH."
THAT IS A LOGICAL DEDUCTION, FATHER.
NYOTA AND I HAVE MANY INTERESTS IN COMMON, AS WELL AS COMPATIBLE TEMPERAMENTS, AS DID MOTHER AND I.
NOT TO MENTION THEY SHARE A HUMAN HERITAGE THAT WOULD HAVE FACILITATED A HARMONIOUS RELATIONSHIP.
I MUST SAY, SPOCK, THE MORE TIME YOU SPEND HERE, THE MORE VULCAN YOU SOUND.
LOGIC ASIDE, I SIMPLY MEAN THAT NYOTA IS A MOST ENJOYABLE COMPANION.
I AM PARTICULARLY IMPRESSED BY THE EASE WITH WHICH SHE HAS ACCLIMATED TO OUR LANGUAGE AND CUSTOMS.
SHE APPEARS TO BE IN NO RUSH TO RETURN TO STARFLEET.

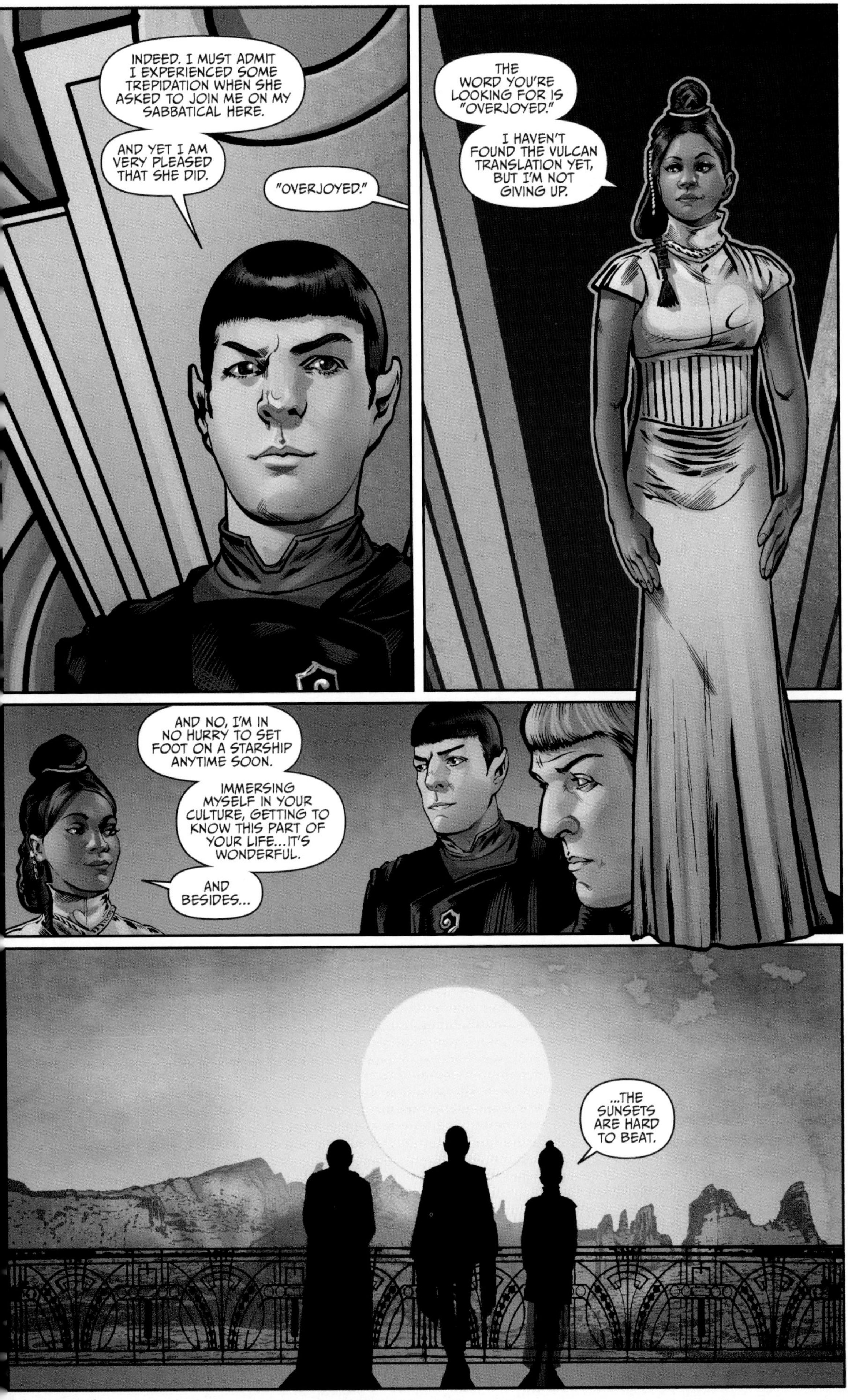
INDEED. I MUST ADMIT I EXPERIENCED SOME TREPIDATION WHEN SHE ASKED TO JOIN ME ON MY SABBATICAL HERE.
AND YET I AM VERY PLEASED THAT SHE DID.
"OVERJOYED."
THE WORD YOU'RE LOOKING FOR IS "OVERJOYED."
I HAVEN'T FOUND THE VULCAN TRANSLATION YET, BUT I'M NOT GIVING UP.
AND NO, I'M IN NO HURRY TO SET FOOT ON A STARSHIP ANYTIME SOON.
IMMERSING MYSELF IN YOUR CULTURE, GETTING TO KNOW THIS PART OF YOUR LIFE...IT'S WONDERFUL.
AND BESIDES...
...THE SUNSETS ARE HARD TO BEAT.

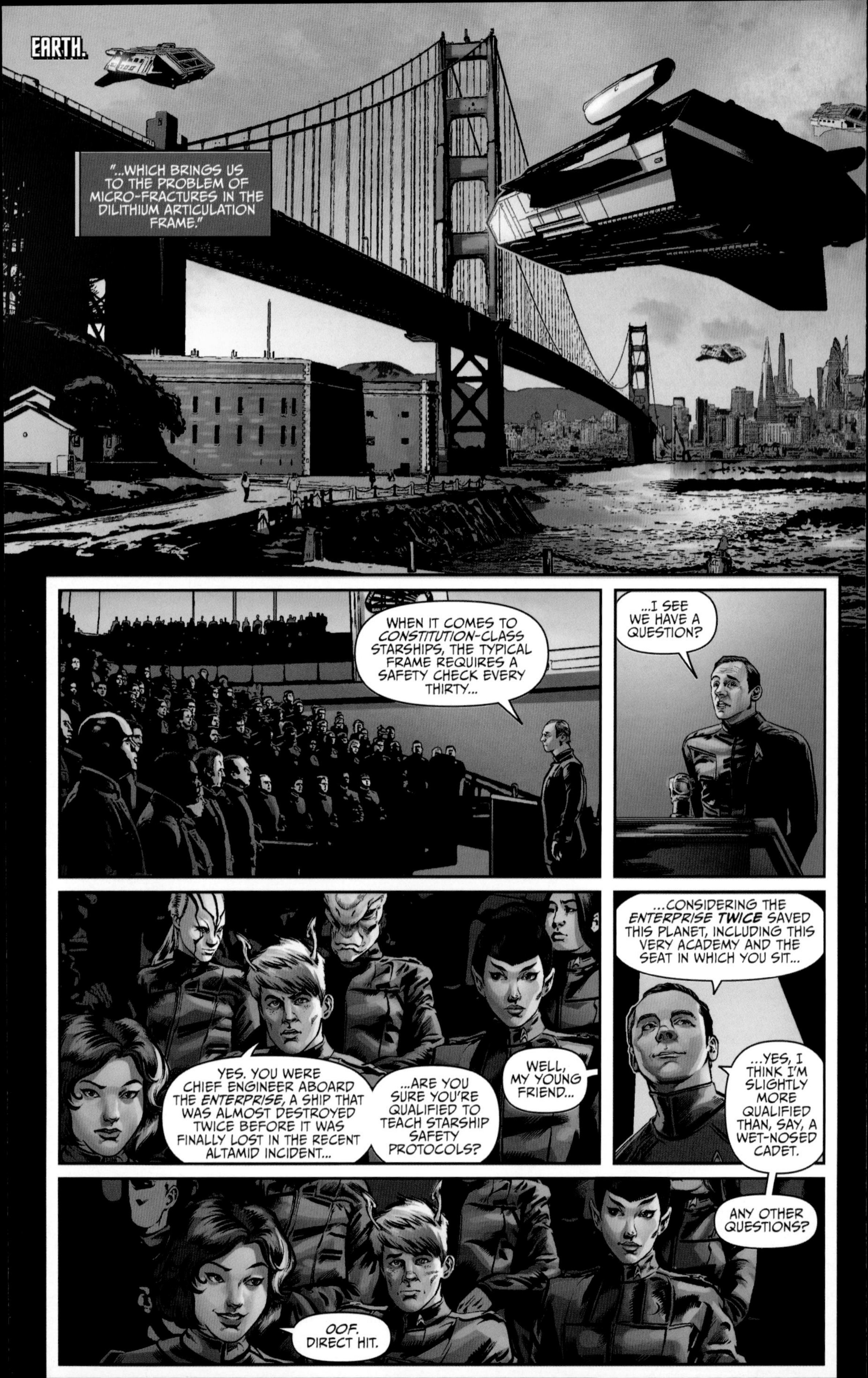
EARTH.
"...WHICH BRINGS US TO THE PROBLEM OF MICRO-FRACTURES IN THE DILITHIUM ARTICULATION FRAME."
WHEN IT COMES TO *CONSTITUTION*-CLASS STARSHIPS, THE TYPICAL FRAME REQUIRES A SAFETY CHECK EVERY THIRTY...
...I SEE WE HAVE A QUESTION?
YES. YOU WERE CHIEF ENGINEER ABOARD THE *ENTERPRISE*, A SHIP THAT WAS ALMOST DESTROYED TWICE BEFORE IT WAS FINALLY LOST IN THE RECENT ALTAMID INCIDENT...
...ARE YOU SURE YOU'RE QUALIFIED TO TEACH STARSHIP SAFETY PROTOCOLS?
WELL, MY YOUNG FRIEND...
...CONSIDERING THE *ENTERPRISE* ***TWICE*** SAVED THIS PLANET, INCLUDING THIS VERY ACADEMY AND THE SEAT IN WHICH YOU SIT...
...YES, I THINK I'M SLIGHTLY MORE QUALIFIED THAN, SAY, A WET-NOSED CADET.
ANY OTHER QUESTIONS?
OOF. DIRECT HIT.

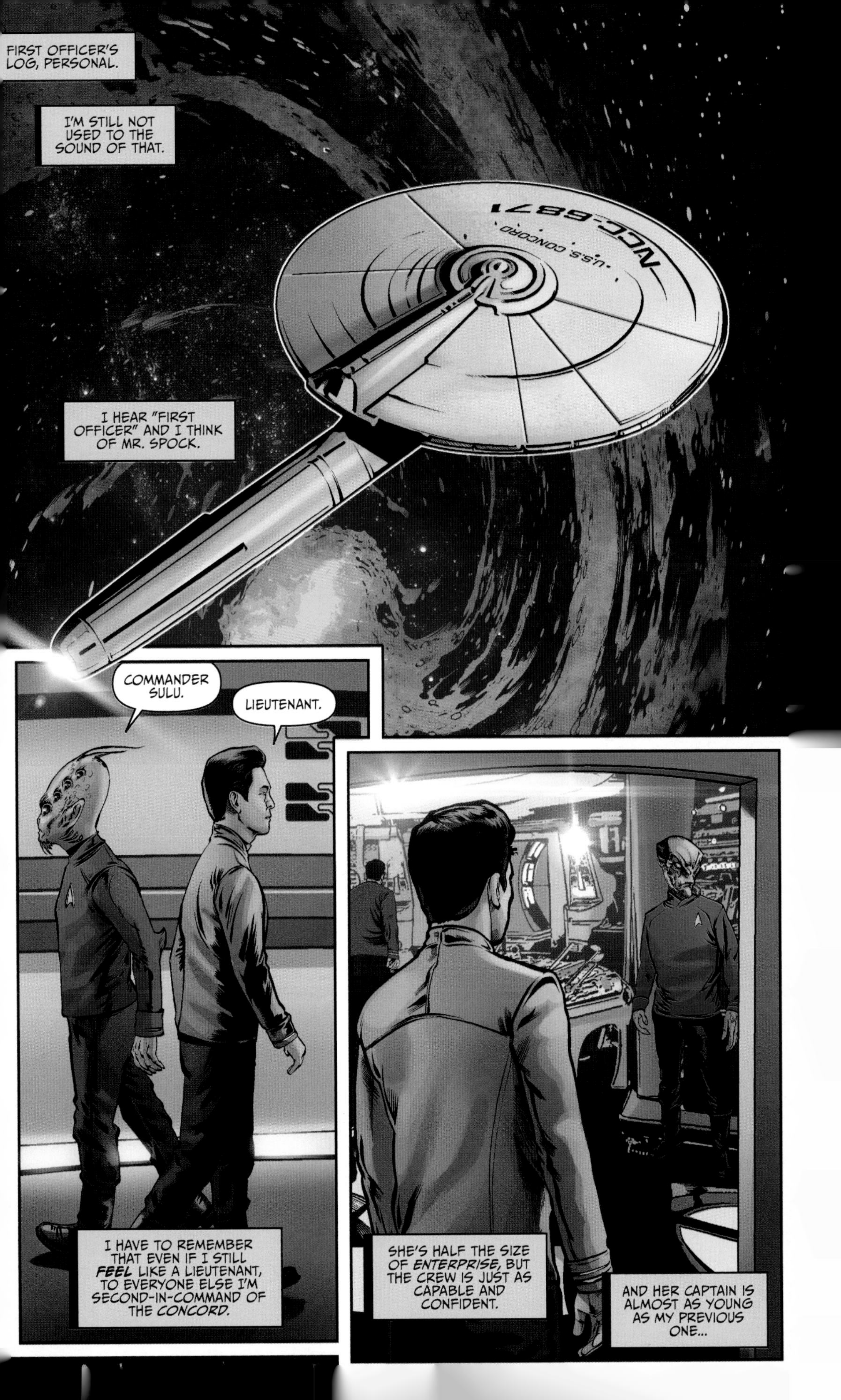
FIRST OFFICER'S LOG, PERSONAL.
I'M STILL NOT USED TO THE SOUND OF THAT.
NCC-6871
U.S.S. CONCORD
I HEAR "FIRST OFFICER" AND I THINK OF MR. SPOCK.
COMMANDER SULU.
LIEUTENANT.
I HAVE TO REMEMBER THAT EVEN IF I STILL **FEEL** LIKE A LIEUTENANT, TO EVERYONE ELSE I'M SECOND-IN-COMMAND OF THE *CONCORD.*
SHE'S HALF THE SIZE OF *ENTERPRISE*, BUT THE CREW IS JUST AS CAPABLE AND CONFIDENT.
AND HER CAPTAIN IS ALMOST AS YOUNG AS MY PREVIOUS ONE...

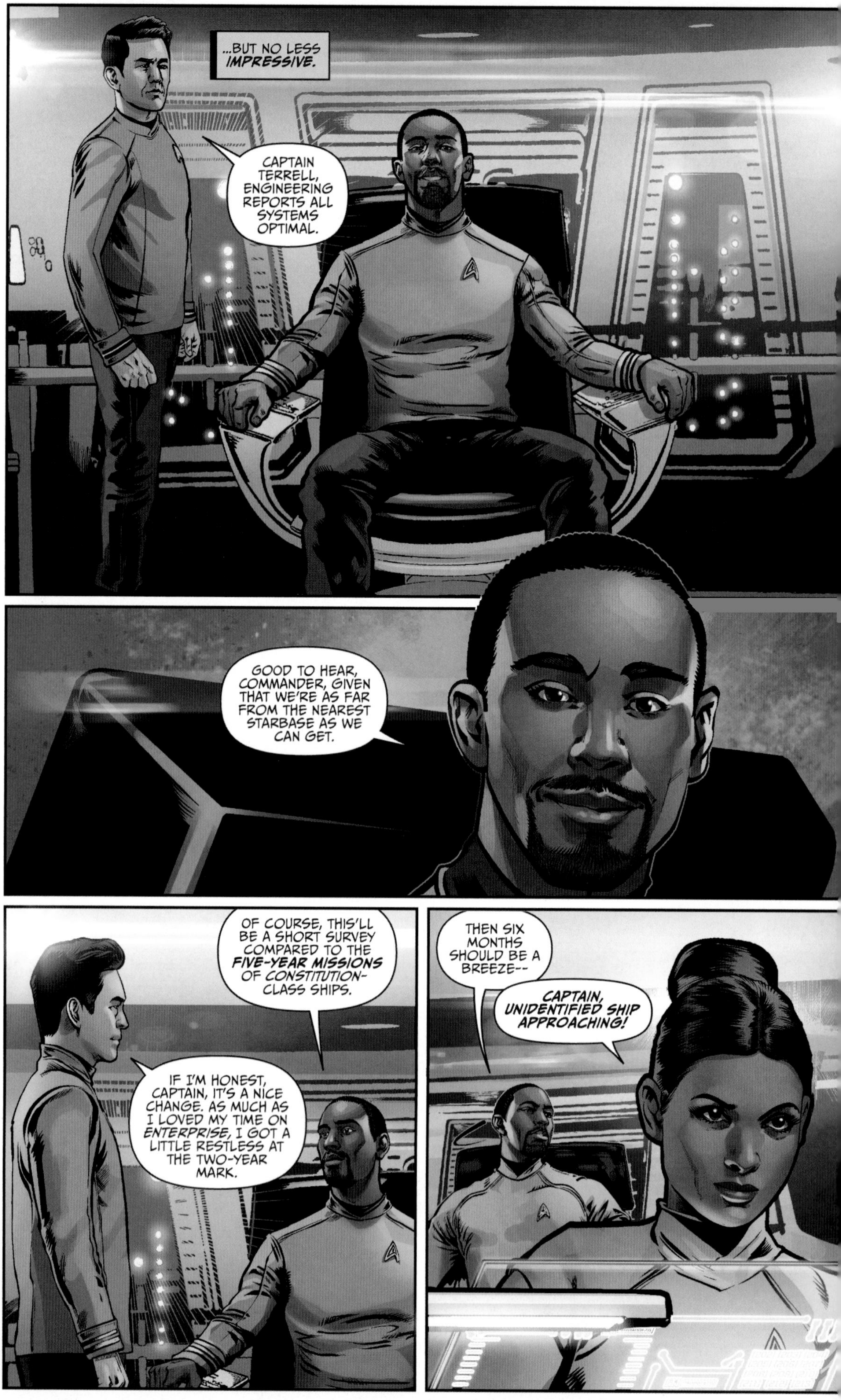
...BUT NO LESS IMPRESSIVE.
CAPTAIN TERRELL, ENGINEERING REPORTS ALL SYSTEMS OPTIMAL.
GOOD TO HEAR, COMMANDER, GIVEN THAT WE'RE AS FAR FROM THE NEAREST STARBASE AS WE CAN GET.
IF I'M HONEST, CAPTAIN, IT'S A NICE CHANGE. AS MUCH AS I LOVED MY TIME ON ENTERPRISE, I GOT A LITTLE RESTLESS AT THE TWO-YEAR MARK.
OF COURSE, THIS'LL BE A SHORT SURVEY COMPARED TO THE FIVE-YEAR MISSIONS OF CONSTITUTION-CLASS SHIPS.
THEN SIX MONTHS SHOULD BE A BREEZE--
CAPTAIN, UNIDENTIFIED SHIP APPROACHING!

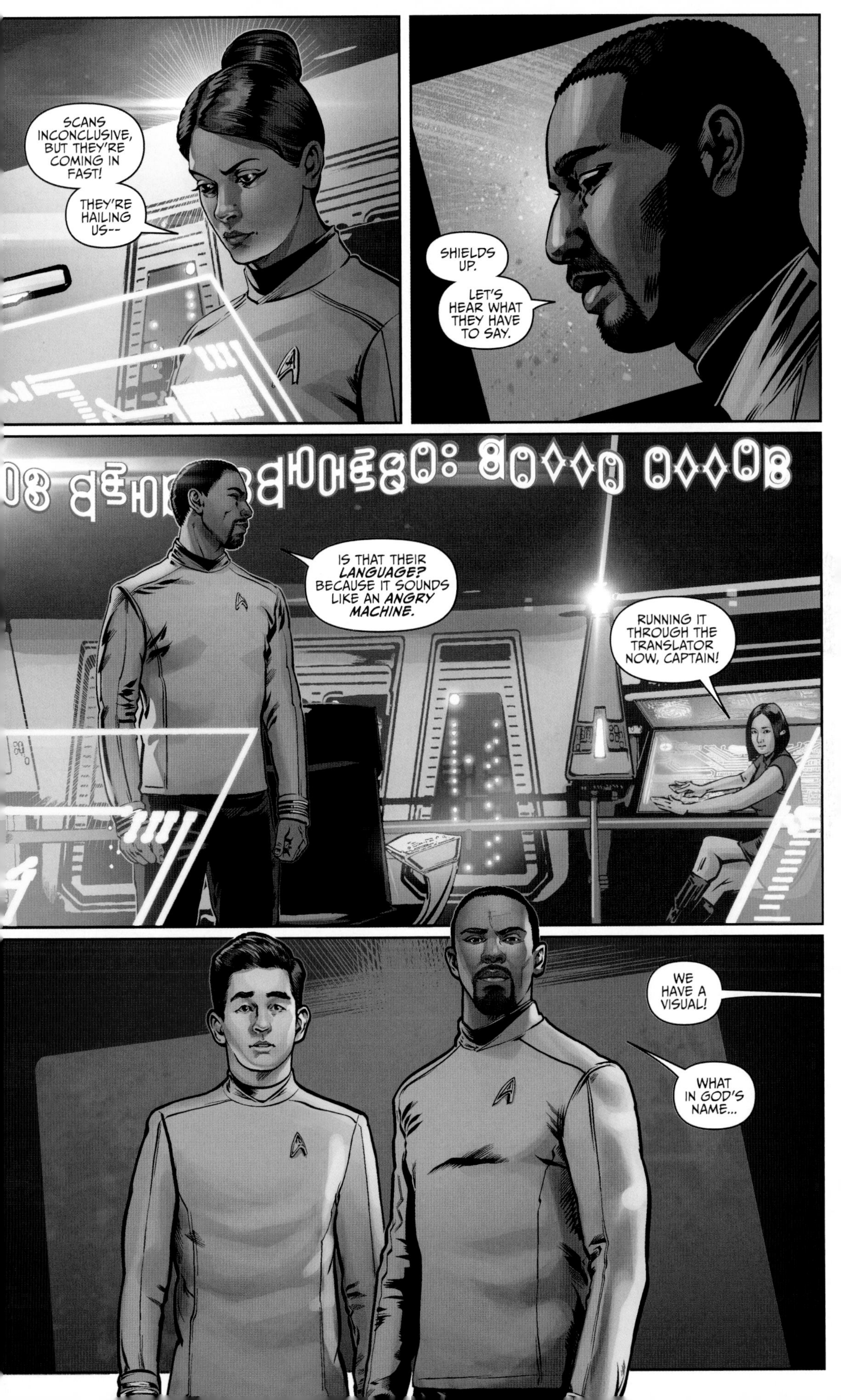
SCANS INCONCLUSIVE, BUT THEY'RE COMING IN FAST!
THEY'RE HAILING US--
SHIELDS UP.
LET'S HEAR WHAT THEY HAVE TO SAY.
IS THAT THEIR *LANGUAGE?* BECAUSE IT SOUNDS LIKE AN *ANGRY MACHINE.*
RUNNING IT THROUGH THE TRANSLATOR NOW, CAPTAIN!
WE HAVE A VISUAL!
WHAT IN GOD'S NAME...

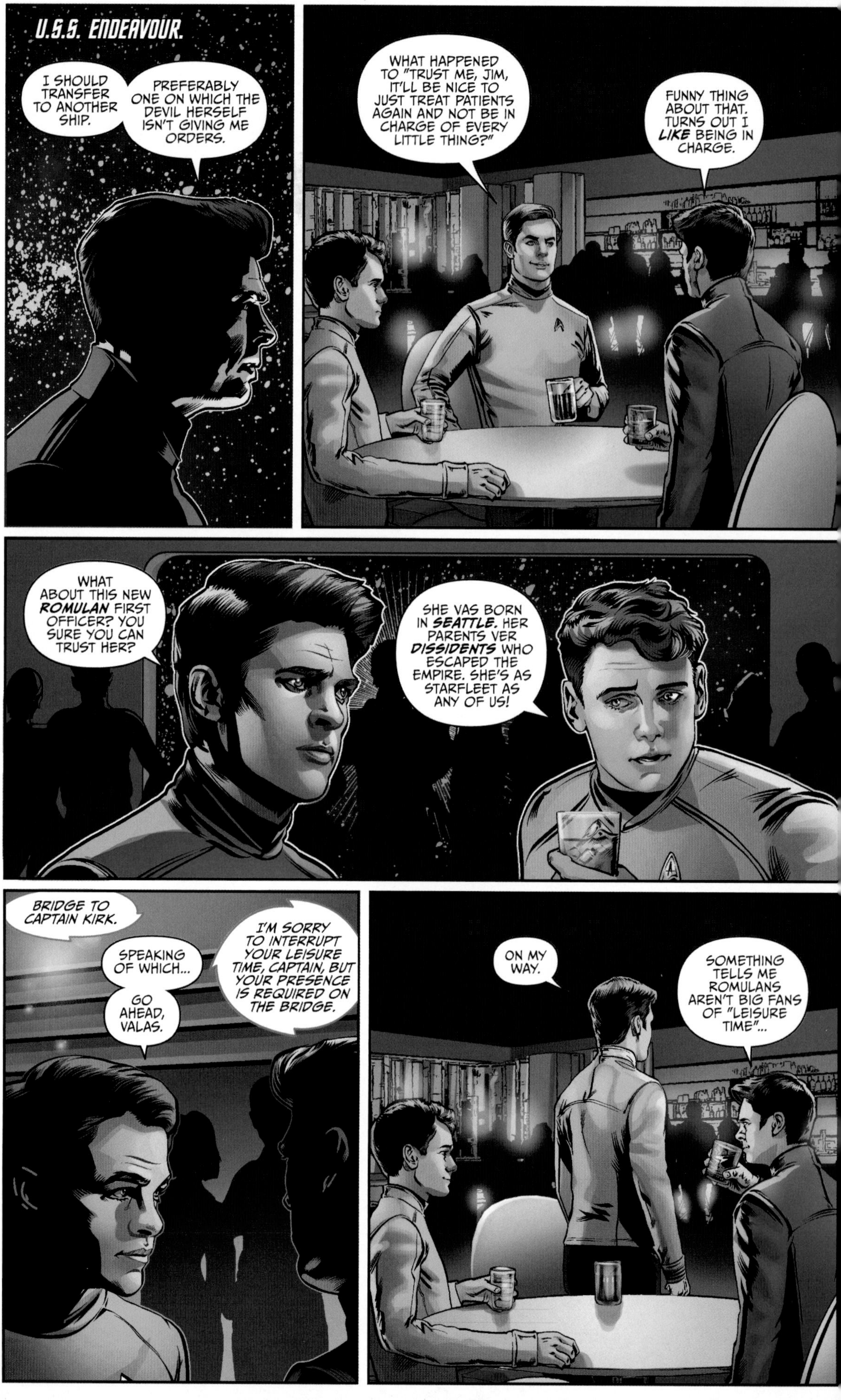
U.S.S. ENDEAVOUR.
I SHOULD TRANSFER TO ANOTHER SHIP.
PREFERABLY ONE ON WHICH THE DEVIL HERSELF ISN'T GIVING ME ORDERS.
WHAT HAPPENED TO "TRUST ME, JIM, IT'LL BE NICE TO JUST TREAT PATIENTS AGAIN AND NOT BE IN CHARGE OF EVERY LITTLE THING?"
FUNNY THING ABOUT THAT. TURNS OUT I LIKE BEING IN CHARGE.
WHAT ABOUT THIS NEW ROMULAN FIRST OFFICER? YOU SURE YOU CAN TRUST HER?
SHE VAS BORN IN SEATTLE. HER PARENTS VER DISSIDENTS WHO ESCAPED THE EMPIRE. SHE'S AS STARFLEET AS ANY OF US!
BRIDGE TO CAPTAIN KIRK.
SPEAKING OF WHICH...
GO AHEAD, VALAS.
I'M SORRY TO INTERRUPT YOUR LEISURE TIME, CAPTAIN, BUT YOUR PRESENCE IS REQUIRED ON THE BRIDGE.
ON MY WAY.
SOMETHING TELLS ME ROMULANS AREN'T BIG FANS OF "LEISURE TIME"...

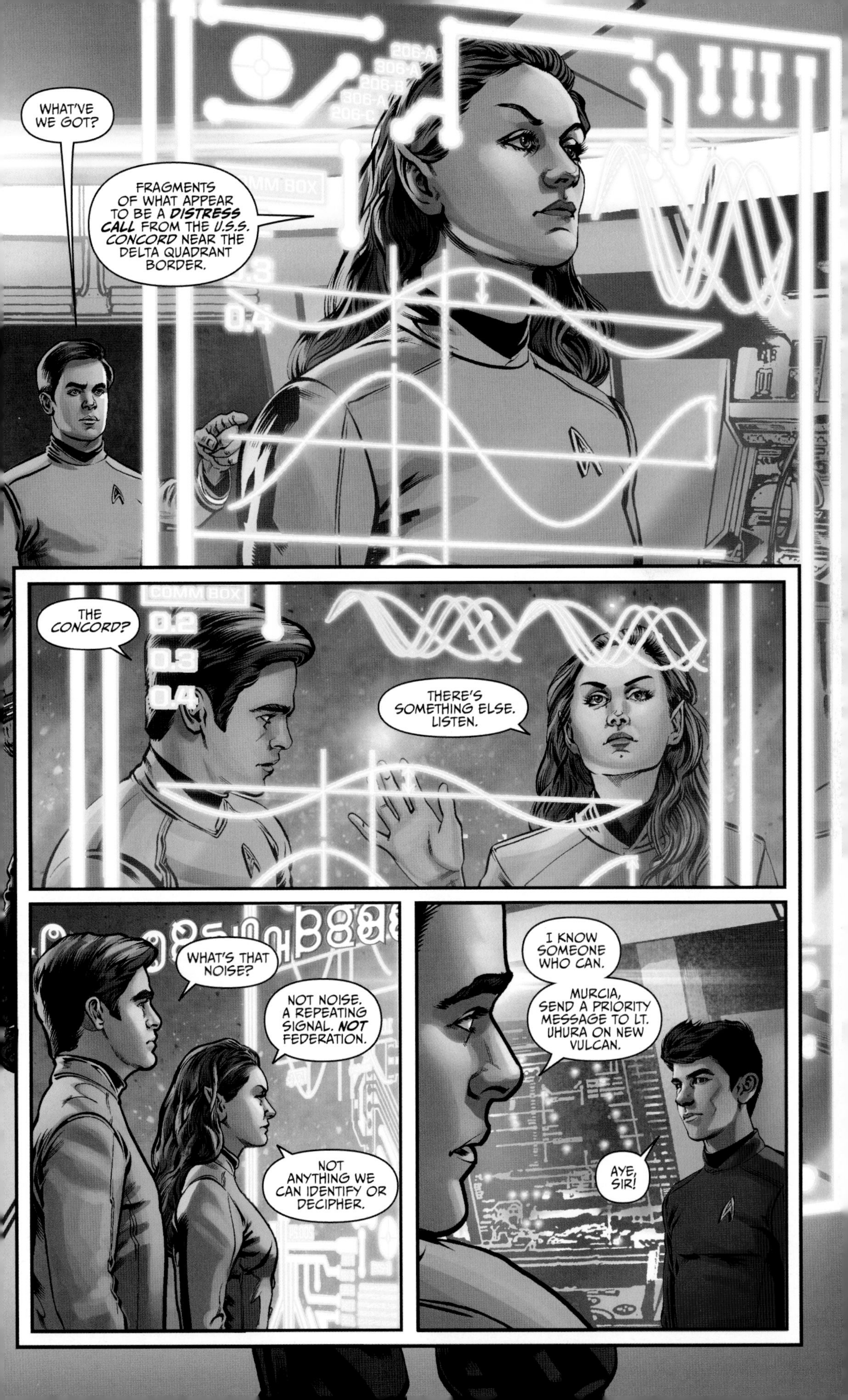
WHAT'VE WE GOT?
FRAGMENTS OF WHAT APPEAR TO BE A *DISTRESS CALL* FROM THE *U.S.S. CONCORD* NEAR THE DELTA QUADRANT BORDER.
THE *CONCORD?*
THERE'S SOMETHING ELSE. LISTEN.
WHAT'S THAT NOISE?
NOT NOISE. A REPEATING SIGNAL. *NOT* FEDERATION.
NOT ANYTHING WE CAN IDENTIFY OR DECIPHER.
I KNOW SOMEONE WHO CAN.
MURCIA, SEND A PRIORITY MESSAGE TO LT. UHURA ON NEW VULCAN.
AYE, SIR!

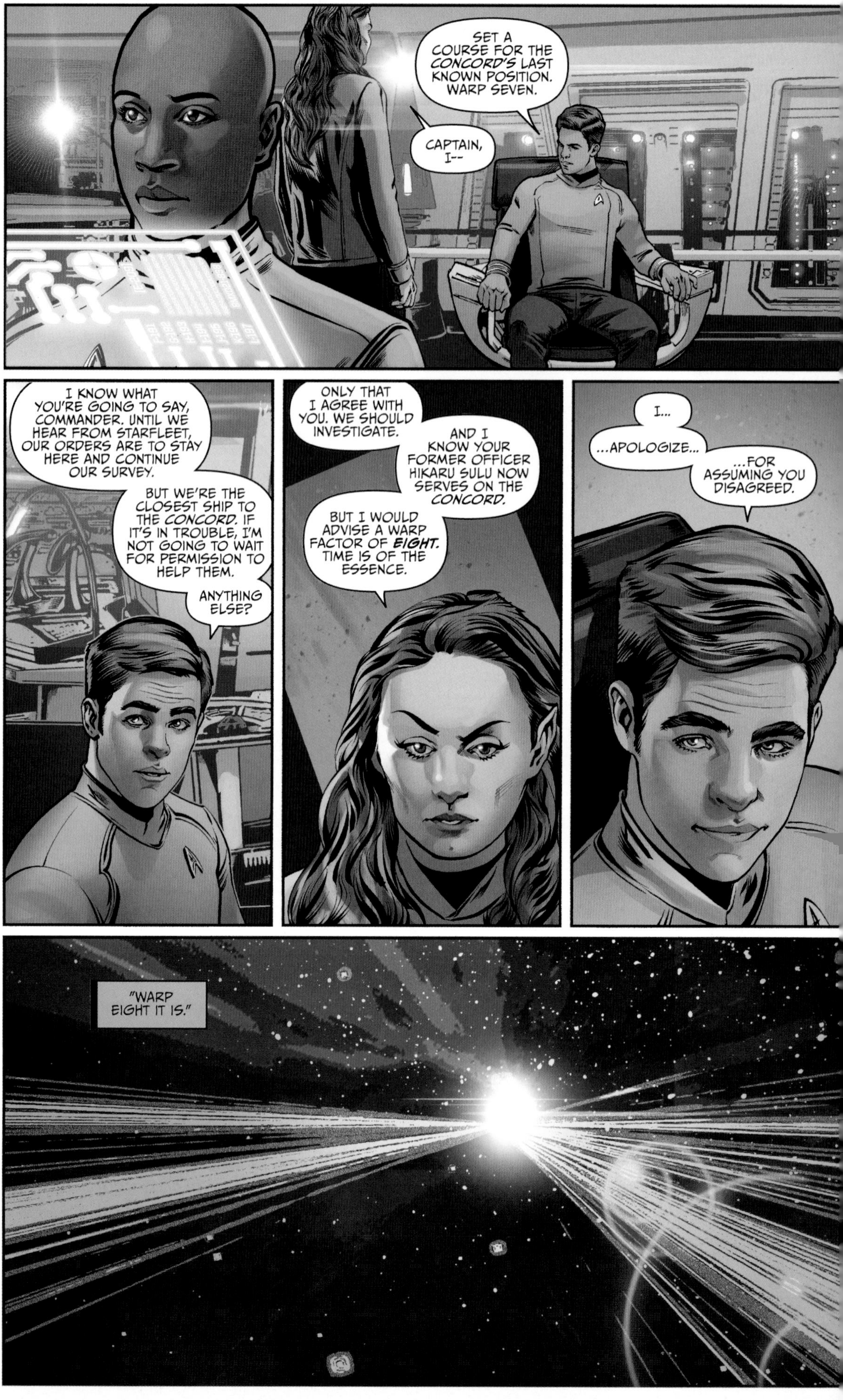
SET A COURSE FOR THE *CONCORD'S* LAST KNOWN POSITION. WARP SEVEN.
CAPTAIN, I--
I KNOW WHAT YOU'RE GOING TO SAY, COMMANDER. UNTIL WE HEAR FROM STARFLEET, OUR ORDERS ARE TO STAY HERE AND CONTINUE OUR SURVEY.
BUT WE'RE THE CLOSEST SHIP TO THE *CONCORD*. IF IT'S IN TROUBLE, I'M NOT GOING TO WAIT FOR PERMISSION TO HELP THEM.
ANYTHING ELSE?
ONLY THAT I AGREE WITH YOU. WE SHOULD INVESTIGATE.
AND I KNOW YOUR FORMER OFFICER HIKARU SULU NOW SERVES ON THE *CONCORD*.
BUT I WOULD ADVISE A WARP FACTOR OF ***EIGHT***. TIME IS OF THE ESSENCE.
I...
...APOLOGIZE...
...FOR ASSUMING YOU DISAGREED.
"WARP EIGHT IT IS."

NEW VULCAN.

FASCINATING...

NYOTA?

MY FATHER IS WAITING. HE HAS PREPARED A SPECIAL *PLOMEEK* SOUP OF HIS OWN RECIPE FOR US.

...DEFINITELY SOME KIND OF VOCALIZATION...

NYOTA...?

I RECEIVED A TRANSMISSION FROM THE *ENDEAVOUR*.

FROM CAPTAIN KIRK.

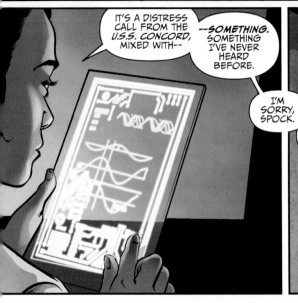

IT'S A DISTRESS CALL FROM THE *U.S.S. CONCORD*, MIXED WITH--

--SOMETHING. SOMETHING I'VE NEVER HEARD BEFORE.

I'M SORRY, SPOCK.

I'M AFRAID THE *PLOMEEK* SOUP WILL HAVE TO WAIT.

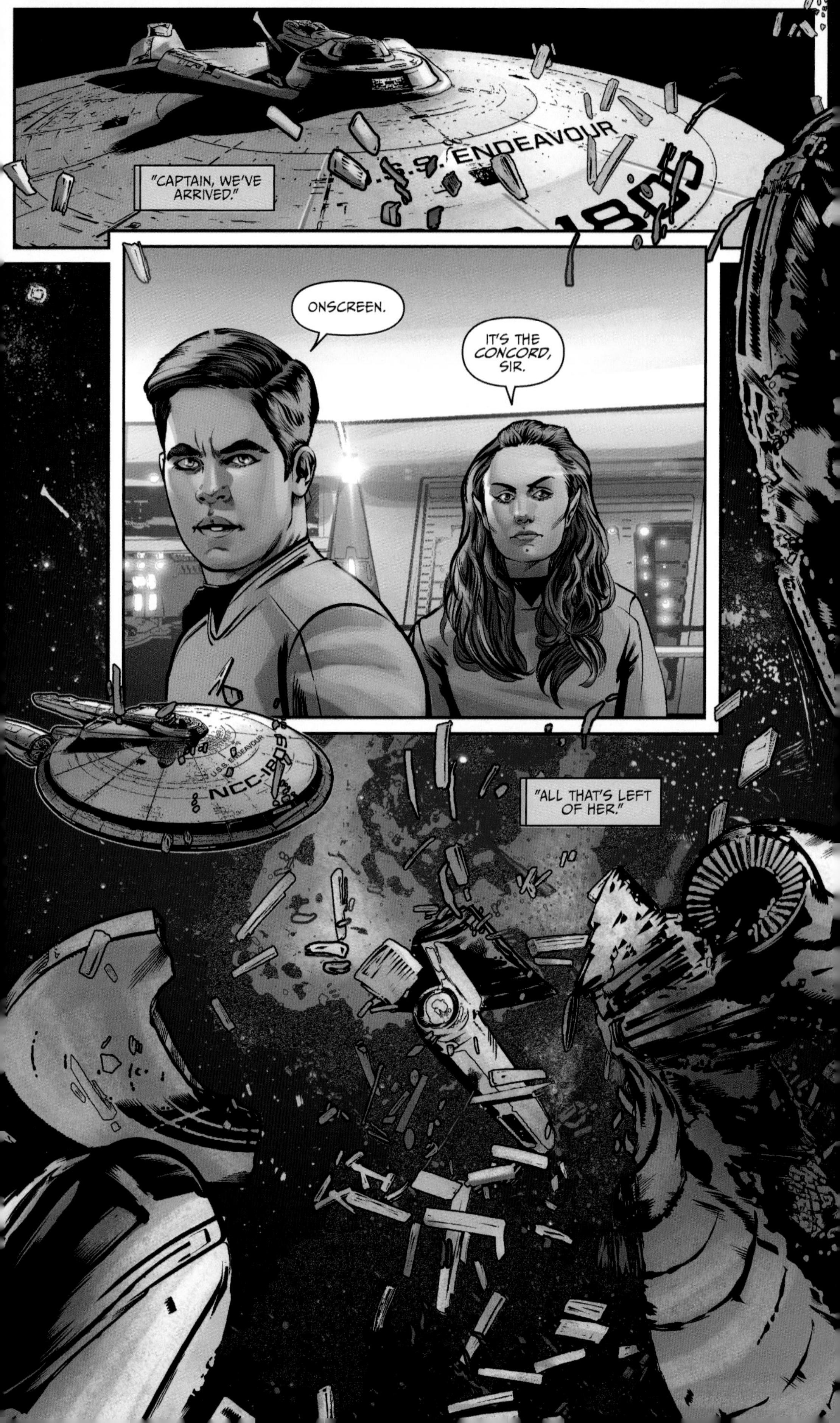
"CAPTAIN, WE'VE ARRIVED."
ONSCREEN.
IT'S THE CONCORD, SIR.
"ALL THAT'S LEFT OF HER."

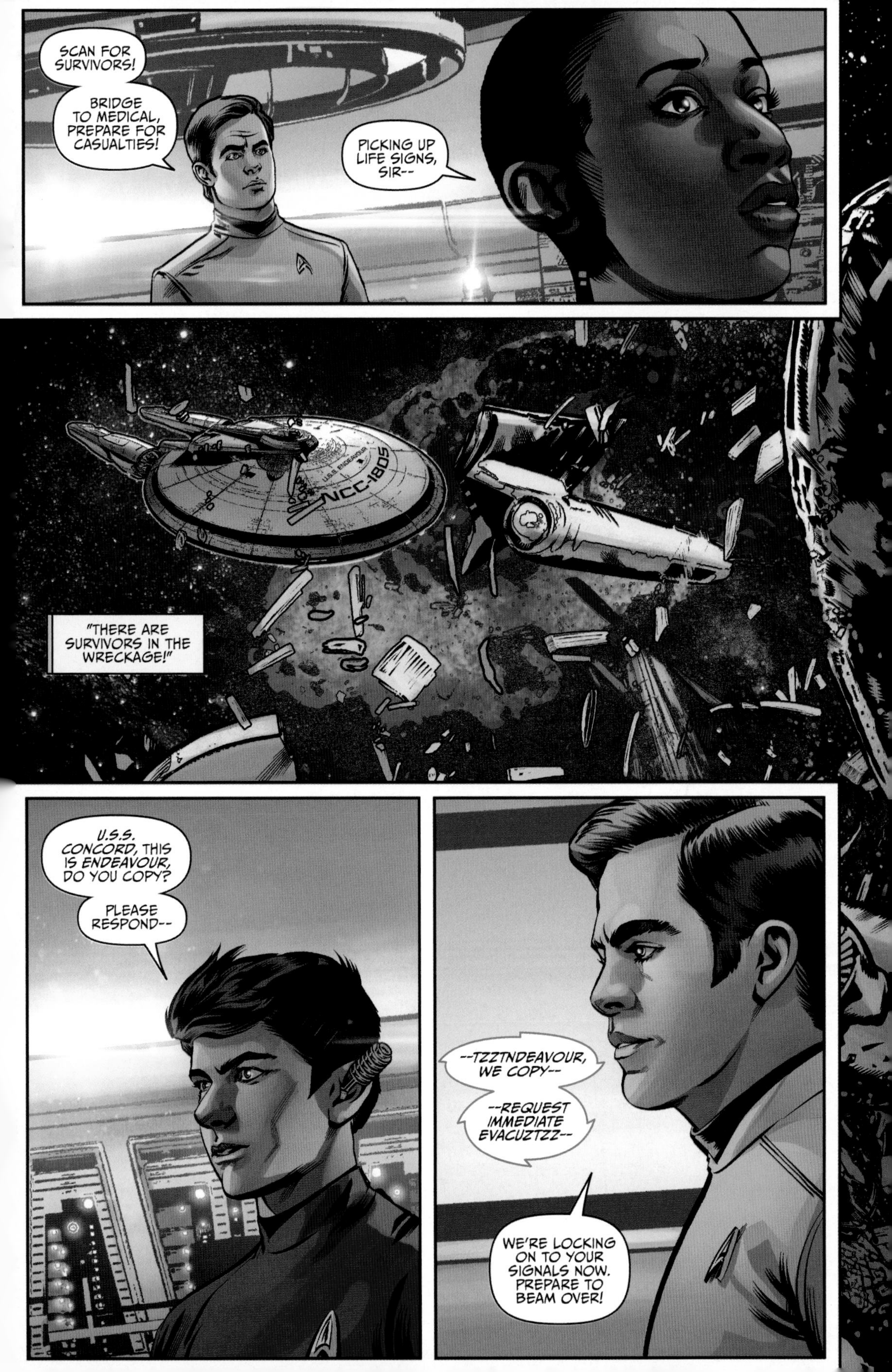
SCAN FOR SURVIVORS!
BRIDGE TO MEDICAL, PREPARE FOR CASUALTIES!
PICKING UP LIFE SIGNS, SIR--
U.S.S. ENDEAVOUR
NCC-1805
"THERE ARE SURVIVORS IN THE WRECKAGE!"
U.S.S. CONCORD, THIS IS ENDEAVOUR, DO YOU COPY?
PLEASE RESPOND--
--TZZTNDEAVOUR, WE COPY--
--REQUEST IMMEDIATE EVACUZTZZ--
WE'RE LOCKING ON TO YOUR SIGNALS NOW. PREPARE TO BEAM OVER!

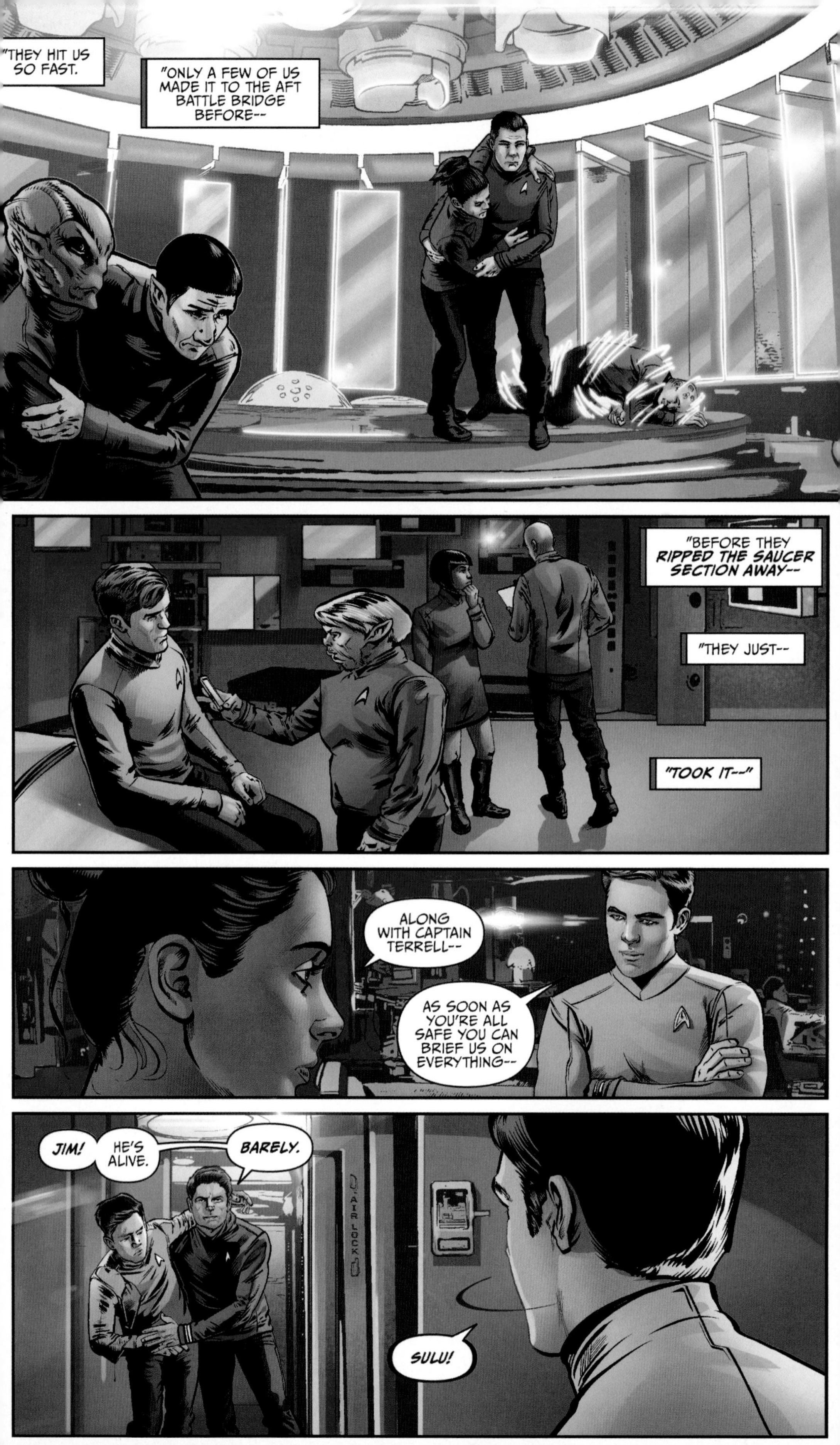
"THEY HIT US SO FAST.
"ONLY A FEW OF US MADE IT TO THE AFT BATTLE BRIDGE BEFORE--
"BEFORE THEY RIPPED THE SAUCER SECTION AWAY--
"THEY JUST--
"TOOK IT--"
ALONG WITH CAPTAIN TERRELL--
AS SOON AS YOU'RE ALL SAFE YOU CAN BRIEF US ON EVERYTHING--
JIM!
HE'S ALIVE.
BARELY.
SULU!
AIR LOCK

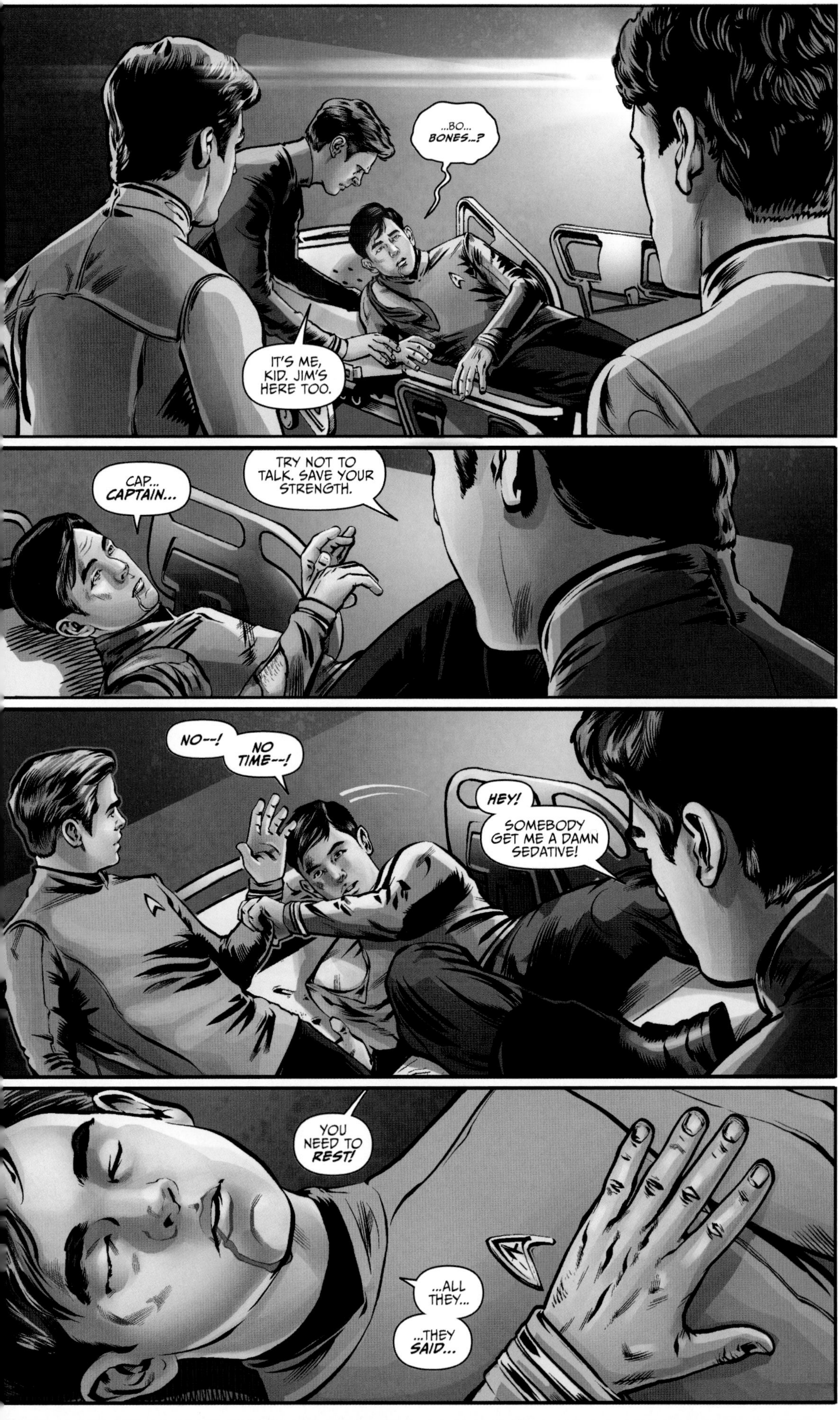
...BO... BONES...?
IT'S ME, KID. JIM'S HERE TOO.
CAP... CAPTAIN...
TRY NOT TO TALK. SAVE YOUR STRENGTH.
NO--!
NO TIME--!
HEY!
SOMEBODY GET ME A DAMN SEDATIVE!
YOU NEED TO REST!
...ALL THEY...
...THEY SAID...

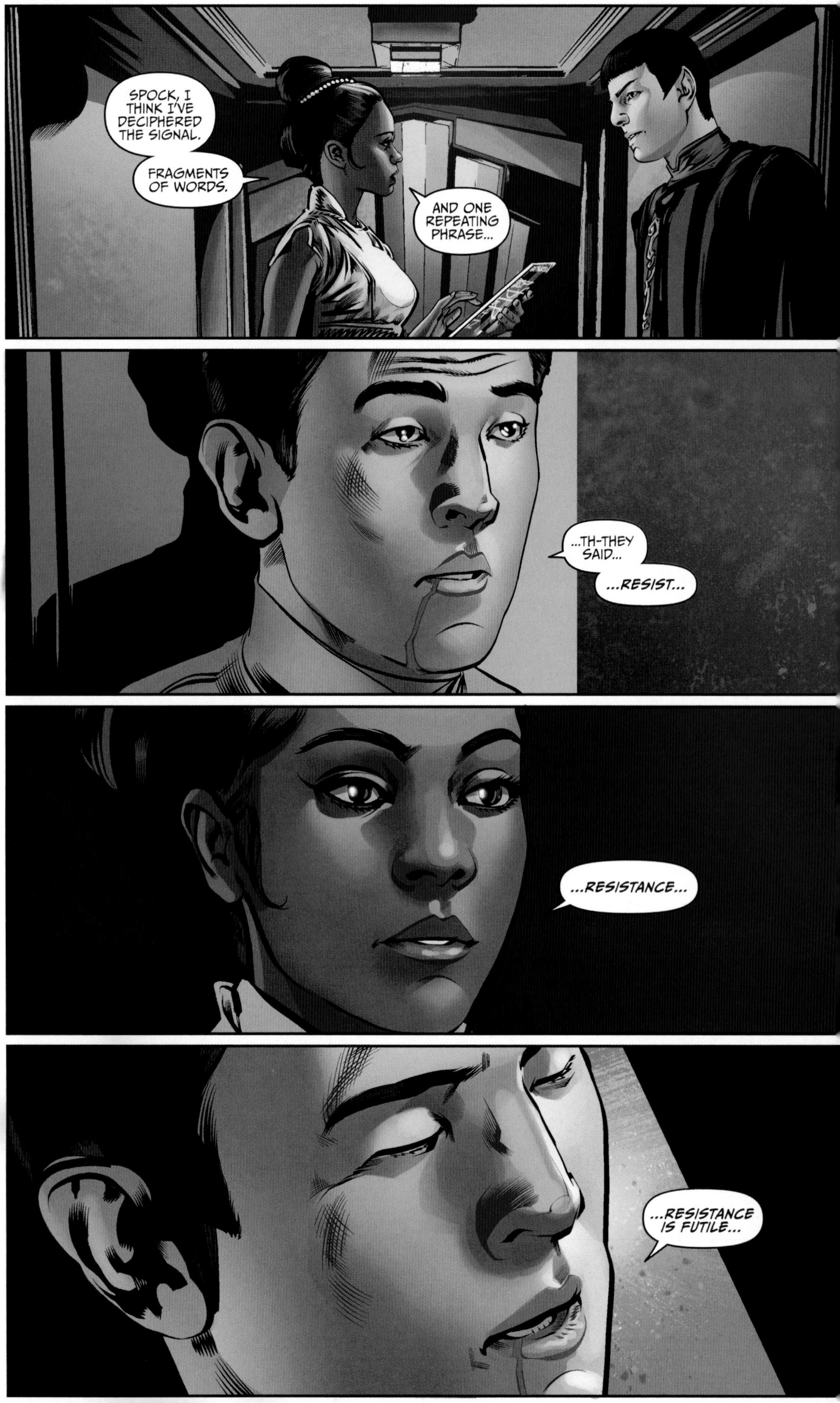
SPOCK, I THINK I'VE DECIPHERED THE SIGNAL.
FRAGMENTS OF WORDS.
AND ONE REPEATING PHRASE...
...TH-THEY SAID...
...RESIST...
...RESISTANCE...
...RESISTANCE IS FUTILE...

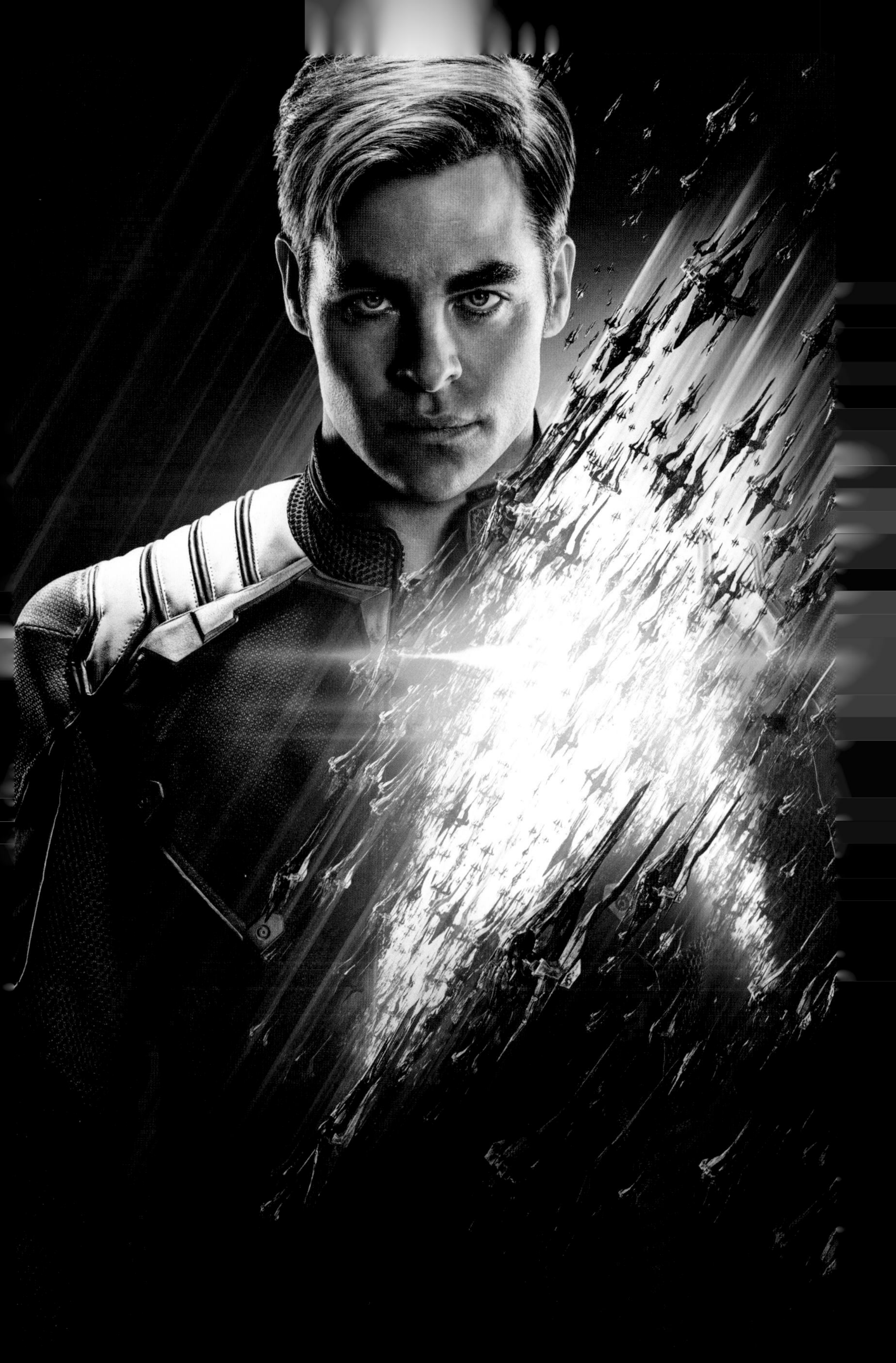

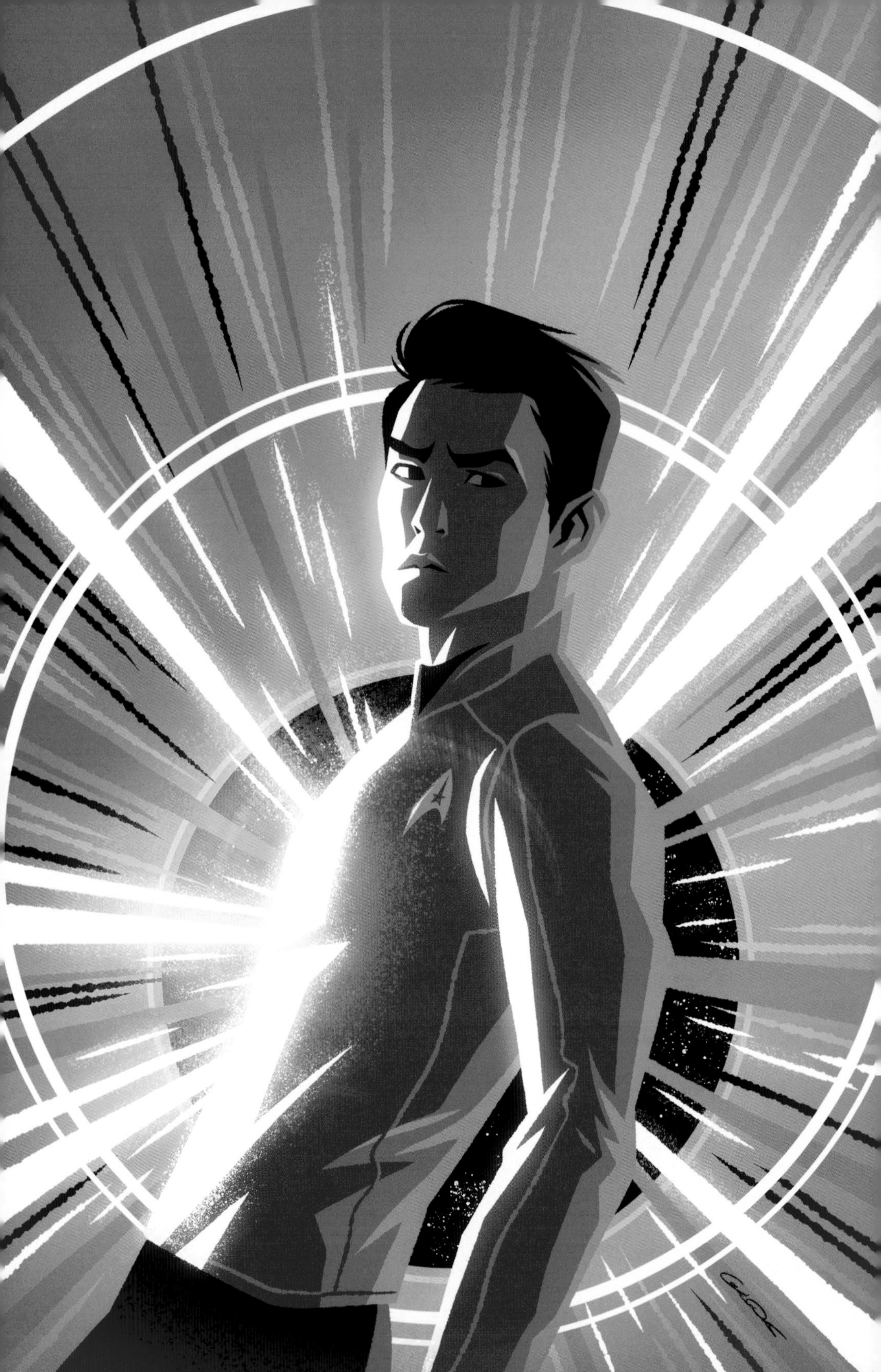

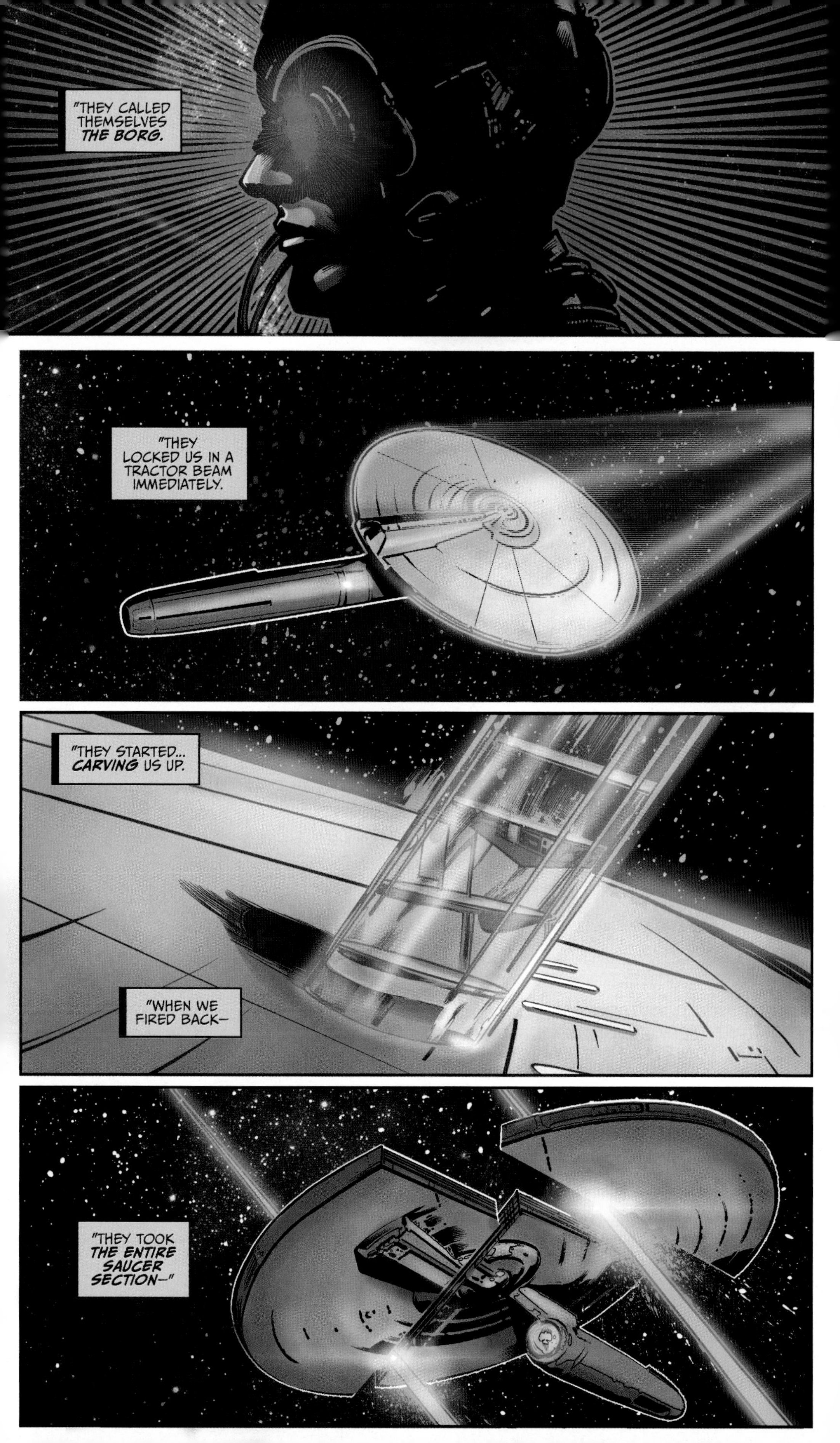
"THEY CALLED THEMSELVES THE BORG.
"THEY LOCKED US IN A TRACTOR BEAM IMMEDIATELY.
"THEY STARTED... CARVING US UP.
"WHEN WE FIRED BACK—
"THEY TOOK THE ENTIRE SAUCER SECTION—"

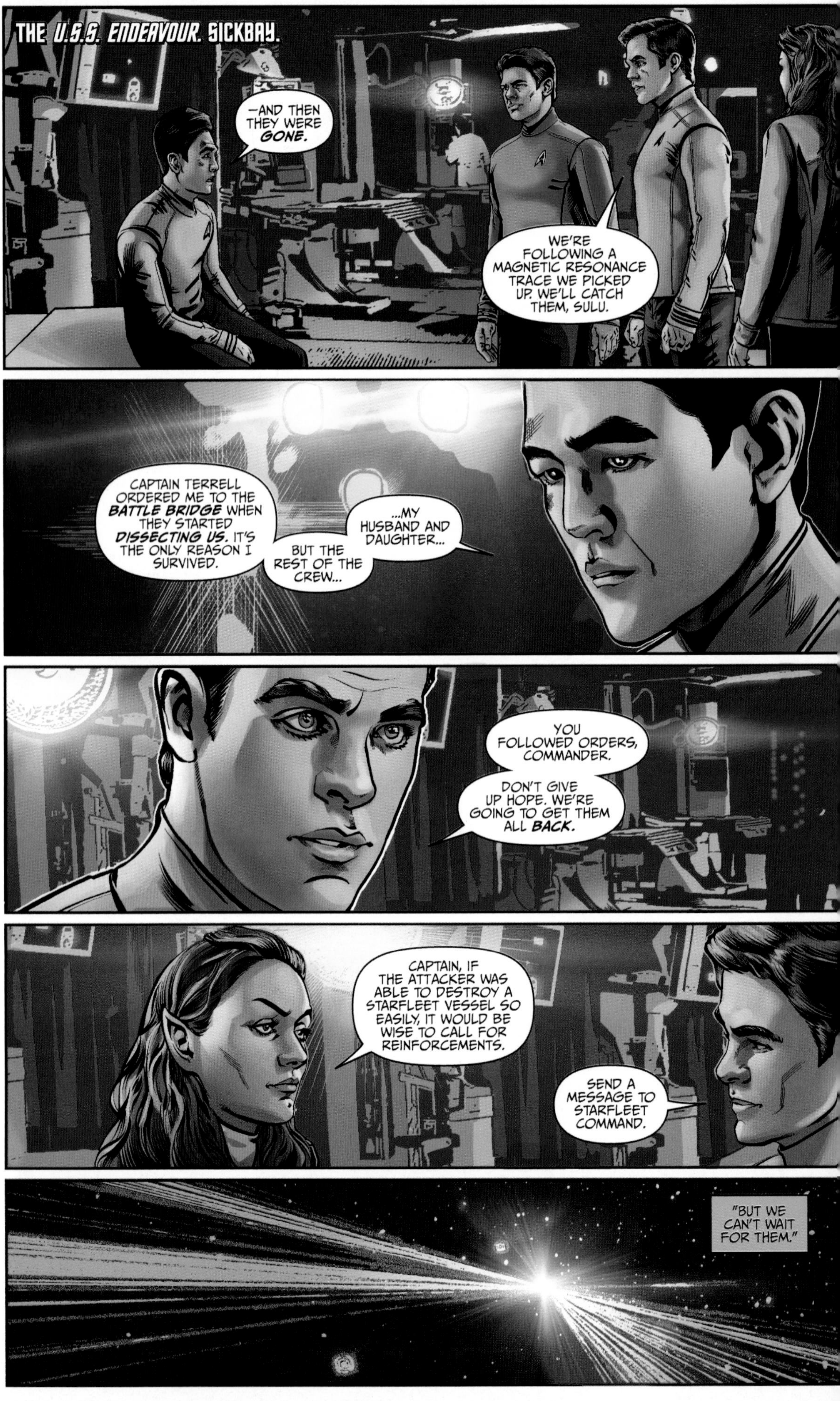
THE U.S.S. ENDEAVOUR. SICKBAY.
—AND THEN THEY WERE GONE.
WE'RE FOLLOWING A MAGNETIC RESONANCE TRACE WE PICKED UP. WE'LL CATCH THEM, SULU.
CAPTAIN TERRELL ORDERED ME TO THE BATTLE BRIDGE WHEN THEY STARTED DISSECTING US. IT'S THE ONLY REASON I SURVIVED.
BUT THE REST OF THE CREW...
...MY HUSBAND AND DAUGHTER...
YOU FOLLOWED ORDERS, COMMANDER.
DON'T GIVE UP HOPE. WE'RE GOING TO GET THEM ALL BACK.
CAPTAIN, IF THE ATTACKER WAS ABLE TO DESTROY A STARFLEET VESSEL SO EASILY, IT WOULD BE WISE TO CALL FOR REINFORCEMENTS.
SEND A MESSAGE TO STARFLEET COMMAND.
"BUT WE CAN'T WAIT FOR THEM."

SPOCK, LOOK AT THIS.

I CROSS-REFERENCED THE AUDIO FRAGMENT JIM SENT US FROM THE *ENDEAVOUR*...

"...RESISTANCE IS FUTILE..."

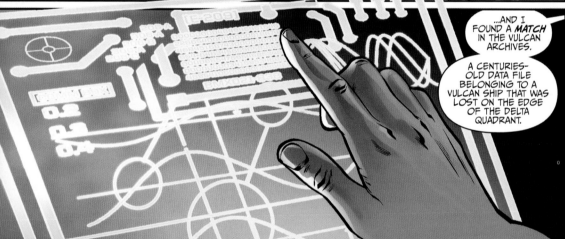

...AND I FOUND A *MATCH* IN THE VULCAN ARCHIVES.

A CENTURIES-OLD DATA FILE BELONGING TO A VULCAN SHIP THAT WAS LOST ON THE EDGE OF THE DELTA QUADRANT.

MOST CURIOUS. WE SHOULD INVESTIGATE FURTHER.

WE CAN'T DO IT FROM HERE.

HOW DO YOU FEEL ABOUT A BREAK FROM OUR SABBATICAL?

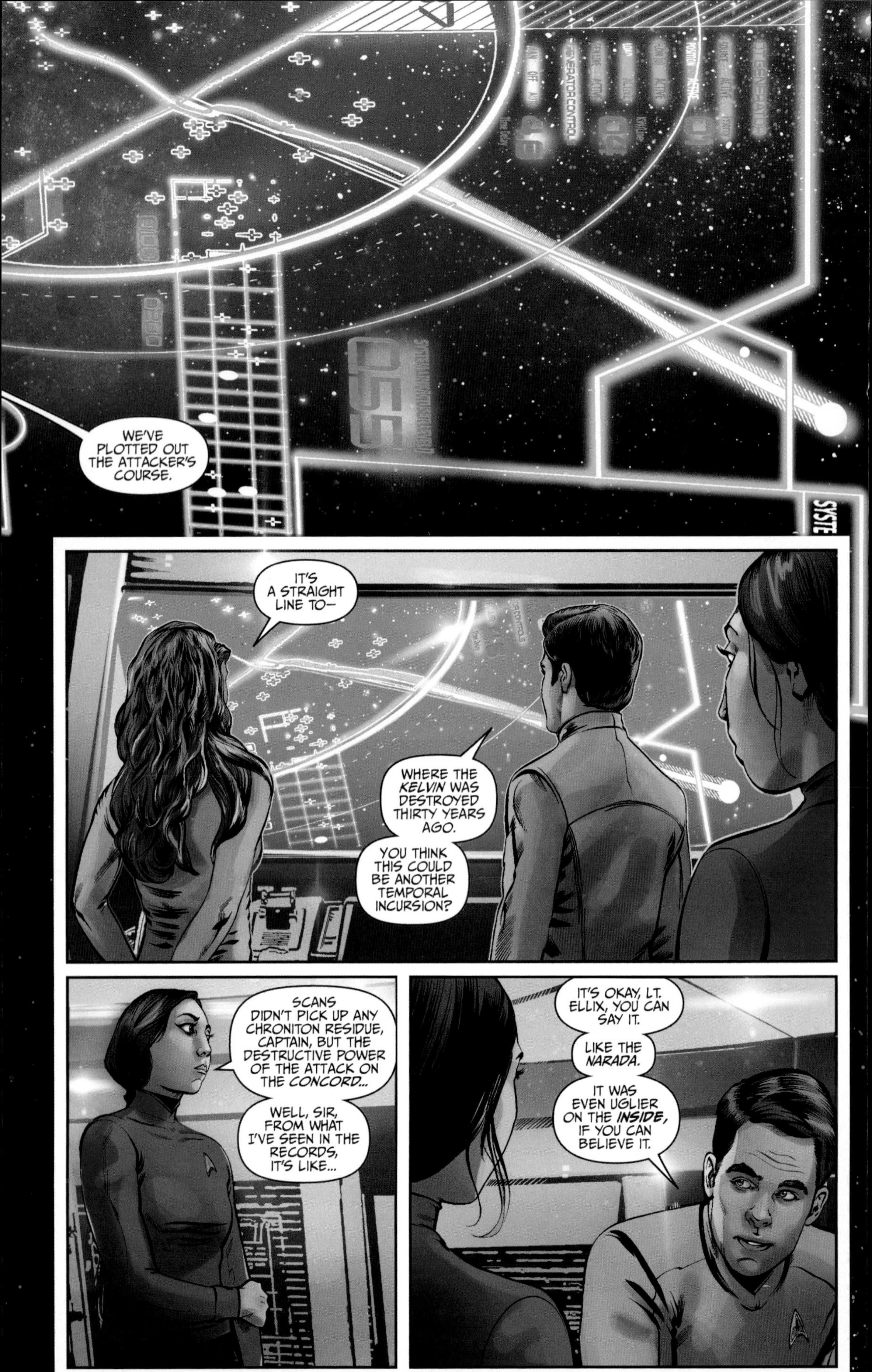
WE'VE PLOTTED OUT THE ATTACKER'S COURSE.
IT'S A STRAIGHT LINE TO—
WHERE THE *KELVIN* WAS DESTROYED THIRTY YEARS AGO.
YOU THINK THIS COULD BE ANOTHER TEMPORAL INCURSION?
SCANS DIDN'T PICK UP ANY CHRONITON RESIDUE, CAPTAIN, BUT THE DESTRUCTIVE POWER OF THE ATTACK ON THE *CONCORD*...
WELL, SIR, FROM WHAT I'VE SEEN IN THE RECORDS, IT'S LIKE...
IT'S OKAY, LT. ELLIX, YOU CAN SAY IT.
LIKE THE *NARADA.*
IT WAS EVEN UGLIER ON THE *INSIDE,* IF YOU CAN BELIEVE IT.

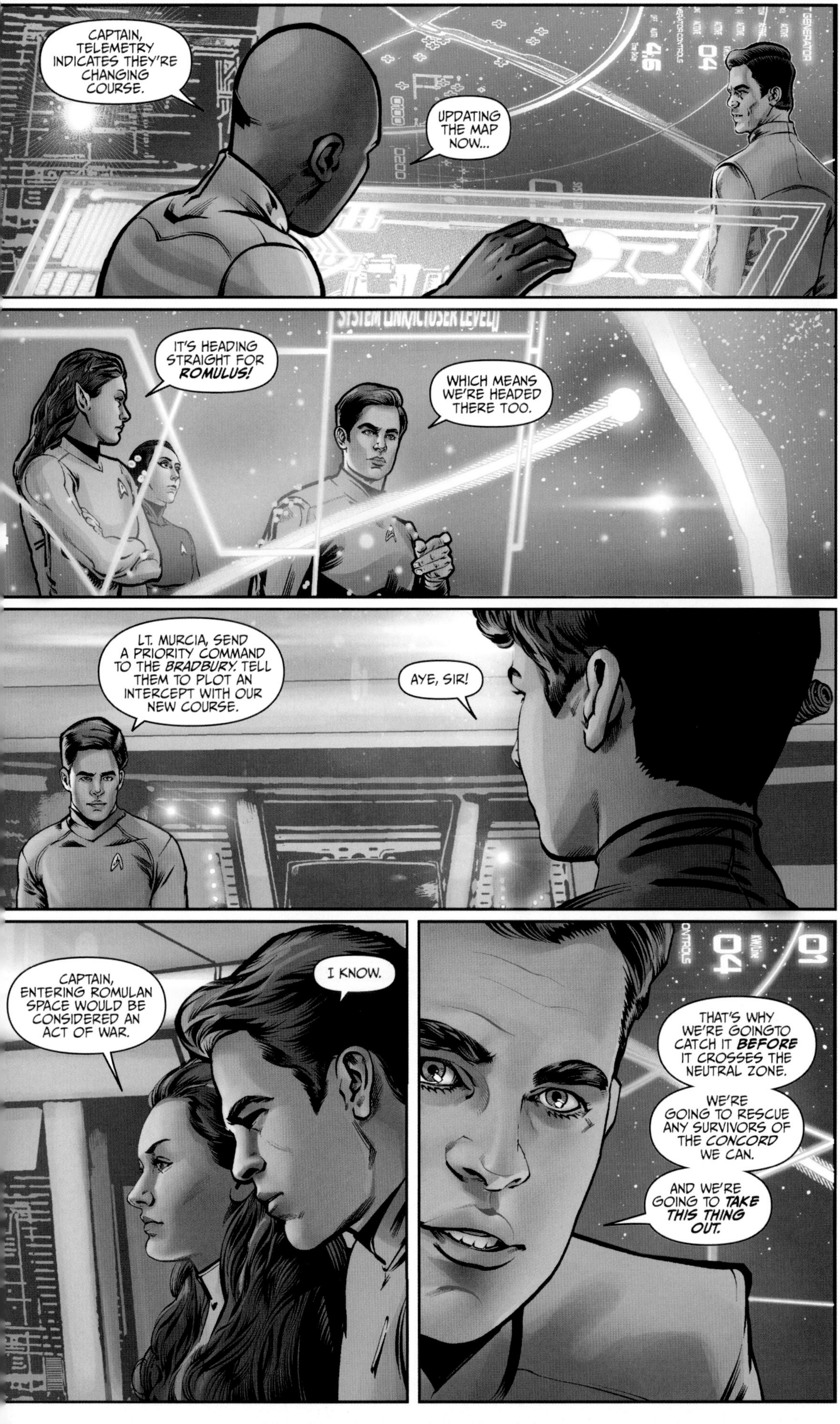
CAPTAIN, TELEMETRY INDICATES THEY'RE CHANGING COURSE.
UPDATING THE MAP NOW...
IT'S HEADING STRAIGHT FOR ROMULUS!
WHICH MEANS WE'RE HEADED THERE TOO.
LT. MURCIA, SEND A PRIORITY COMMAND TO THE BRADBURY. TELL THEM TO PLOT AN INTERCEPT WITH OUR NEW COURSE.
AYE, SIR!
CAPTAIN, ENTERING ROMULAN SPACE WOULD BE CONSIDERED AN ACT OF WAR.
I KNOW.
THAT'S WHY WE'RE GOINGTO CATCH IT BEFORE IT CROSSES THE NEUTRAL ZONE.
WE'RE GOING TO RESCUE ANY SURVIVORS OF THE CONCORD WE CAN.
AND WE'RE GOING TO TAKE THIS THING OUT.

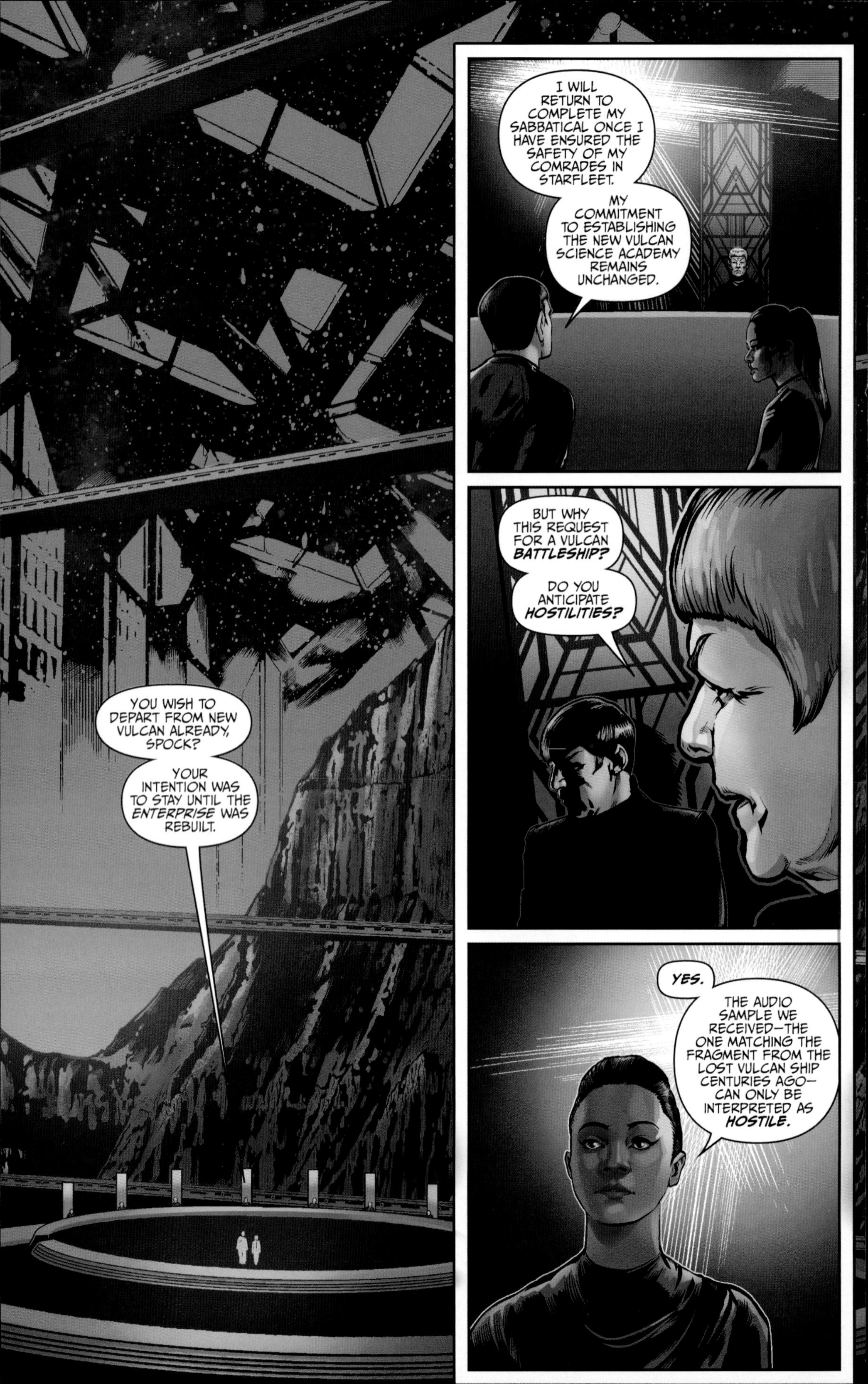
YOU WISH TO DEPART FROM NEW VULCAN ALREADY, SPOCK?
YOUR INTENTION WAS TO STAY UNTIL THE ENTERPRISE WAS REBUILT.
I WILL RETURN TO COMPLETE MY SABBATICAL ONCE I HAVE ENSURED THE SAFETY OF MY COMRADES IN STARFLEET.
MY COMMITMENT TO ESTABLISHING THE NEW VULCAN SCIENCE ACADEMY REMAINS UNCHANGED.
BUT WHY THIS REQUEST FOR A VULCAN BATTLESHIP?
DO YOU ANTICIPATE HOSTILITIES?
YES.
THE AUDIO SAMPLE WE RECEIVED—THE ONE MATCHING THE FRAGMENT FROM THE LOST VULCAN SHIP CENTURIES AGO—CAN ONLY BE INTERPRETED AS HOSTILE.

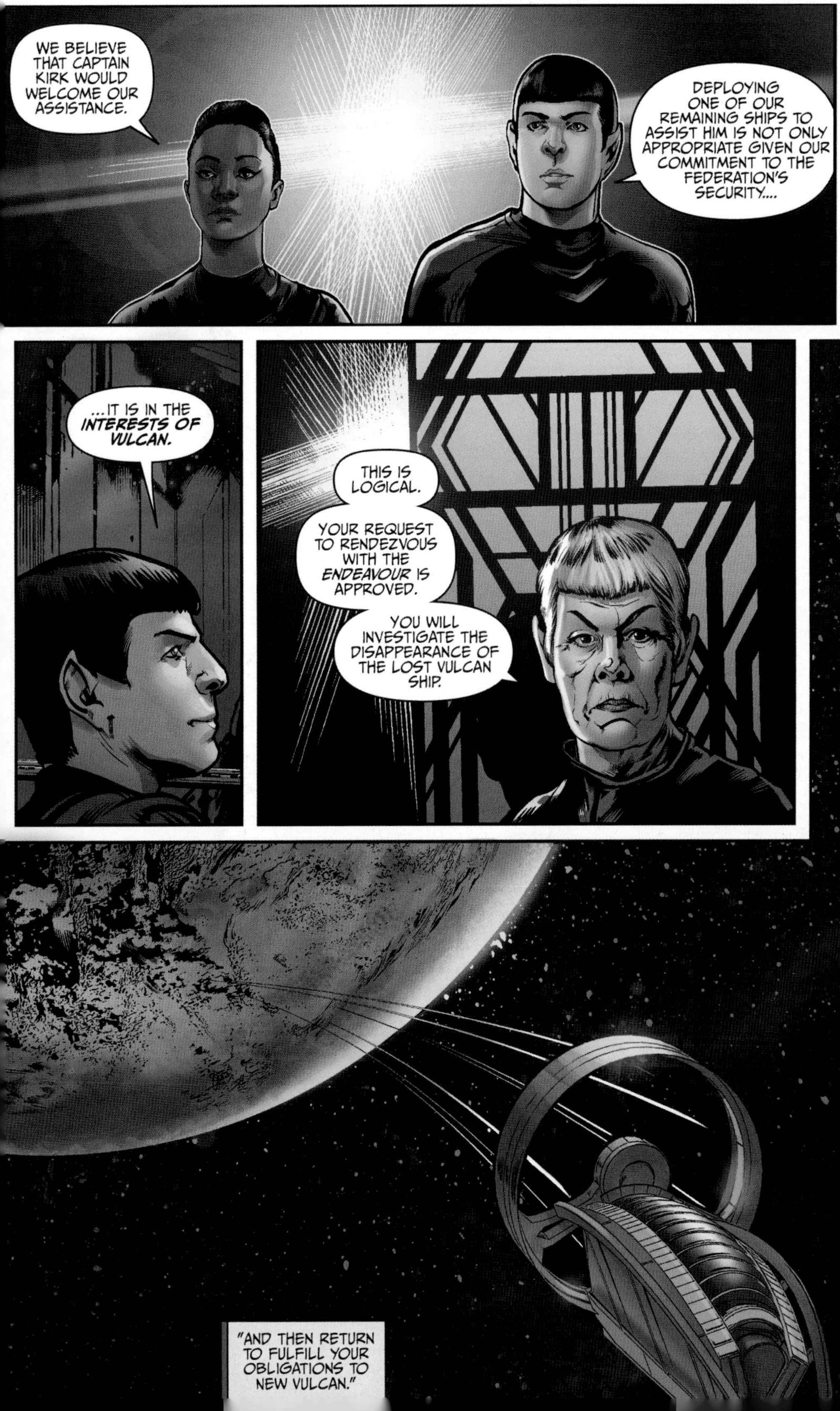
WE BELIEVE THAT CAPTAIN KIRK WOULD WELCOME OUR ASSISTANCE.
DEPLOYING ONE OF OUR REMAINING SHIPS TO ASSIST HIM IS NOT ONLY APPROPRIATE GIVEN OUR COMMITMENT TO THE FEDERATION'S SECURITY....
...IT IS IN THE *INTERESTS OF VULCAN.*
THIS IS LOGICAL.
YOUR REQUEST TO RENDEZVOUS WITH THE *ENDEAVOUR* IS APPROVED.
YOU WILL INVESTIGATE THE DISAPPEARANCE OF THE LOST VULCAN SHIP.
"AND THEN RETURN TO FULFILL YOUR OBLIGATIONS TO NEW VULCAN."

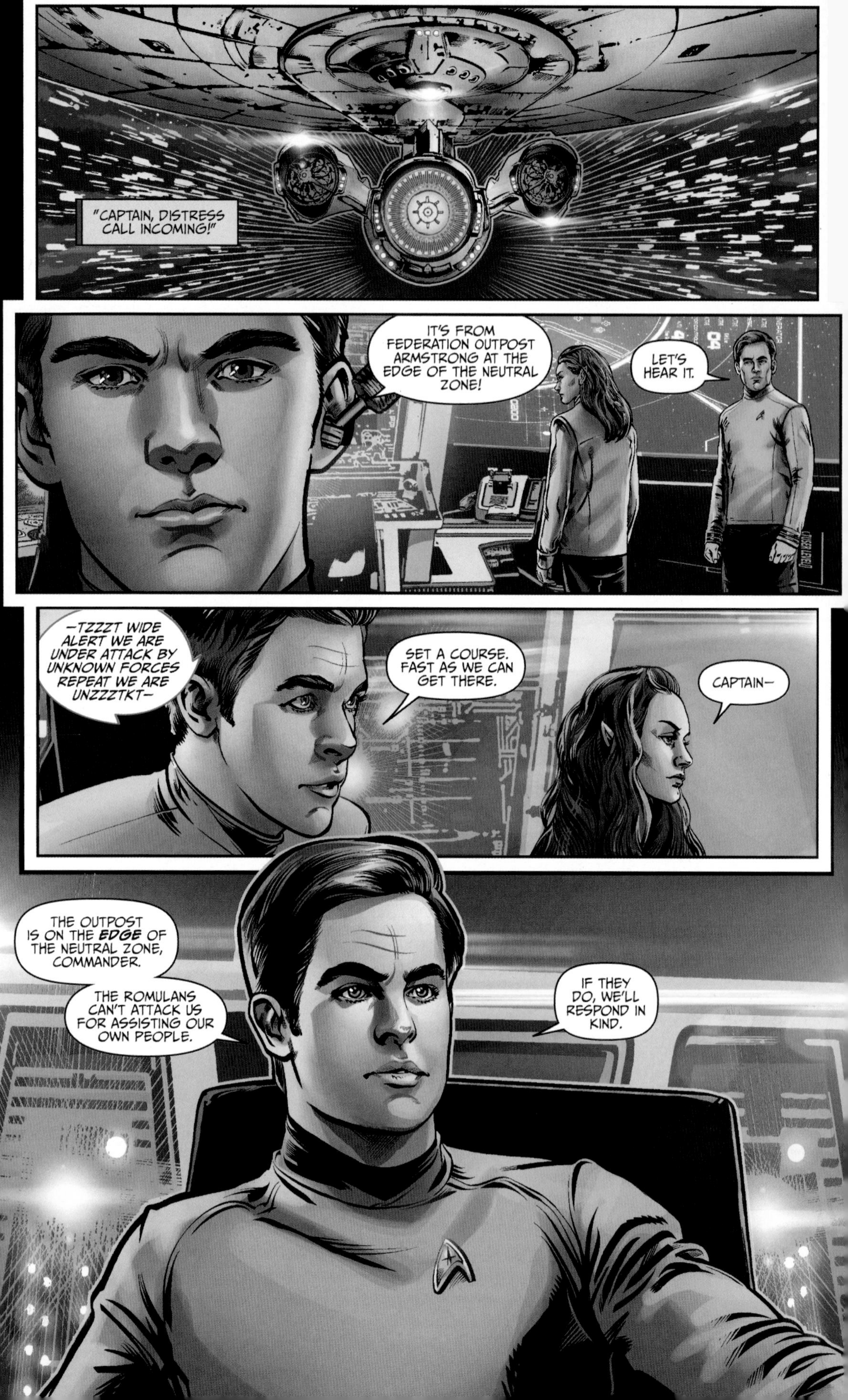
"CAPTAIN, DISTRESS CALL INCOMING!"
IT'S FROM FEDERATION OUTPOST ARMSTRONG AT THE EDGE OF THE NEUTRAL ZONE!
LET'S HEAR IT.
—TZZZT WIDE ALERT WE ARE UNDER ATTACK BY UNKNOWN FORCES REPEAT WE ARE UNZZZTKT—
SET A COURSE. FAST AS WE CAN GET THERE.
CAPTAIN—
THE OUTPOST IS ON THE EDGE OF THE NEUTRAL ZONE, COMMANDER.
THE ROMULANS CAN'T ATTACK US FOR ASSISTING OUR OWN PEOPLE.
IF THEY DO, WE'LL RESPOND IN KIND.

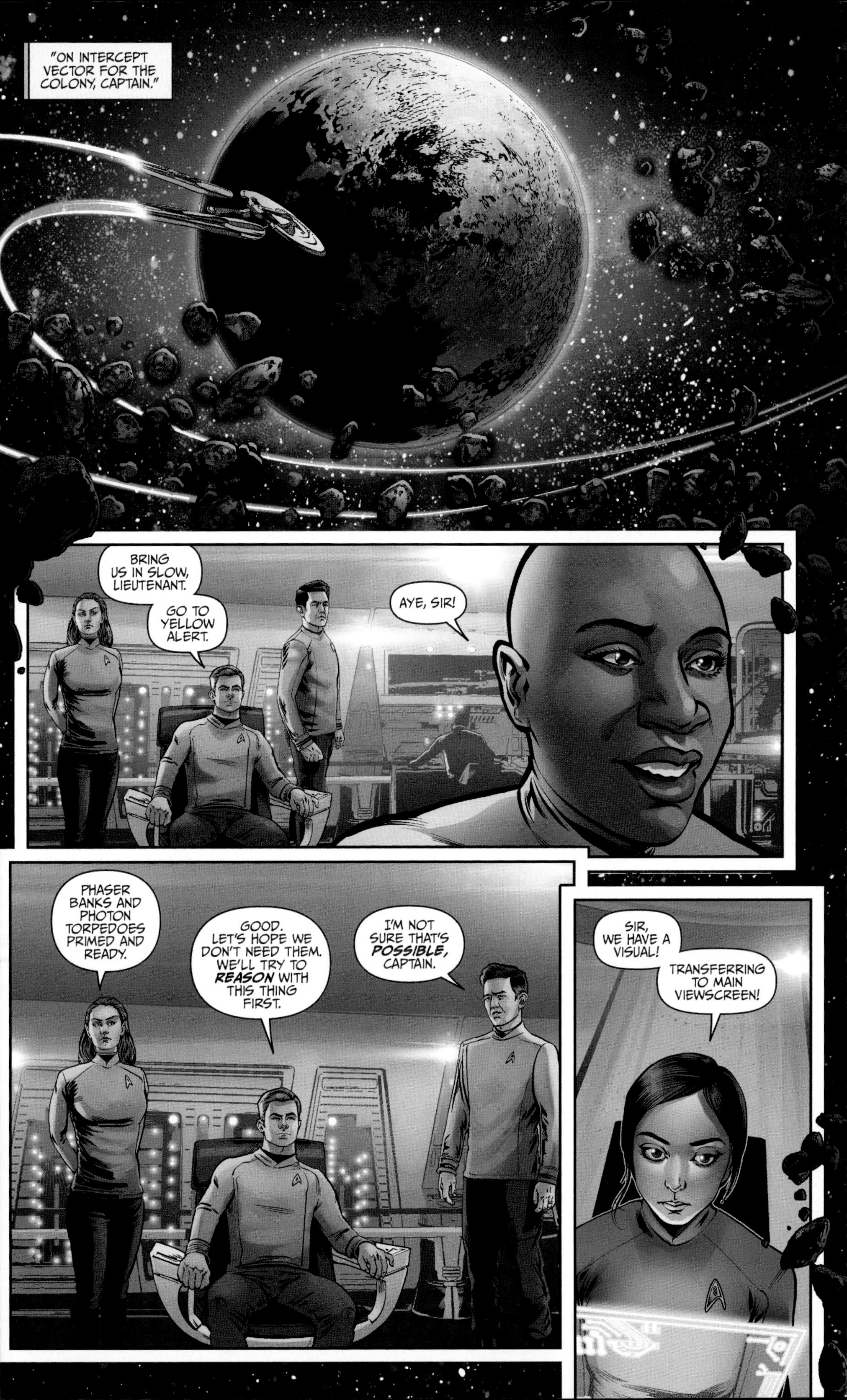
"ON INTERCEPT VECTOR FOR THE COLONY, CAPTAIN."
BRING US IN SLOW, LIEUTENANT.
GO TO YELLOW ALERT.
AYE, SIR!
PHASER BANKS AND PHOTON TORPEDOES PRIMED AND READY.
GOOD. LET'S HOPE WE DON'T NEED THEM. WE'LL TRY TO **REASON** WITH THIS THING FIRST.
I'M NOT SURE THAT'S **POSSIBLE,** CAPTAIN.
SIR, WE HAVE A VISUAL!
TRANSFERRING TO MAIN VIEWSCREEN!

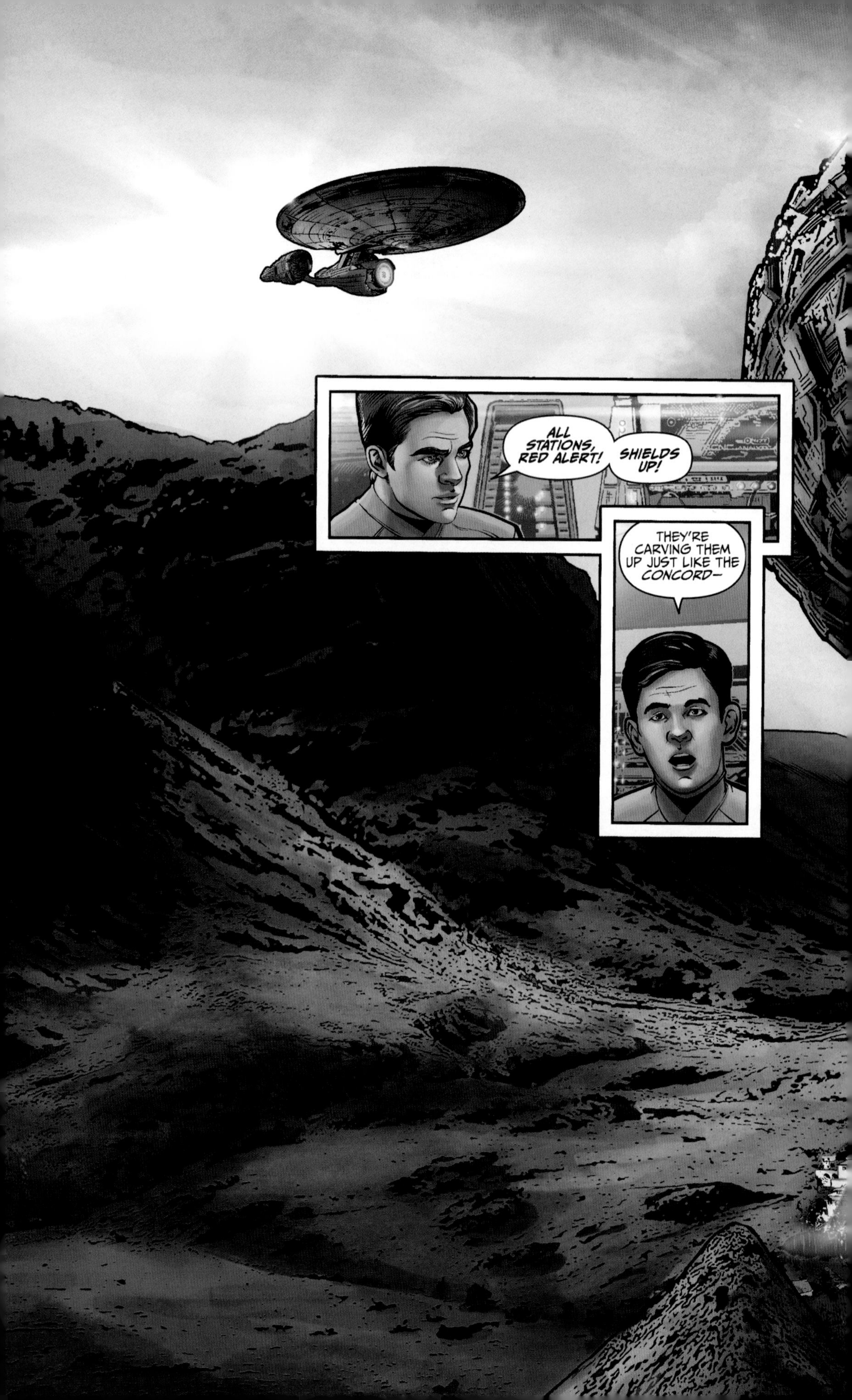
ALL STATIONS, RED ALERT!
SHIELDS UP!
THEY'RE CARVING THEM UP JUST LIKE THE CONCORD—

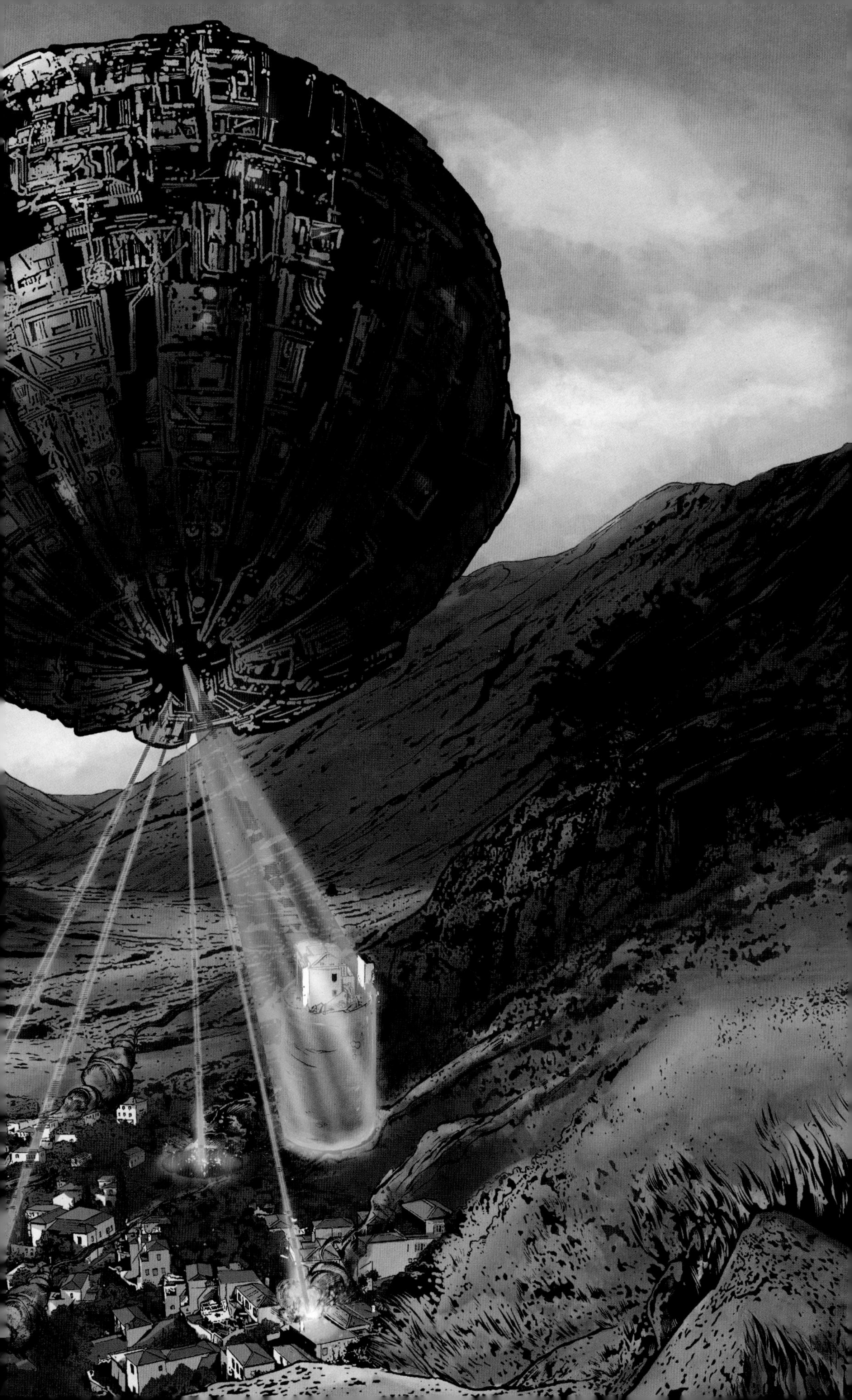

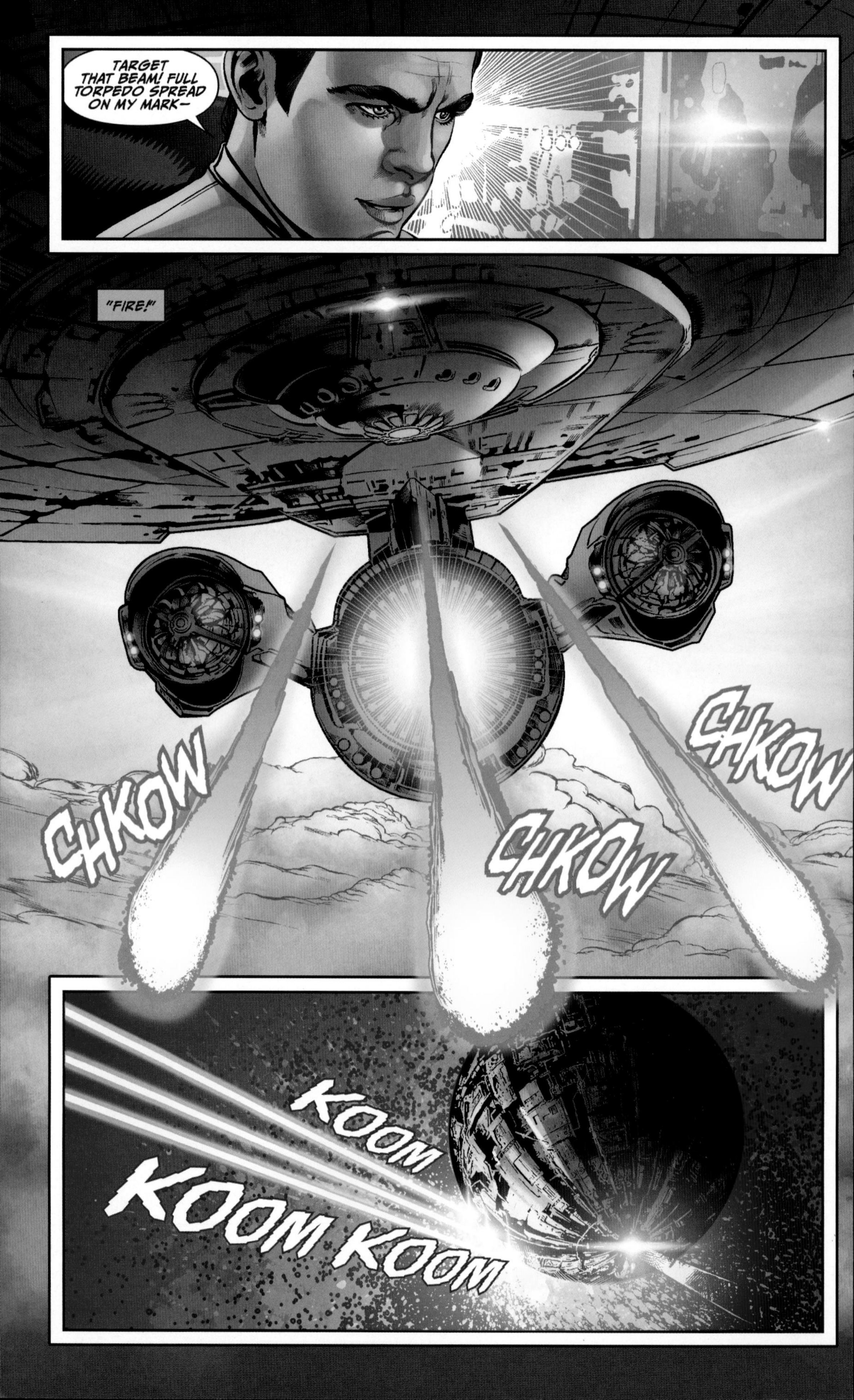
TARGET THAT BEAM! FULL TORPEDO SPREAD ON MY MARK—
"FIRE!"
CHKOW
CHKOW
CHKOW
KOOM
KOOM KOOM

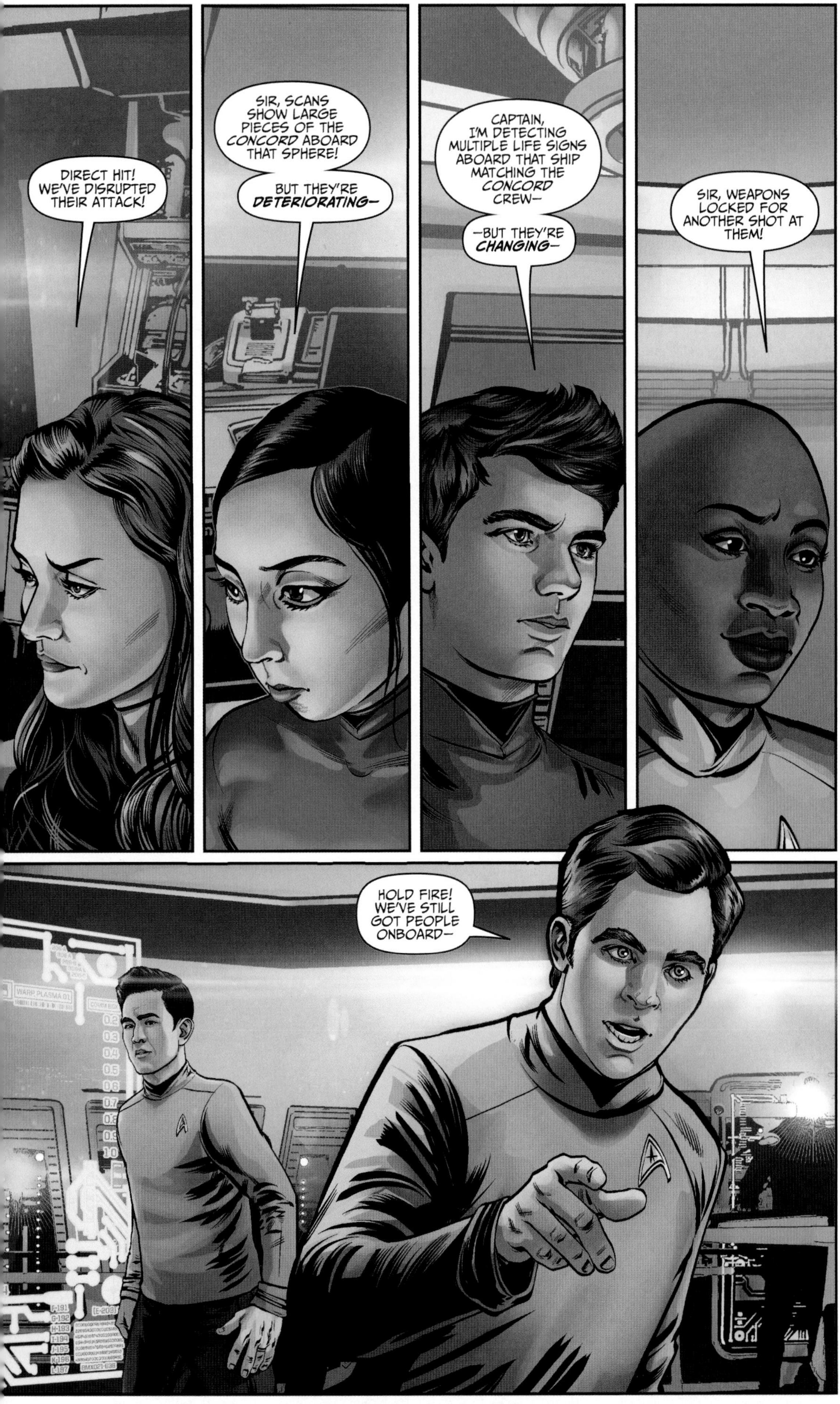

DIRECT HIT! WE'VE DISRUPTED THEIR ATTACK!
SIR, SCANS SHOW LARGE PIECES OF THE *CONCORD* ABOARD THAT SPHERE!
BUT THEY'RE ***DETERIORATING—***
CAPTAIN, I'M DETECTING MULTIPLE LIFE SIGNS ABOARD THAT SHIP MATCHING THE *CONCORD* CREW—
—BUT THEY'RE ***CHANGING—***
SIR, WEAPONS LOCKED FOR ANOTHER SHOT AT THEM!
HOLD FIRE! WE'VE STILL GOT PEOPLE ONBOARD—
WARP PLASMA 01

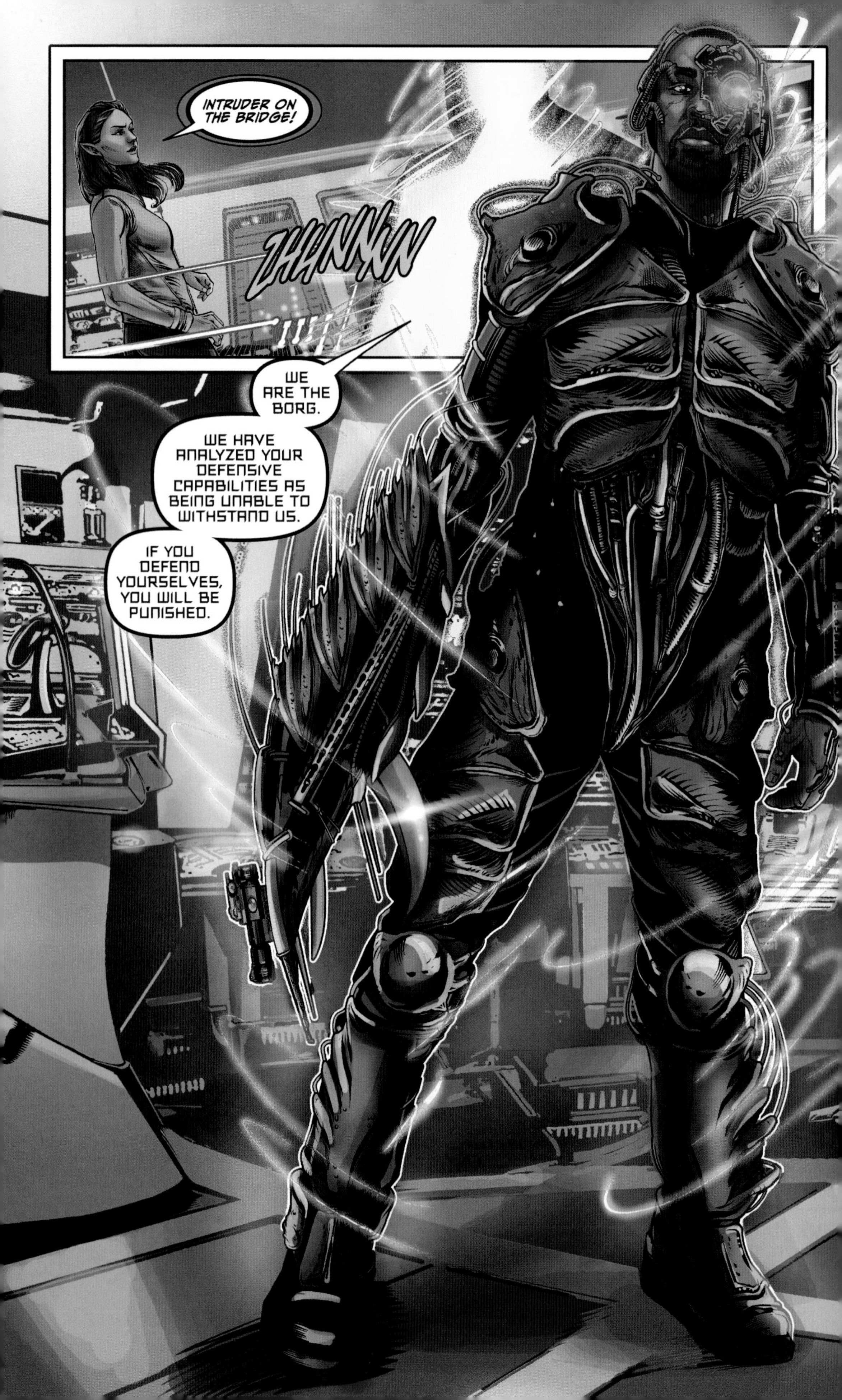
INTRUDER ON THE BRIDGE!
ZHUNNNN
WE ARE THE BORG.
WE HAVE ANALYZED YOUR DEFENSIVE CAPABILITIES AS BEING UNABLE TO WITHSTAND US.
IF YOU DEFEND YOURSELVES, YOU WILL BE PUNISHED.

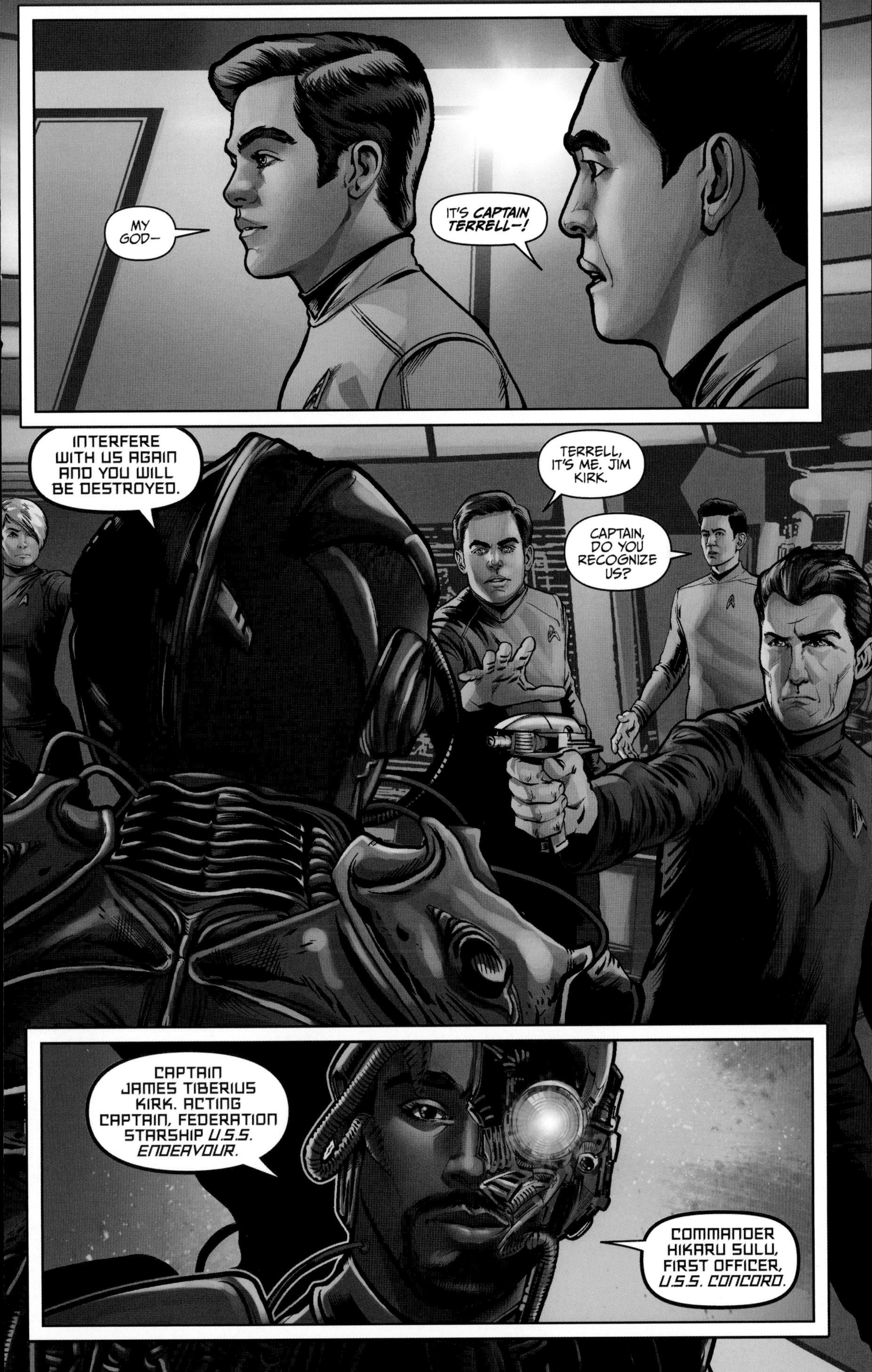
MY GOD—
IT'S CAPTAIN TERRELL—!
INTERFERE WITH US AGAIN AND YOU WILL BE DESTROYED.
TERRELL, IT'S ME. JIM KIRK.
CAPTAIN, DO YOU RECOGNIZE US?
CAPTAIN JAMES TIBERIUS KIRK. ACTING CAPTAIN, FEDERATION STARSHIP U.S.S. ENDEAVOUR.
COMMANDER HIKARU SULU, FIRST OFFICER, U.S.S. CONCORD.

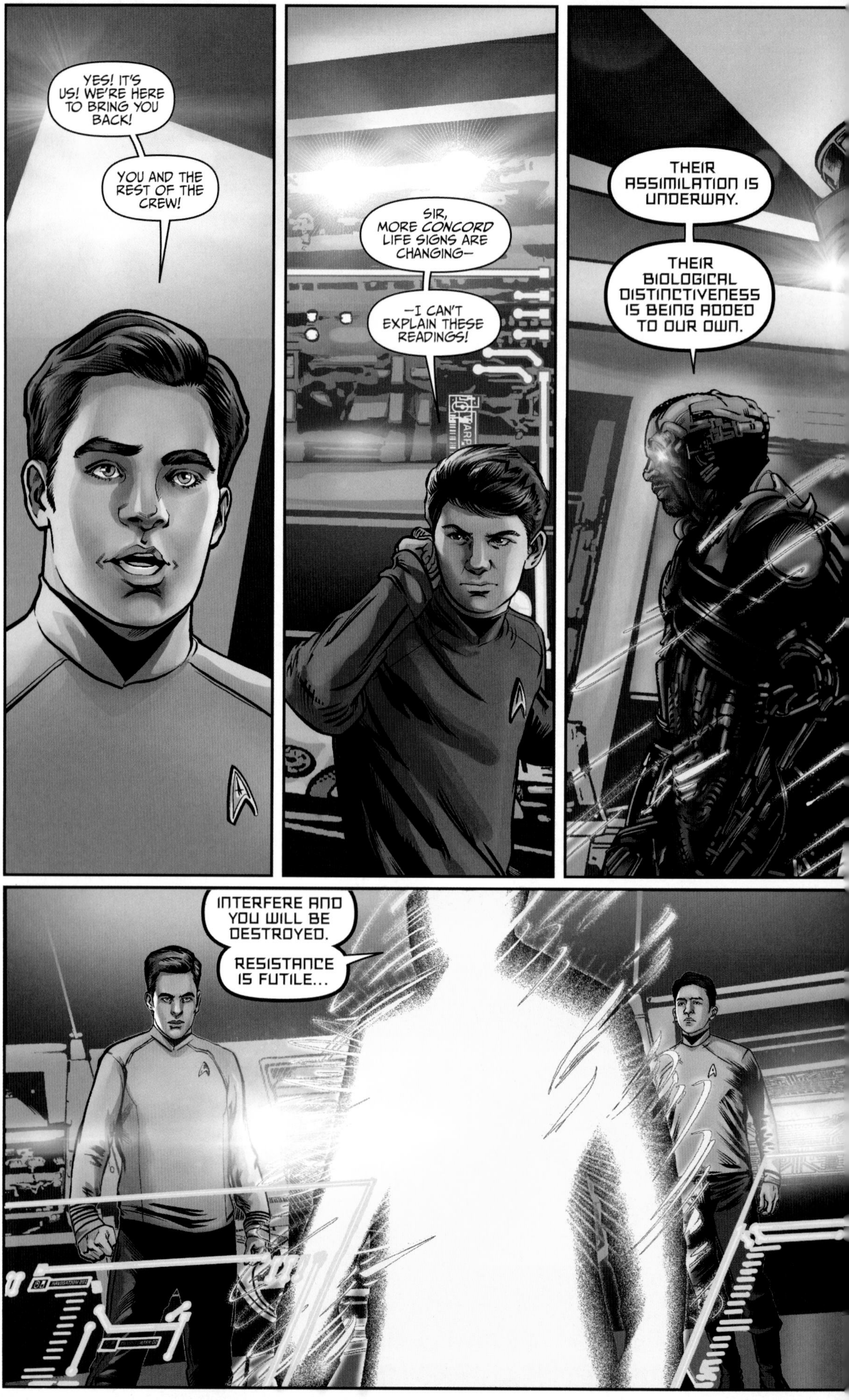
YES! IT'S US! WE'RE HERE TO BRING YOU BACK!
YOU AND THE REST OF THE CREW!
SIR, MORE CONCORD LIFE SIGNS ARE CHANGING—
—I CAN'T EXPLAIN THESE READINGS!
THEIR ASSIMILATION IS UNDERWAY.
THEIR BIOLOGICAL DISTINCTIVENESS IS BEING ADDED TO OUR OWN.
INTERFERE AND YOU WILL BE DESTROYED.
RESISTANCE IS FUTILE...

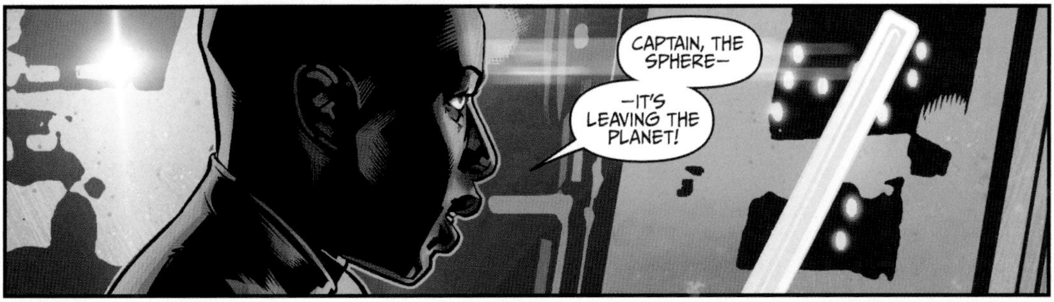
CAPTAIN, THE SPHERE—
—IT'S LEAVING THE PLANET!

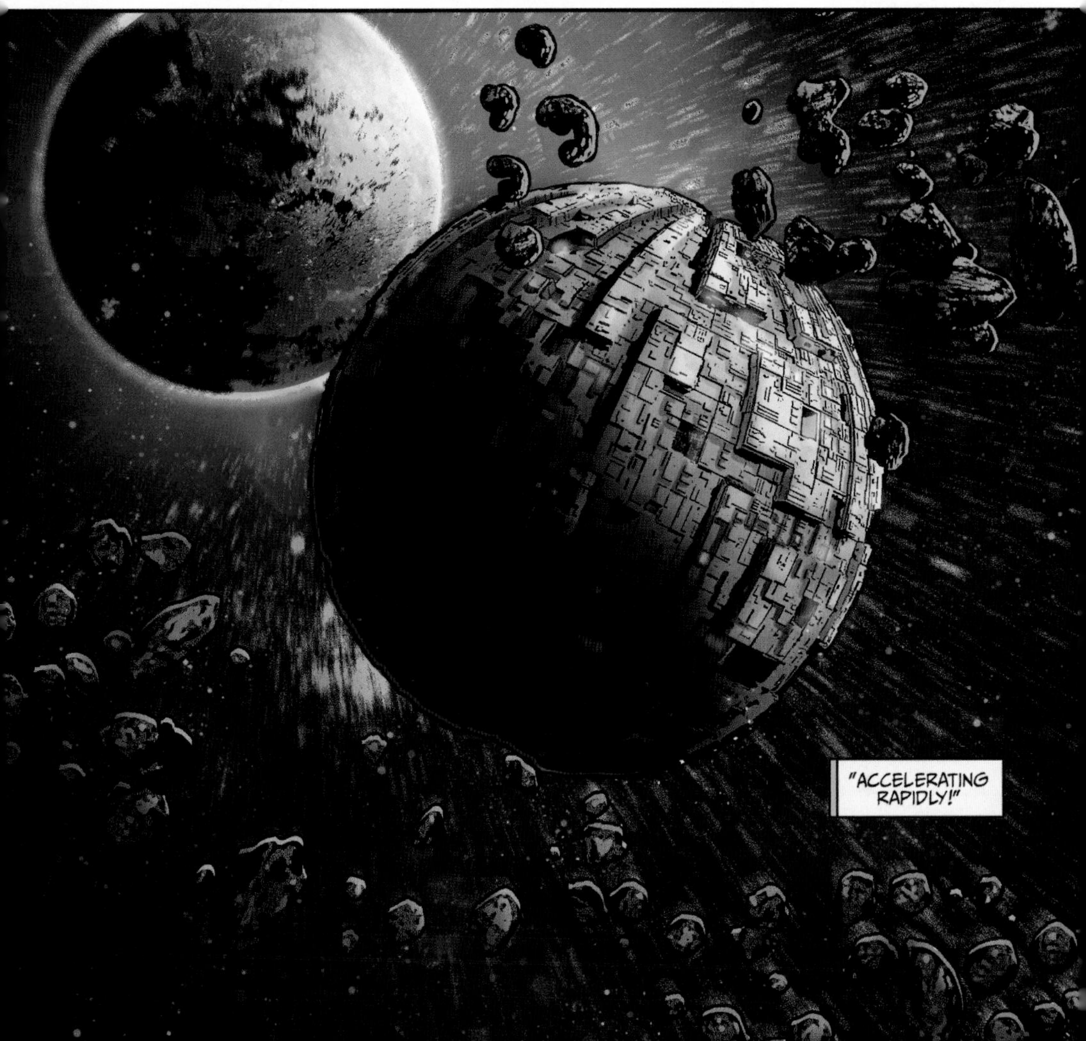
"ACCELERATING RAPIDLY!"

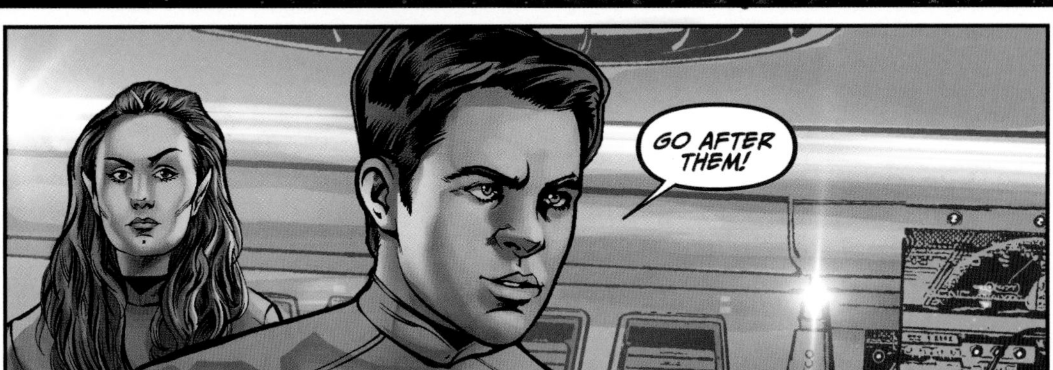
GO AFTER THEM!

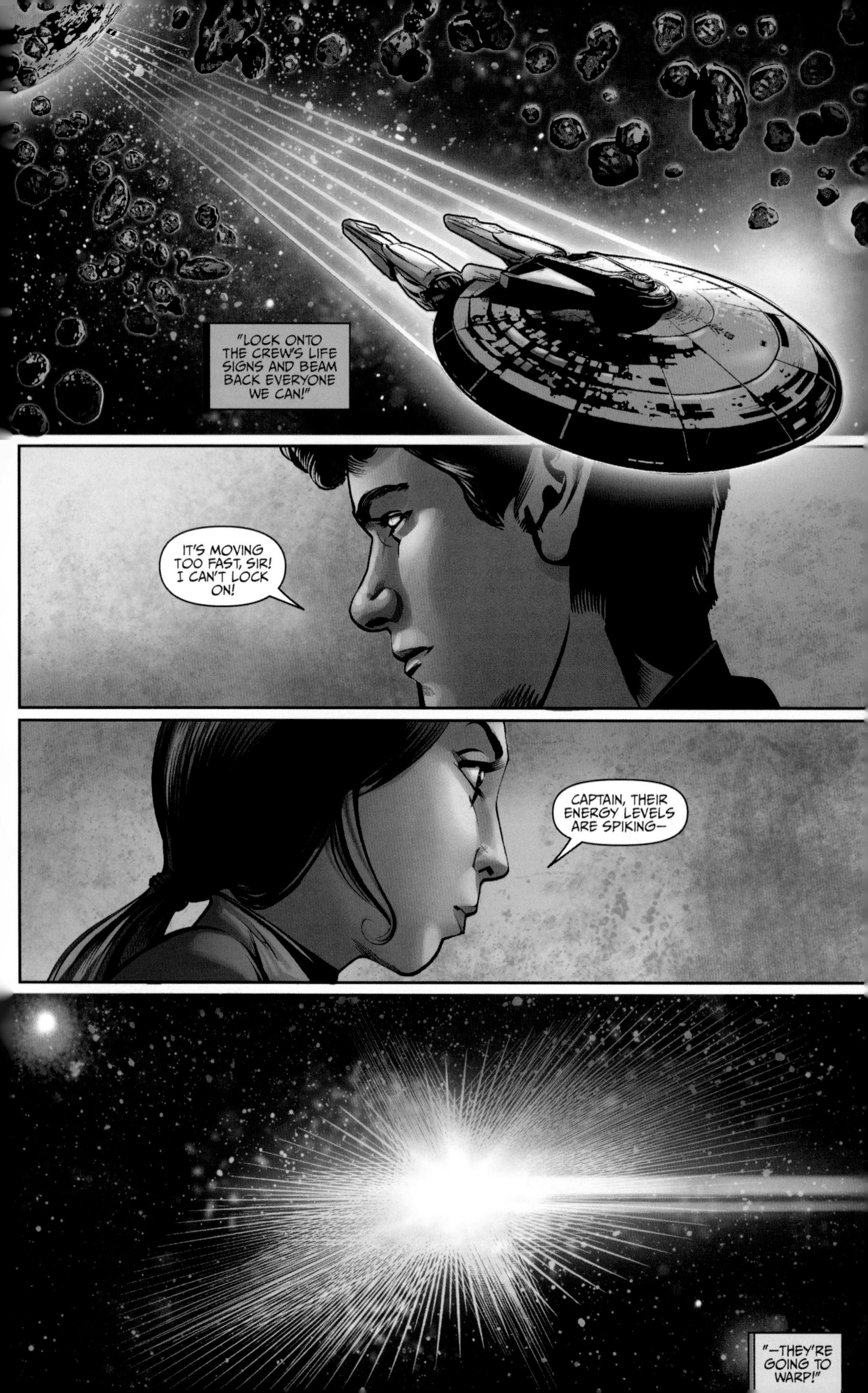
"LOCK ONTO THE CREW'S LIFE SIGNS AND BEAM BACK EVERYONE WE CAN!"
IT'S MOVING TOO FAST, SIR! I CAN'T LOCK ON!
CAPTAIN, THEIR ENERGY LEVELS ARE SPIKING—
"—THEY'RE GOING TO WARP!"

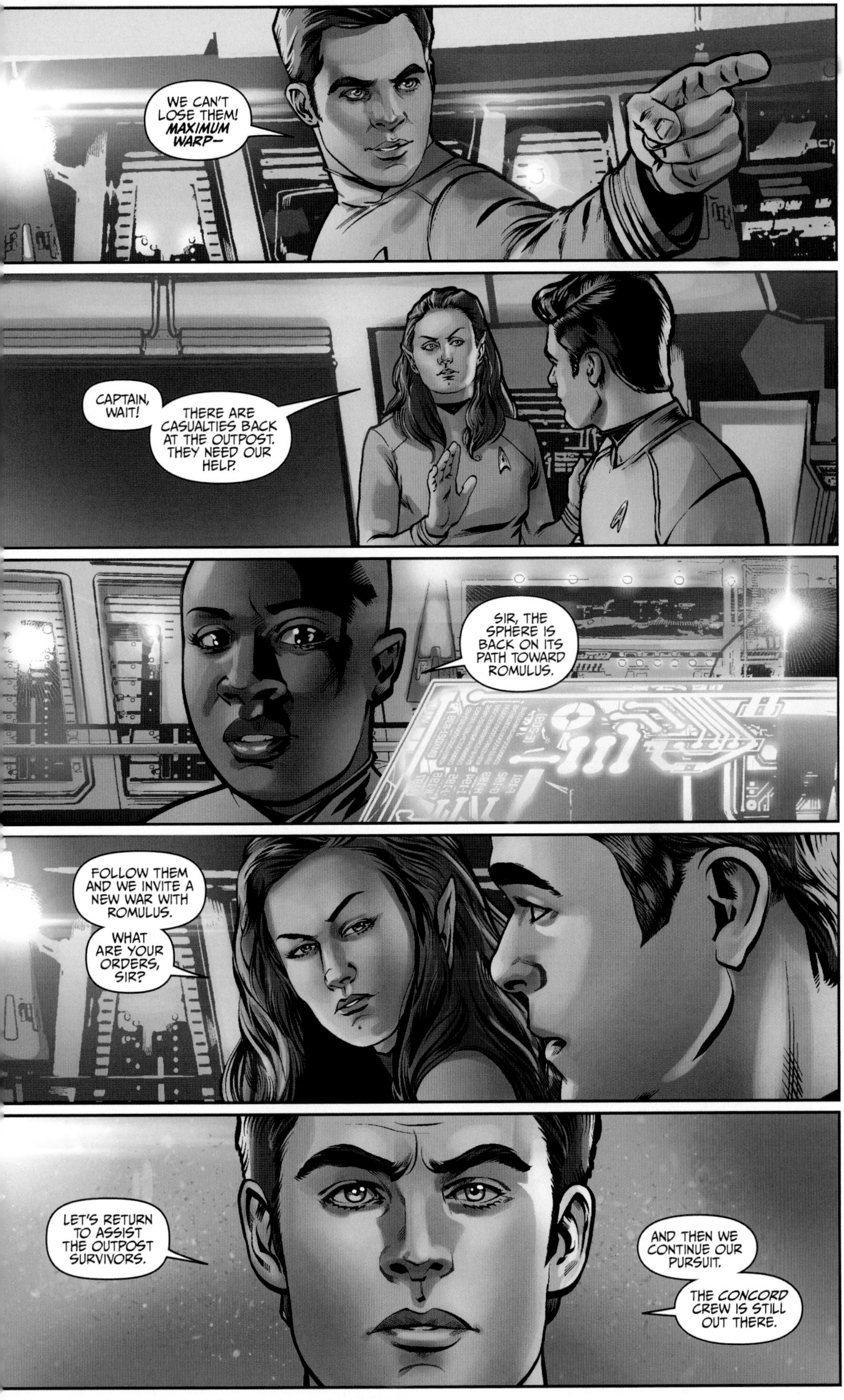
WE CAN'T LOSE THEM! *MAXIMUM WARP—*
CAPTAIN, WAIT!
THERE ARE CASUALTIES BACK AT THE OUTPOST. THEY NEED OUR HELP.
SIR, THE SPHERE IS BACK ON ITS PATH TOWARD ROMULUS.
FOLLOW THEM AND WE INVITE A NEW WAR WITH ROMULUS.
WHAT ARE YOUR ORDERS, SIR?
LET'S RETURN TO ASSIST THE OUTPOST SURVIVORS.
AND THEN WE CONTINUE OUR PURSUIT.
THE *CONCORD* CREW IS STILL OUT THERE.

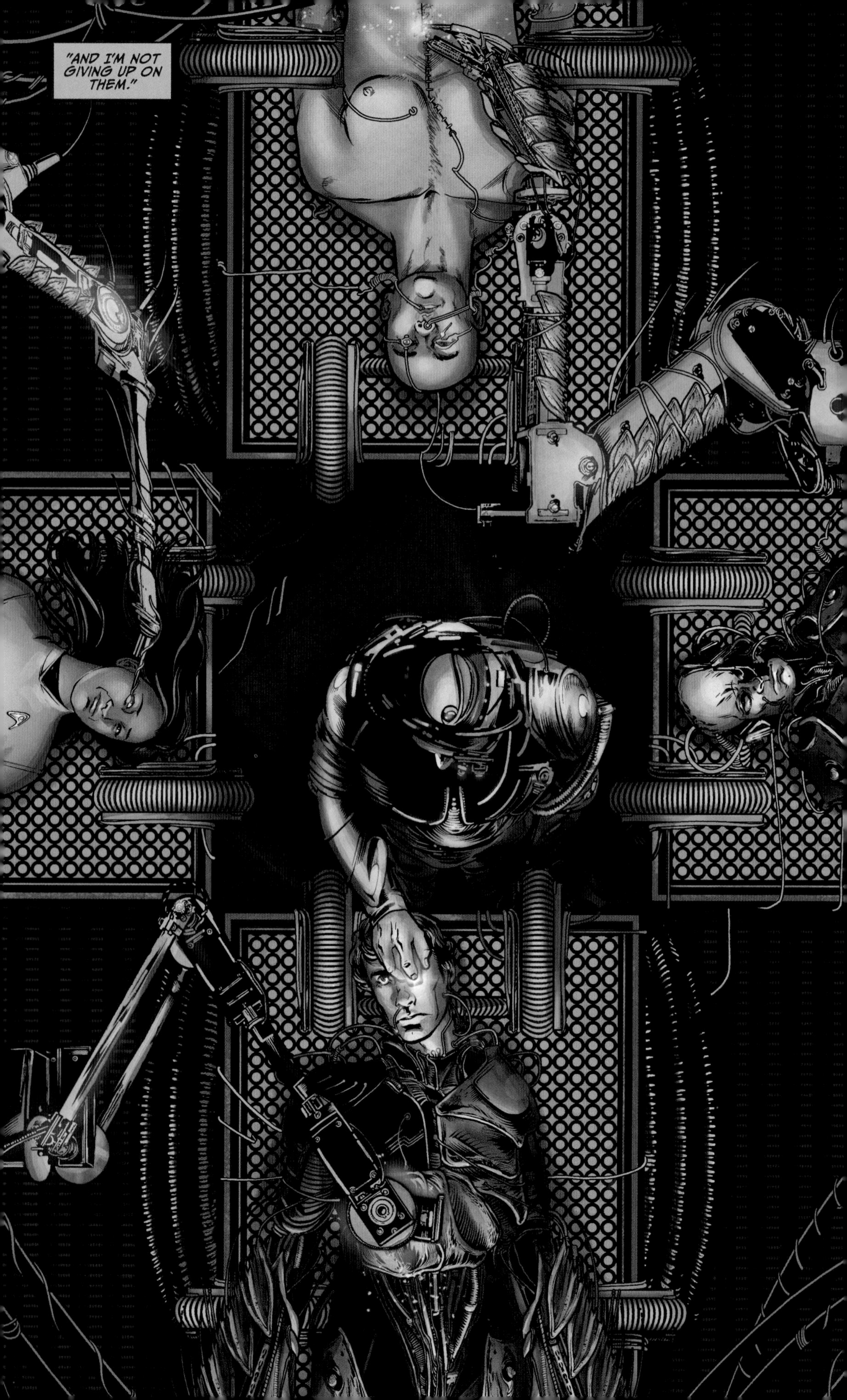
"AND I'M NOT GIVING UP ON THEM."

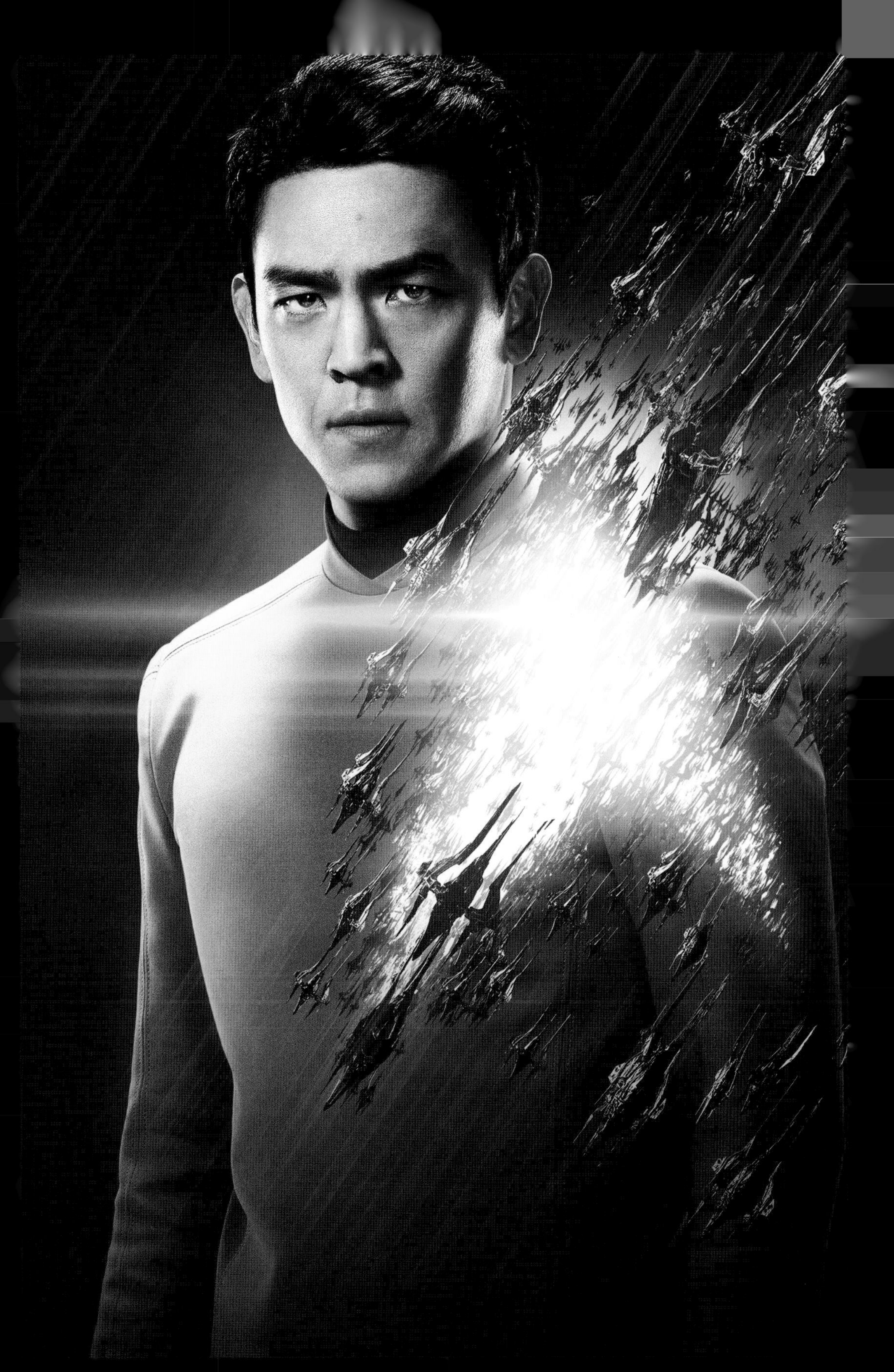

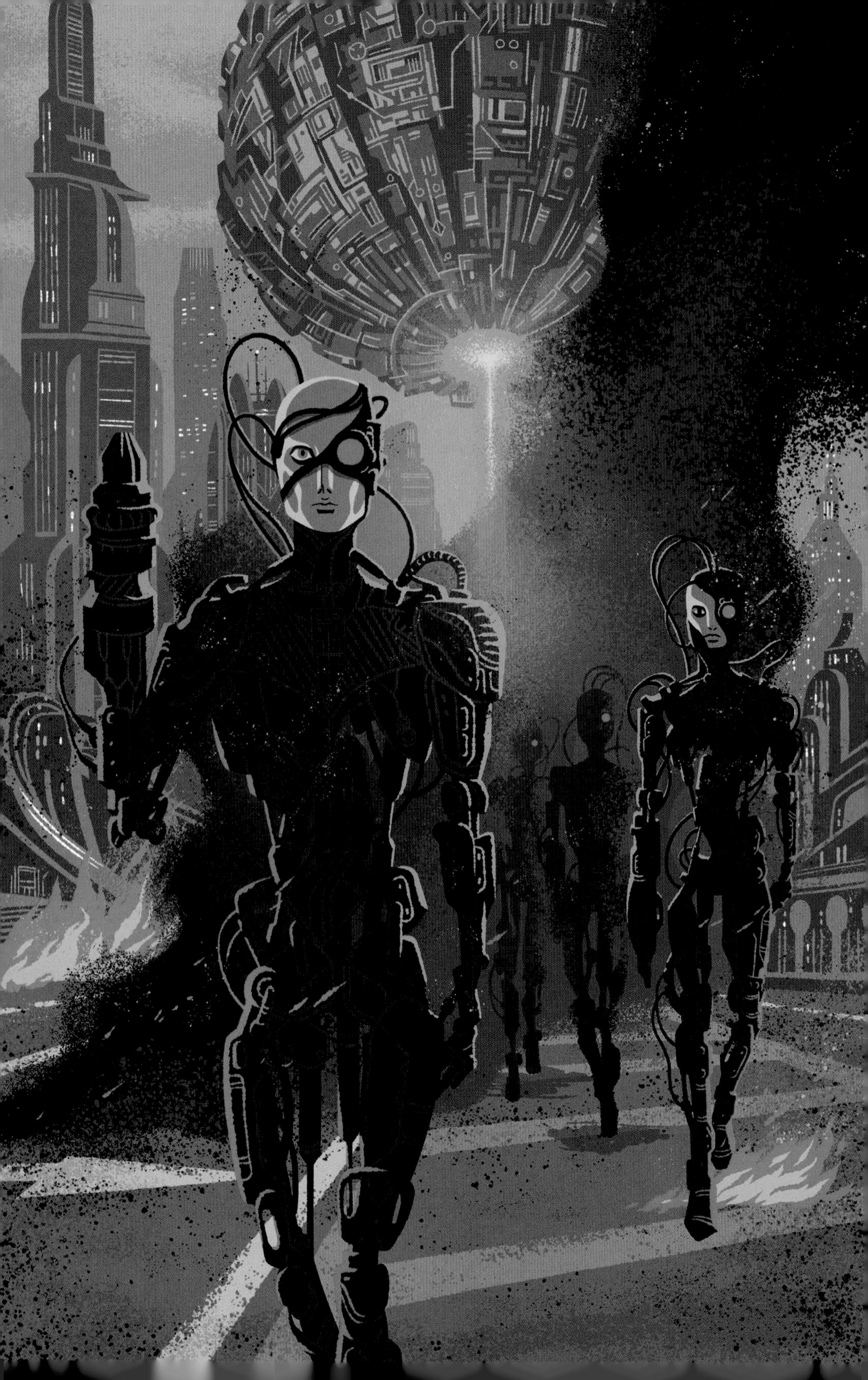

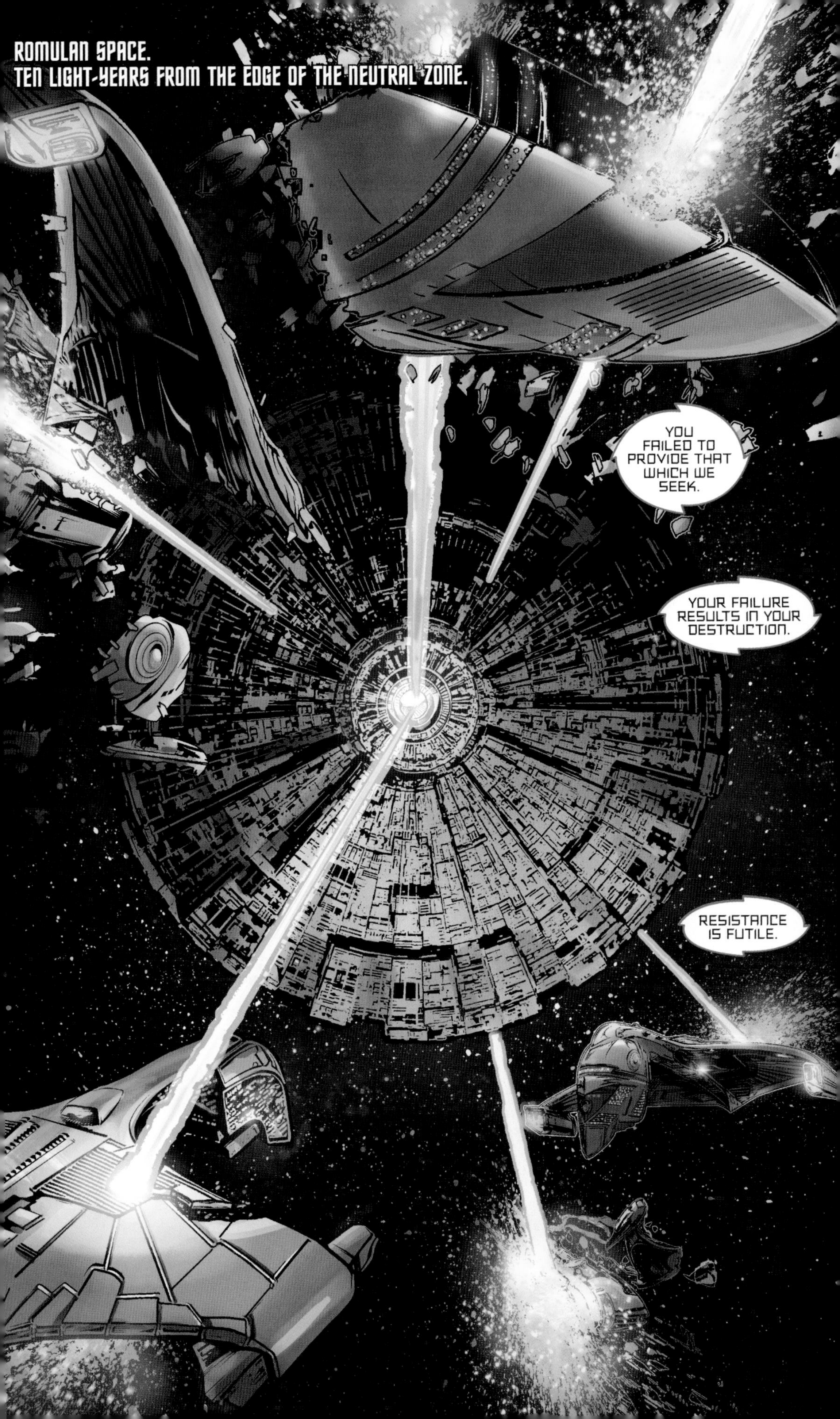
ROMULAN SPACE.
TEN LIGHT-YEARS FROM THE EDGE OF THE NEUTRAL ZONE.
YOU FAILED TO PROVIDE THAT WHICH WE SEEK.
YOUR FAILURE RESULTS IN YOUR DESTRUCTION.
RESISTANCE IS FUTILE.

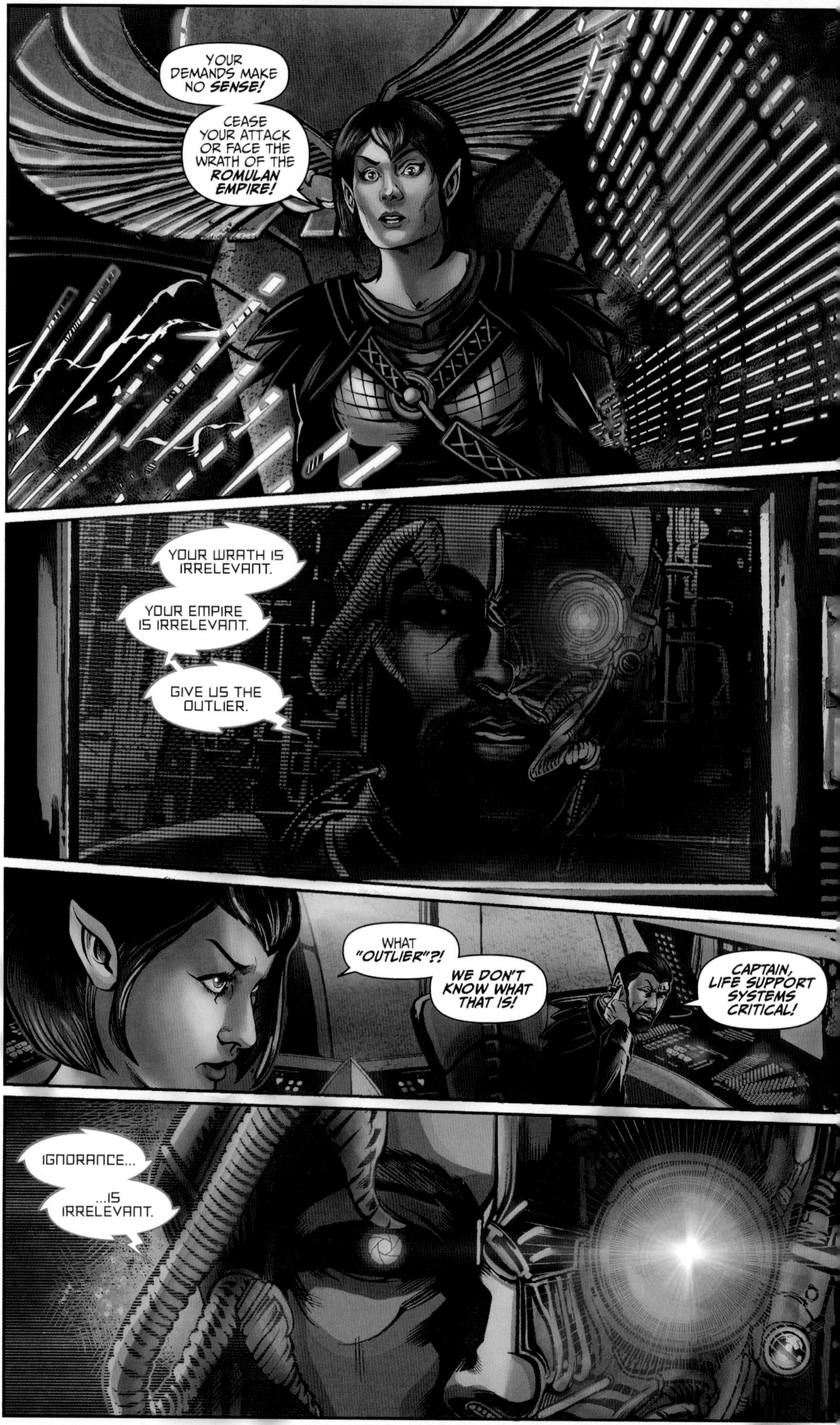
YOUR DEMANDS MAKE NO SENSE!
CEASE YOUR ATTACK OR FACE THE WRATH OF THE ROMULAN EMPIRE!
YOUR WRATH IS IRRELEVANT.
YOUR EMPIRE IS IRRELEVANT.
GIVE US THE OUTLIER.
WHAT "OUTLIER"?!
WE DON'T KNOW WHAT THAT IS!
CAPTAIN, LIFE SUPPORT SYSTEMS CRITICAL!
IGNORANCE...
...IS IRRELEVANT.

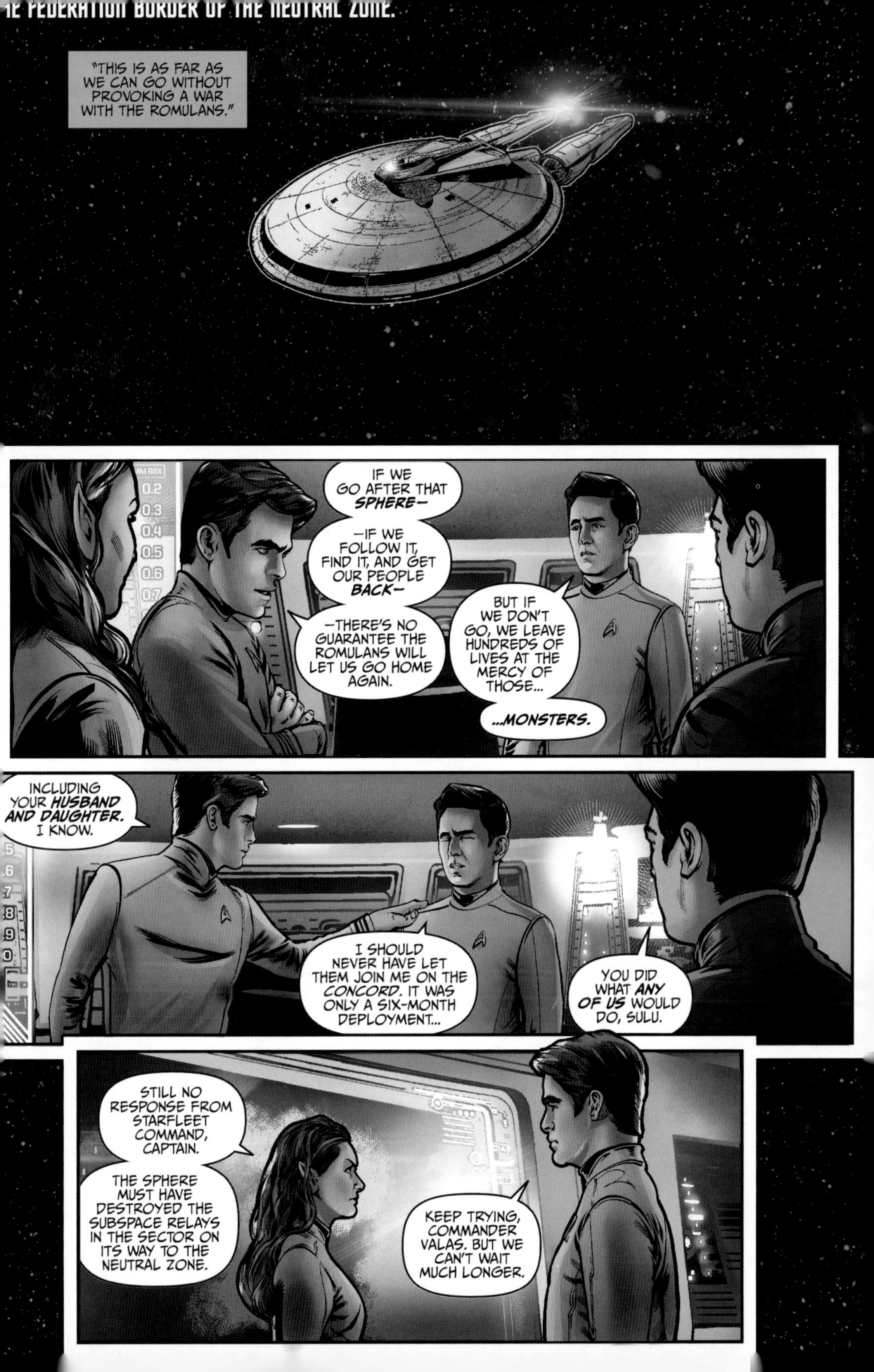
FEDERATION BORDER OF THE NEUTRAL ZONE.
"THIS IS AS FAR AS WE CAN GO WITHOUT PROVOKING A WAR WITH THE ROMULANS."
IF WE GO AFTER THAT SPHERE—
—IF WE FOLLOW IT, FIND IT, AND GET OUR PEOPLE BACK—
—THERE'S NO GUARANTEE THE ROMULANS WILL LET US GO HOME AGAIN.
BUT IF WE DON'T GO, WE LEAVE HUNDREDS OF LIVES AT THE MERCY OF THOSE...
...MONSTERS.
INCLUDING YOUR HUSBAND AND DAUGHTER. I KNOW.
I SHOULD NEVER HAVE LET THEM JOIN ME ON THE CONCORD. IT WAS ONLY A SIX-MONTH DEPLOYMENT...
YOU DID WHAT ANY OF US WOULD DO, SULU.
STILL NO RESPONSE FROM STARFLEET COMMAND, CAPTAIN.
THE SPHERE MUST HAVE DESTROYED THE SUBSPACE RELAYS IN THE SECTOR ON ITS WAY TO THE NEUTRAL ZONE.
KEEP TRYING, COMMANDER VALAS. BUT WE CAN'T WAIT MUCH LONGER.

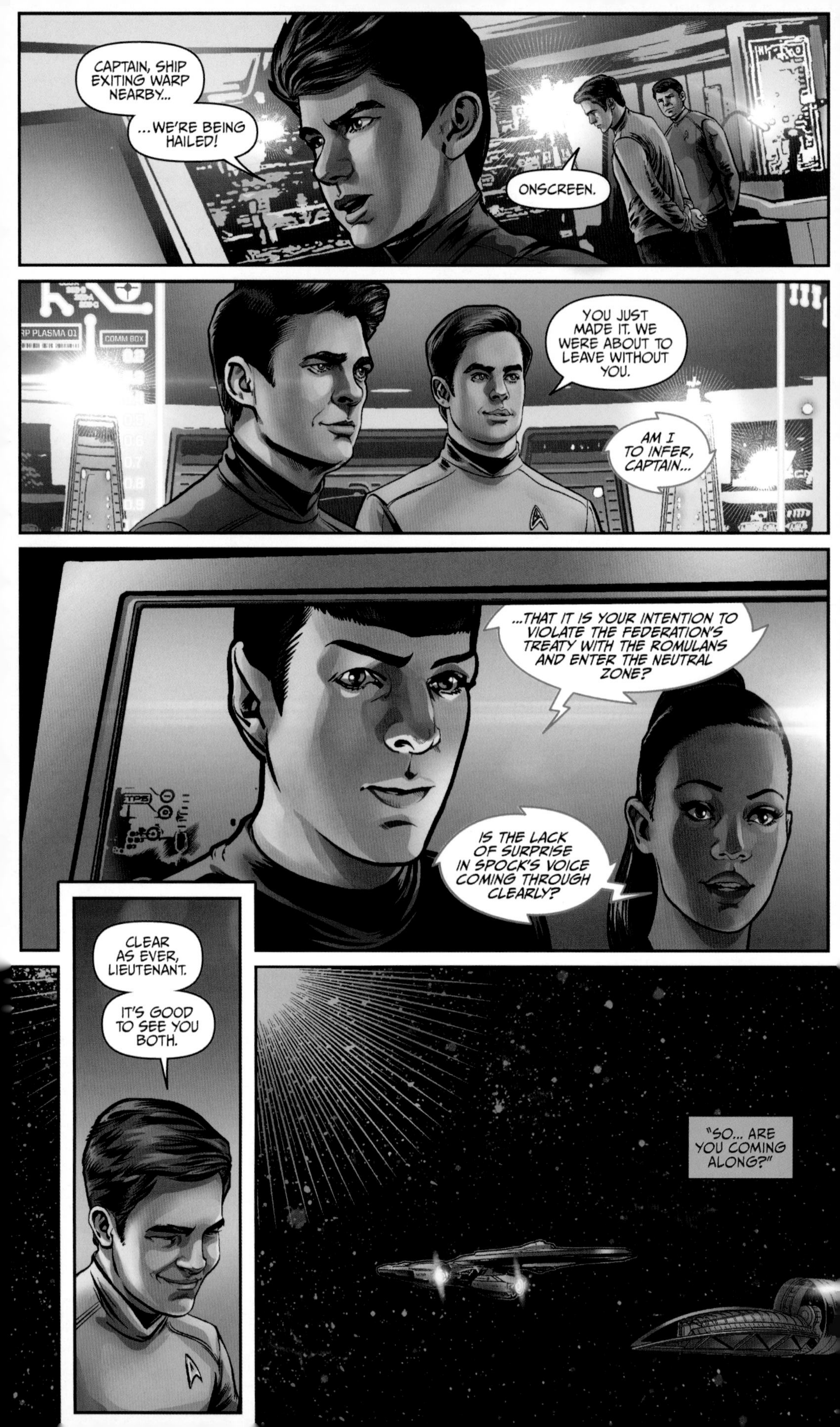

CAPTAIN, SHIP EXITING WARP NEARBY...
...WE'RE BEING HAILED!
ONSCREEN.
RP PLASMA 01
COMM BOX
YOU JUST MADE IT. WE WERE ABOUT TO LEAVE WITHOUT YOU.
AM I TO INFER, CAPTAIN...
...THAT IT IS YOUR INTENTION TO VIOLATE THE FEDERATION'S TREATY WITH THE ROMULANS AND ENTER THE NEUTRAL ZONE?
IS THE LACK OF SURPRISE IN SPOCK'S VOICE COMING THROUGH CLEARLY?
CLEAR AS EVER, LIEUTENANT.
IT'S GOOD TO SEE YOU BOTH.
"SO... ARE YOU COMING ALONG?"

BEFORE YOU TRY TO TALK ME OUT OF IT—

—I HAVE A PLAN.

HIKARU! I'M SO SORRY...

THANK YOU, NYOTA. WE'RE GOING TO GET THEM *BACK*.

I WISH THIS REUNION WAS FOR A *HAPPIER* REASON.

AS DO I, DOCTOR. CAPTAIN, I WOULD LIKE TO REVIEW ALL OF THE DATA YOU HAVE ACQUIRED ON THE SUBJECT OF THESE...

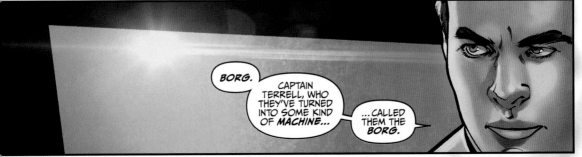

BORG.

CAPTAIN TERRELL, WHO THEY'VE TURNED INTO SOME KIND OF *MACHINE*...

...CALLED THEM THE BORG.

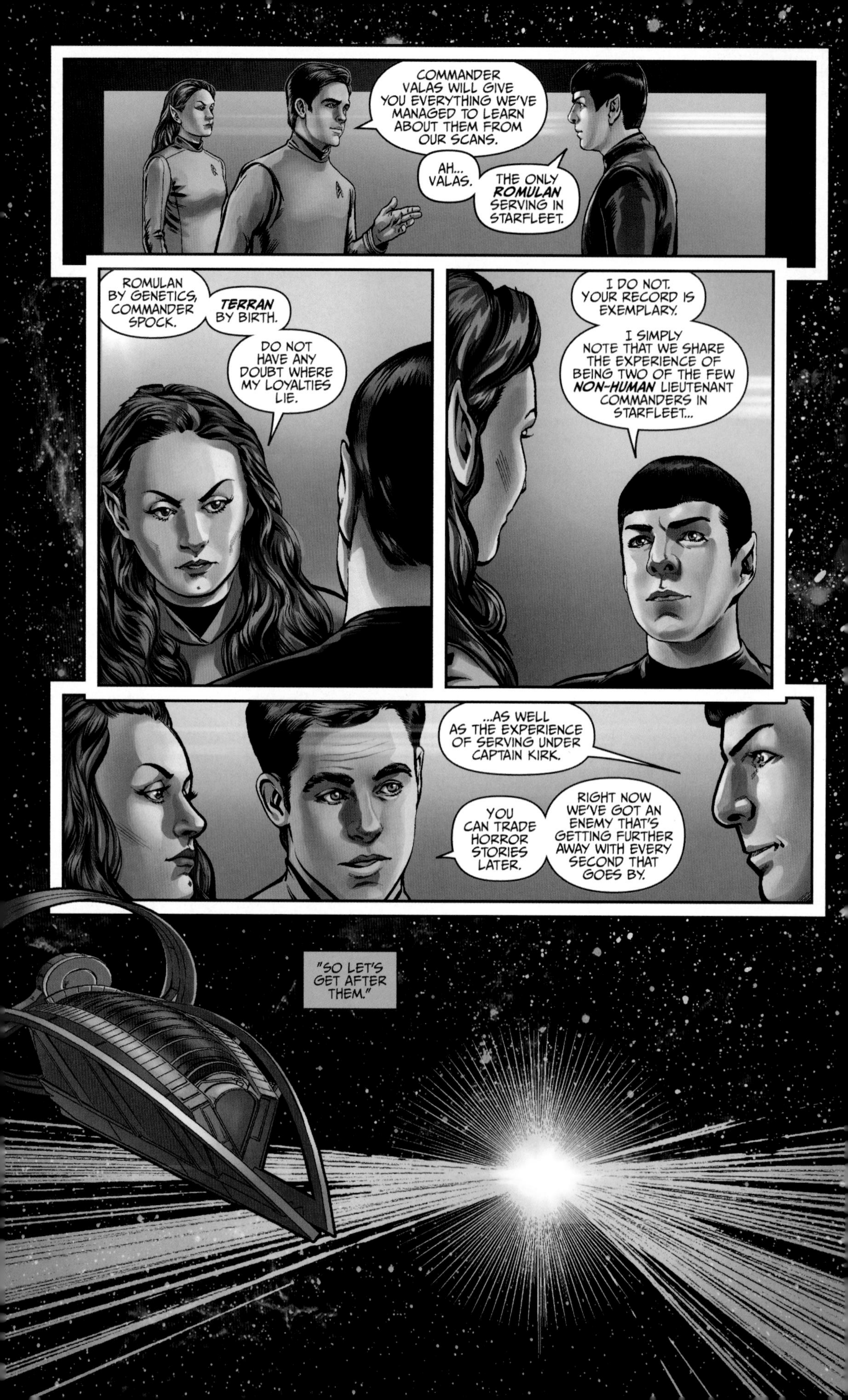
COMMANDER VALAS WILL GIVE YOU EVERYTHING WE'VE MANAGED TO LEARN ABOUT THEM FROM OUR SCANS.
AH... VALAS.
THE ONLY ROMULAN SERVING IN STARFLEET.
ROMULAN BY GENETICS, COMMANDER SPOCK.
TERRAN BY BIRTH.
DO NOT HAVE ANY DOUBT WHERE MY LOYALTIES LIE.
I DO NOT. YOUR RECORD IS EXEMPLARY.
I SIMPLY NOTE THAT WE SHARE THE EXPERIENCE OF BEING TWO OF THE FEW NON-HUMAN LIEUTENANT COMMANDERS IN STARFLEET...
...AS WELL AS THE EXPERIENCE OF SERVING UNDER CAPTAIN KIRK.
YOU CAN TRADE HORROR STORIES LATER.
RIGHT NOW WE'VE GOT AN ENEMY THAT'S GETTING FURTHER AWAY WITH EVERY SECOND THAT GOES BY.
"SO LET'S GET AFTER THEM."

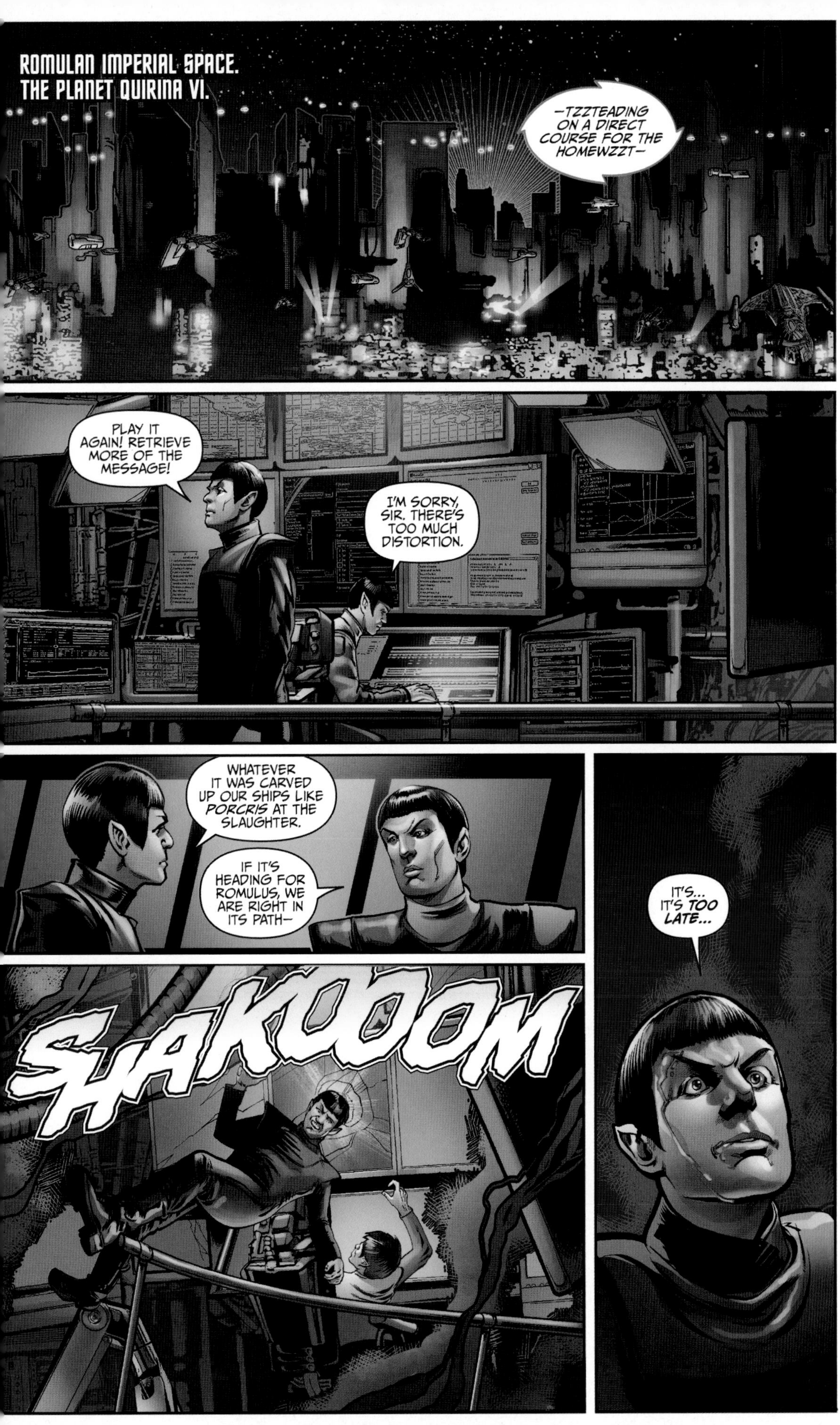
ROMULAN IMPERIAL SPACE. THE PLANET QUIRINA VI.
—TZZTEADING ON A DIRECT COURSE FOR THE HOMEWZZT—
PLAY IT AGAIN! RETRIEVE MORE OF THE MESSAGE!
I'M SORRY, SIR. THERE'S TOO MUCH DISTORTION.
WHATEVER IT WAS CARVED UP OUR SHIPS LIKE PORCRIS AT THE SLAUGHTER.
IF IT'S HEADING FOR ROMULUS, WE ARE RIGHT IN ITS PATH—
IT'S... IT'S TOO LATE...
SHAKOOM

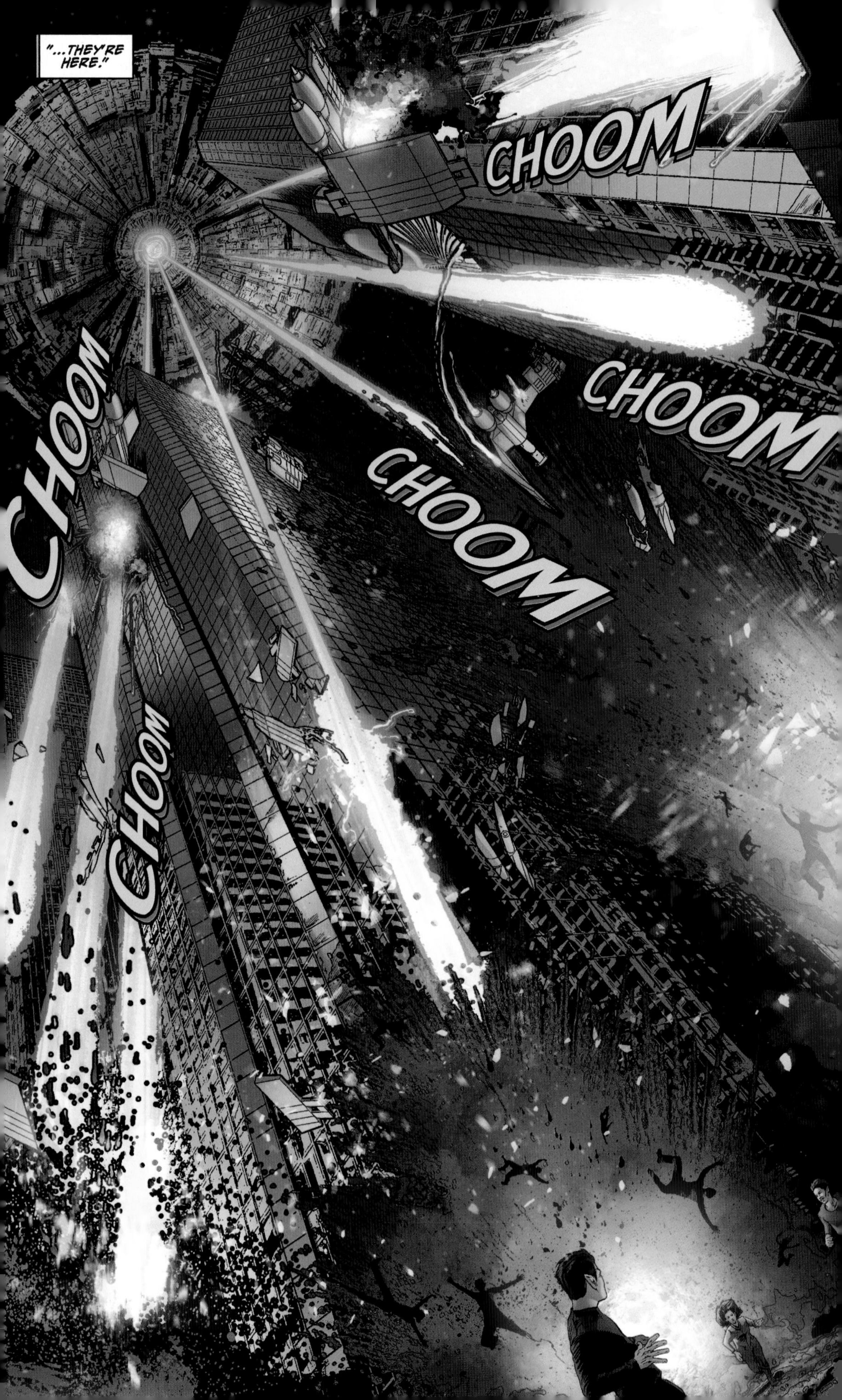
"...THEY'RE HERE."
CHOOM
CHOOM
CHOOM
CHOOM
CHOOM
CHOOM

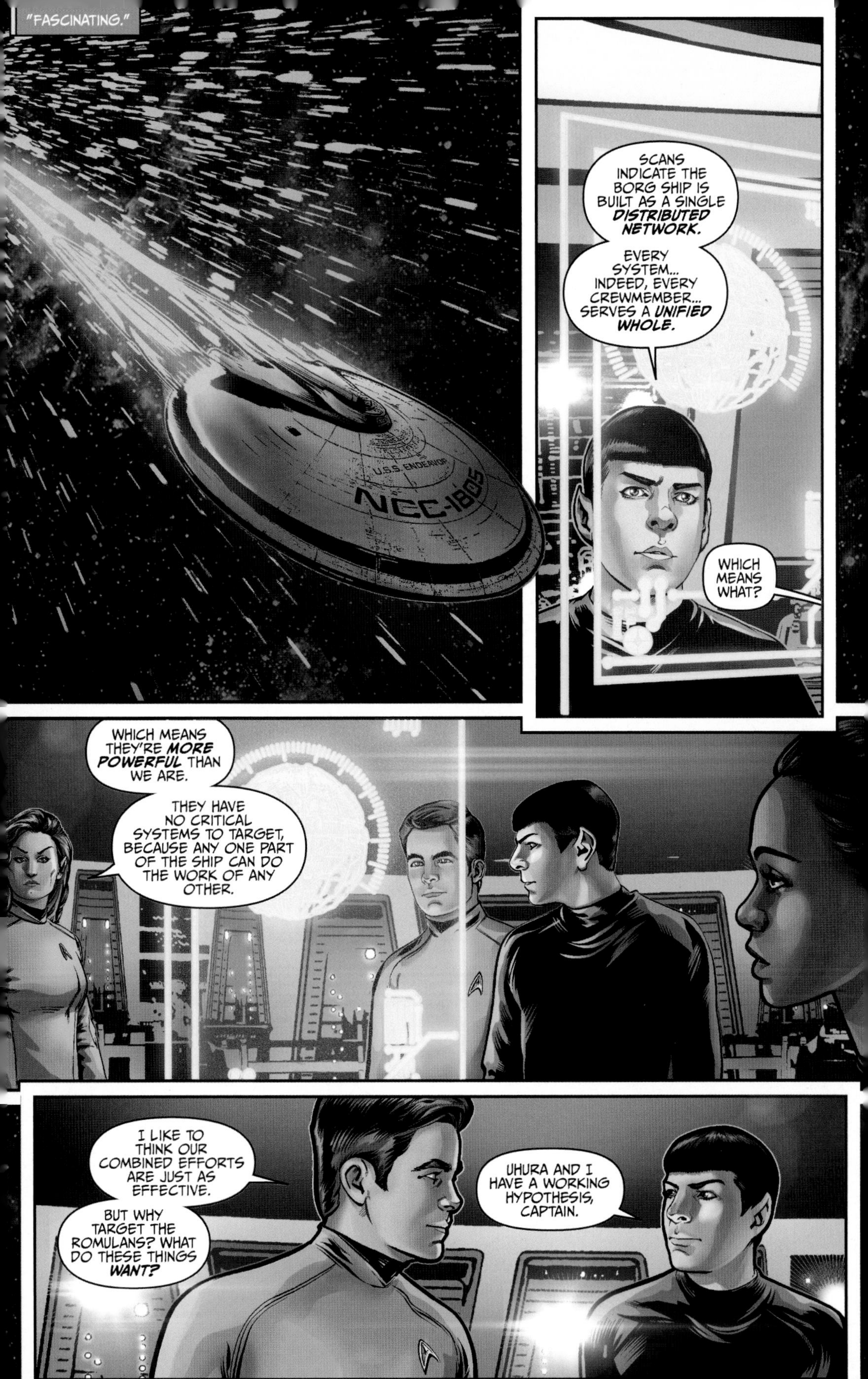
"FASCINATING."
U.S.S. ENDEAVOR
NCC-1805
SCANS INDICATE THE BORG SHIP IS BUILT AS A SINGLE DISTRIBUTED NETWORK.
EVERY SYSTEM... INDEED, EVERY CREWMEMBER... SERVES A UNIFIED WHOLE.
WHICH MEANS WHAT?
WHICH MEANS THEY'RE MORE POWERFUL THAN WE ARE.
THEY HAVE NO CRITICAL SYSTEMS TO TARGET, BECAUSE ANY ONE PART OF THE SHIP CAN DO THE WORK OF ANY OTHER.
I LIKE TO THINK OUR COMBINED EFFORTS ARE JUST AS EFFECTIVE.
BUT WHY TARGET THE ROMULANS? WHAT DO THESE THINGS WANT?
UHURA AND I HAVE A WORKING HYPOTHESIS, CAPTAIN.

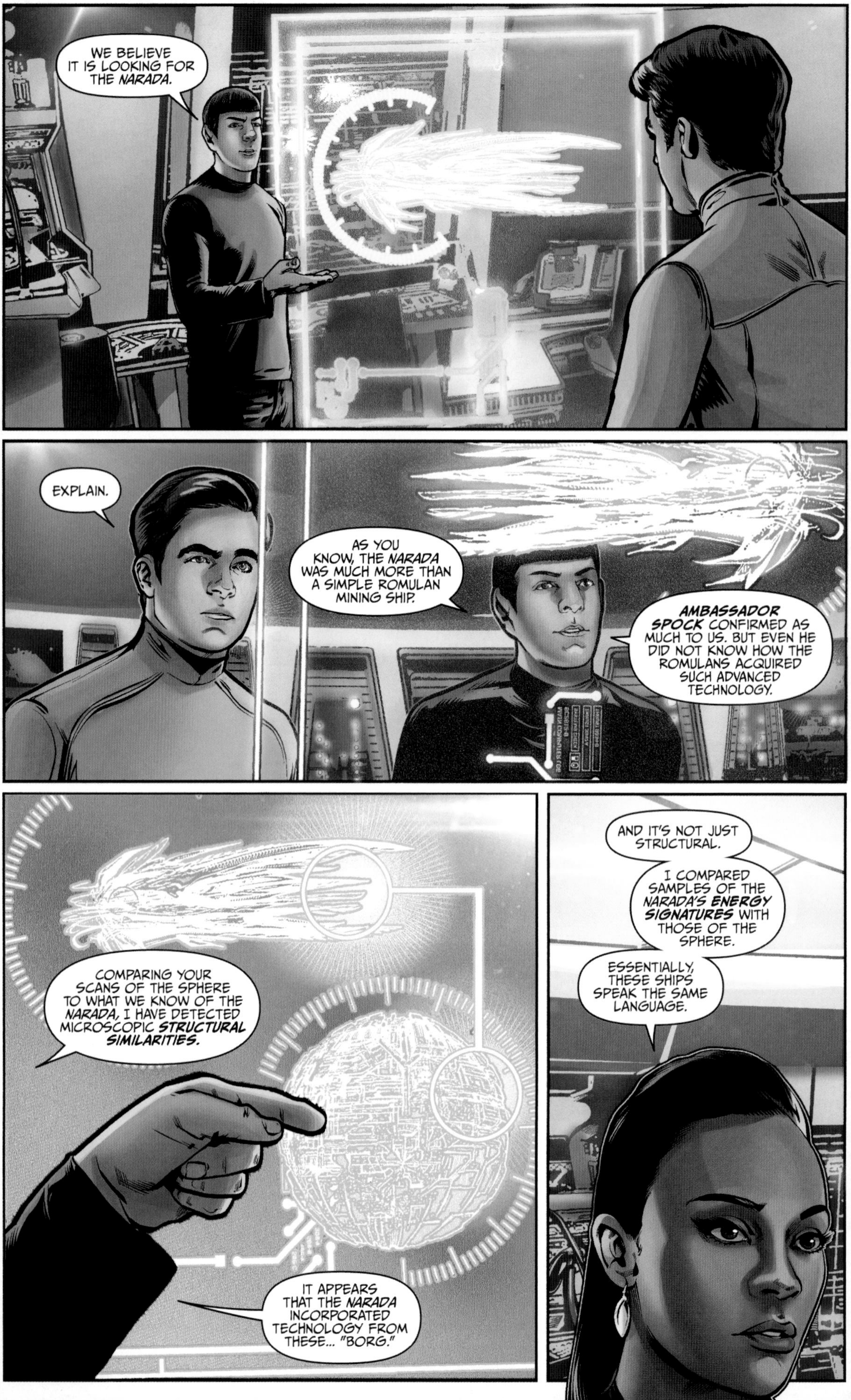
WE BELIEVE IT IS LOOKING FOR THE NARADA.
EXPLAIN.
AS YOU KNOW, THE NARADA WAS MUCH MORE THAN A SIMPLE ROMULAN MINING SHIP.
AMBASSADOR SPOCK CONFIRMED AS MUCH TO US. BUT EVEN HE DID NOT KNOW HOW THE ROMULANS ACQUIRED SUCH ADVANCED TECHNOLOGY.
COMPARING YOUR SCANS OF THE SPHERE TO WHAT WE KNOW OF THE NARADA, I HAVE DETECTED MICROSCOPIC STRUCTURAL SIMILARITIES.
IT APPEARS THAT THE NARADA INCORPORATED TECHNOLOGY FROM THESE... "BORG."
AND IT'S NOT JUST STRUCTURAL.
I COMPARED SAMPLES OF THE NARADA'S ENERGY SIGNATURES WITH THOSE OF THE SPHERE.
ESSENTIALLY, THESE SHIPS SPEAK THE SAME LANGUAGE.

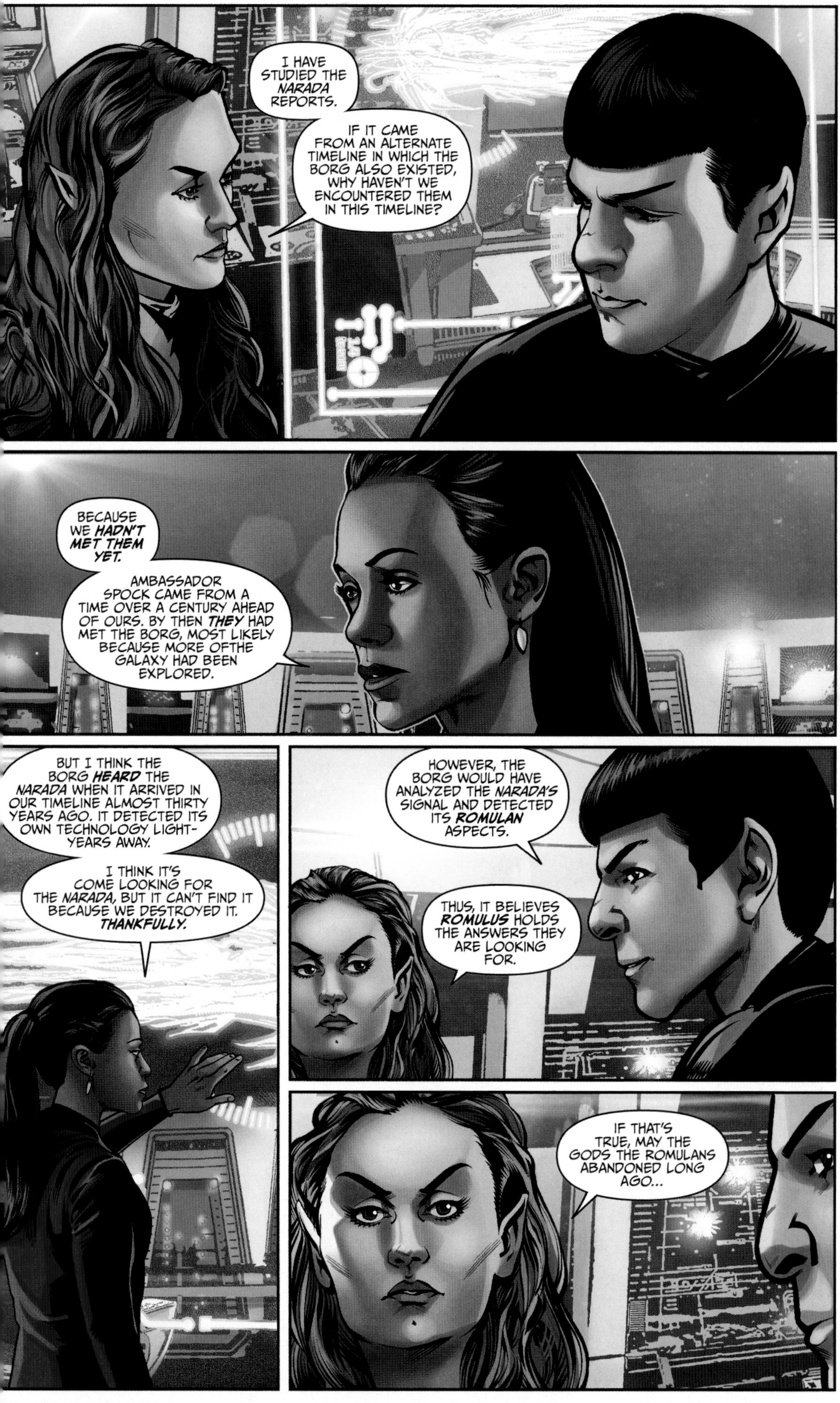

I HAVE STUDIED THE *NARADA* REPORTS.
IF IT CAME FROM AN ALTERNATE TIMELINE IN WHICH THE BORG ALSO EXISTED, WHY HAVEN'T WE ENCOUNTERED THEM IN THIS TIMELINE?
BECAUSE WE ***HADN'T MET THEM YET.***
AMBASSADOR SPOCK CAME FROM A TIME OVER A CENTURY AHEAD OF OURS. BY THEN ***THEY*** HAD MET THE BORG, MOST LIKELY BECAUSE MORE OFTHE GALAXY HAD BEEN EXPLORED.
BUT I THINK THE BORG ***HEARD*** THE *NARADA* WHEN IT ARRIVED IN OUR TIMELINE ALMOST THIRTY YEARS AGO. IT DETECTED ITS OWN TECHNOLOGY LIGHT-YEARS AWAY.
I THINK IT'S COME LOOKING FOR THE *NARADA*, BUT IT CAN'T FIND IT BECAUSE WE DESTROYED IT. ***THANKFULLY.***
HOWEVER, THE BORG WOULD HAVE ANALYZED THE *NARADA'S* SIGNAL AND DETECTED ITS ***ROMULAN*** ASPECTS.
THUS, IT BELIEVES ***ROMULUS*** HOLDS THE ANSWERS THEY ARE LOOKING FOR.
IF THAT'S TRUE, MAY THE GODS THE ROMULANS ABANDONED LONG AGO...

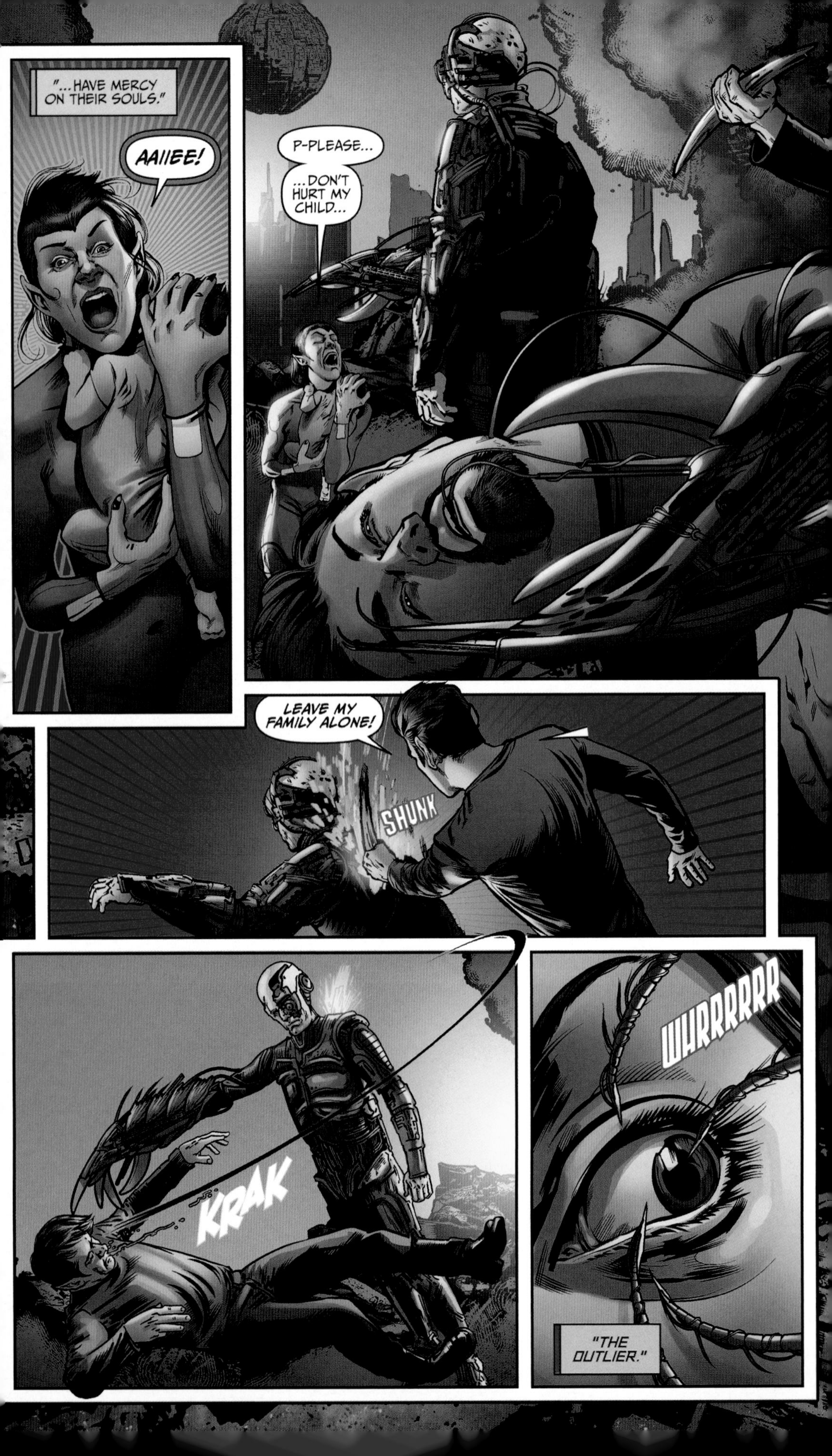
"...HAVE MERCY ON THEIR SOULS."
AAIIEE!
P-PLEASE...
...DON'T HURT MY CHILD...
LEAVE MY FAMILY ALONE!
SHUNK
KRAK
WHRRRRRR
"THE OUTLIER."

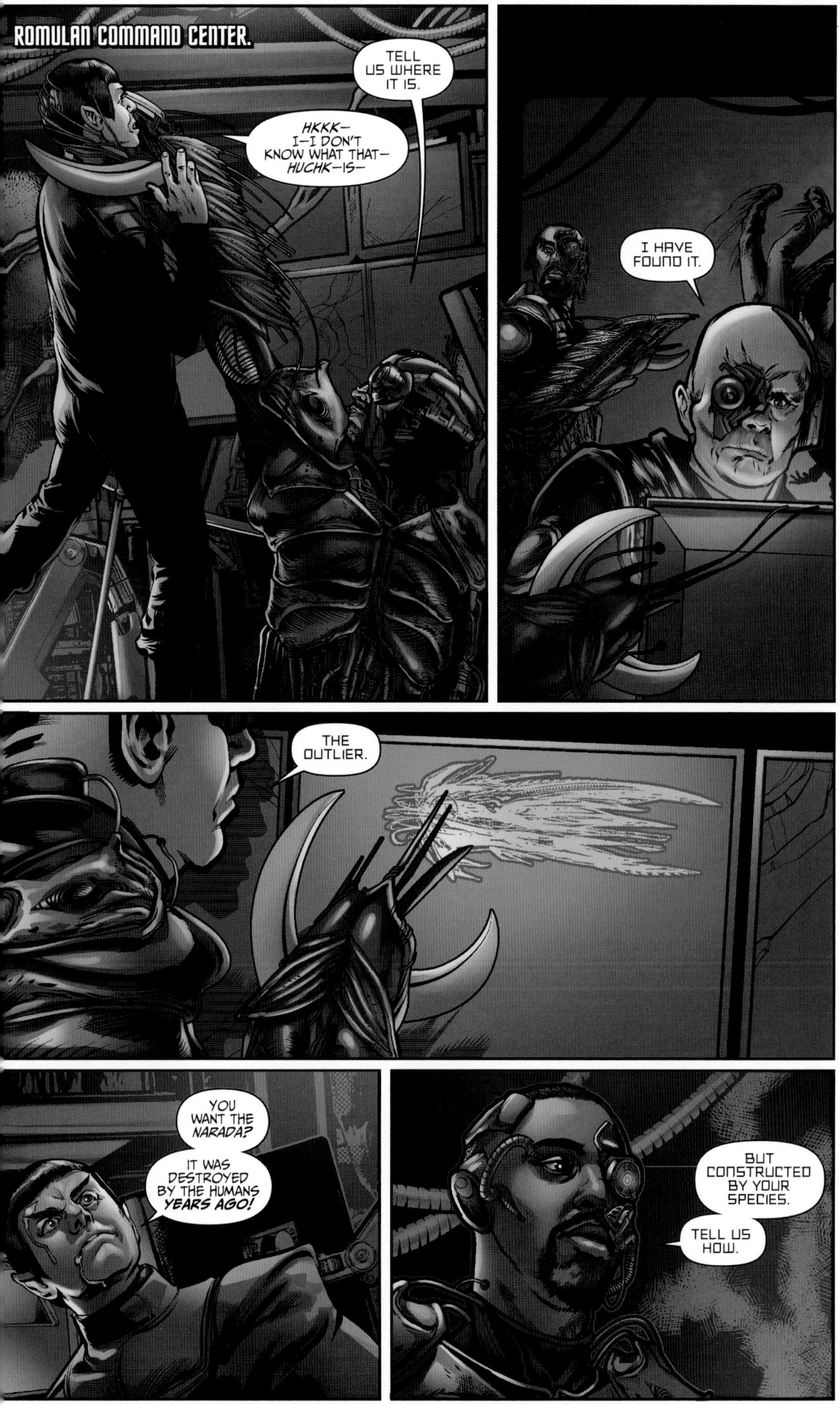
ROMULAN COMMAND CENTER.
TELL US WHERE IT IS.
HKKK— I—I DON'T KNOW WHAT THAT— HUCHK—IS—
I HAVE FOUND IT.
THE OUTLIER.
YOU WANT THE NARADA?
IT WAS DESTROYED BY THE HUMANS YEARS AGO!
BUT CONSTRUCTED BY YOUR SPECIES.
TELL US HOW.

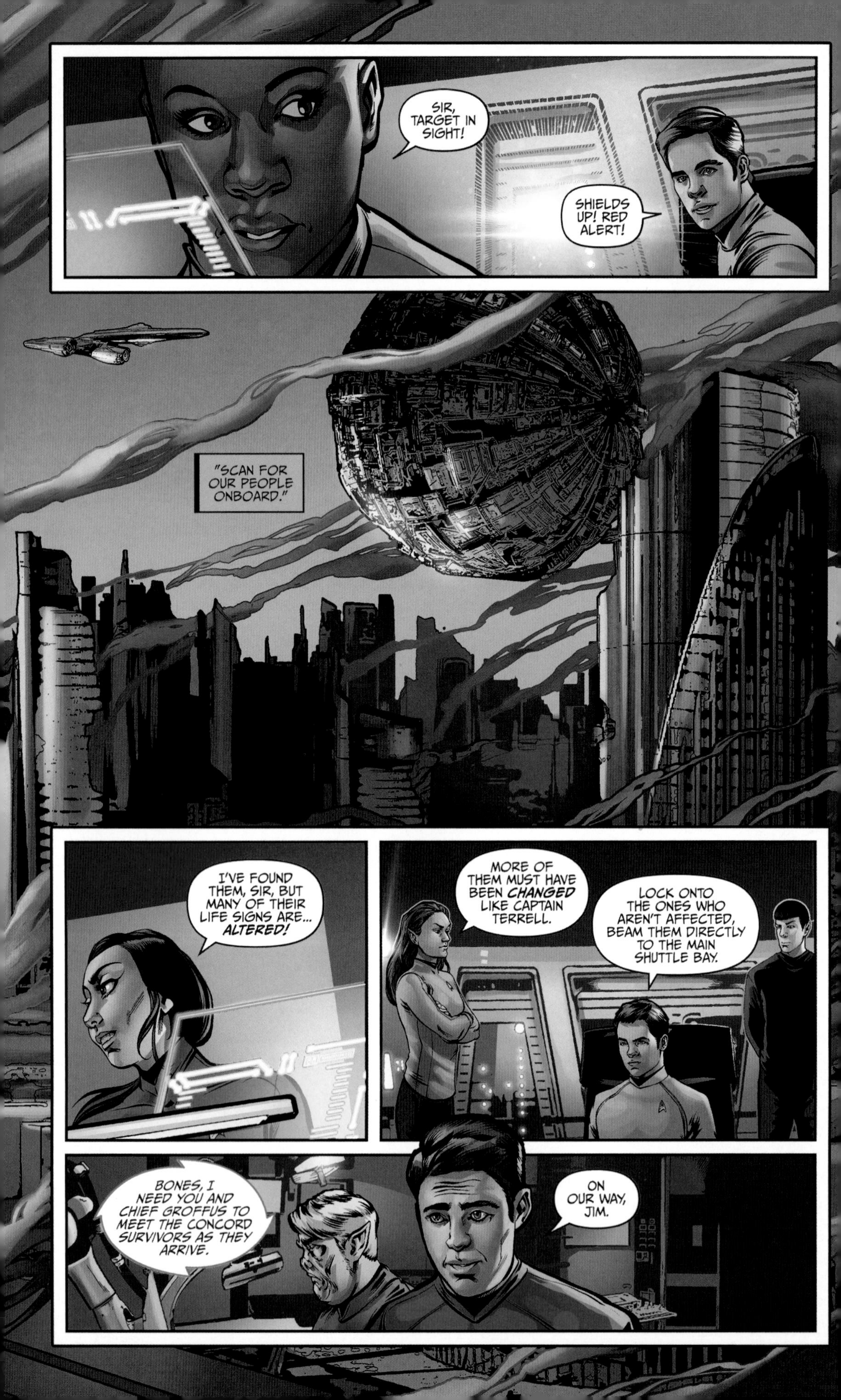

SIR, TARGET IN SIGHT!
SHIELDS UP! RED ALERT!
"SCAN FOR OUR PEOPLE ONBOARD."
I'VE FOUND THEM, SIR, BUT MANY OF THEIR LIFE SIGNS ARE... ALTERED!
MORE OF THEM MUST HAVE BEEN CHANGED LIKE CAPTAIN TERRELL.
LOCK ONTO THE ONES WHO AREN'T AFFECTED, BEAM THEM DIRECTLY TO THE MAIN SHUTTLE BAY.
BONES, I NEED YOU AND CHIEF GROFFUS TO MEET THE CONCORD SURVIVORS AS THEY ARRIVE.
ON OUR WAY, JIM.

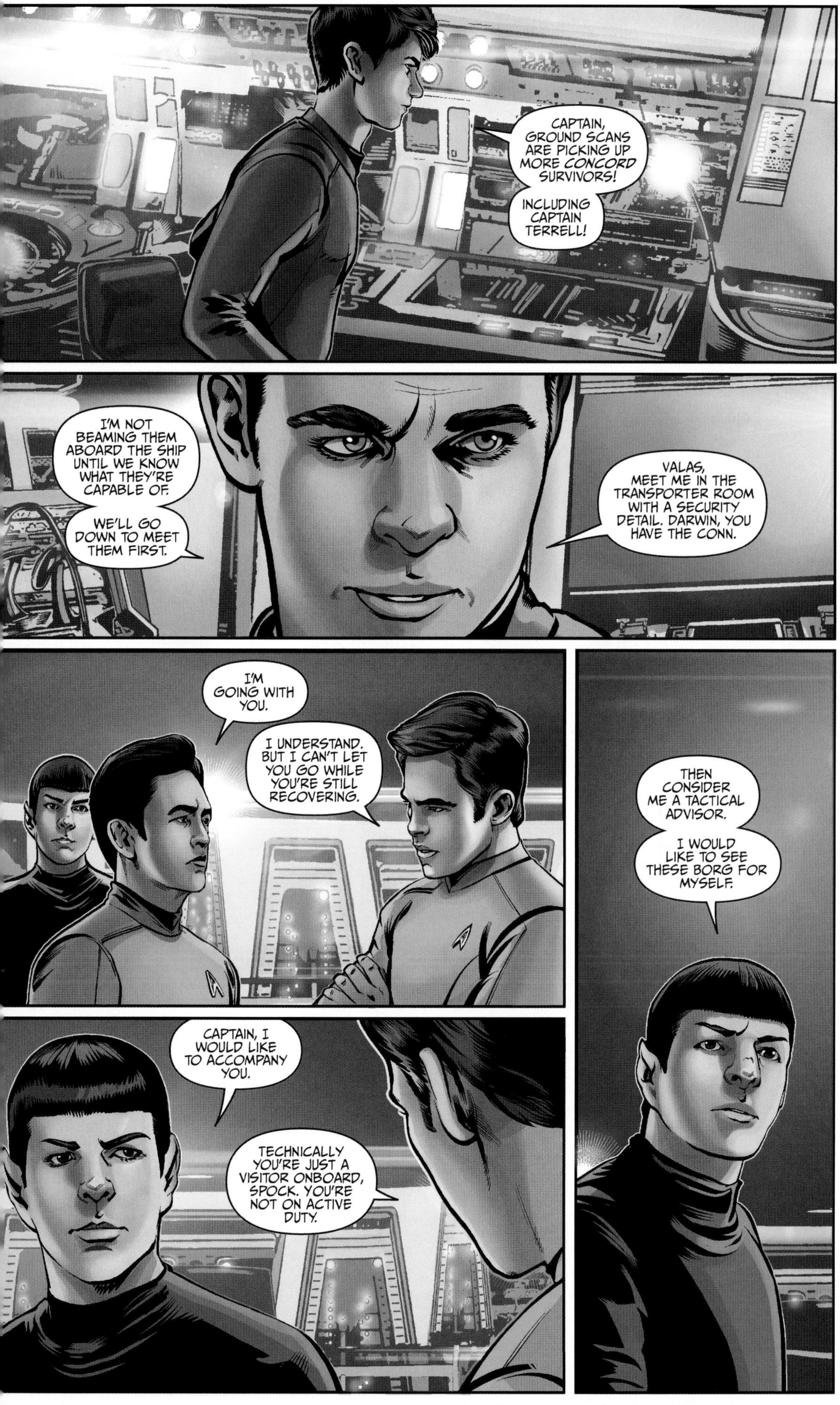
CAPTAIN, GROUND SCANS ARE PICKING UP MORE CONCORD SURVIVORS!
INCLUDING CAPTAIN TERRELL!
I'M NOT BEAMING THEM ABOARD THE SHIP UNTIL WE KNOW WHAT THEY'RE CAPABLE OF.
WE'LL GO DOWN TO MEET THEM FIRST.
VALAS, MEET ME IN THE TRANSPORTER ROOM WITH A SECURITY DETAIL. DARWIN, YOU HAVE THE CONN.
I'M GOING WITH YOU.
I UNDERSTAND. BUT I CAN'T LET YOU GO WHILE YOU'RE STILL RECOVERING.
CAPTAIN, I WOULD LIKE TO ACCOMPANY YOU.
TECHNICALLY YOU'RE JUST A VISITOR ONBOARD, SPOCK. YOU'RE NOT ON ACTIVE DUTY.
THEN CONSIDER ME A TACTICAL ADVISOR.
I WOULD LIKE TO SEE THESE BORG FOR MYSELF.

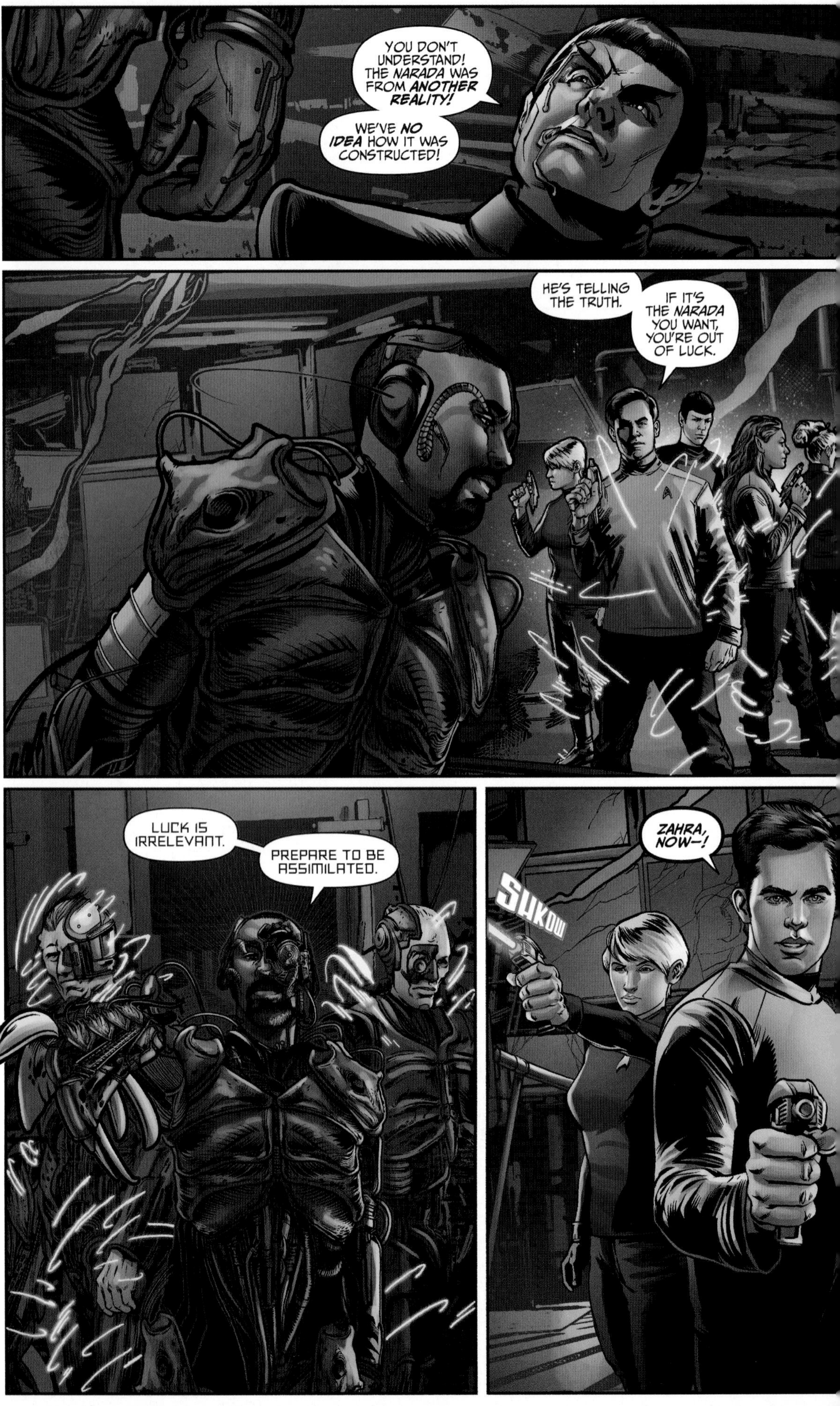
YOU DON'T UNDERSTAND! THE *NARADA* WAS FROM **ANOTHER REALITY!**
WE'VE **NO IDEA** HOW IT WAS CONSTRUCTED!
HE'S TELLING THE TRUTH.
IF IT'S THE *NARADA* YOU WANT, YOU'RE OUT OF LUCK.
LUCK IS IRRELEVANT.
PREPARE TO BE ASSIMILATED.
SUKOW
ZAHRA, NOW--!

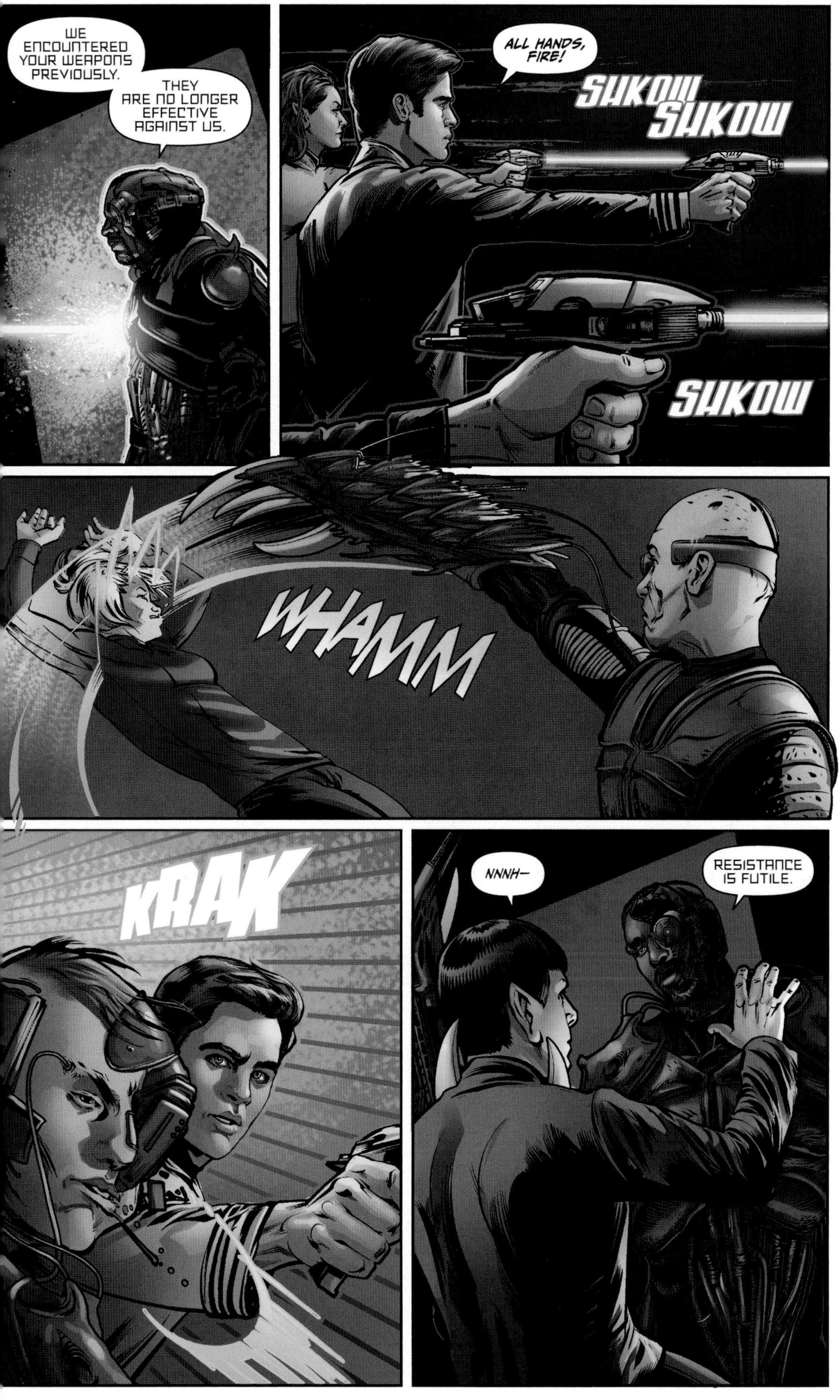
WE ENCOUNTERED YOUR WEAPONS PREVIOUSLY.
THEY ARE NO LONGER EFFECTIVE AGAINST US.
ALL HANDS, FIRE!
SHKOW SHKOW
SHKOW
WHAMM
KRAK
NNNH—
RESISTANCE IS FUTILE.

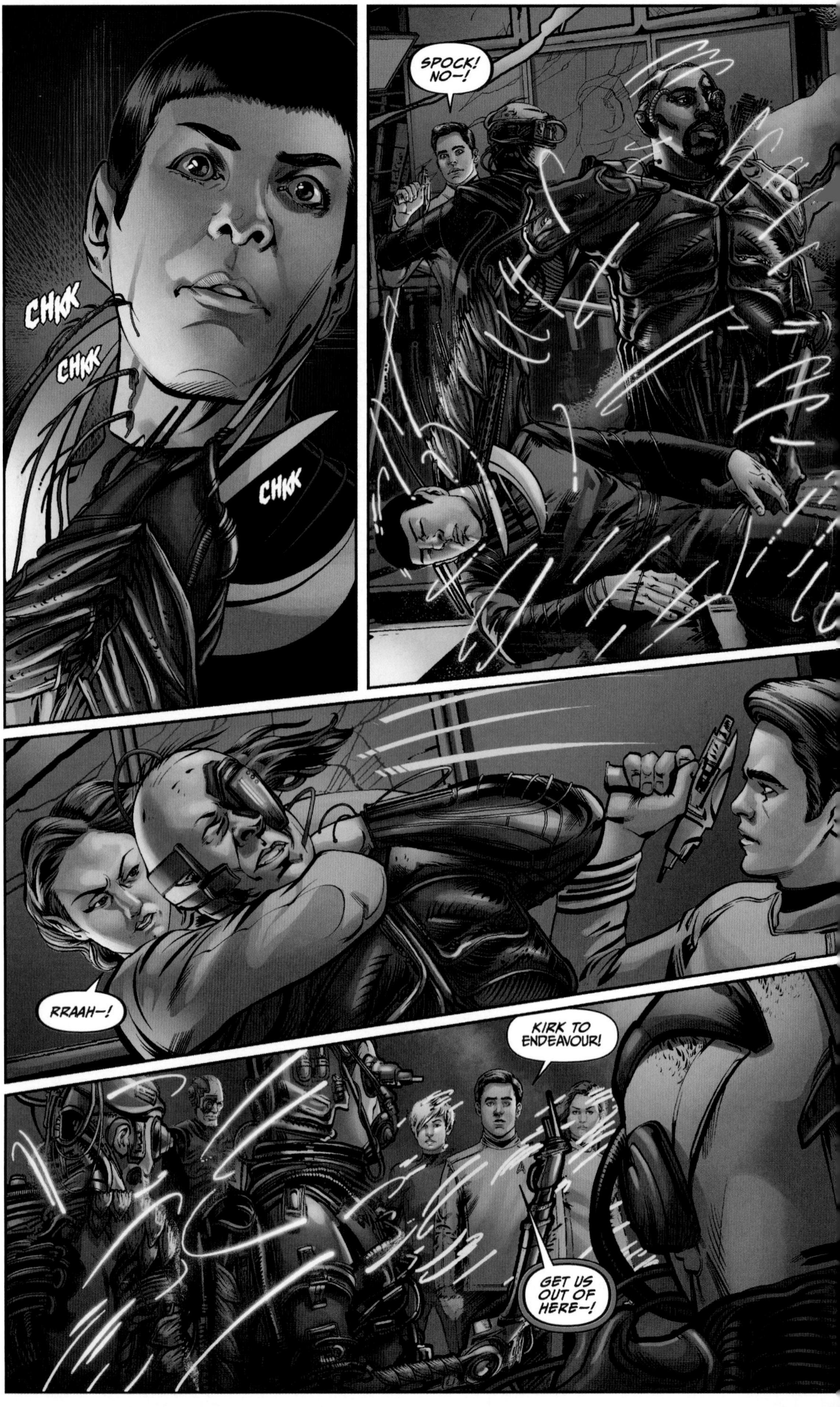
CHKK
CHKK
CHKK
SPOCK! NO--!
RRAAH--!
KIRK TO ENDEAVOUR!
GET US OUT OF HERE--!

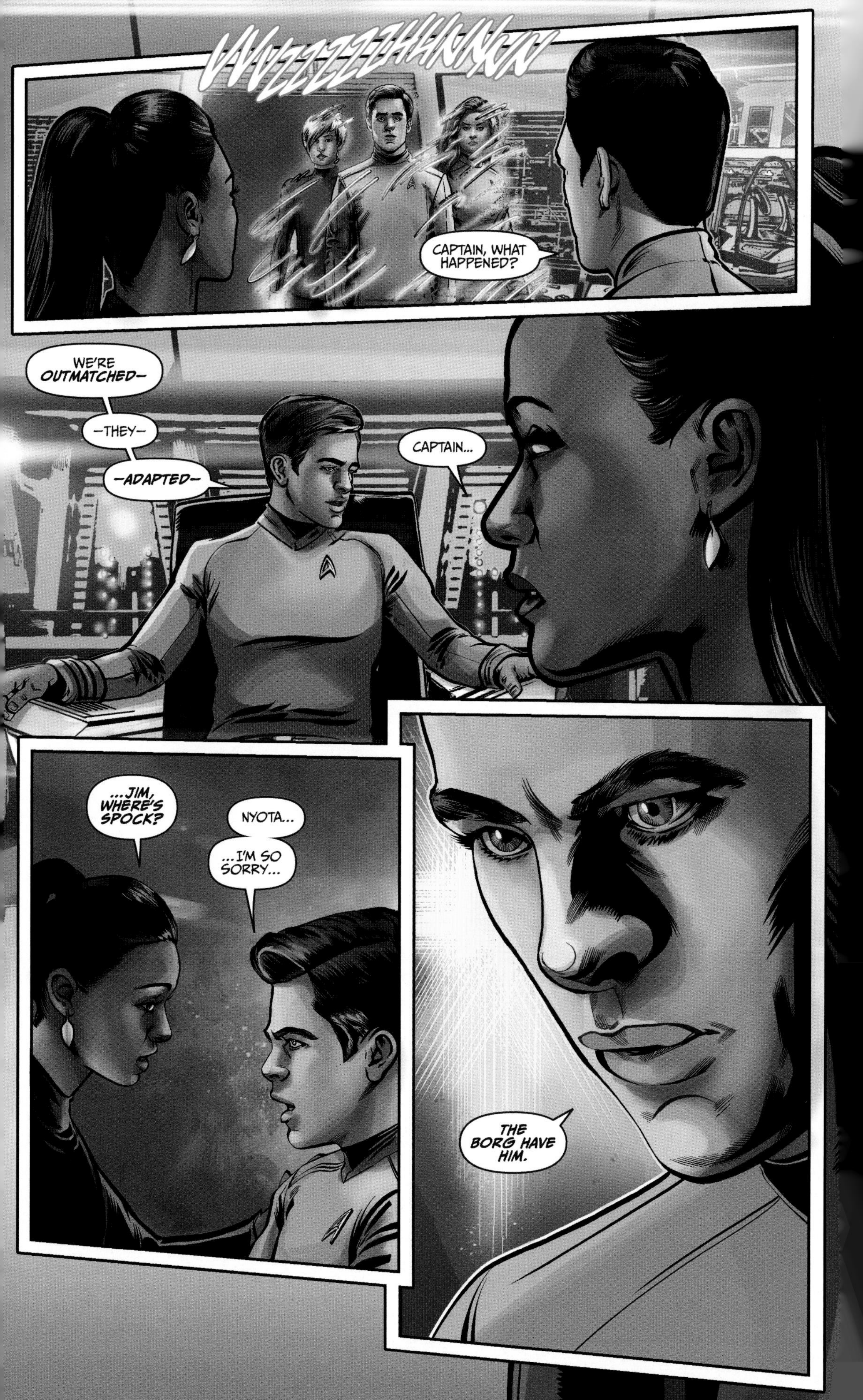
VVVZZZZZHHNNNGN
CAPTAIN, WHAT HAPPENED?
WE'RE OUTMATCHED—
—THEY—
—ADAPTED—
CAPTAIN...
...JIM, WHERE'S SPOCK?
NYOTA...
...I'M SO SORRY...
THE BORG HAVE HIM.

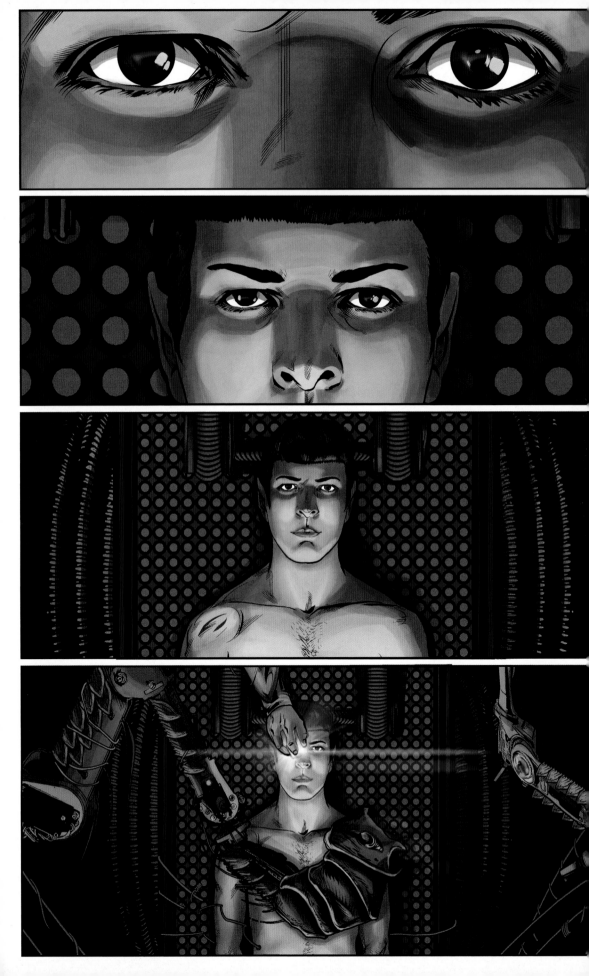

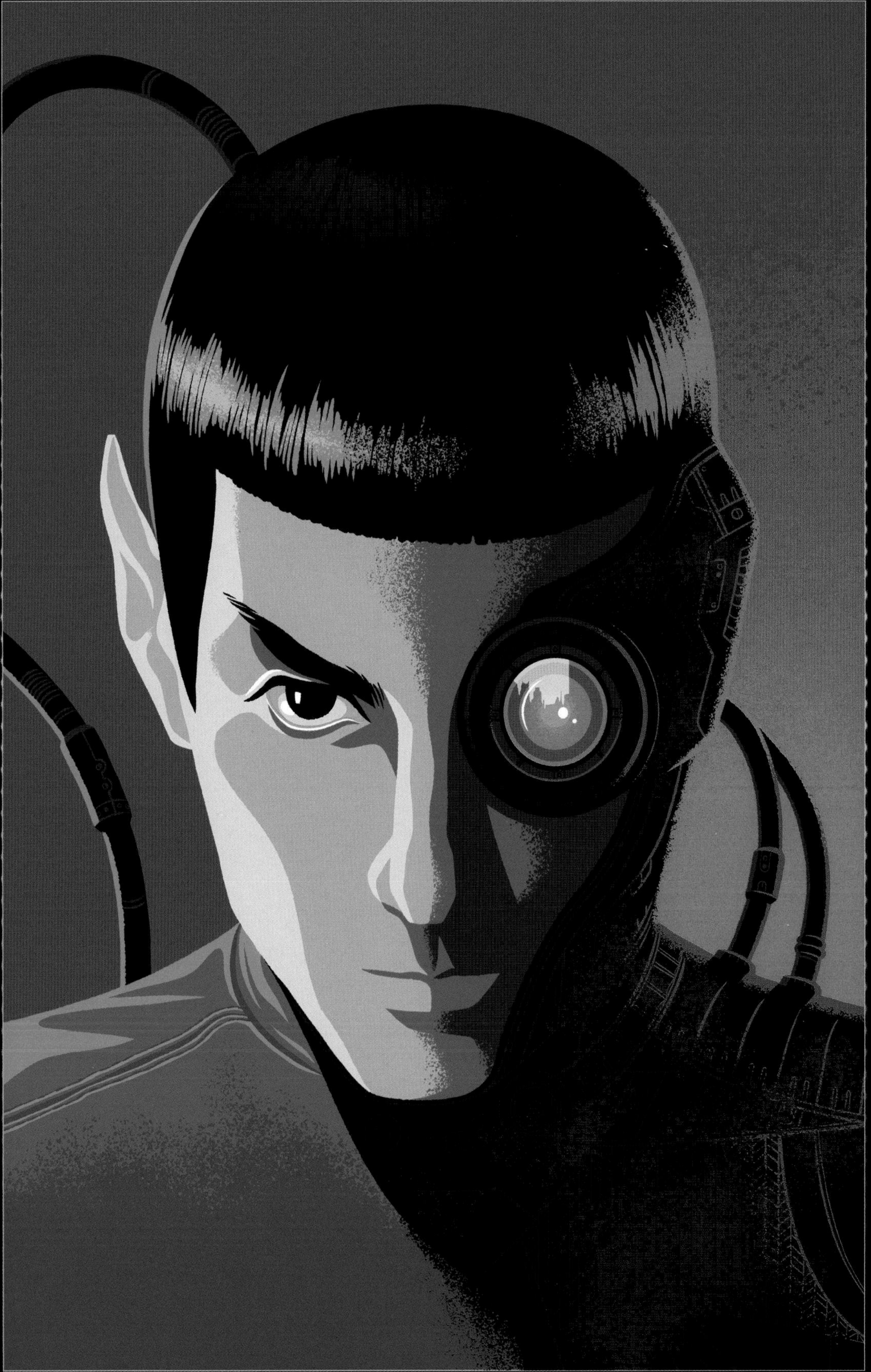

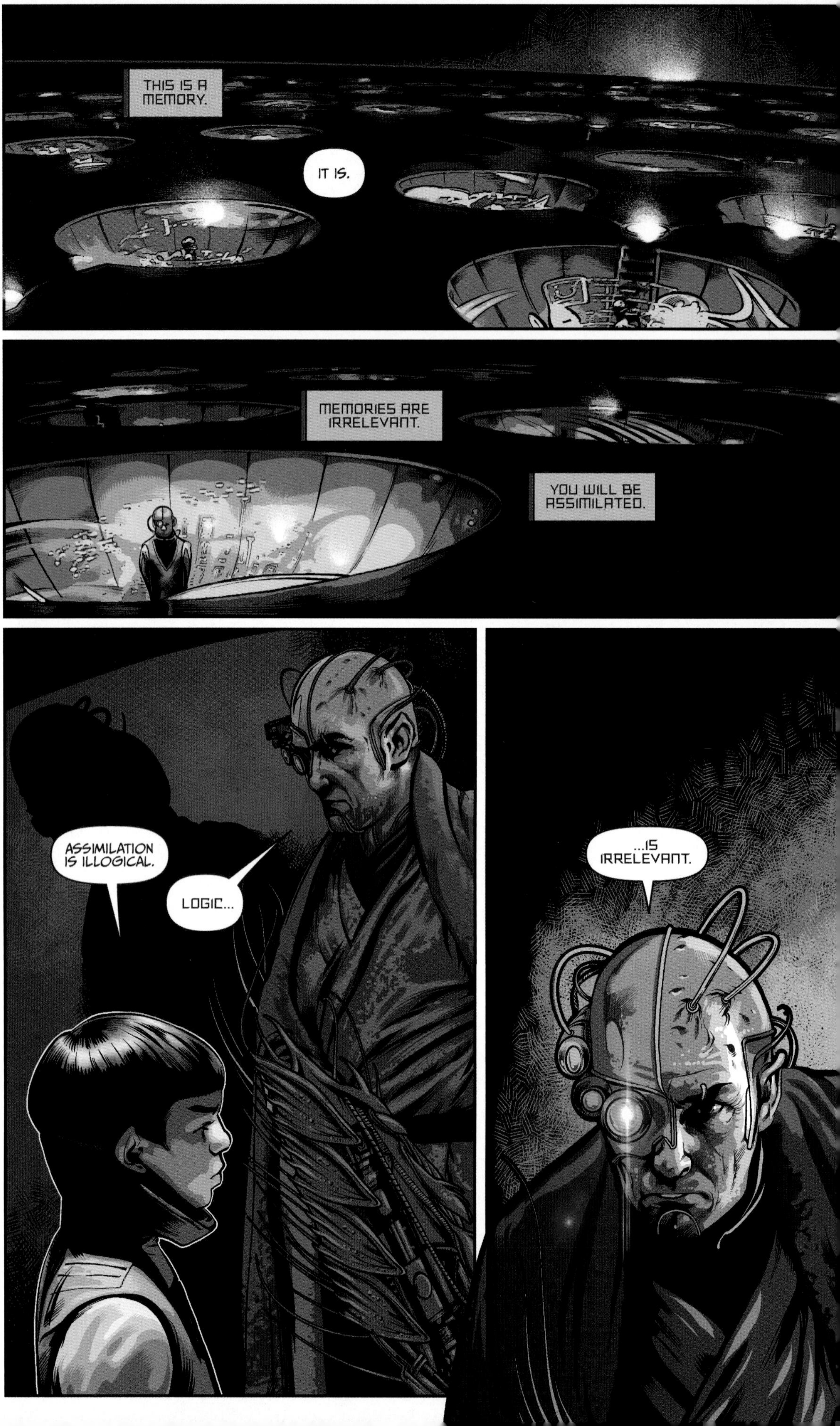
THIS IS A MEMORY.
IT IS.
MEMORIES ARE IRRELEVANT.
YOU WILL BE ASSIMILATED.
ASSIMILATION IS ILLOGICAL.
LOGIC...
...IS IRRELEVANT.

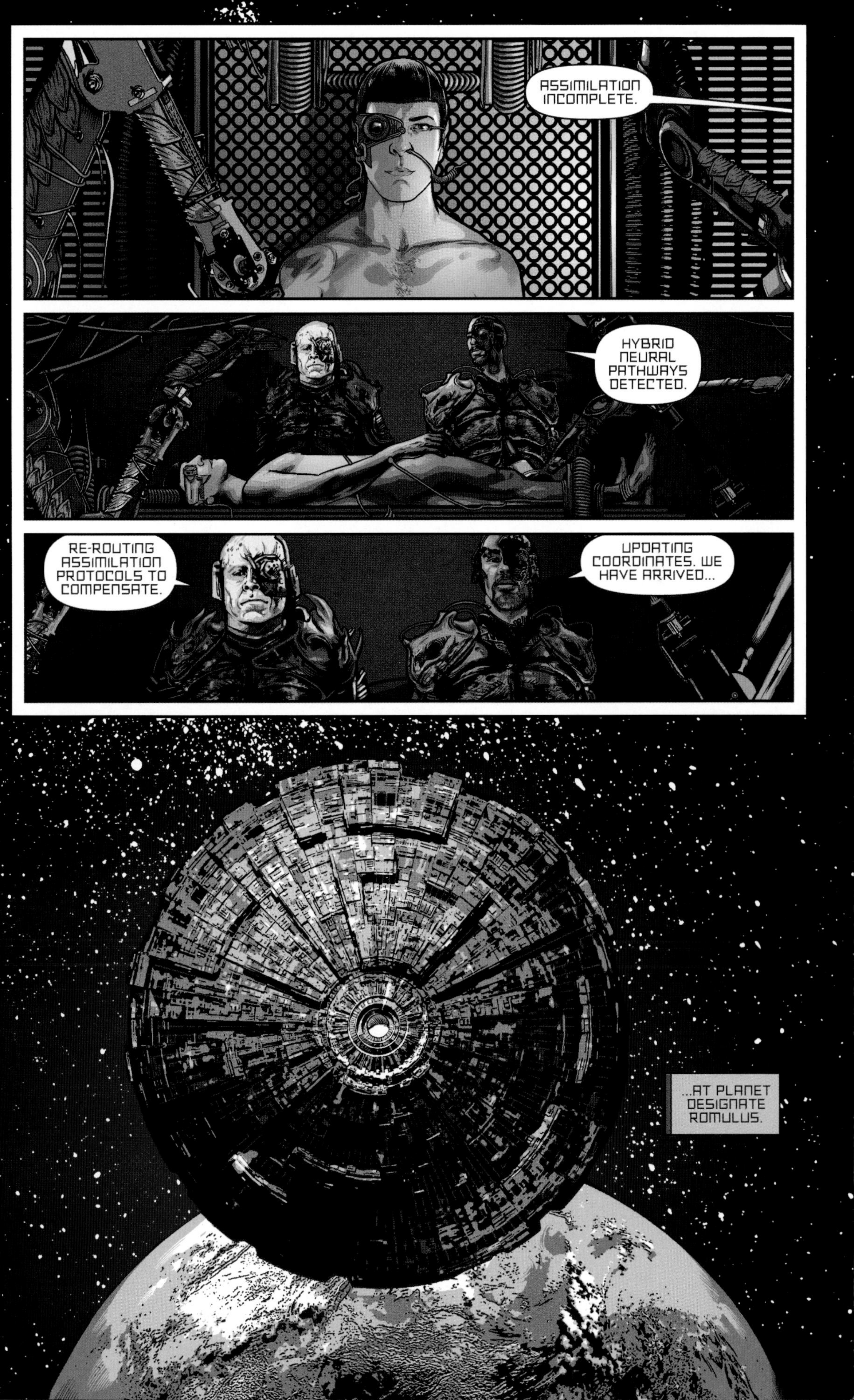
ASSIMILATION INCOMPLETE.
HYBRID NEURAL PATHWAYS DETECTED.
RE-ROUTING ASSIMILATION PROTOCOLS TO COMPENSATE.
UPDATING COORDINATES. WE HAVE ARRIVED...
...AT PLANET DESIGNATE ROMULUS.

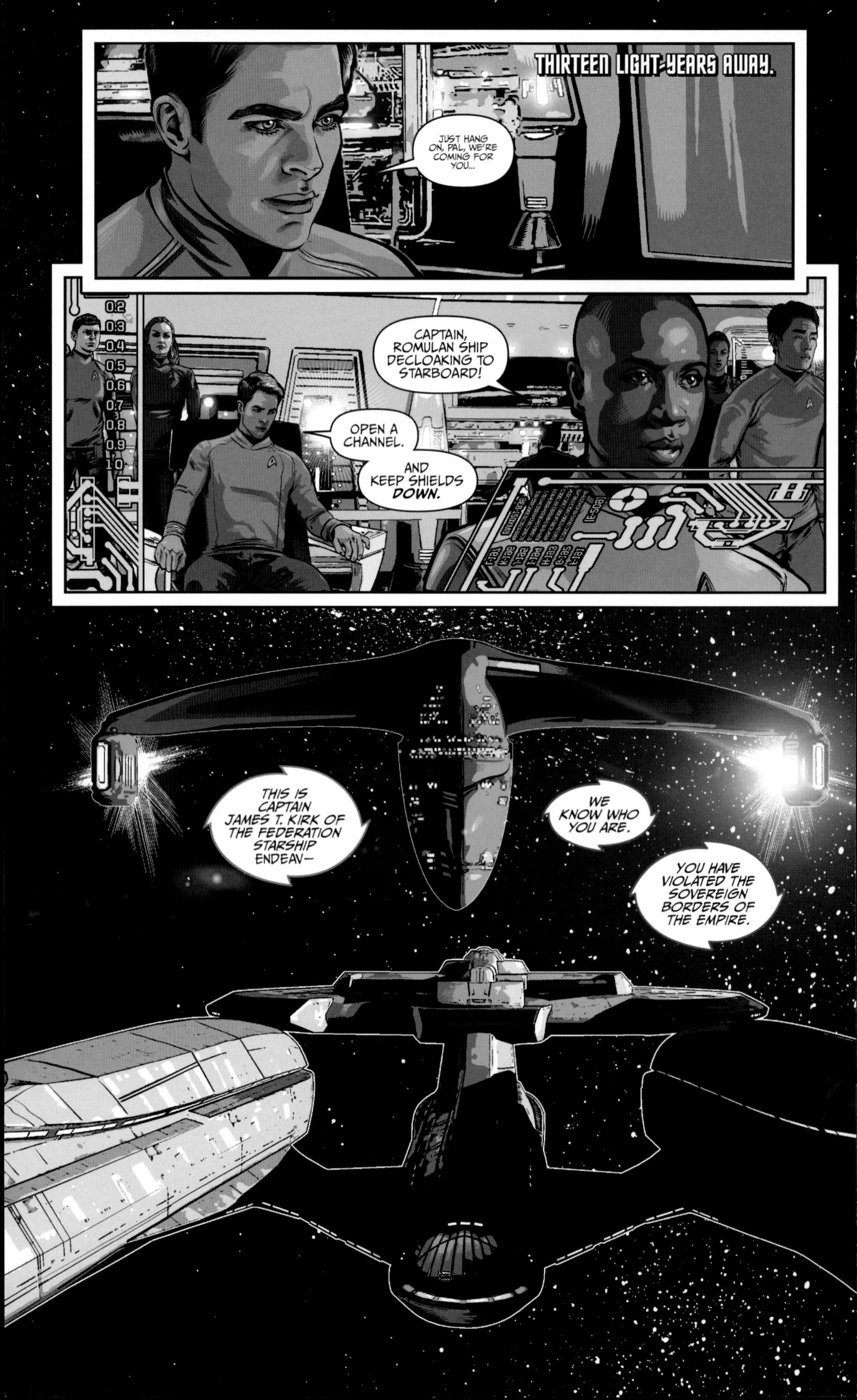
THIRTEEN LIGHT-YEARS AWAY.
JUST HANG ON, PAL, WE'RE COMING FOR YOU...
CAPTAIN, ROMULAN SHIP DECLOAKING TO STARBOARD!
OPEN A CHANNEL.
AND KEEP SHIELDS *DOWN.*
THIS IS CAPTAIN JAMES T. KIRK OF THE FEDERATION STARSHIP ENDEAV—
WE KNOW WHO YOU ARE.
YOU HAVE VIOLATED THE SOVEREIGN BORDERS OF THE EMPIRE.

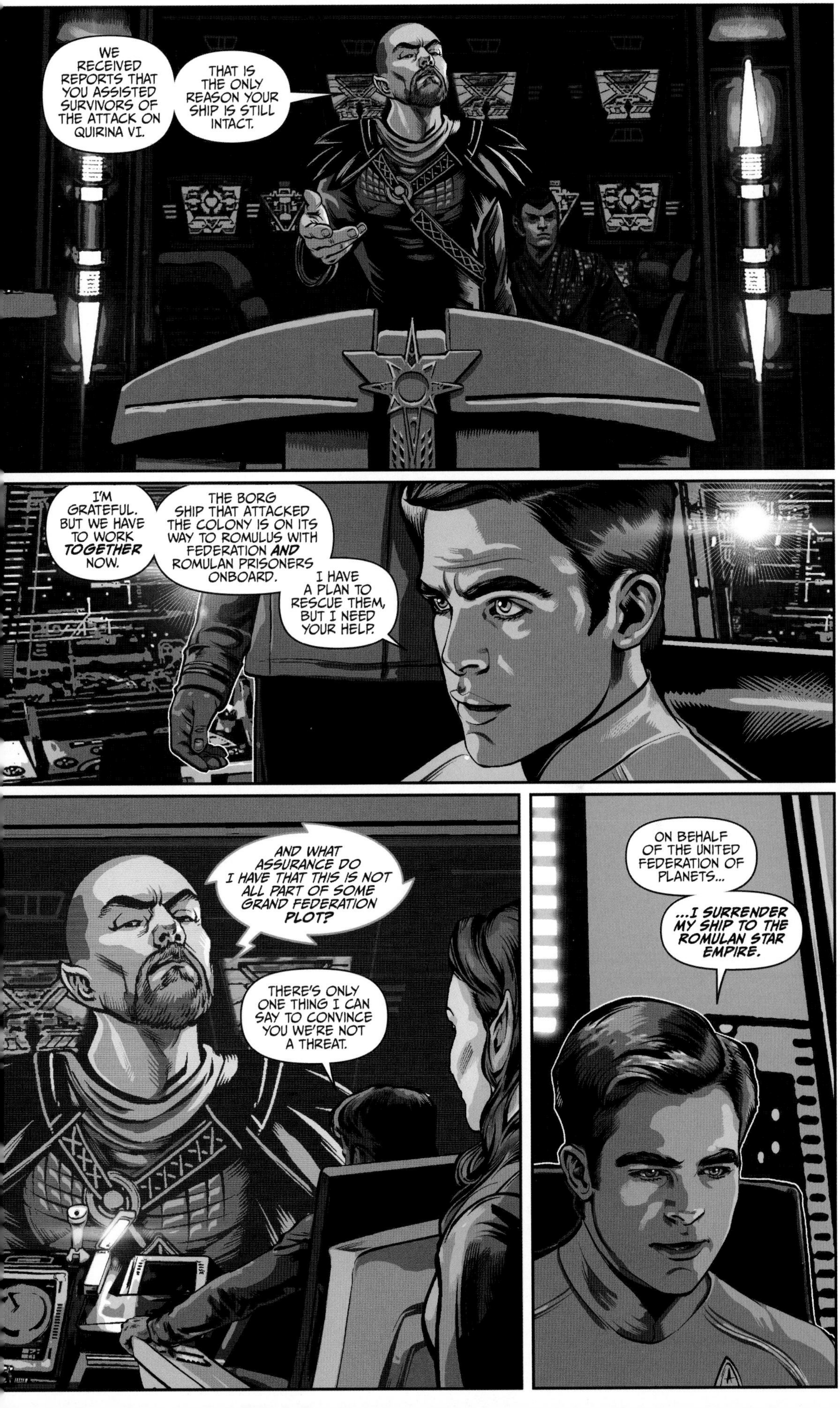
WE RECEIVED REPORTS THAT YOU ASSISTED SURVIVORS OF THE ATTACK ON QUIRINA VI.
THAT IS THE ONLY REASON YOUR SHIP IS STILL INTACT.
I'M GRATEFUL. BUT WE HAVE TO WORK ***TOGETHER*** NOW.
THE BORG SHIP THAT ATTACKED THE COLONY IS ON ITS WAY TO ROMULUS WITH FEDERATION ***AND*** ROMULAN PRISONERS ONBOARD.
I HAVE A PLAN TO RESCUE THEM, BUT I NEED YOUR HELP.
AND WHAT ASSURANCE DO I HAVE THAT THIS IS NOT ALL PART OF SOME GRAND FEDERATION ***PLOT?***
THERE'S ONLY ONE THING I CAN SAY TO CONVINCE YOU WE'RE NOT A THREAT.
ON BEHALF OF THE UNITED FEDERATION OF PLANETS...
...I SURRENDER MY SHIP TO THE ROMULAN STAR EMPIRE.

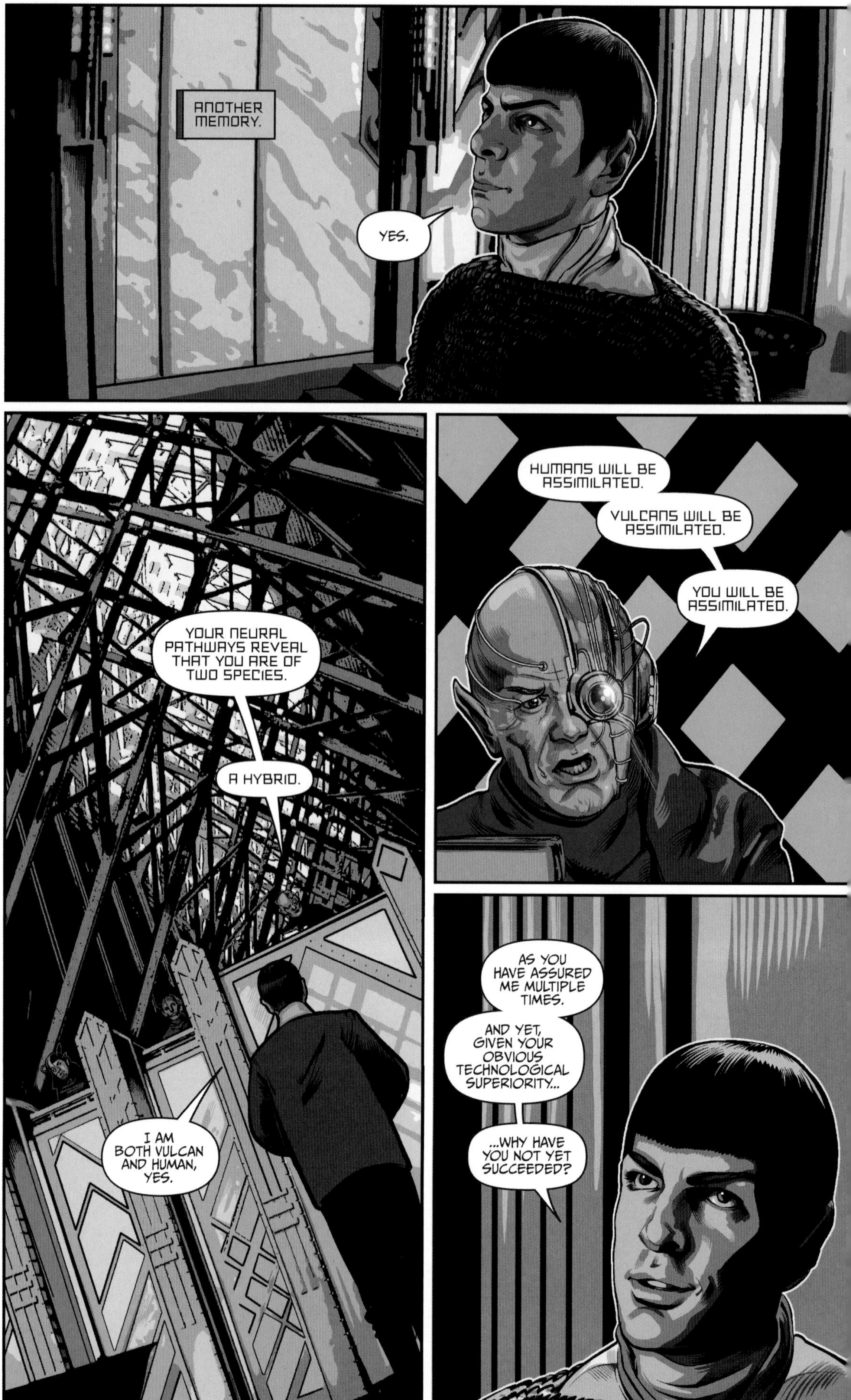
ANOTHER MEMORY.
YES.
YOUR NEURAL PATHWAYS REVEAL THAT YOU ARE OF TWO SPECIES.
A HYBRID.
I AM BOTH VULCAN AND HUMAN, YES.
HUMANS WILL BE ASSIMILATED.
VULCANS WILL BE ASSIMILATED.
YOU WILL BE ASSIMILATED.
AS YOU HAVE ASSURED ME MULTIPLE TIMES.
AND YET, GIVEN YOUR OBVIOUS TECHNOLOGICAL SUPERIORITY...
...WHY HAVE YOU NOT YET SUCCEEDED?

"EVEN IF WE GET OUR PEOPLE BACK..."

...THE ROMULANS WILL NEVER LET US GO.

HEY, YOU AGREED TO THIS PLAN, VALAS.

OUR OPTIONS WERE LIMITED.

BUT THIS SHIP IS TOO GREAT A PRIZE FOR THE ROMULANS TO GIVE UP. WE'LL BE USED AS LEVERAGE AGAINST THE FEDERATION.

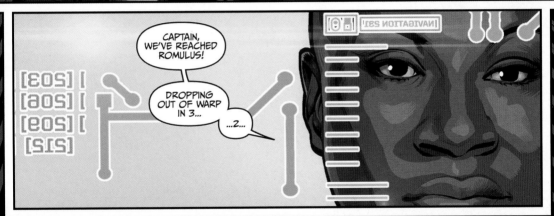

CAPTAIN, WE'VE REACHED ROMULUS!

DROPPING OUT OF WARP IN 3...

...2...

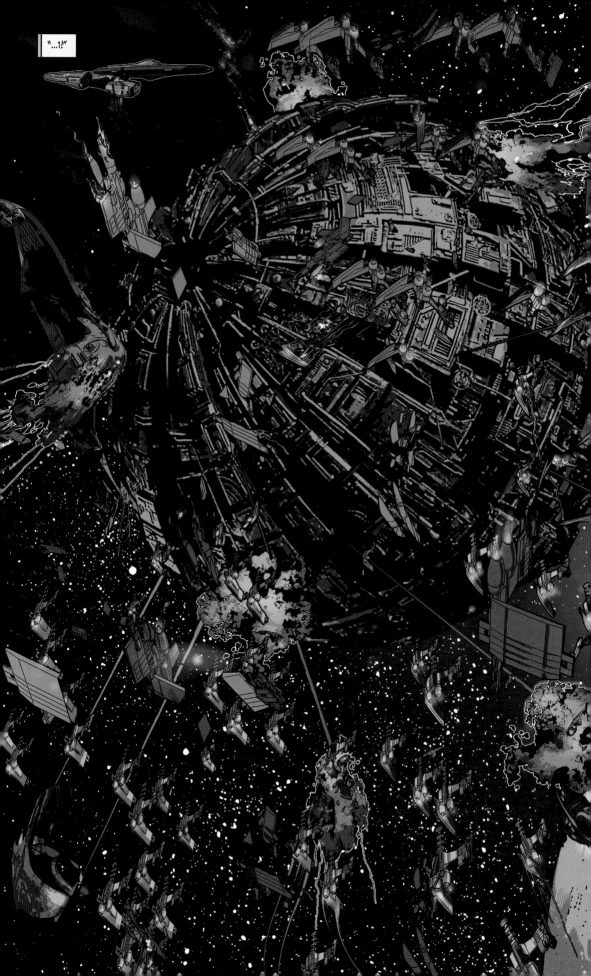

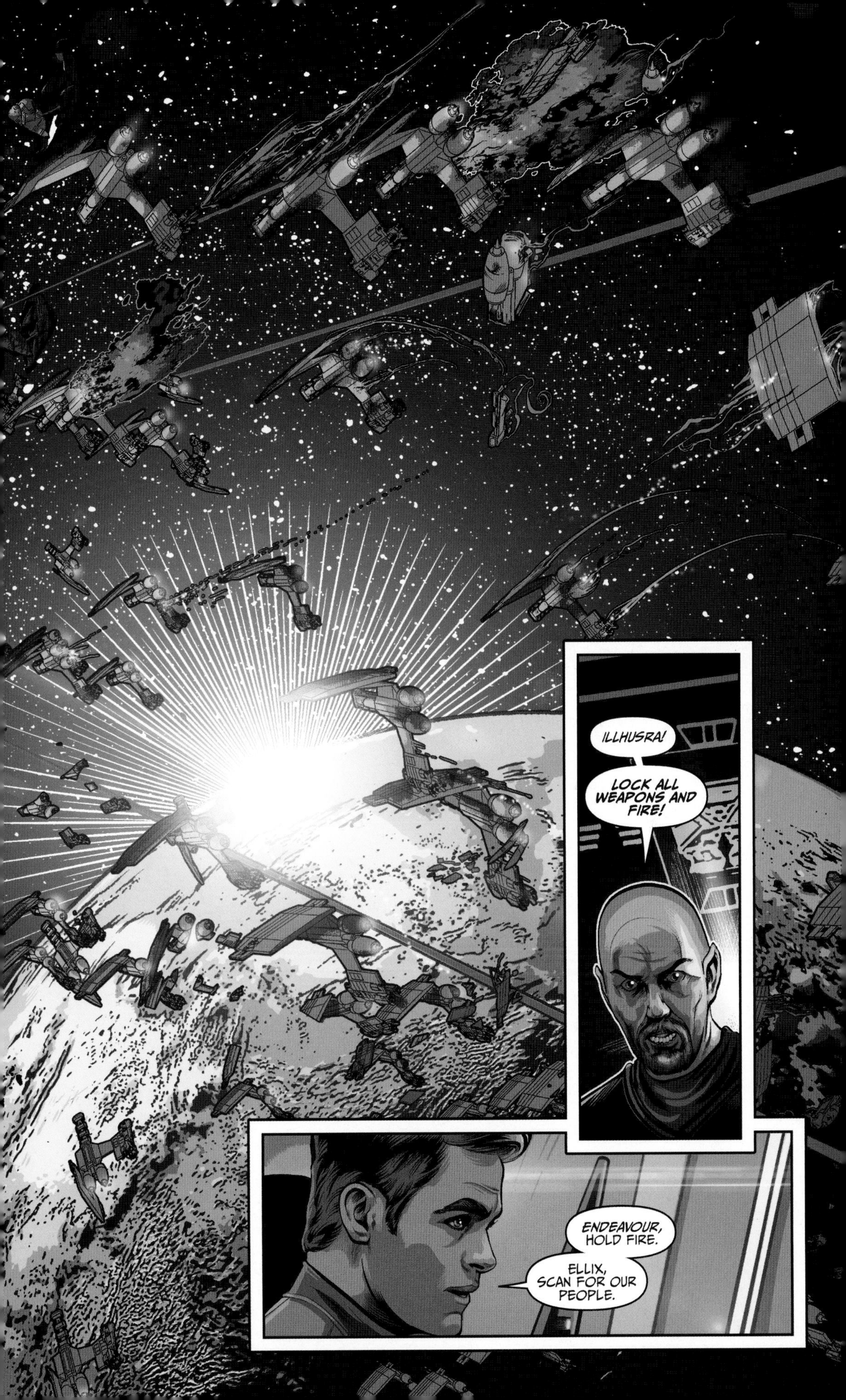
ILLHUSRA!
LOCK ALL WEAPONS AND FIRE!
ENDEAVOUR, HOLD FIRE.
ELLIX, SCAN FOR OUR PEOPLE.

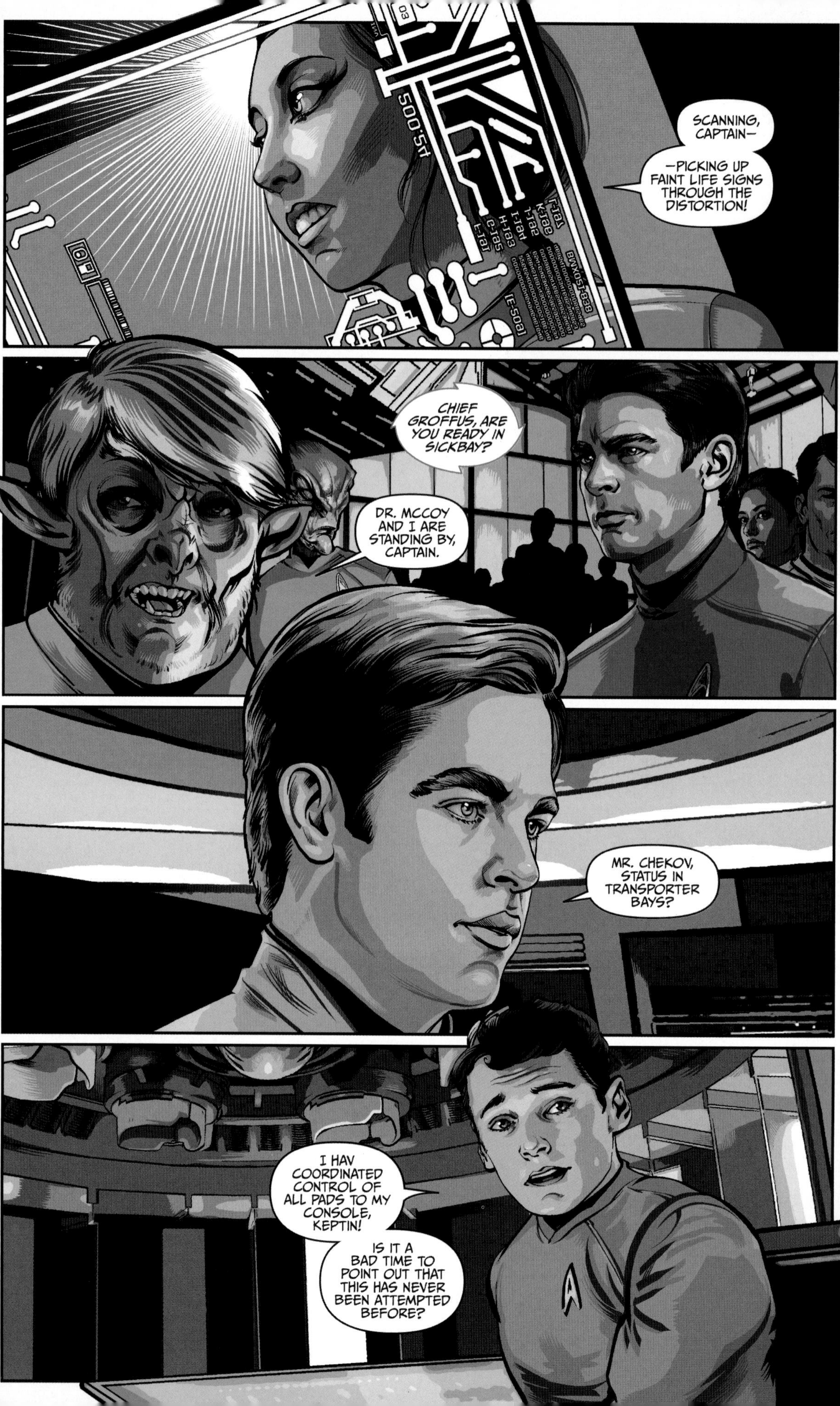
SCANNING, CAPTAIN—
—PICKING UP FAINT LIFE SIGNS THROUGH THE DISTORTION!
CHIEF GROFFUS, ARE YOU READY IN SICKBAY?
DR. MCCOY AND I ARE STANDING BY, CAPTAIN.
MR. CHEKOV, STATUS IN TRANSPORTER BAYS?
I HAV COORDINATED CONTROL OF ALL PADS TO MY CONSOLE, KEPTIN!
IS IT A BAD TIME TO POINT OUT THAT THIS HAS NEVER BEEN ATTEMPTED BEFORE?

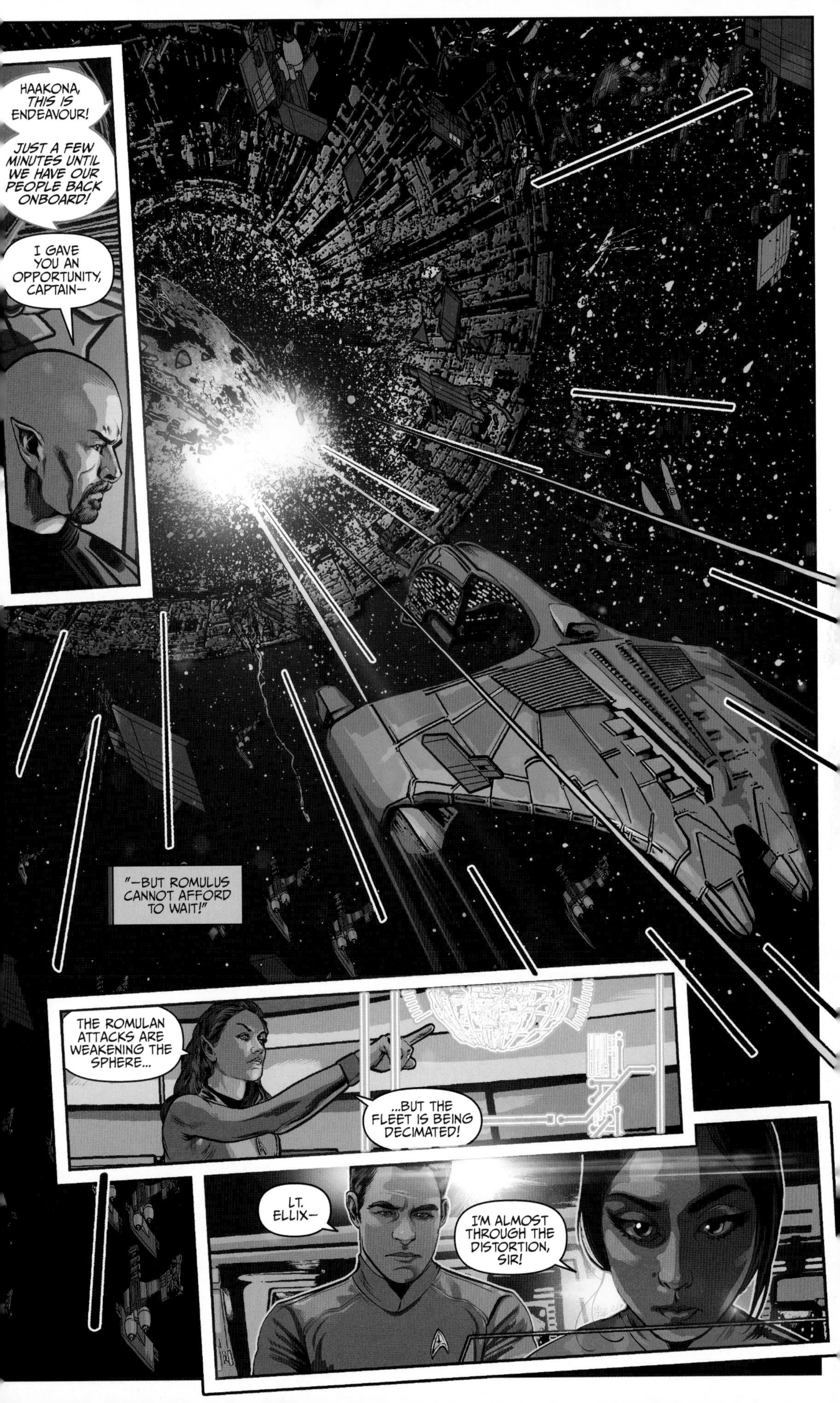

HAAKONA, THIS IS ENDEAVOUR!
JUST A FEW MINUTES UNTIL WE HAVE OUR PEOPLE BACK ONBOARD!
I GAVE YOU AN OPPORTUNITY, CAPTAIN—
"—BUT ROMULUS CANNOT AFFORD TO WAIT!"
THE ROMULAN ATTACKS ARE WEAKENING THE SPHERE...
...BUT THE FLEET IS BEING DECIMATED!
LT. ELLIX—
I'M ALMOST THROUGH THE DISTORTION, SIR!

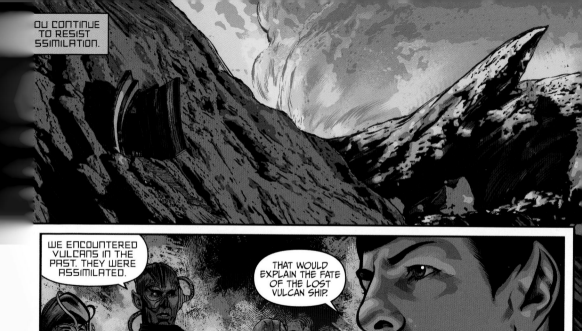

OU CONTINUE TO RESIST SSIMILATION.
WE ENCOUNTERED VULCANS IN THE PAST. THEY WERE ASSIMILATED.
THAT WOULD EXPLAIN THE FATE OF THE LOST VULCAN SHIP.
BUT I SUSPECT THAT MY COMBINED VULCAN AND HUMAN DNA IS PROVING MORE OF AN OBSTACLE THAN YOU EXPECTED.
MY VULCAN DISCIPLINE HAS ALLOWED ME TO RESIST THUS FAR.
ALL I REQUIRE TO BREAK YOUR HOLD ON ME...
...IS AN EMOTIONAL STIMULUS.

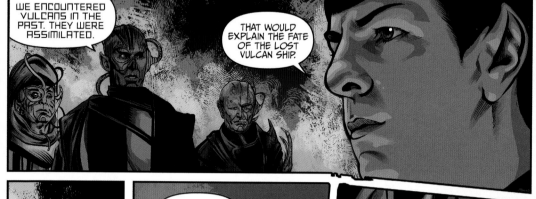

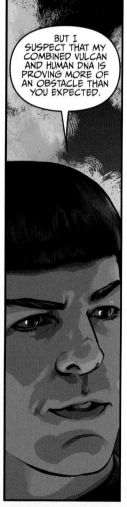

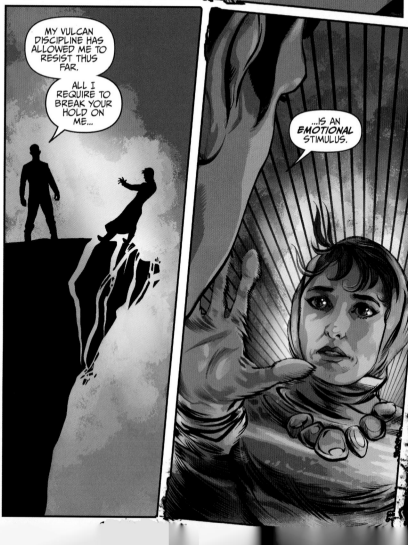

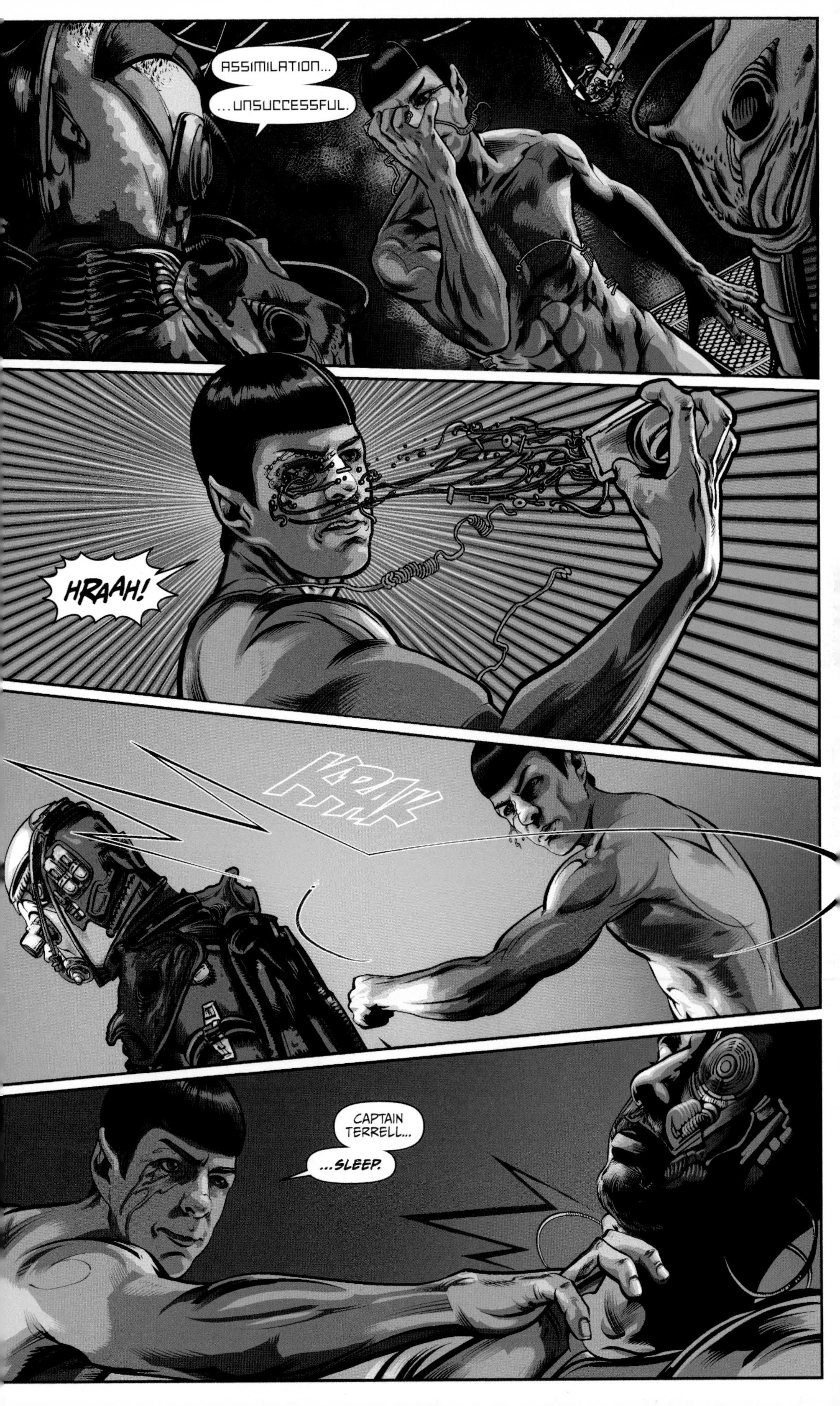
ASSIMILATION...
...UNSUCCESSFUL.
HRAAH!
KRAK
CAPTAIN TERRELL...
...SLEEP.

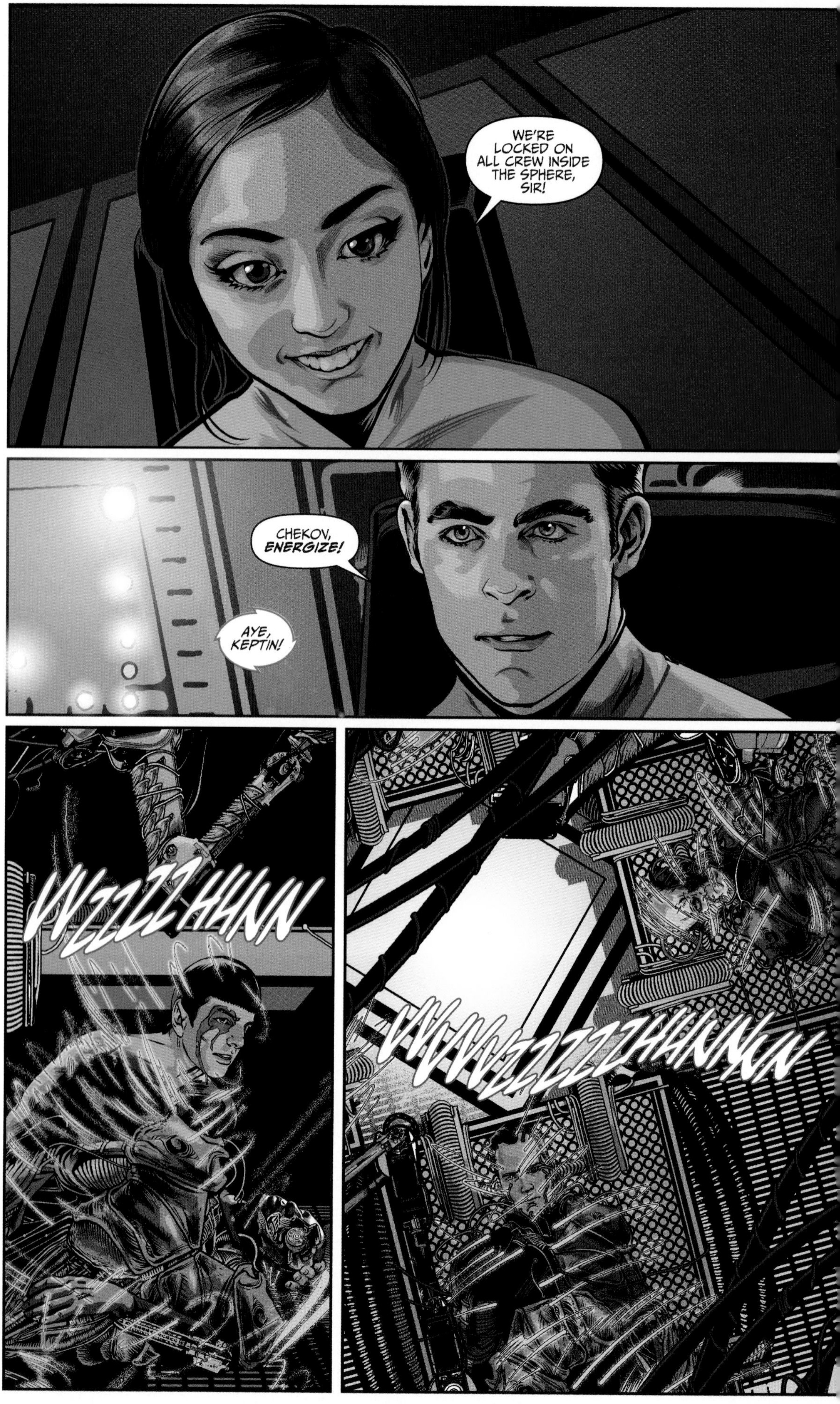
WE'RE LOCKED ON ALL CREW INSIDE THE SPHERE, SIR!
CHEKOV, ENERGIZE!
AYE, KEPTIN!
VVZZZZZHHNN
VVVVVZZZZZZHHNNNN

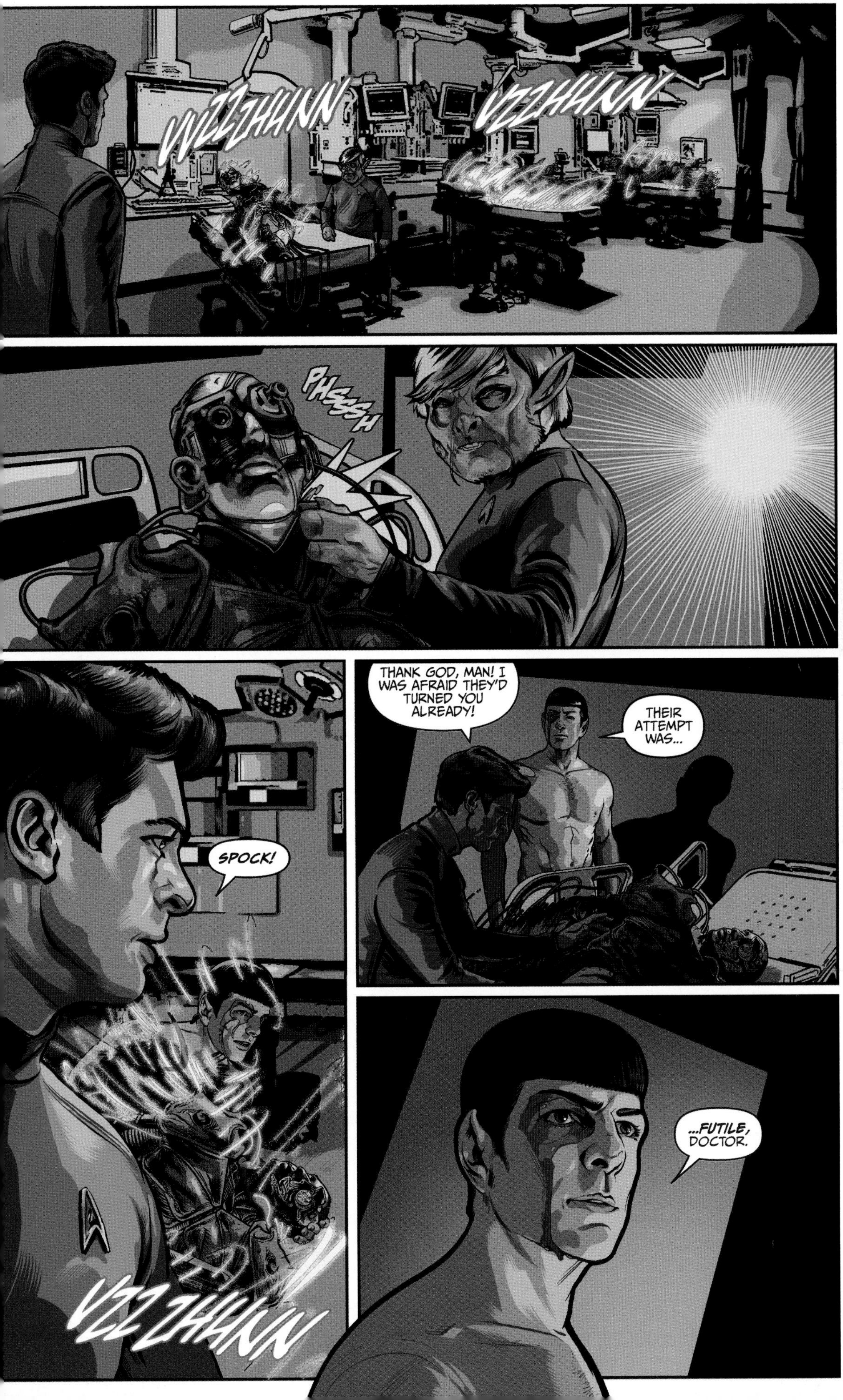
VVZZZHHNN
VZZHHHNN
PHSSSH
SPOCK!
THANK GOD, MAN! I WAS AFRAID THEY'D TURNED YOU ALREADY!
THEIR ATTEMPT WAS...
...FUTILE, DOCTOR.
VZZZHHNN

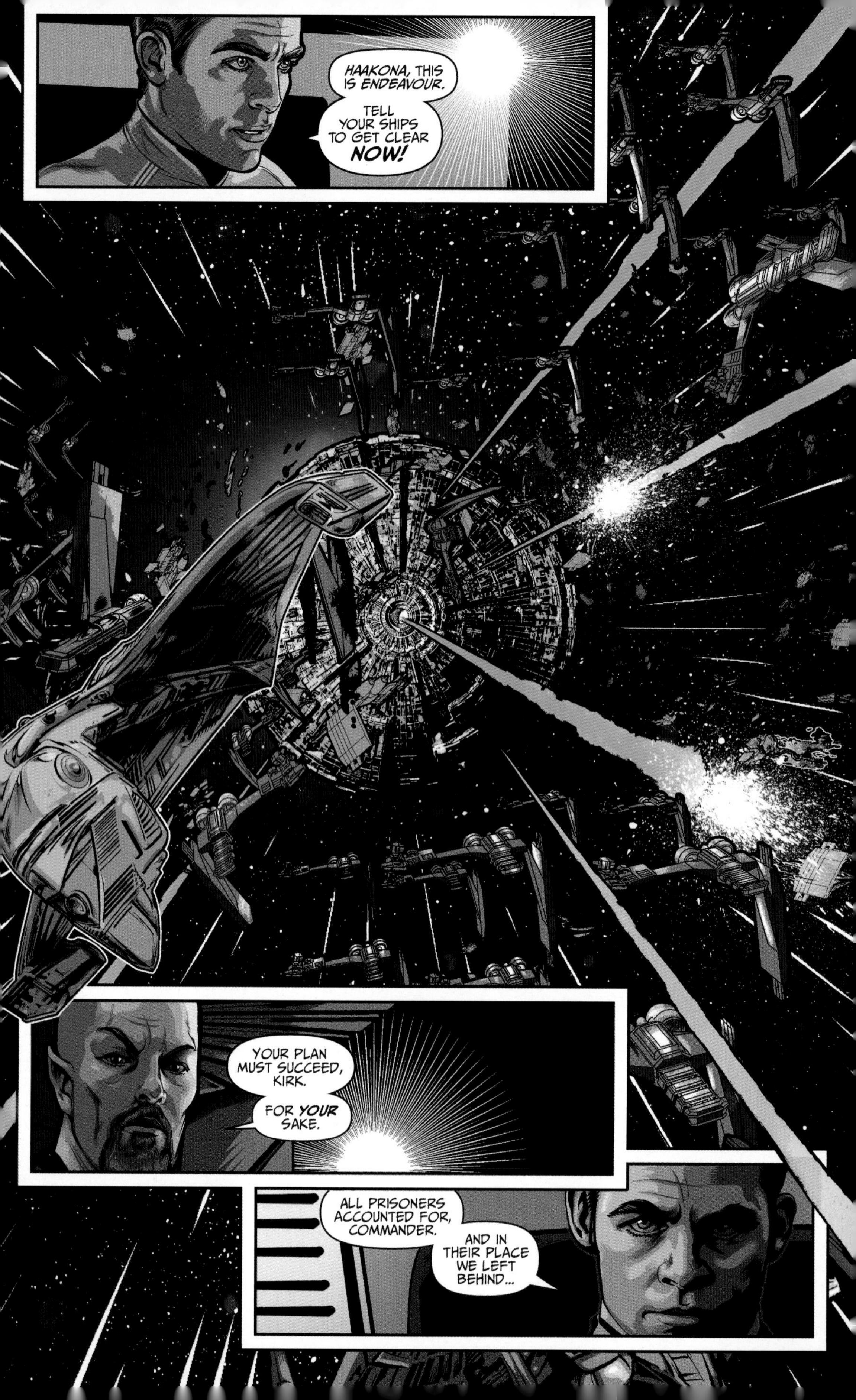
HAAKONA, THIS IS ENDEAVOUR.
TELL YOUR SHIPS TO GET CLEAR NOW!
YOUR PLAN MUST SUCCEED, KIRK.
FOR YOUR SAKE.
ALL PRISONERS ACCOUNTED FOR, COMMANDER.
AND IN THEIR PLACE WE LEFT BEHIND...

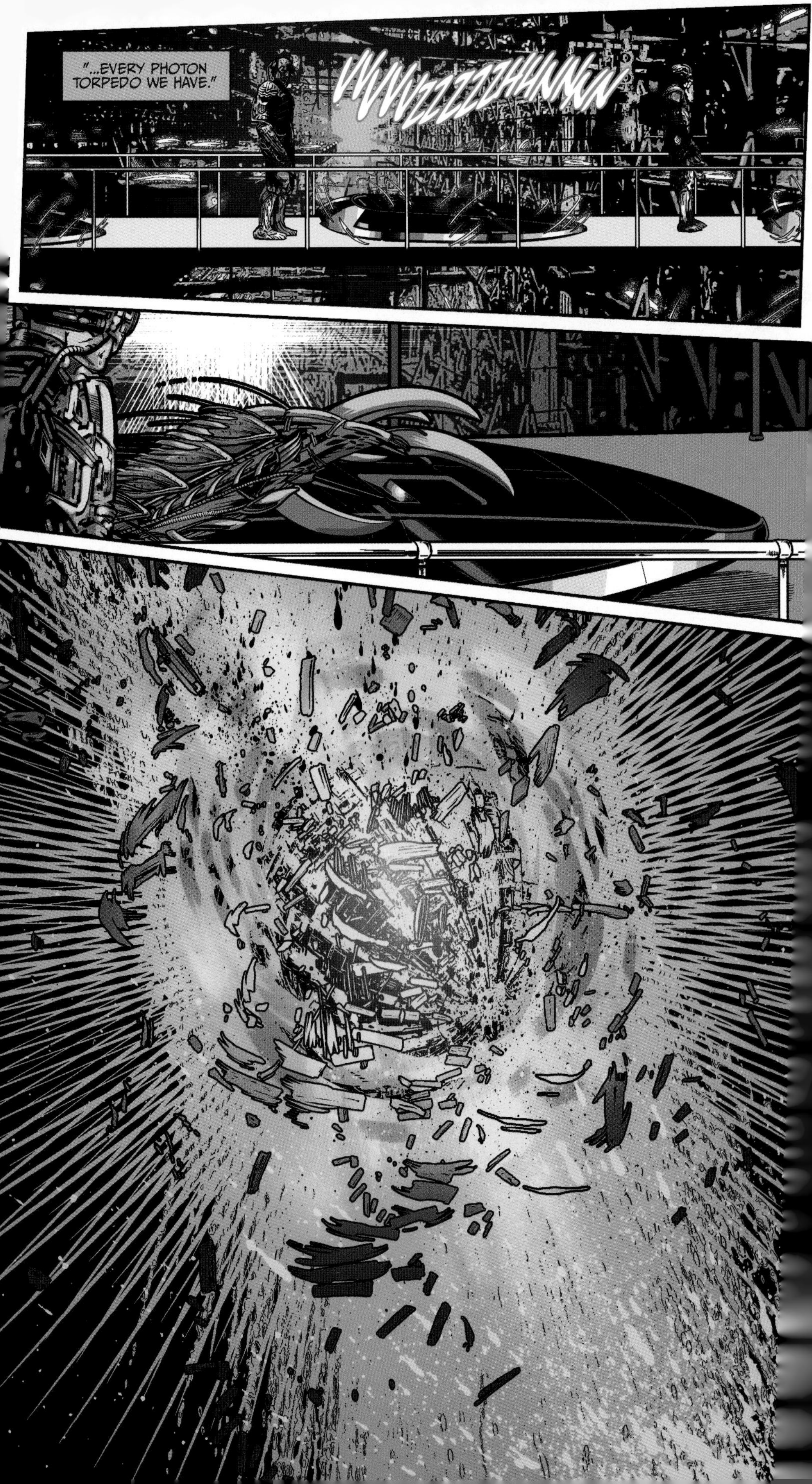
"...EVERY PHOTON TORPEDO WE HAVE."
VVVVVZZZZZHHNNGN

"YOU ARE NO HERO, JAMES TIBERIUS KIRK."

YOU BRAZENLY VIOLATED THE BORDERS OF THE EMPIRE. FOR THE SECOND TIME, I MUST ADD.

THE FIRST TIME, YOUR ASSISTANCE IN UNCOVERING THE VULCAN TERRORIST PLOT WAS ENOUGH TO GRANT YOUR RELEASE.

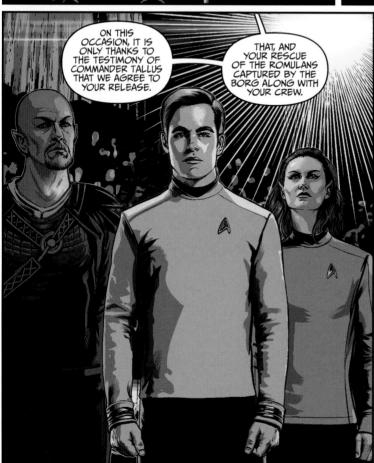

ON THIS OCCASION, IT IS ONLY THANKS TO THE TESTIMONY OF COMMANDER TALLUS THAT WE AGREE TO YOUR RELEASE.

THAT, AND YOUR RESCUE OF THE ROMULANS CAPTURED BY THE BORG ALONG WITH YOUR CREW.

BUT YOUR RELEASE IS *NOT* UNCONDITIONAL.

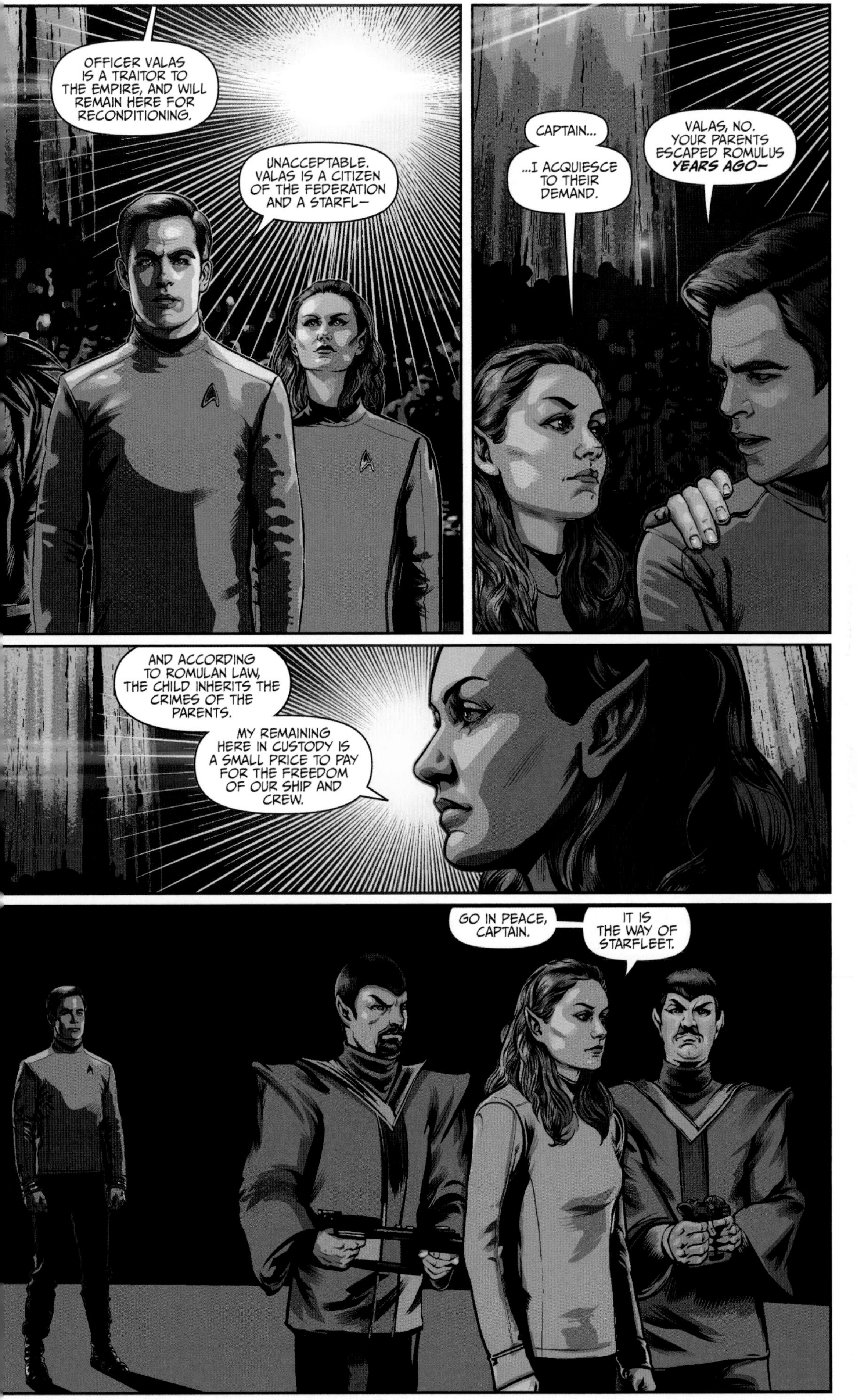
OFFICER VALAS IS A TRAITOR TO THE EMPIRE, AND WILL REMAIN HERE FOR RECONDITIONING.
UNACCEPTABLE. VALAS IS A CITIZEN OF THE FEDERATION AND A STARFL—
CAPTAIN...
...I ACQUIESCE TO THEIR DEMAND.
VALAS, NO. YOUR PARENTS ESCAPED ROMULUS YEARS AGO—
AND ACCORDING TO ROMULAN LAW, THE CHILD INHERITS THE CRIMES OF THE PARENTS.
MY REMAINING HERE IN CUSTODY IS A SMALL PRICE TO PAY FOR THE FREEDOM OF OUR SHIP AND CREW.
GO IN PEACE, CAPTAIN.
IT IS THE WAY OF STARFLEET.

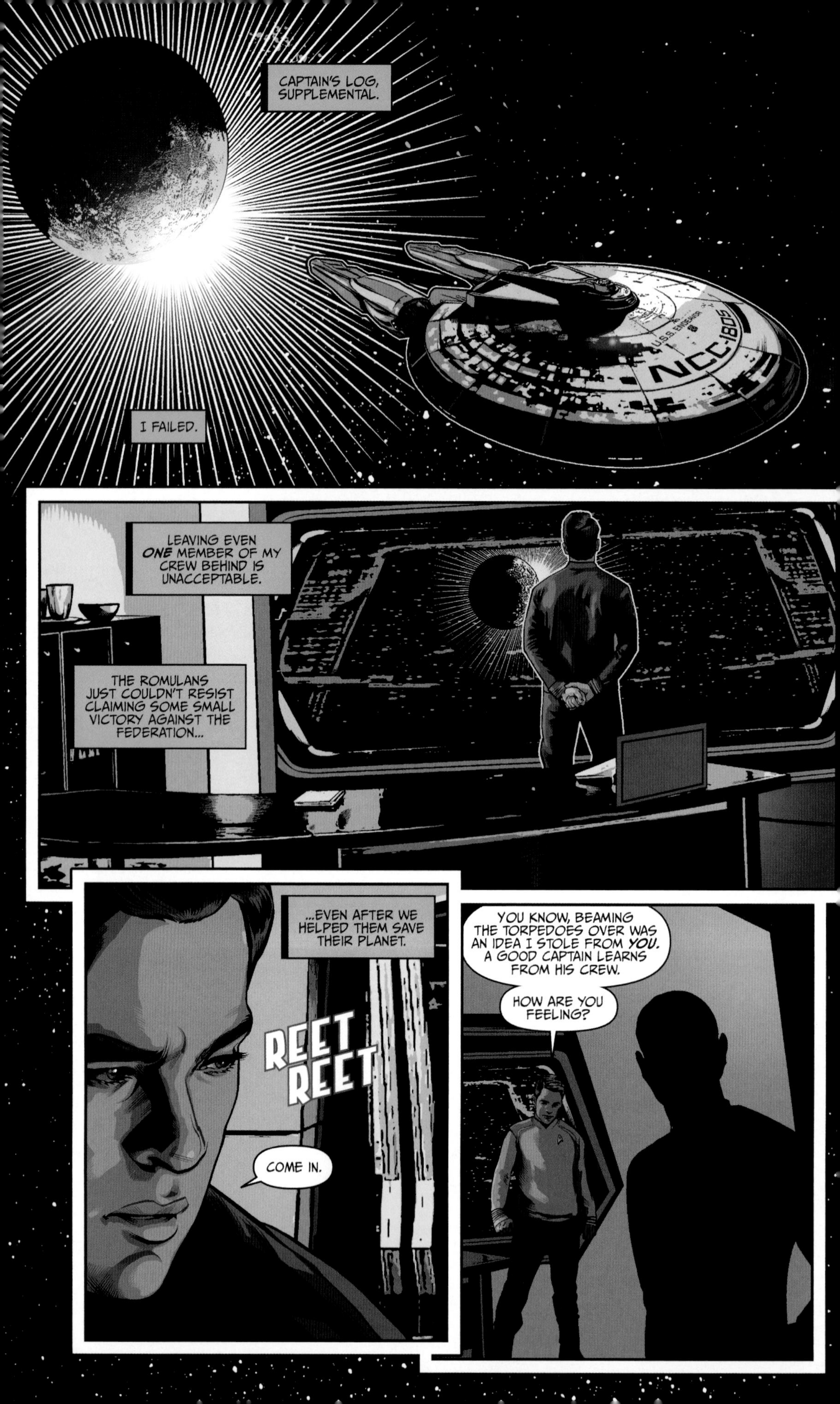
CAPTAIN'S LOG, SUPPLEMENTAL.
I FAILED.
LEAVING EVEN *ONE* MEMBER OF MY CREW BEHIND IS UNACCEPTABLE.
THE ROMULANS JUST COULDN'T RESIST CLAIMING SOME SMALL VICTORY AGAINST THE FEDERATION...
...EVEN AFTER WE HELPED THEM SAVE THEIR PLANET.
REET REET
COME IN.
YOU KNOW, BEAMING THE TORPEDOES OVER WAS AN IDEA I STOLE FROM *YOU.* A GOOD CAPTAIN LEARNS FROM HIS CREW.
HOW ARE YOU FEELING?

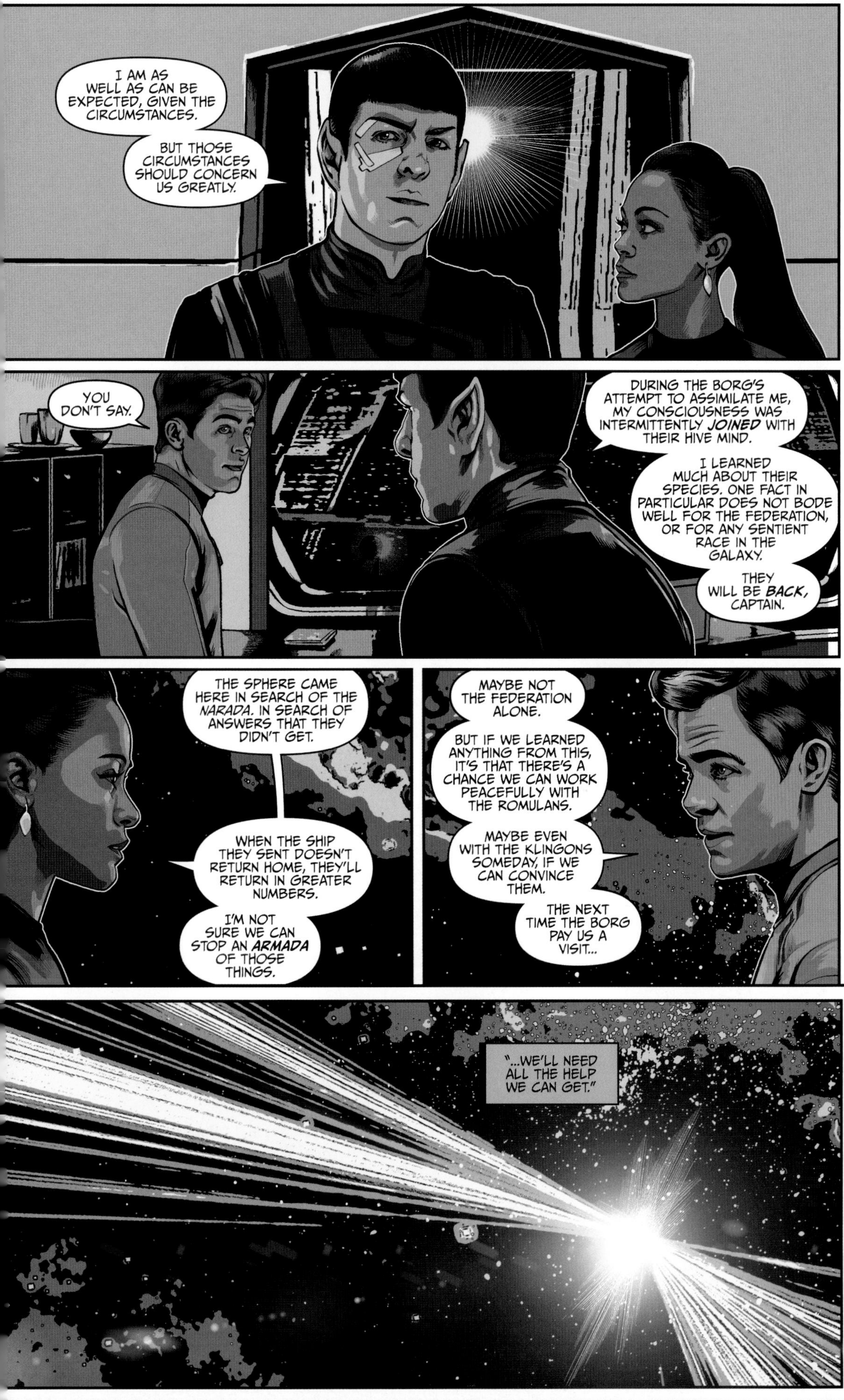
I AM AS WELL AS CAN BE EXPECTED, GIVEN THE CIRCUMSTANCES.
BUT THOSE CIRCUMSTANCES SHOULD CONCERN US GREATLY.
YOU DON'T SAY.
DURING THE BORG'S ATTEMPT TO ASSIMILATE ME, MY CONSCIOUSNESS WAS INTERMITTENTLY *JOINED* WITH THEIR HIVE MIND.
I LEARNED MUCH ABOUT THEIR SPECIES. ONE FACT IN PARTICULAR DOES NOT BODE WELL FOR THE FEDERATION, OR FOR ANY SENTIENT RACE IN THE GALAXY.
THEY WILL BE ***BACK,*** CAPTAIN.
THE SPHERE CAME HERE IN SEARCH OF THE *NARADA.* IN SEARCH OF ANSWERS THAT THEY DIDN'T GET.
WHEN THE SHIP THEY SENT DOESN'T RETURN HOME, THEY'LL RETURN IN GREATER NUMBERS.
I'M NOT SURE WE CAN STOP AN ***ARMADA*** OF THOSE THINGS.
MAYBE NOT THE FEDERATION ALONE.
BUT IF WE LEARNED ANYTHING FROM THIS, IT'S THAT THERE'S A CHANCE WE CAN WORK PEACEFULLY WITH THE ROMULANS.
MAYBE EVEN WITH THE KLINGONS SOMEDAY, IF WE CAN CONVINCE THEM.
THE NEXT TIME THE BORG PAY US A VISIT...
"...WE'LL NEED ALL THE HELP WE CAN GET."

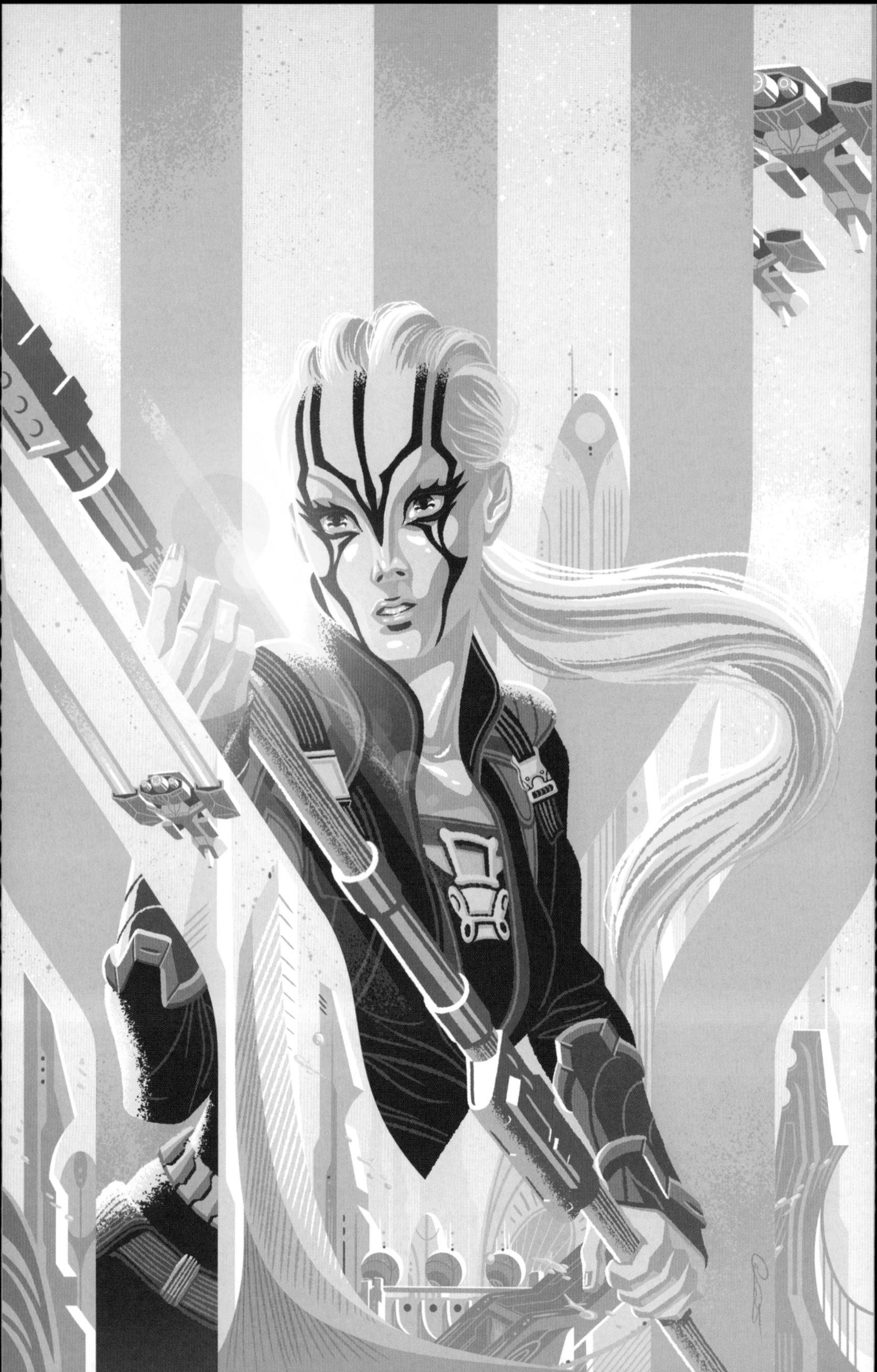

art by
George Caltsoudas

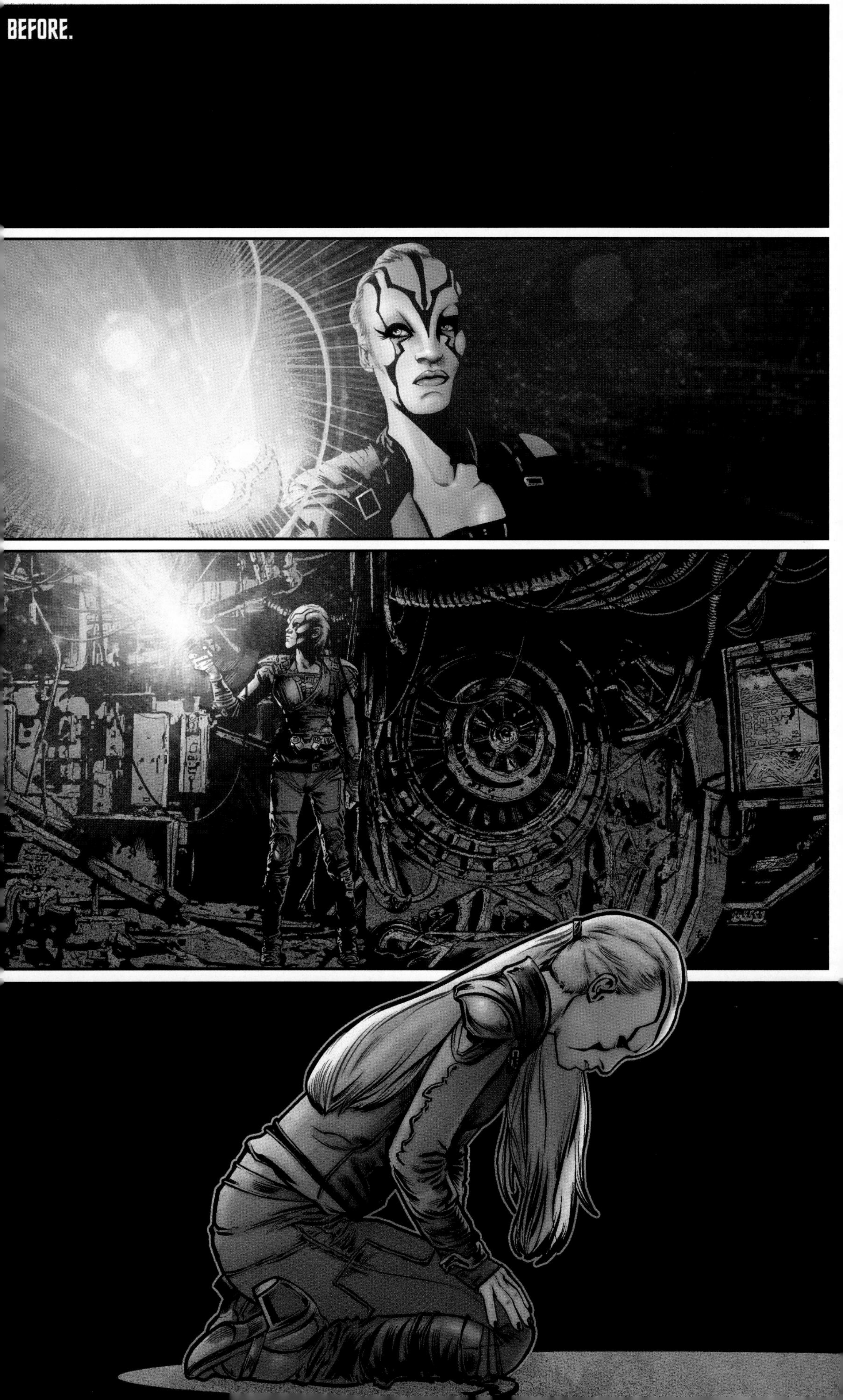
BEFORE.

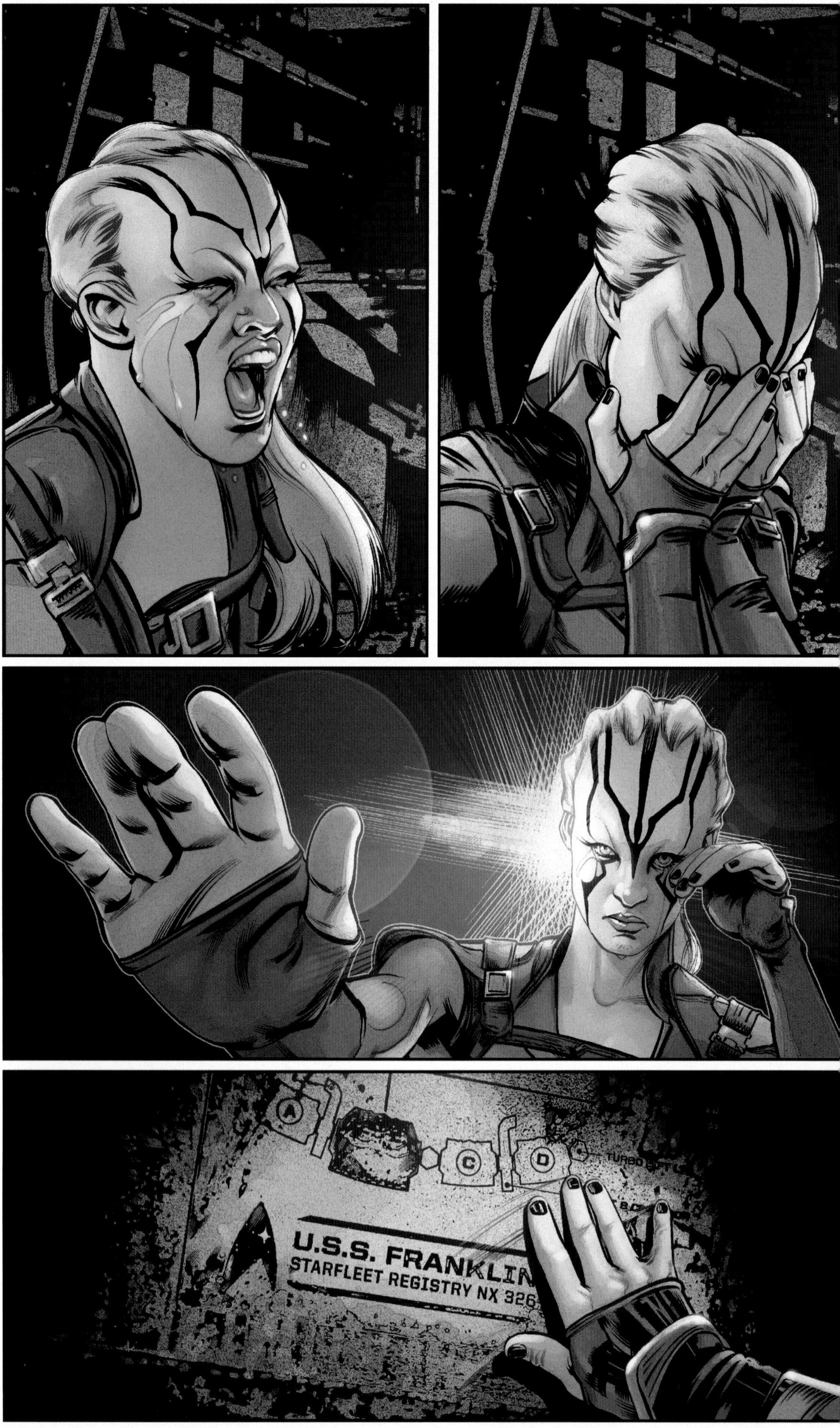
A
C
D
TURBO
U.S.S. FRANKLIN
STARFLEET REGISTRY NX 326

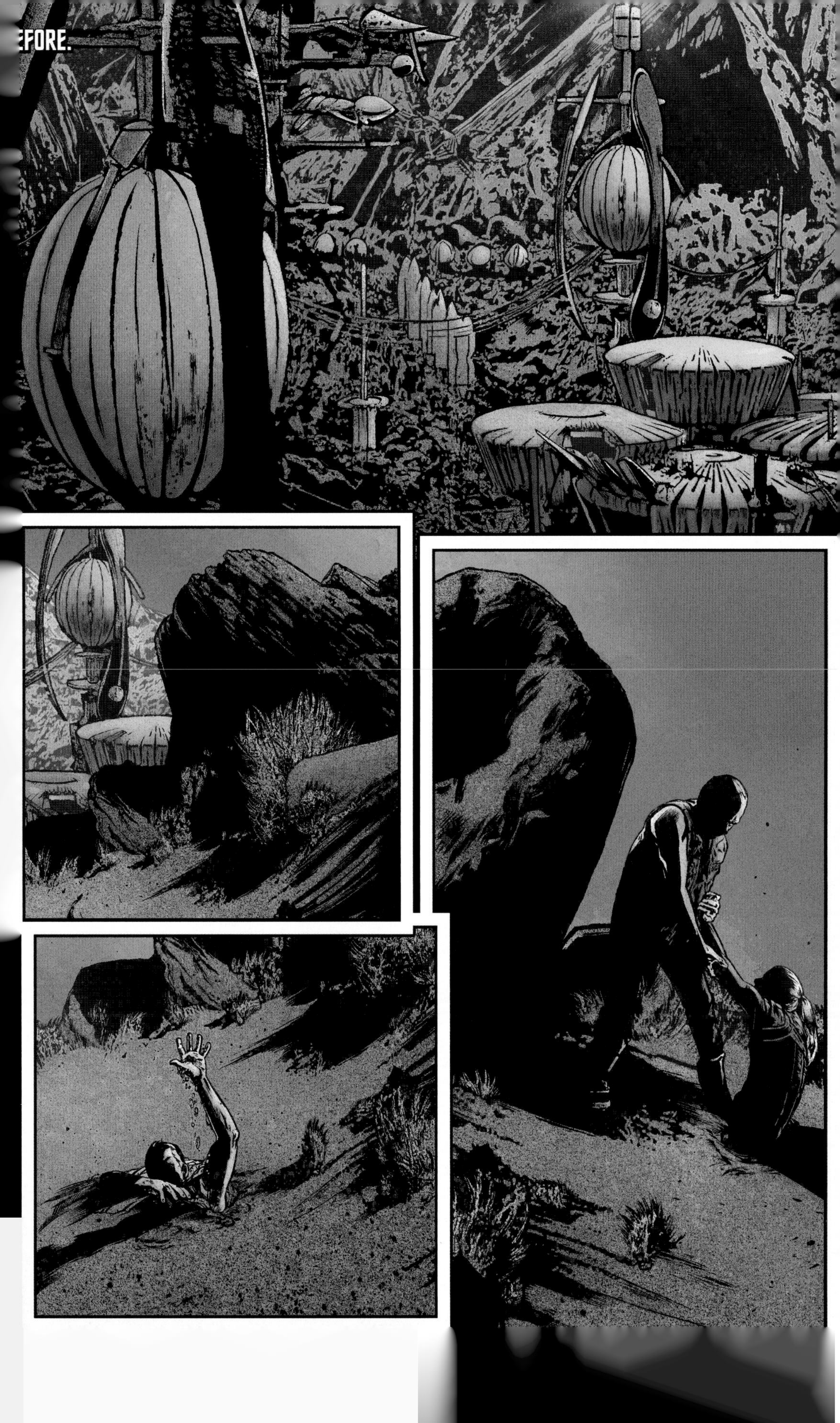
EFORE.

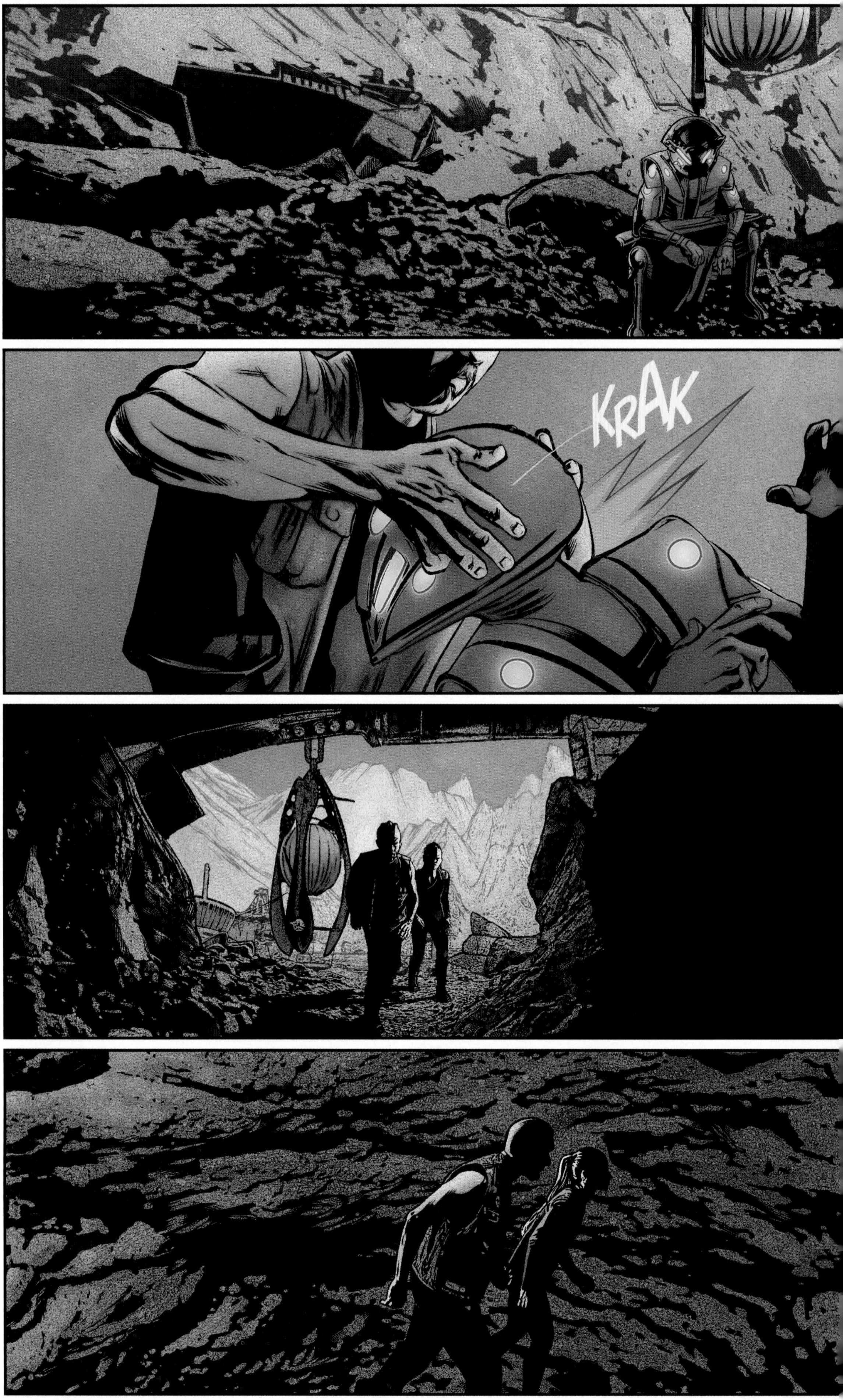
KRAK

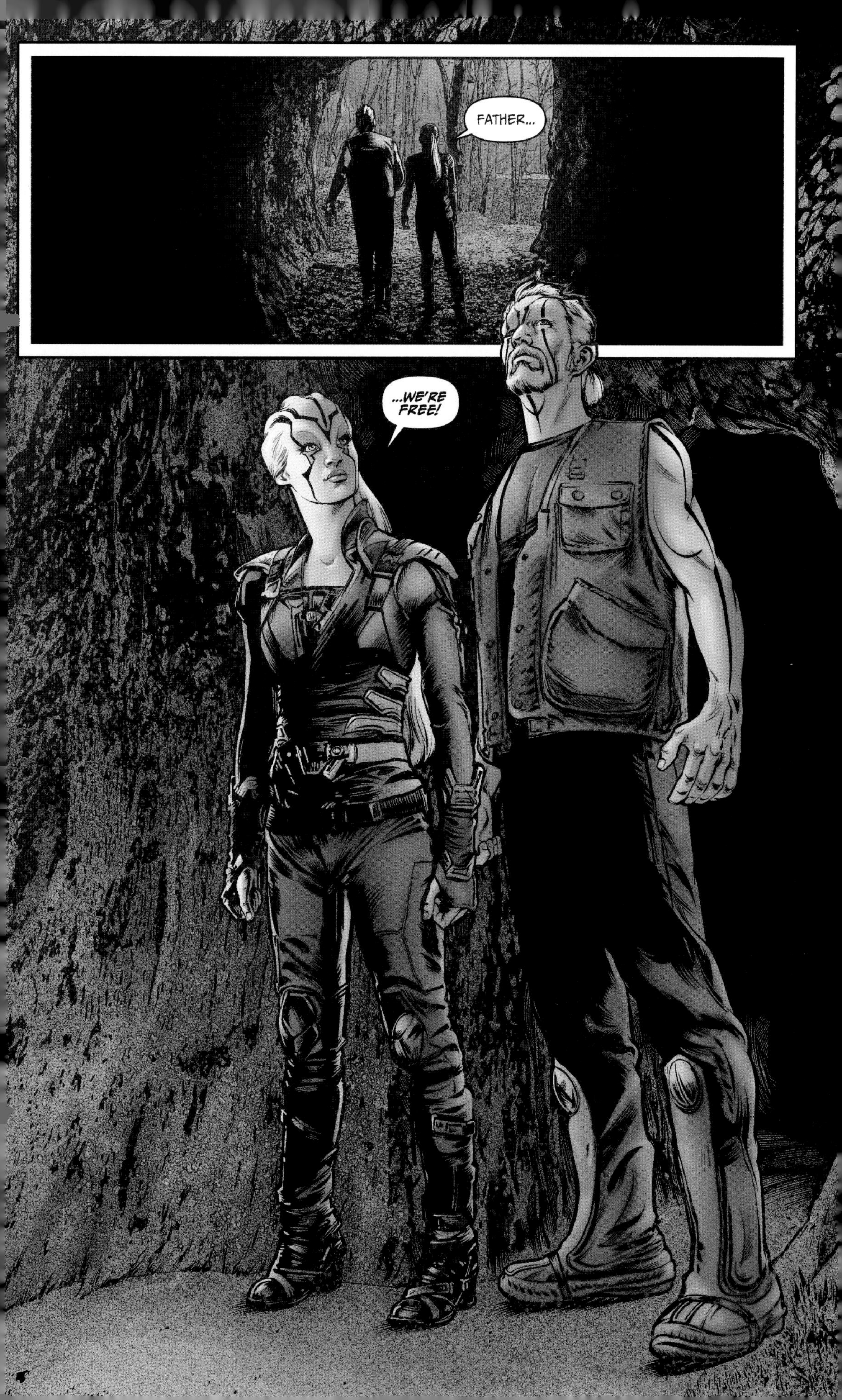
FATHER...
...WE'RE FREE!

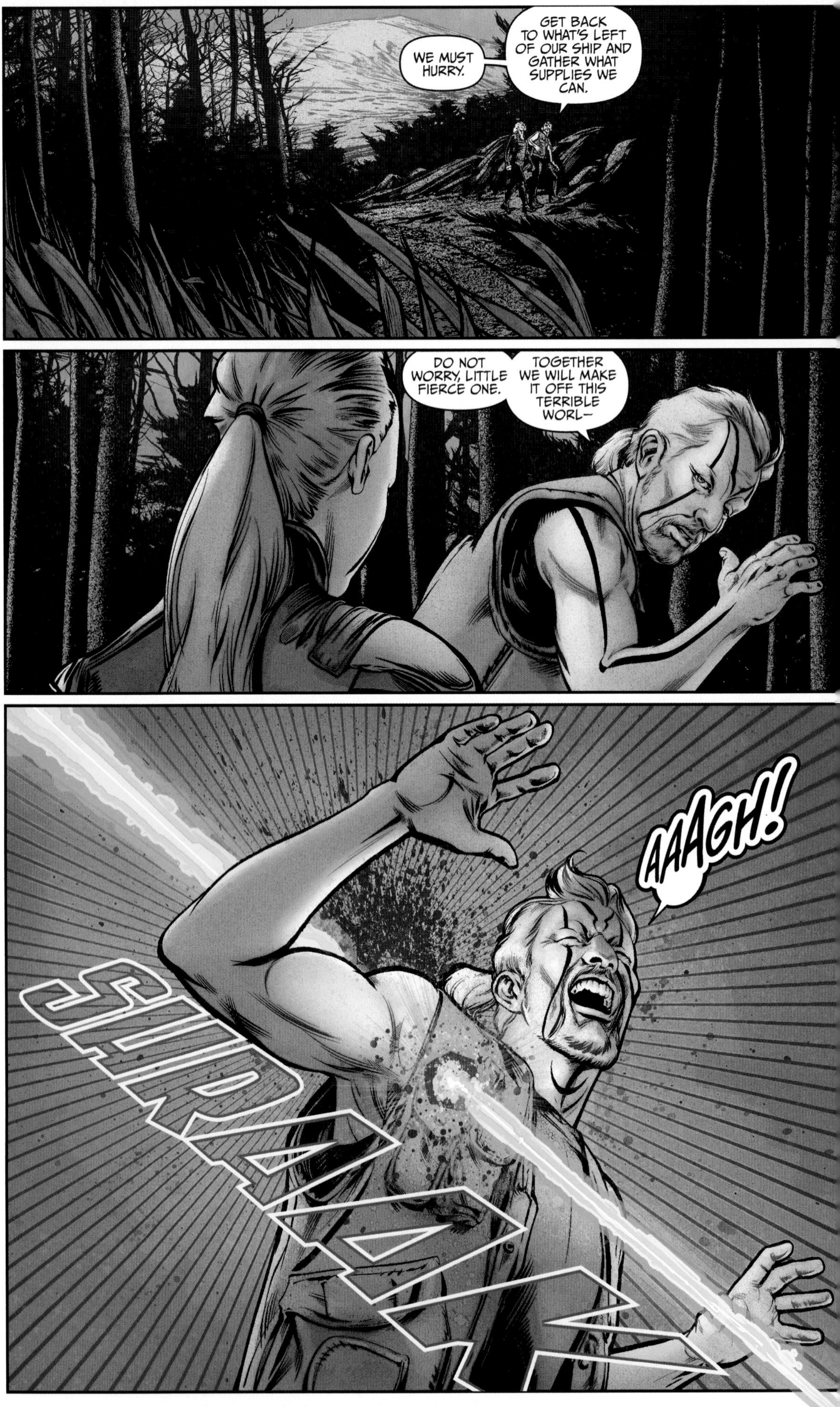
WE MUST HURRY.
GET BACK TO WHAT'S LEFT OF OUR SHIP AND GATHER WHAT SUPPLIES WE CAN.
DO NOT WORRY, LITTLE FIERCE ONE.
TOGETHER WE WILL MAKE IT OFF THIS TERRIBLE WORL—
AAAGH!
SHRAAAAK

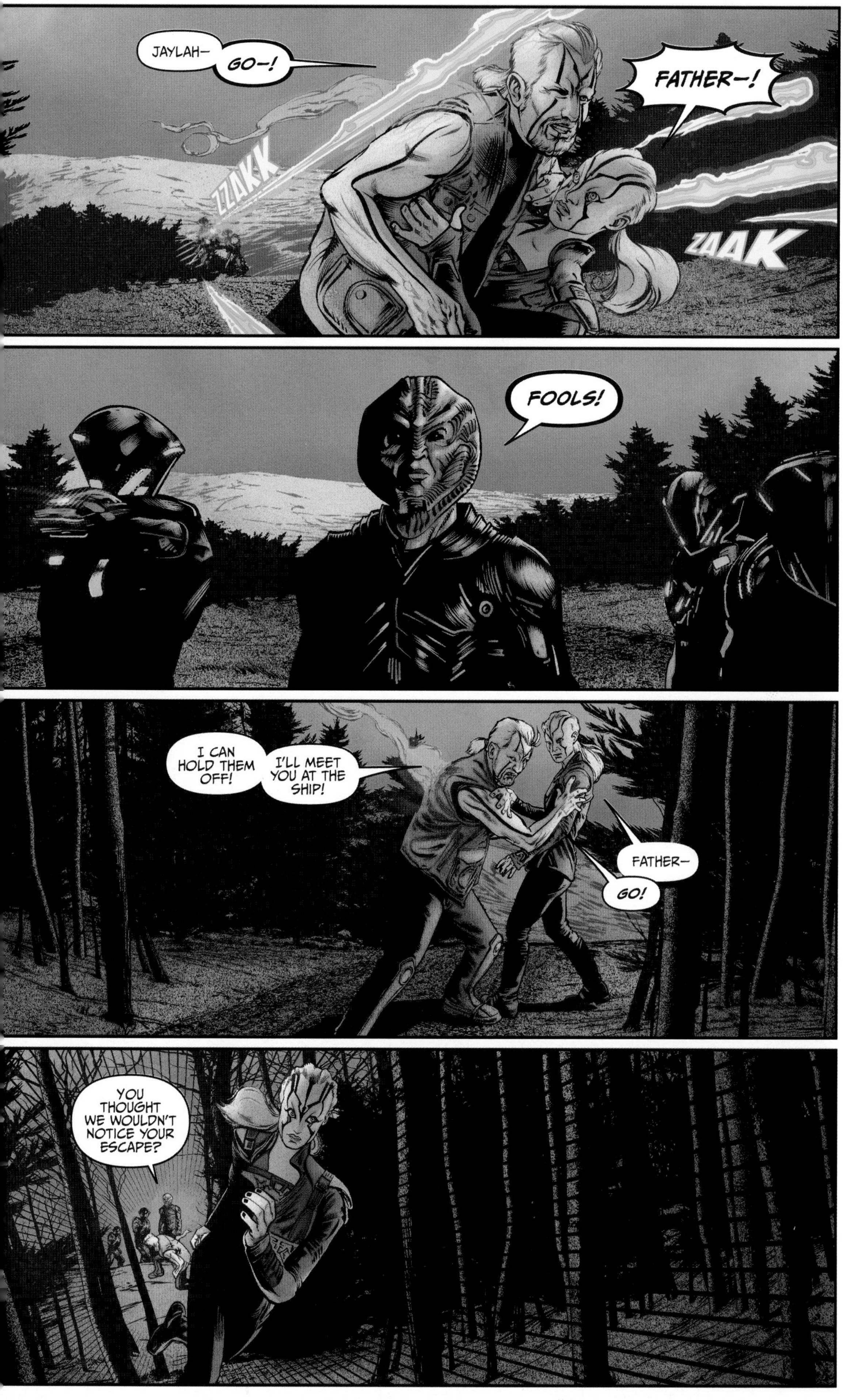
JAYLAH—
GO—!
ZZAKK
FATHER—!
ZAAK
FOOLS!
I CAN HOLD THEM OFF!
I'LL MEET YOU AT THE SHIP!
FATHER—
GO!
YOU THOUGHT WE WOULDN'T NOTICE YOUR ESCAPE?

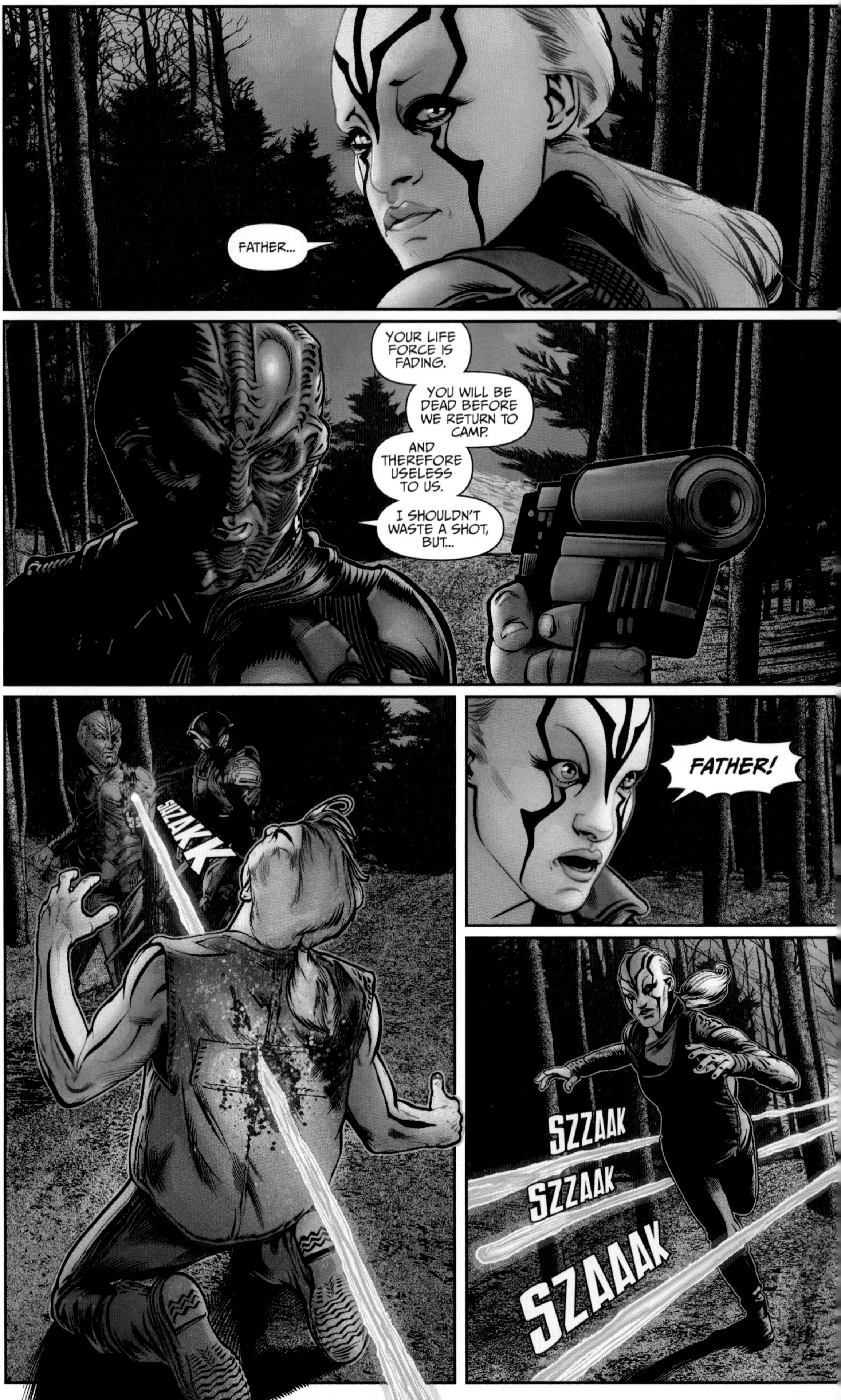
FATHER...
YOUR LIFE FORCE IS FADING.
YOU WILL BE DEAD BEFORE WE RETURN TO CAMP.
AND THEREFORE USELESS TO US.
I SHOULDN'T WASTE A SHOT, BUT...
SZZAKK
FATHER!
SZZAAK
SZZAAK
SZAAAK

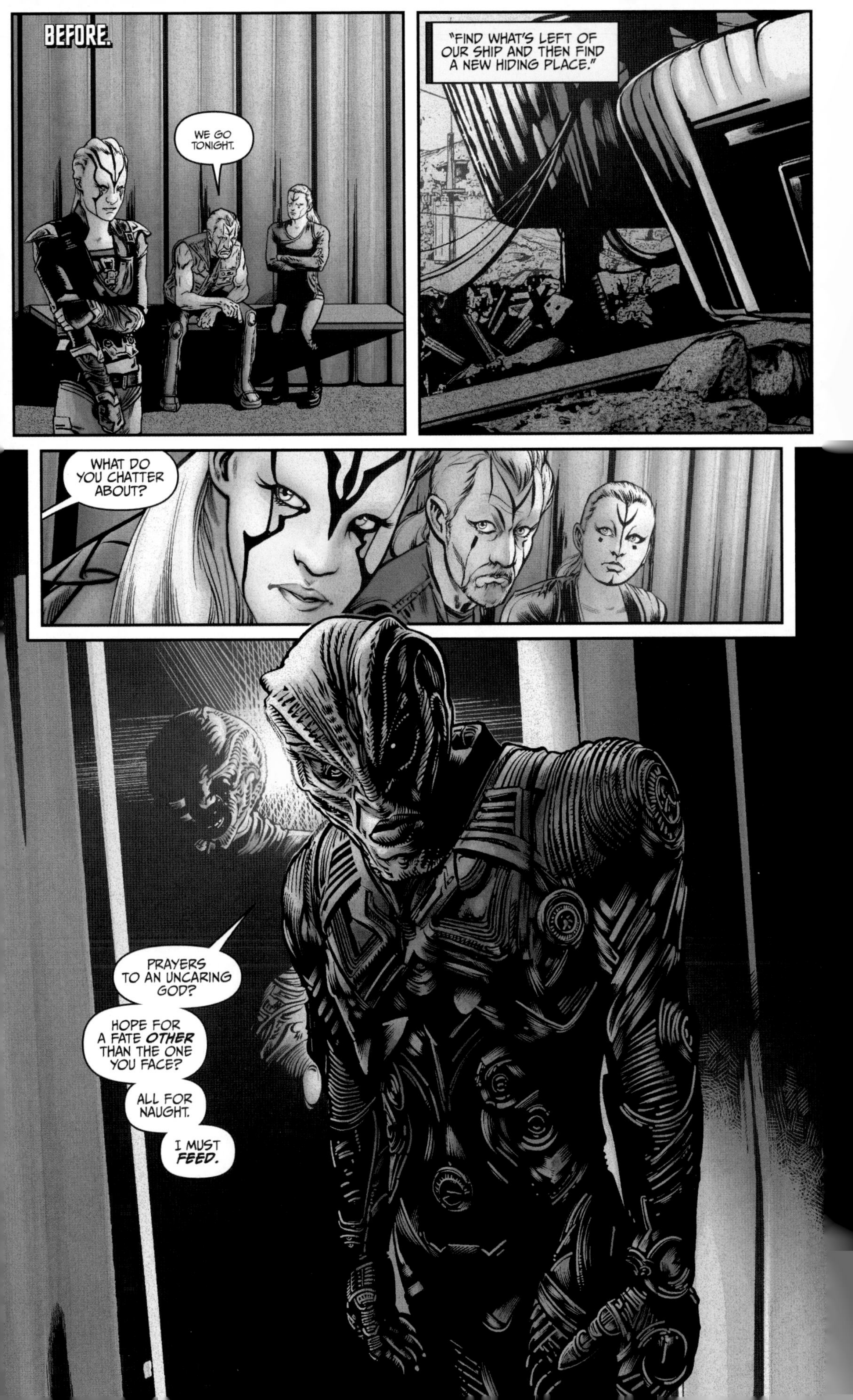
BEFORE.
WE GO TONIGHT.
"FIND WHAT'S LEFT OF OUR SHIP AND THEN FIND A NEW HIDING PLACE."
WHAT DO YOU CHATTER ABOUT?
PRAYERS TO AN UNCARING GOD?
HOPE FOR A FATE OTHER THAN THE ONE YOU FACE?
ALL FOR NAUGHT.
I MUST FEED.

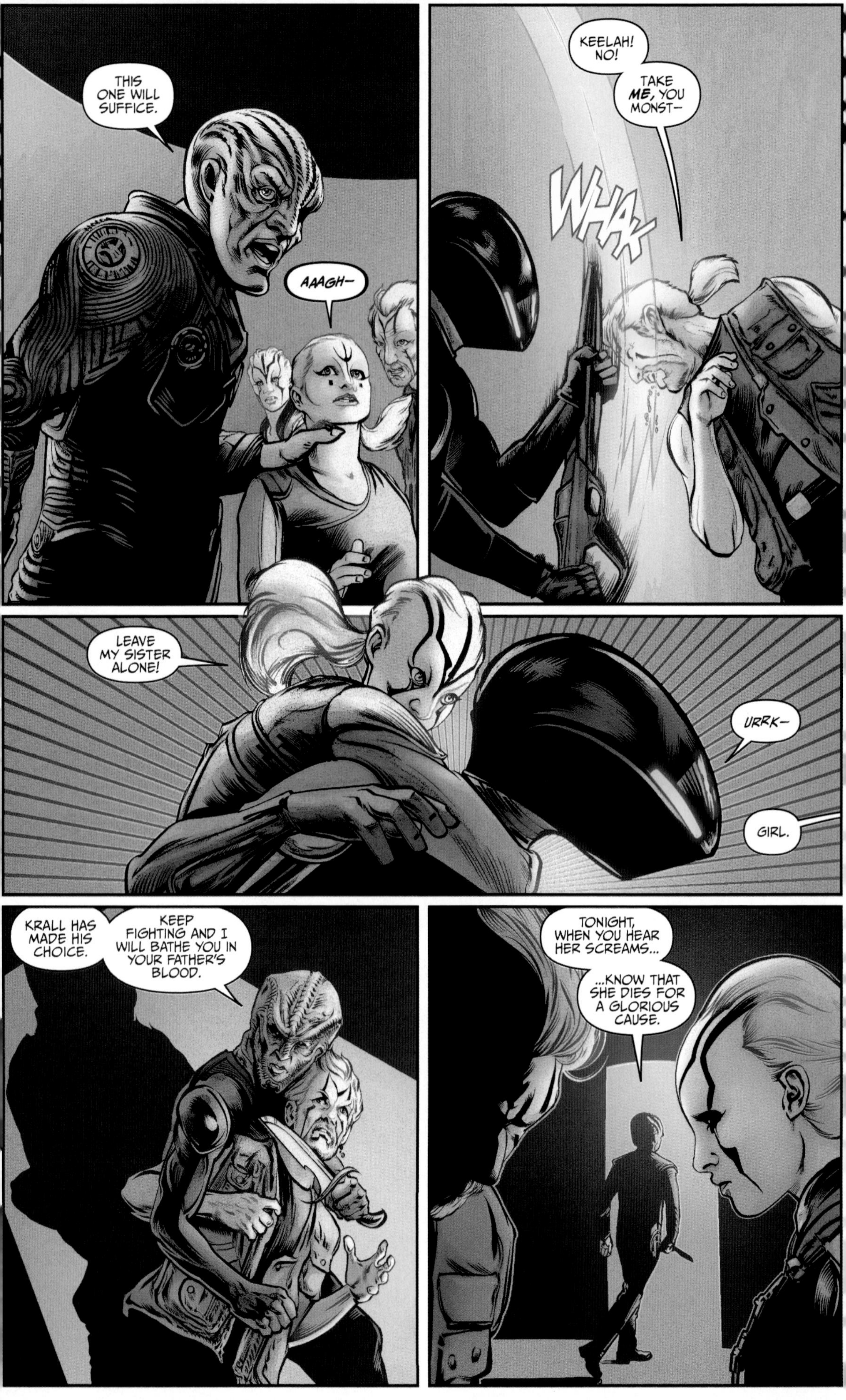
THIS ONE WILL SUFFICE.
AAAGH—
KEELAH! NO!
TAKE ME, YOU MONST—
WHAK
LEAVE MY SISTER ALONE!
URRK—
GIRL.
KRALL HAS MADE HIS CHOICE.
KEEP FIGHTING AND I WILL BATHE YOU IN YOUR FATHER'S BLOOD.
TONIGHT, WHEN YOU HEAR HER SCREAMS...
...KNOW THAT SHE DIES FOR A GLORIOUS CAUSE.

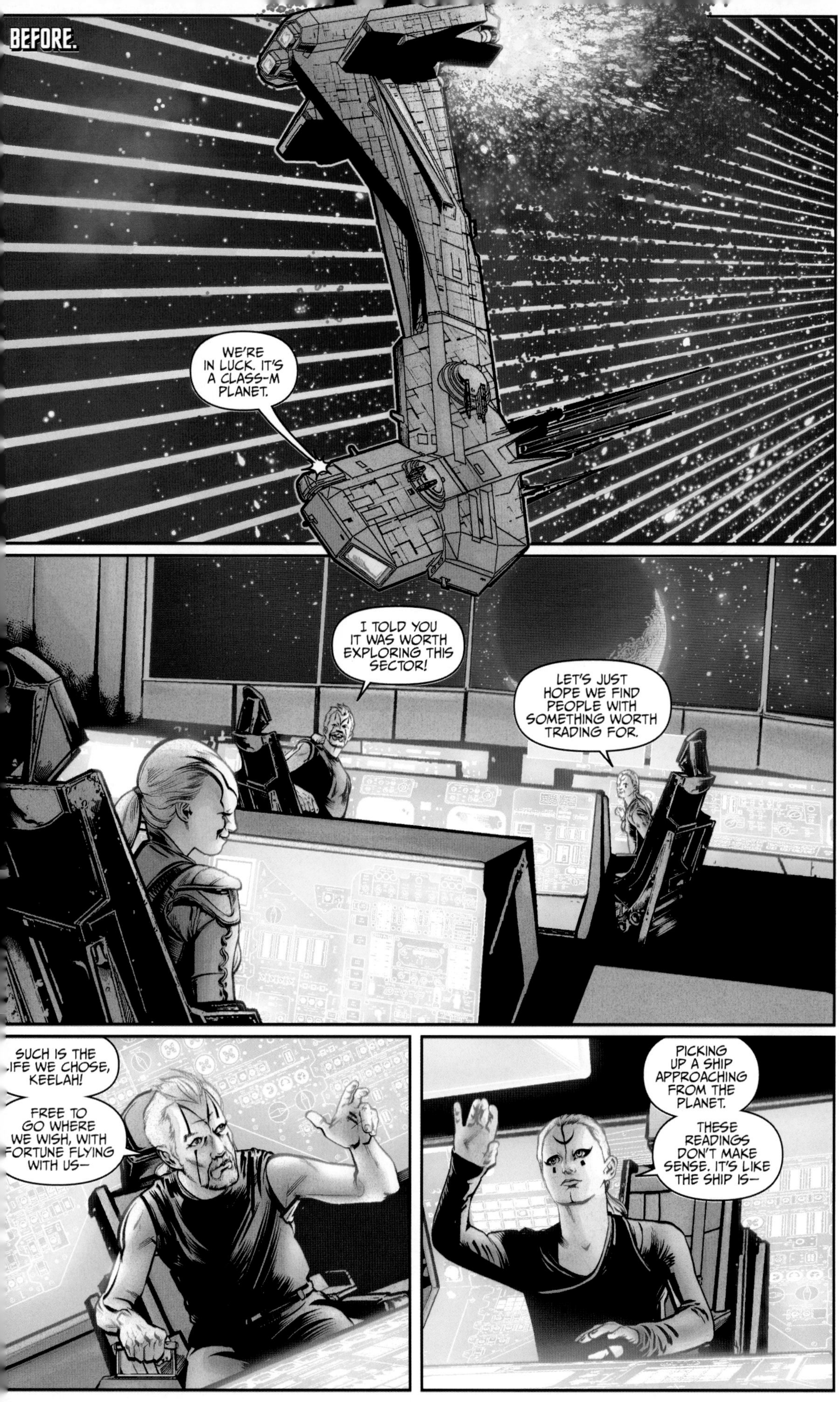
BEFORE.
WE'RE IN LUCK. IT'S A CLASS-M PLANET.
I TOLD YOU IT WAS WORTH EXPLORING THIS SECTOR!
LET'S JUST HOPE WE FIND PEOPLE WITH SOMETHING WORTH TRADING FOR.
SUCH IS THE LIFE WE CHOSE, KEELAH!
FREE TO GO WHERE WE WISH, WITH FORTUNE FLYING WITH US—
PICKING UP A SHIP APPROACHING FROM THE PLANET.
THESE READINGS DON'T MAKE SENSE. IT'S LIKE THE SHIP IS—

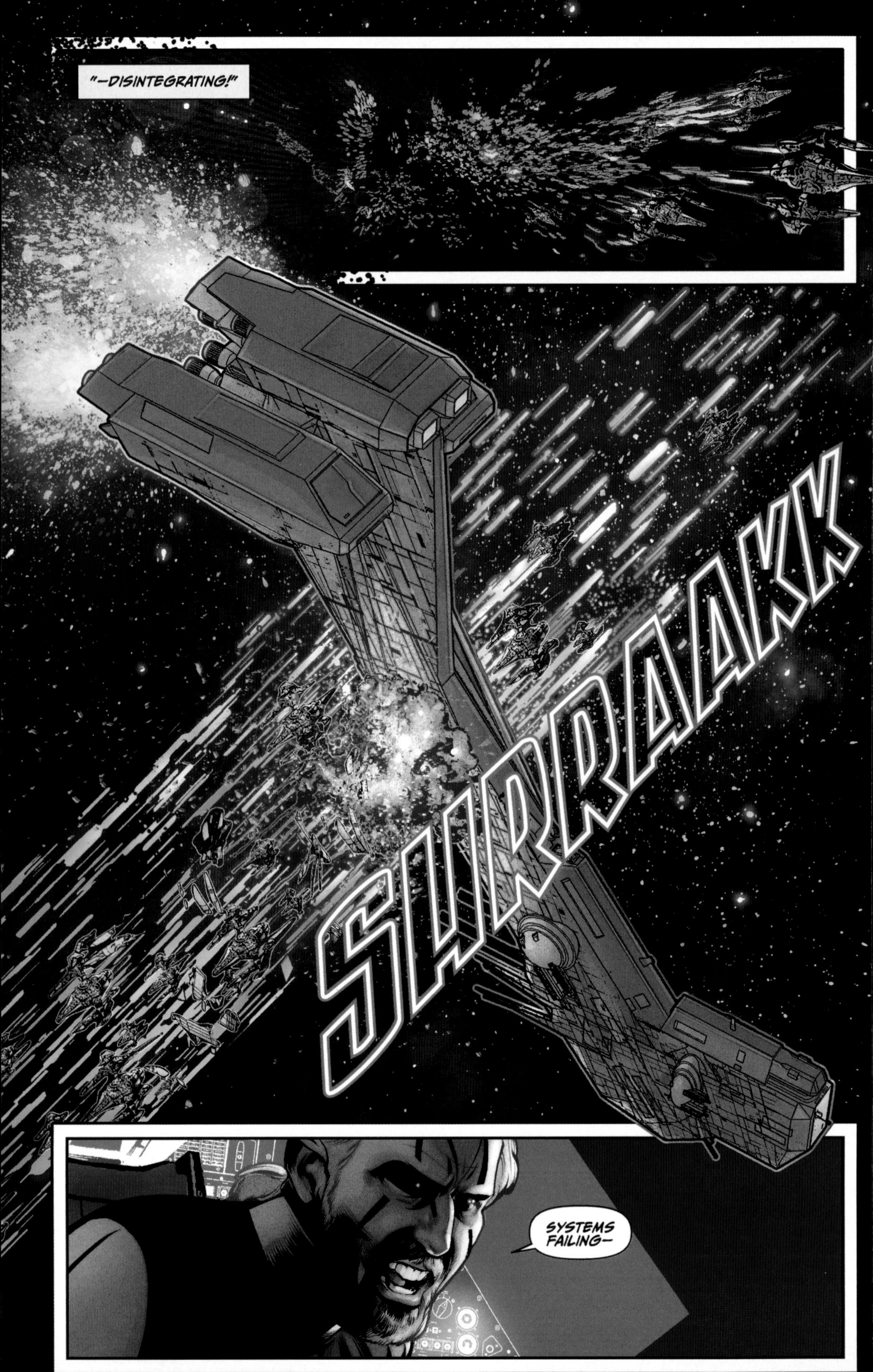
"—DISINTEGRATING!"
SURRAAKK
SYSTEMS FAILING—

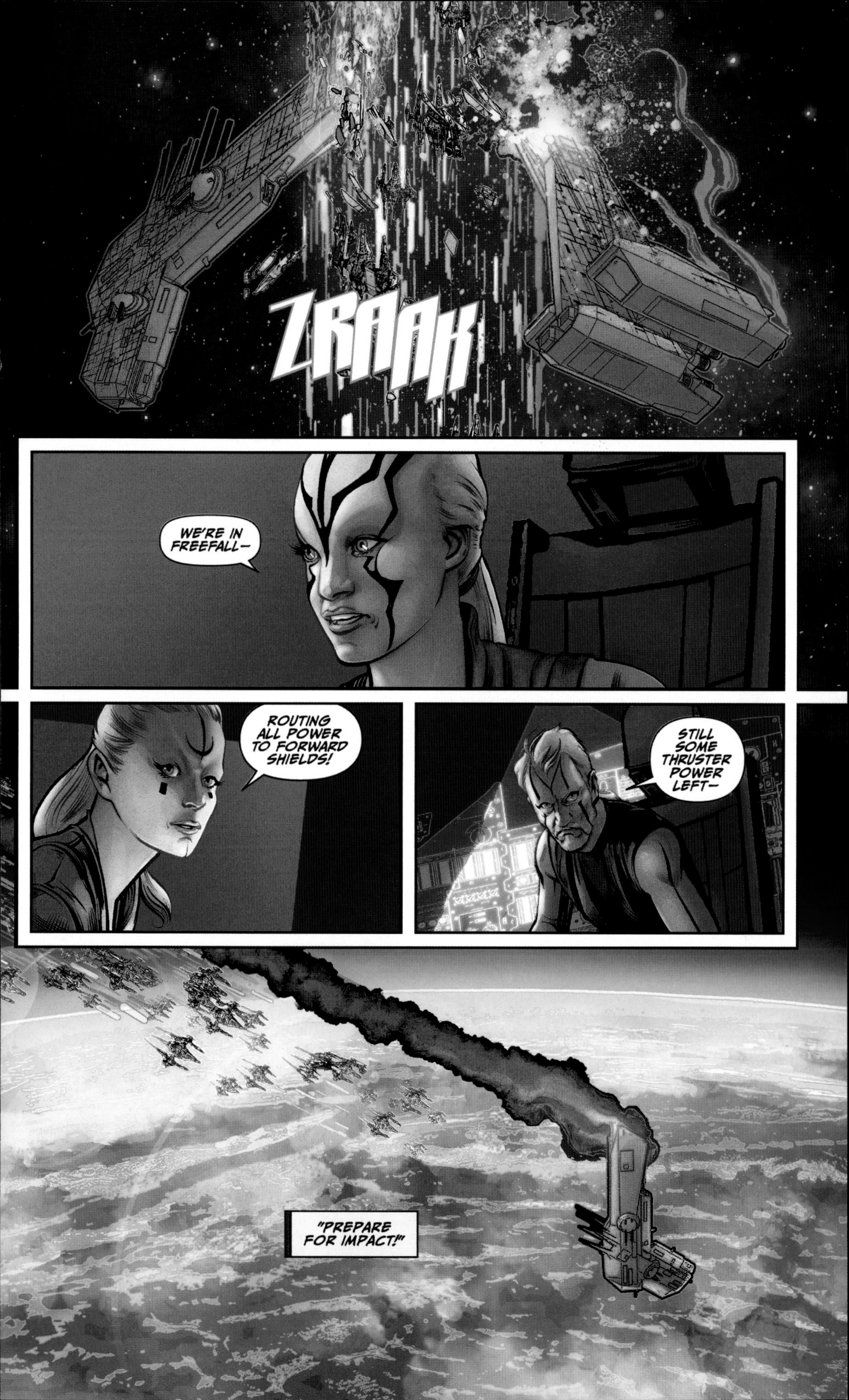
ZRAAK
WE'RE IN FREEFALL—
ROUTING ALL POWER TO FORWARD SHIELDS!
STILL SOME THRUSTER POWER LEFT—
"PREPARE FOR IMPACT!"

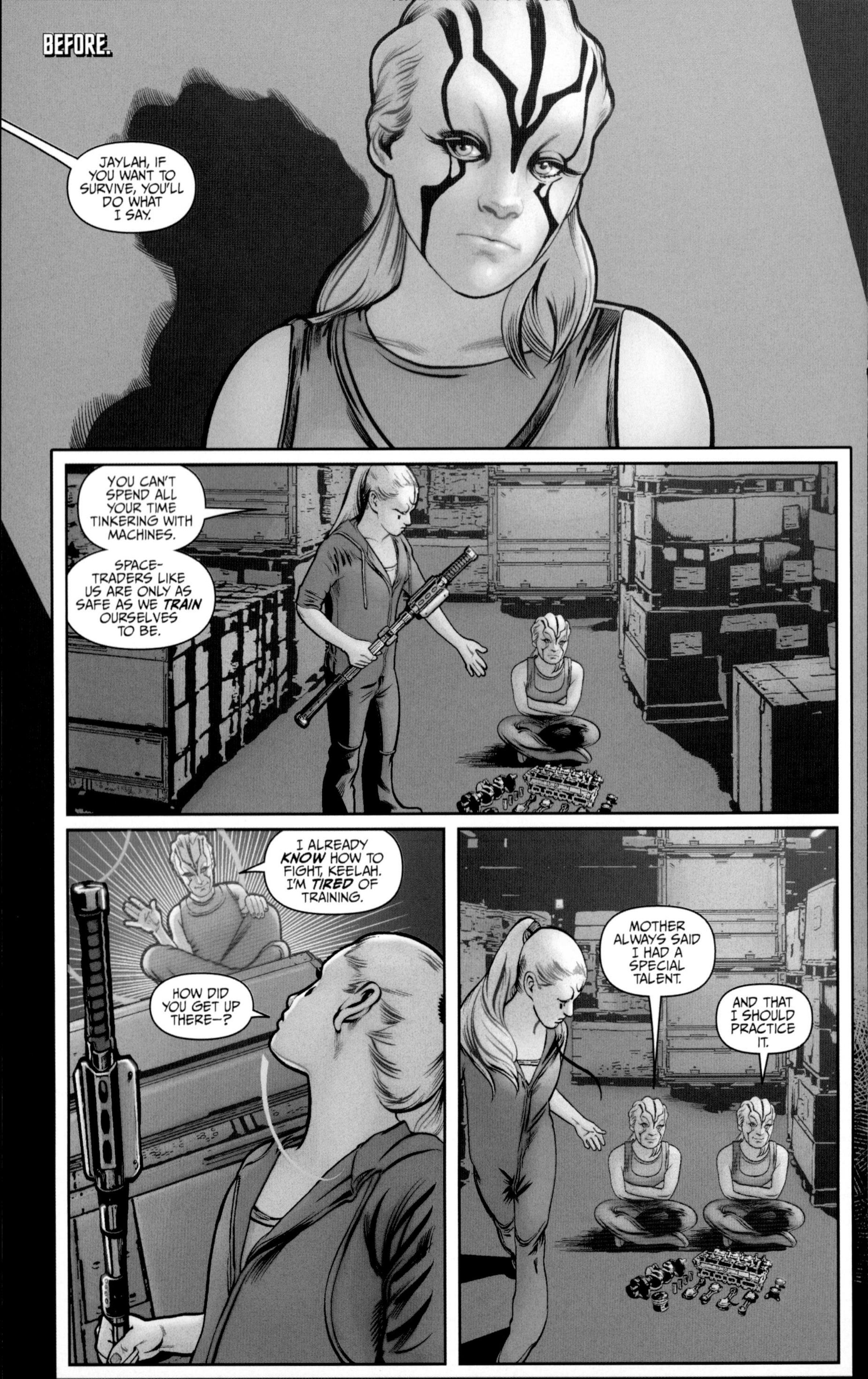
BEFORE.
JAYLAH, IF YOU WANT TO SURVIVE, YOU'LL DO WHAT I SAY.
YOU CAN'T SPEND ALL YOUR TIME TINKERING WITH MACHINES.
SPACE-TRADERS LIKE US ARE ONLY AS SAFE AS WE *TRAIN* OURSELVES TO BE.
I ALREADY ***KNOW*** HOW TO FIGHT, KEELAH. I'M ***TIRED*** OF TRAINING.
HOW DID YOU GET UP THERE—?
MOTHER ALWAYS SAID I HAD A SPECIAL TALENT.
AND THAT I SHOULD PRACTICE IT.

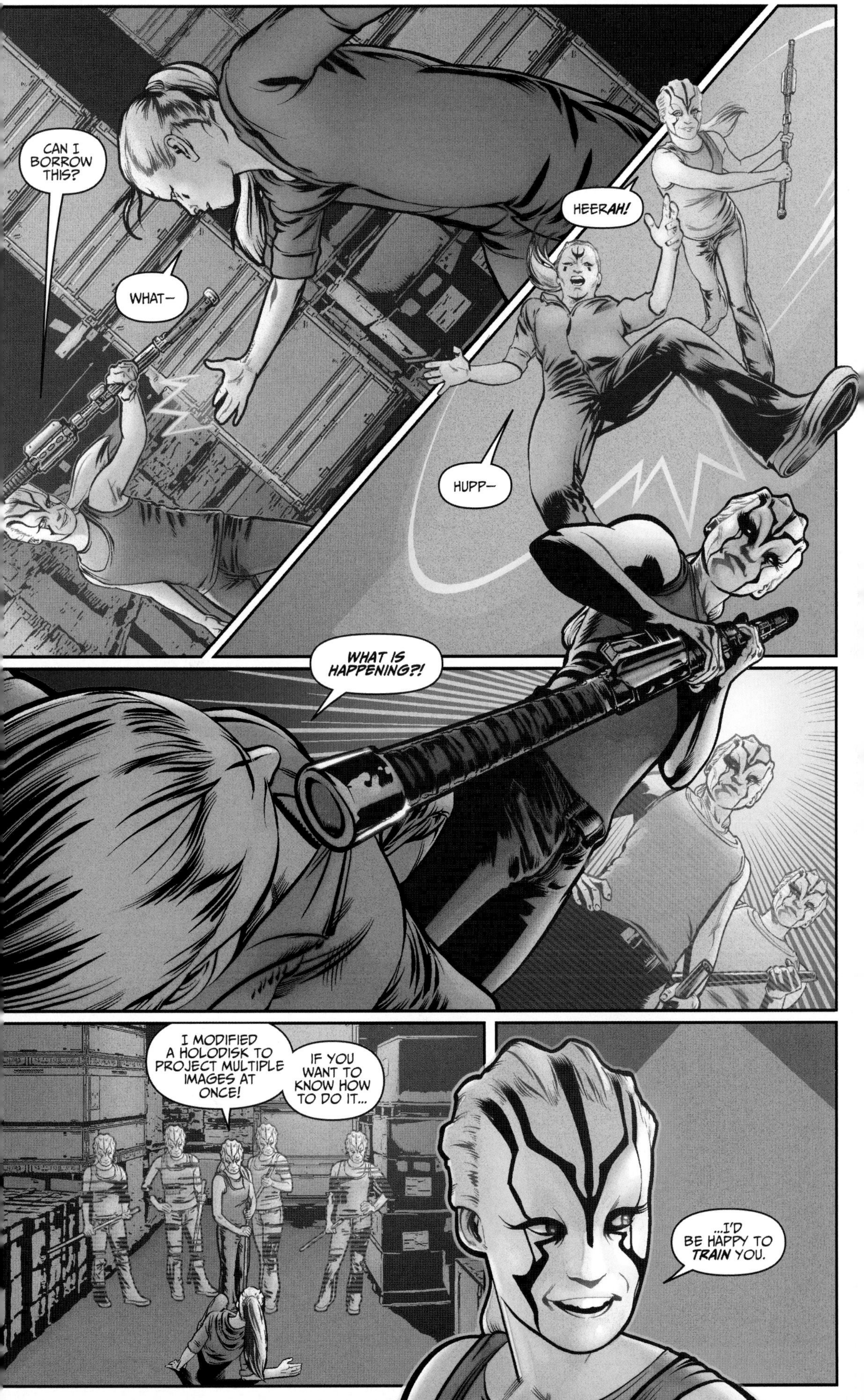
CAN I BORROW THIS?
WHAT–
HEERAH!
HUPP–
WHAT IS HAPPENING?!
I MODIFIED A HOLODISK TO PROJECT MULTIPLE IMAGES AT ONCE!
IF YOU WANT TO KNOW HOW TO DO IT...
...I'D BE HAPPY TO TRAIN YOU.

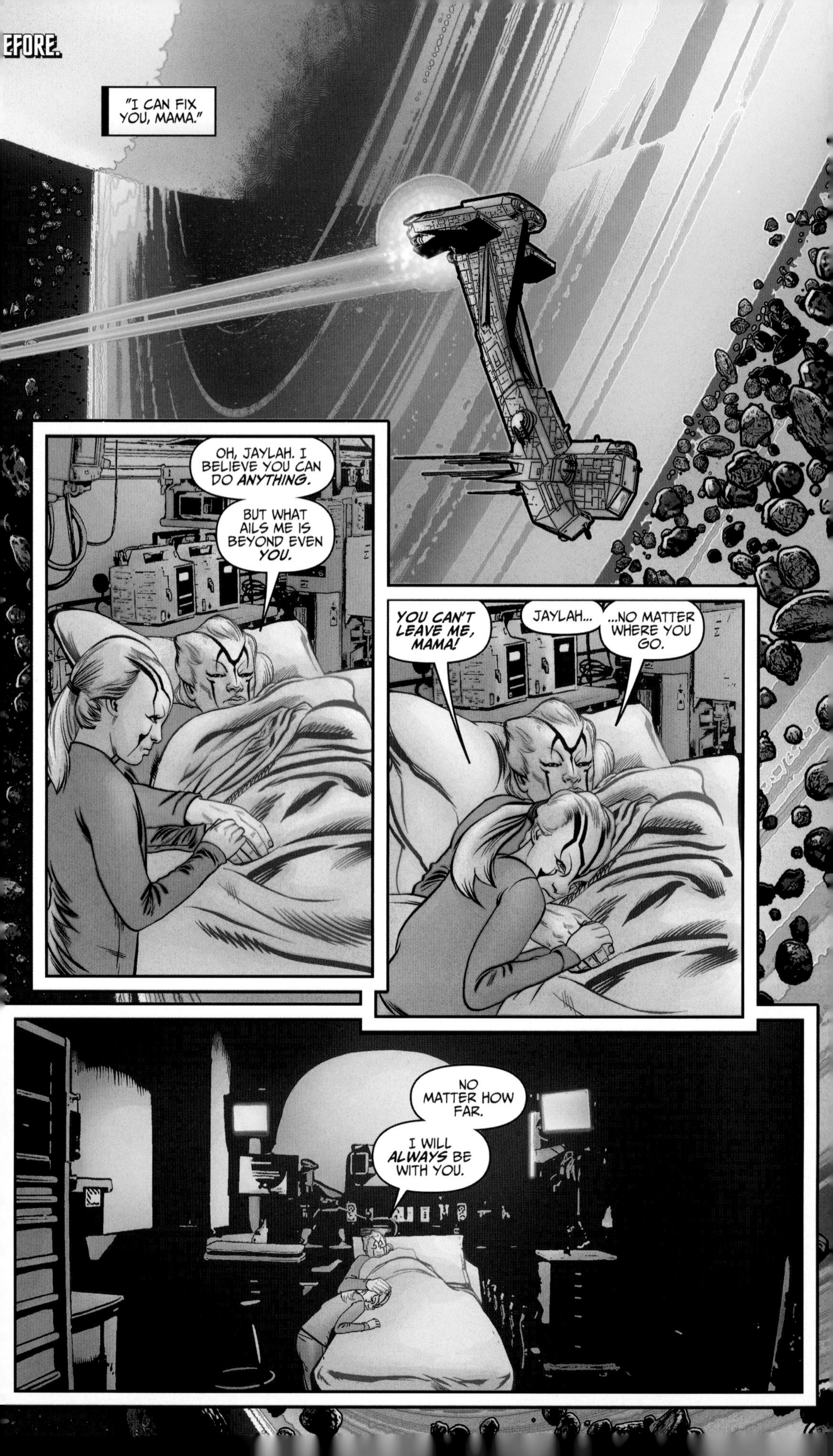
EFORE.
"I CAN FIX YOU, MAMA."
OH, JAYLAH. I BELIEVE YOU CAN DO ANYTHING.
BUT WHAT AILS ME IS BEYOND EVEN YOU.
YOU CAN'T LEAVE ME, MAMA!
JAYLAH...
...NO MATTER WHERE YOU GO.
NO MATTER HOW FAR.
I WILL ALWAYS BE WITH YOU.

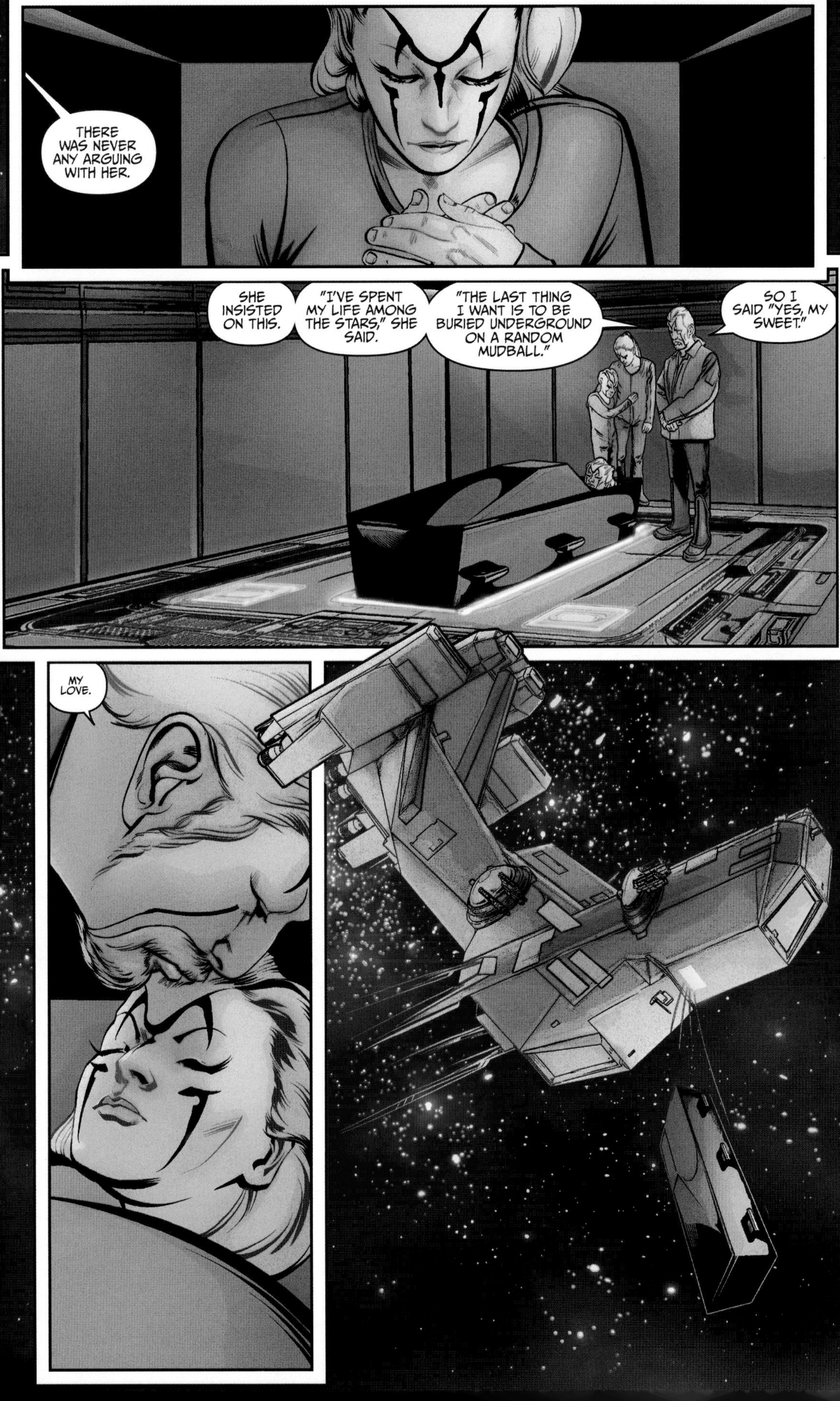
THERE WAS NEVER ANY ARGUING WITH HER.
SHE INSISTED ON THIS.
"I'VE SPENT MY LIFE AMONG THE STARS," SHE SAID.
"THE LAST THING I WANT IS TO BE BURIED UNDERGROUND ON A RANDOM MUDBALL."
SO I SAID "YES, MY SWEET."
MY LOVE.

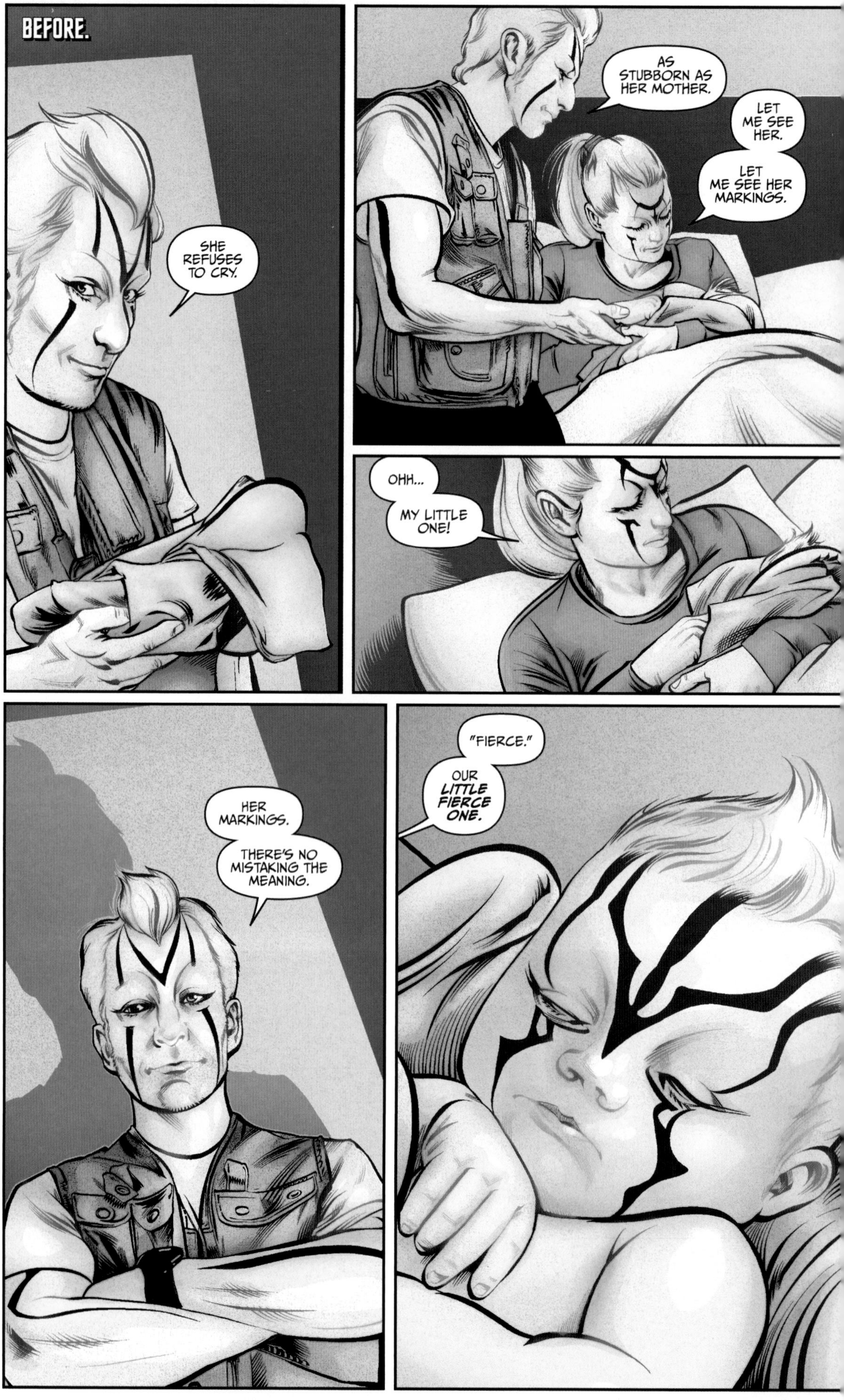
BEFORE.
SHE REFUSES TO CRY.
AS STUBBORN AS HER MOTHER.
LET ME SEE HER.
LET ME SEE HER MARKINGS.
OHH...
MY LITTLE ONE!
HER MARKINGS.
THERE'S NO MISTAKING THE MEANING.
"FIERCE."
OUR *LITTLE FIERCE ONE.*

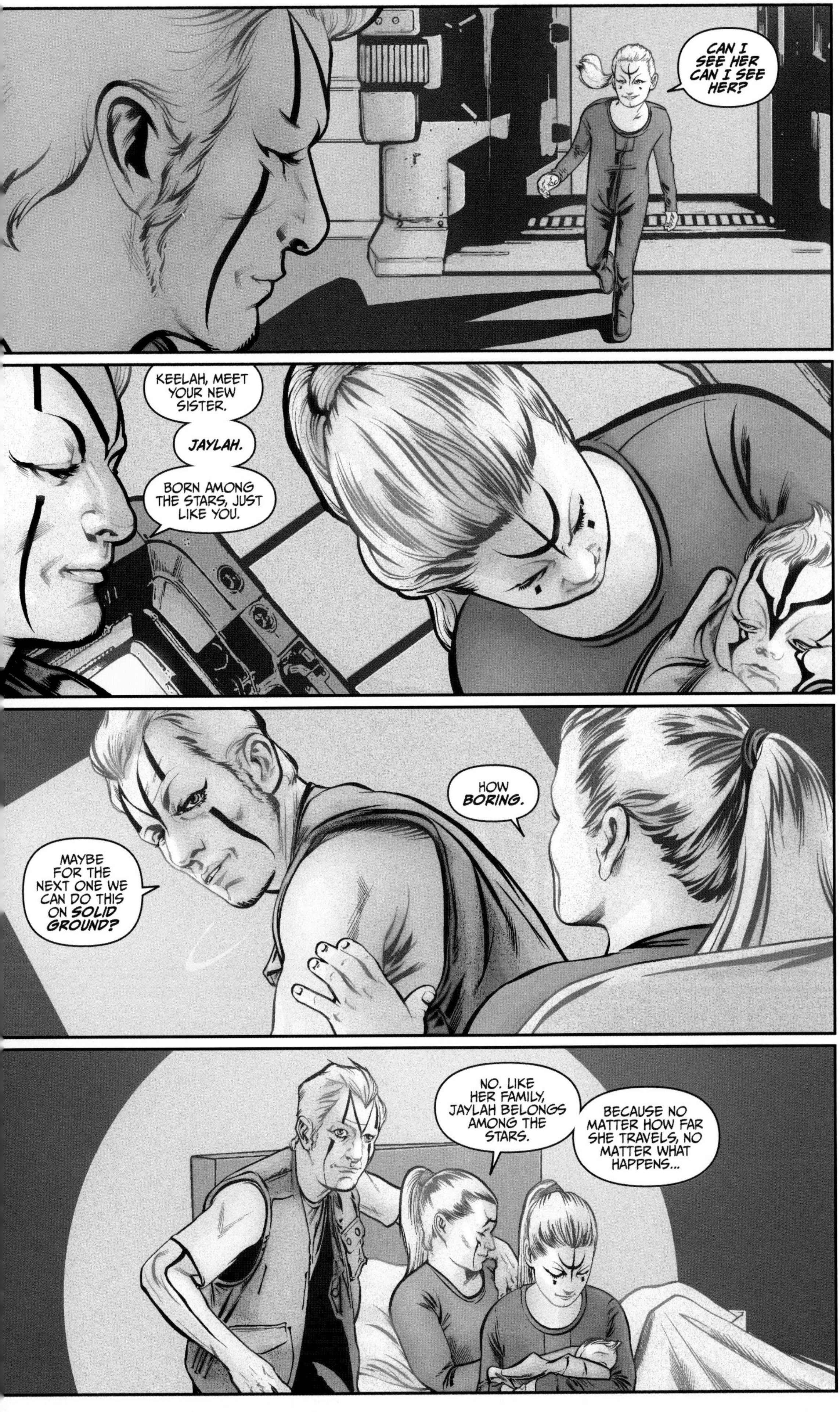

CAN I SEE HER CAN I SEE HER?
KEELAH, MEET YOUR NEW SISTER.
JAYLAH.
BORN AMONG THE STARS, JUST LIKE YOU.
HOW BORING.
MAYBE FOR THE NEXT ONE WE CAN DO THIS ON SOLID GROUND?
NO. LIKE HER FAMILY, JAYLAH BELONGS AMONG THE STARS.
BECAUSE NO MATTER HOW FAR SHE TRAVELS, NO MATTER WHAT HAPPENS...

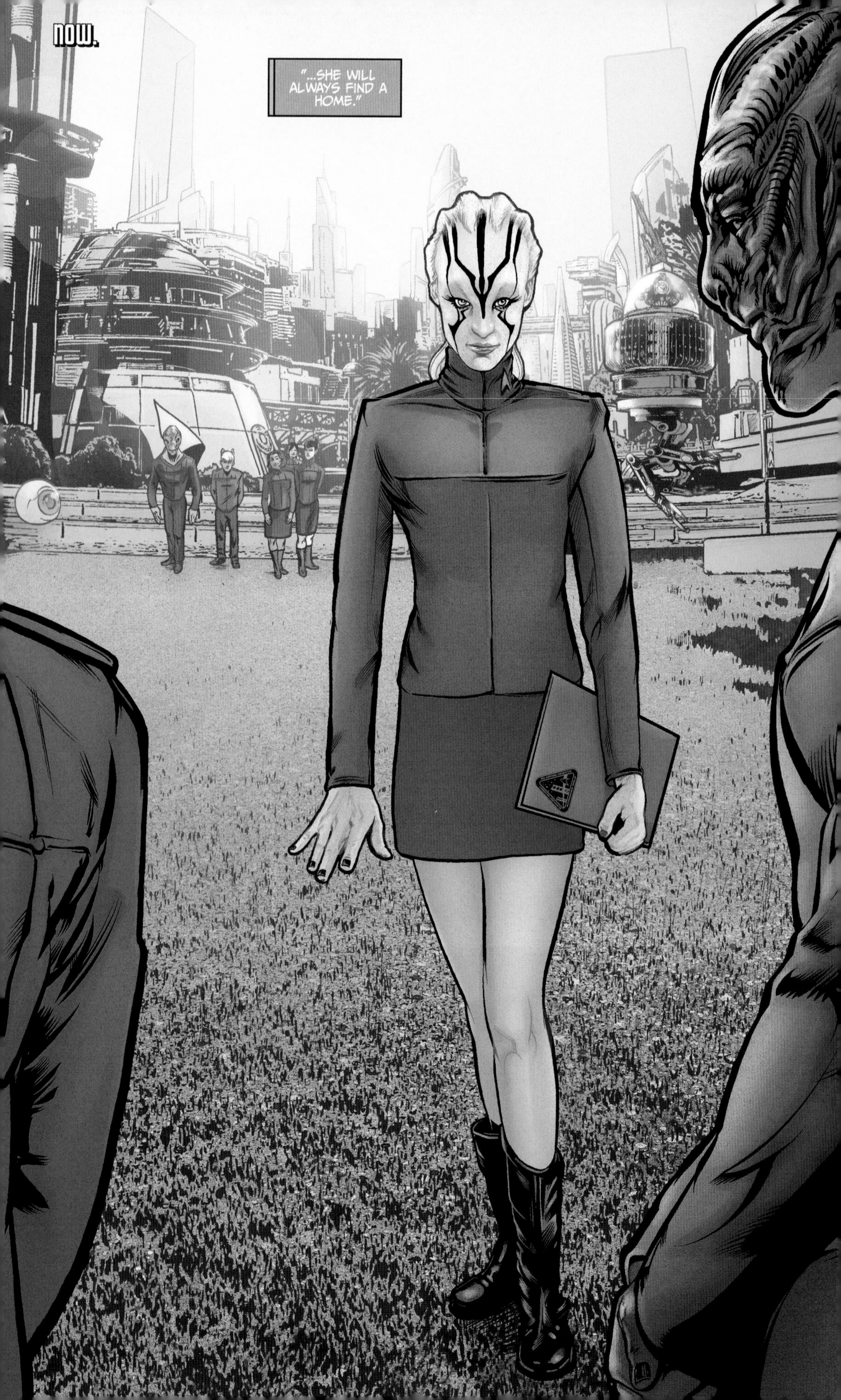
NOW.
"...SHE WILL ALWAYS FIND A HOME."

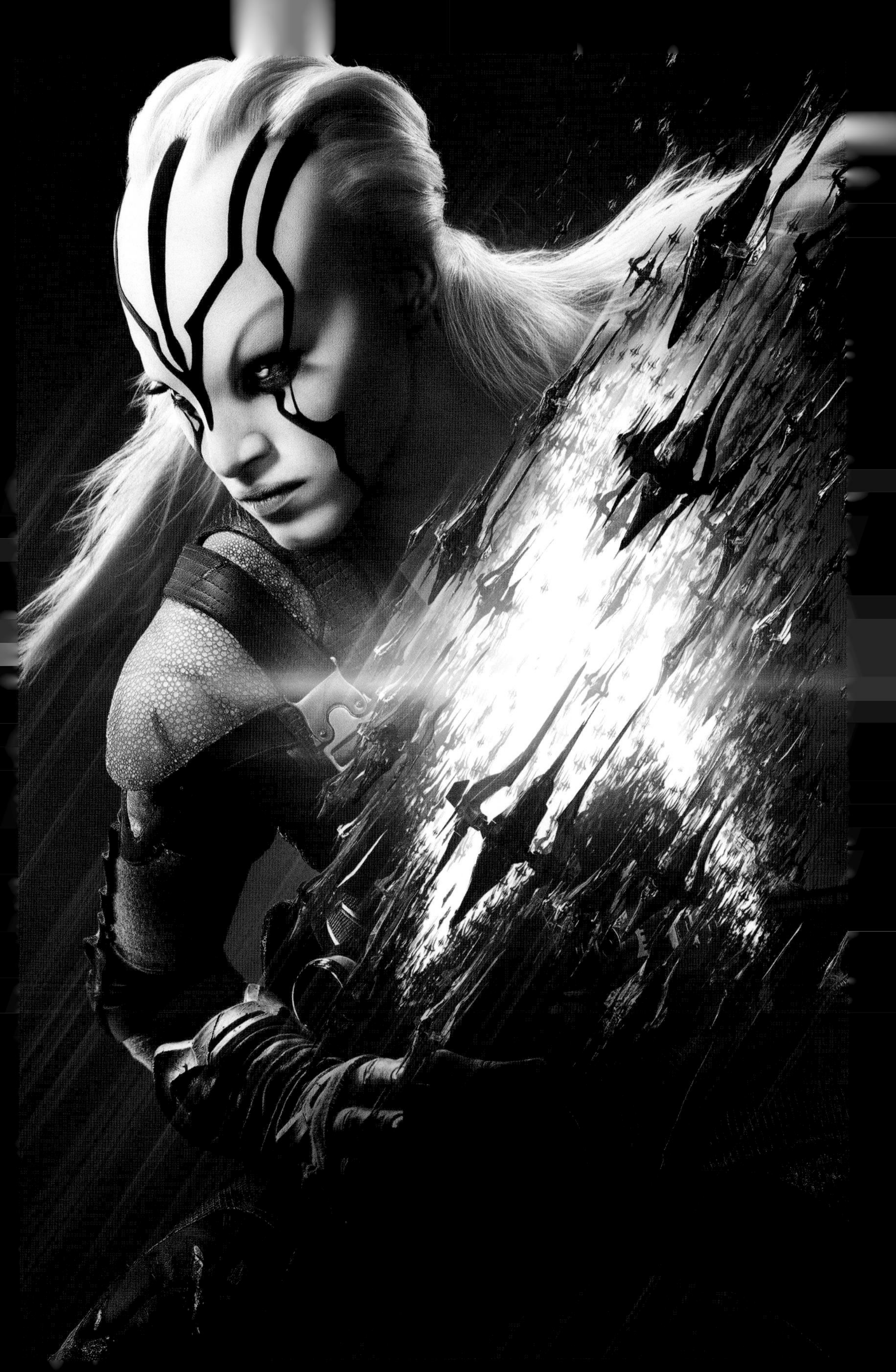

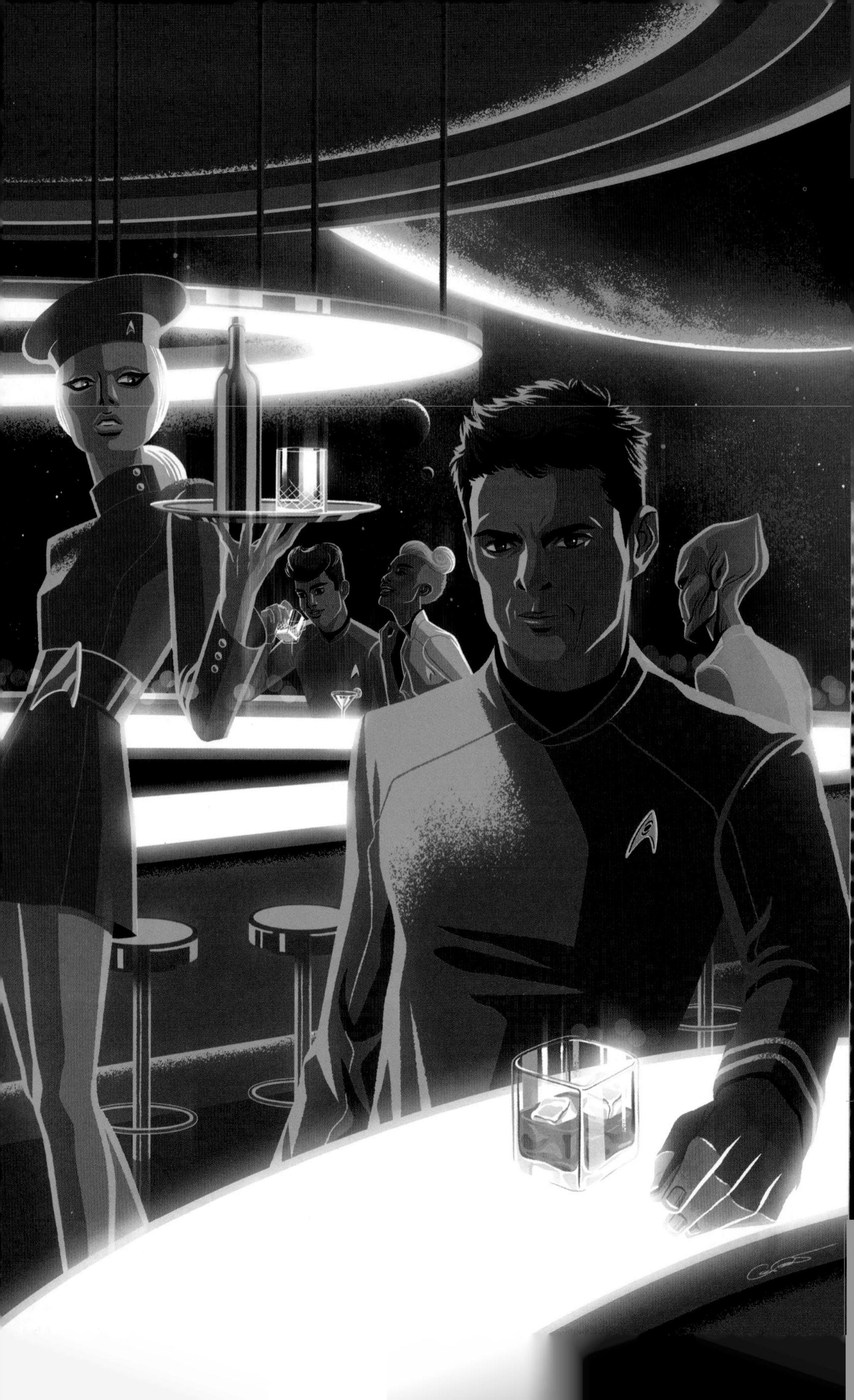

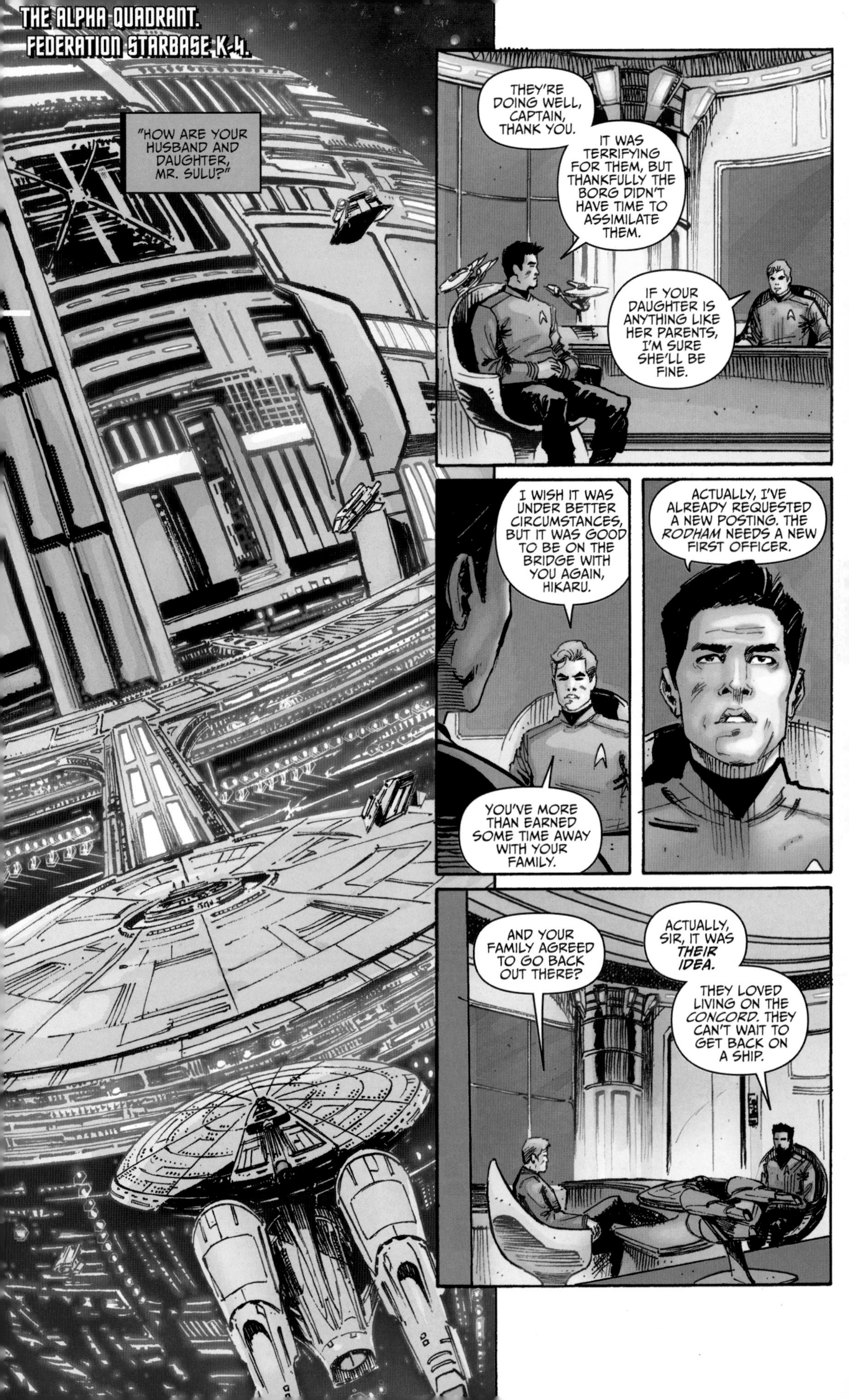
THE ALPHA QUADRANT. FEDERATION STARBASE K-4.
"HOW ARE YOUR HUSBAND AND DAUGHTER, MR. SULU?"
THEY'RE DOING WELL, CAPTAIN, THANK YOU.
IT WAS TERRIFYING FOR THEM, BUT THANKFULLY THE BORG DIDN'T HAVE TIME TO ASSIMILATE THEM.
IF YOUR DAUGHTER IS ANYTHING LIKE HER PARENTS, I'M SURE SHE'LL BE FINE.
I WISH IT WAS UNDER BETTER CIRCUMSTANCES, BUT IT WAS GOOD TO BE ON THE BRIDGE WITH YOU AGAIN, HIKARU.
YOU'VE MORE THAN EARNED SOME TIME AWAY WITH YOUR FAMILY.
ACTUALLY, I'VE ALREADY REQUESTED A NEW POSTING. THE *RODHAM* NEEDS A NEW FIRST OFFICER.
AND YOUR FAMILY AGREED TO GO BACK OUT THERE?
ACTUALLY, SIR, IT WAS ***THEIR IDEA.***
THEY LOVED LIVING ON THE *CONCORD*. THEY CAN'T WAIT TO GET BACK ON A SHIP.

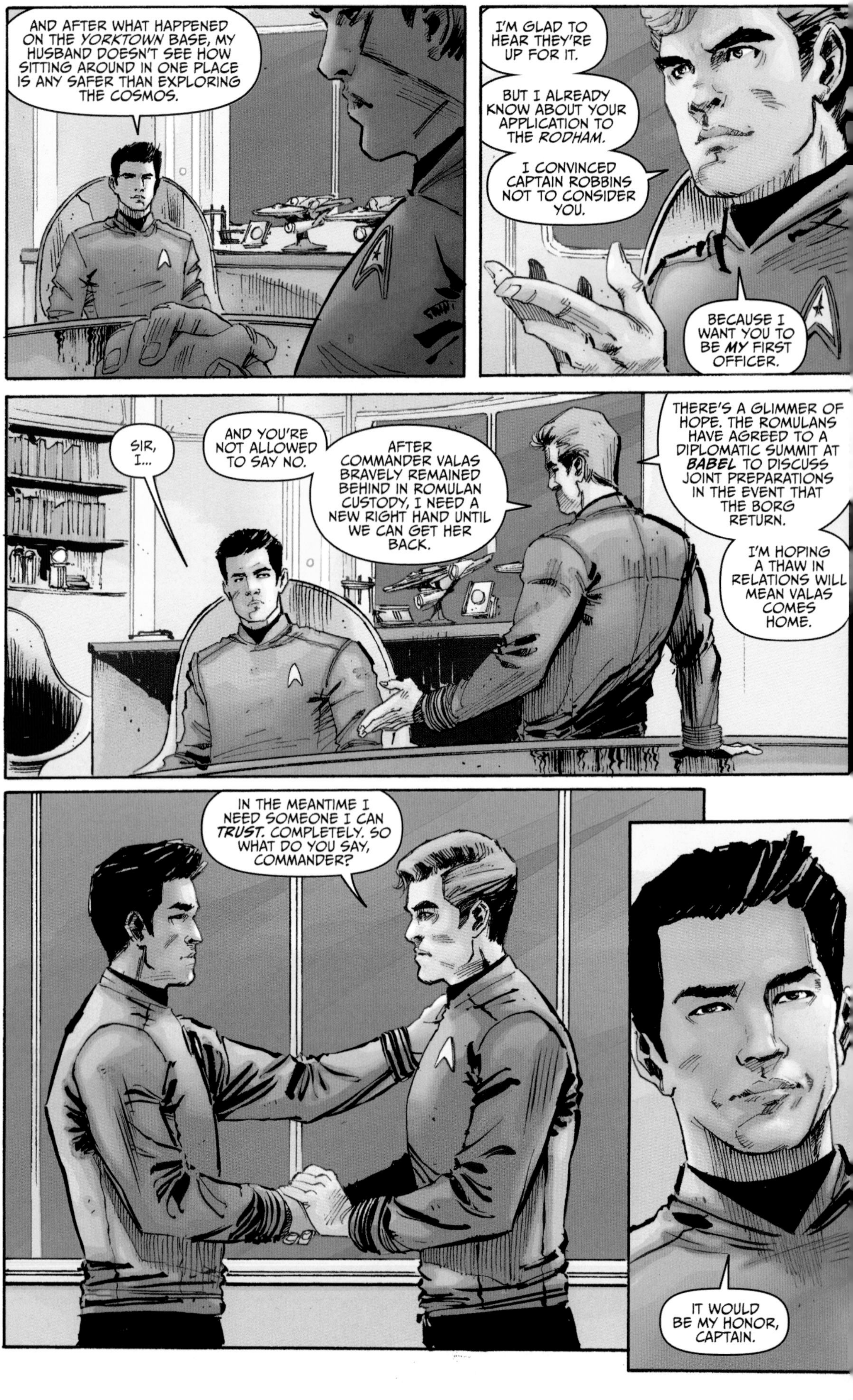
AND AFTER WHAT HAPPENED ON THE *YORKTOWN* BASE, MY HUSBAND DOESN'T SEE HOW SITTING AROUND IN ONE PLACE IS ANY SAFER THAN EXPLORING THE COSMOS.
I'M GLAD TO HEAR THEY'RE UP FOR IT.
BUT I ALREADY KNOW ABOUT YOUR APPLICATION TO THE *RODHAM.*
I CONVINCED CAPTAIN ROBBINS NOT TO CONSIDER YOU.
BECAUSE I WANT YOU TO BE ***MY*** FIRST OFFICER.
SIR, I...
AND YOU'RE NOT ALLOWED TO SAY NO.
AFTER COMMANDER VALAS BRAVELY REMAINED BEHIND IN ROMULAN CUSTODY, I NEED A NEW RIGHT HAND UNTIL WE CAN GET HER BACK.
THERE'S A GLIMMER OF HOPE. THE ROMULANS HAVE AGREED TO A DIPLOMATIC SUMMIT AT ***BABEL*** TO DISCUSS JOINT PREPARATIONS IN THE EVENT THAT THE BORG RETURN.
I'M HOPING A THAW IN RELATIONS WILL MEAN VALAS COMES HOME.
IN THE MEANTIME I NEED SOMEONE I CAN ***TRUST.*** COMPLETELY. SO WHAT DO YOU SAY, COMMANDER?
IT WOULD BE MY HONOR, CAPTAIN.

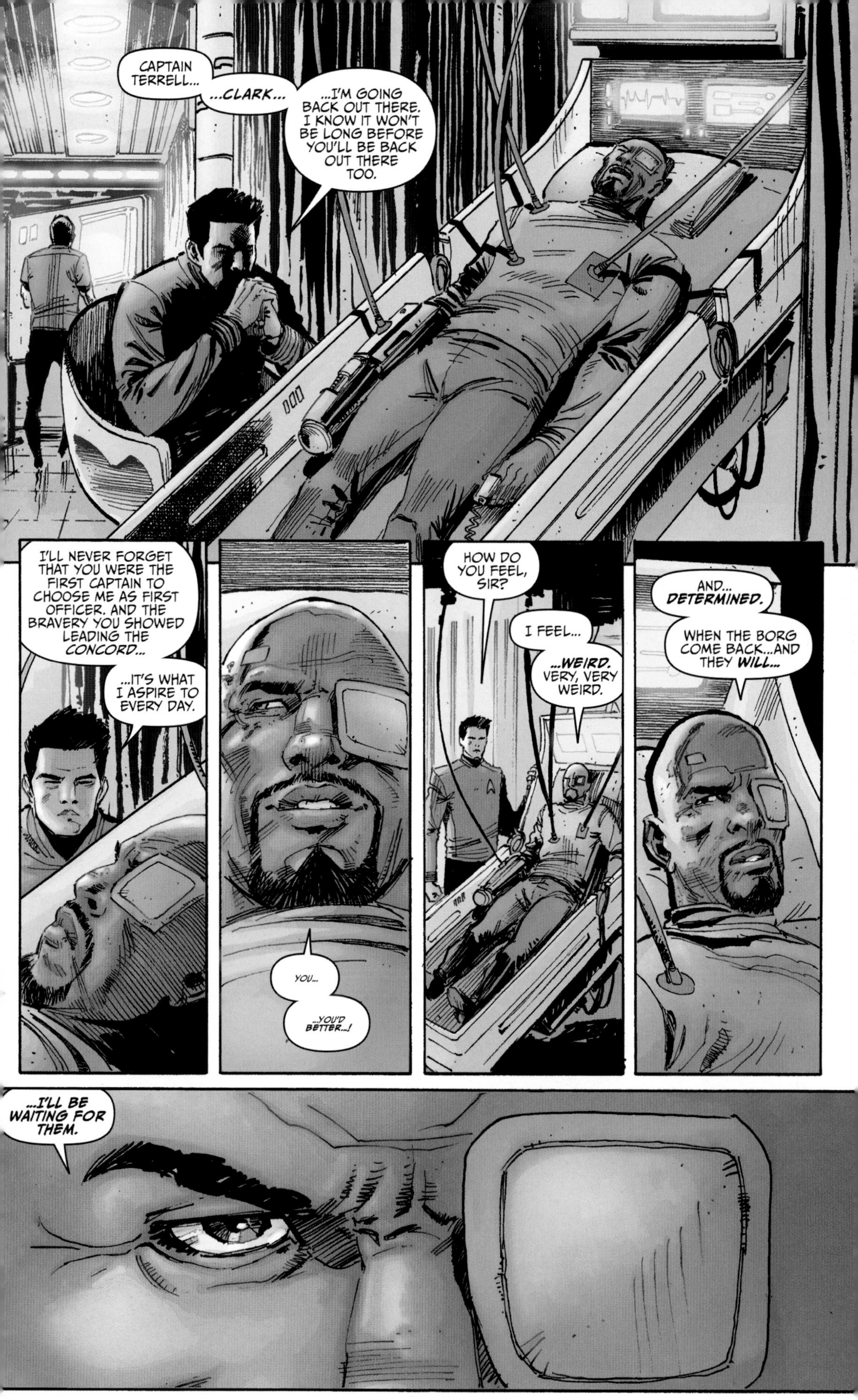
CAPTAIN TERRELL...
...CLARK...
...I'M GOING BACK OUT THERE. I KNOW IT WON'T BE LONG BEFORE YOU'LL BE BACK OUT THERE TOO.
I'LL NEVER FORGET THAT YOU WERE THE FIRST CAPTAIN TO CHOOSE ME AS FIRST OFFICER. AND THE BRAVERY YOU SHOWED LEADING THE CONCORD...
...IT'S WHAT I ASPIRE TO EVERY DAY.
YOU...
...YOU'D BETTER...!
HOW DO YOU FEEL, SIR?
I FEEL...
...WEIRD. VERY, VERY WEIRD.
AND... DETERMINED.
WHEN THE BORG COME BACK...AND THEY WILL...
...I'LL BE WAITING FOR THEM.

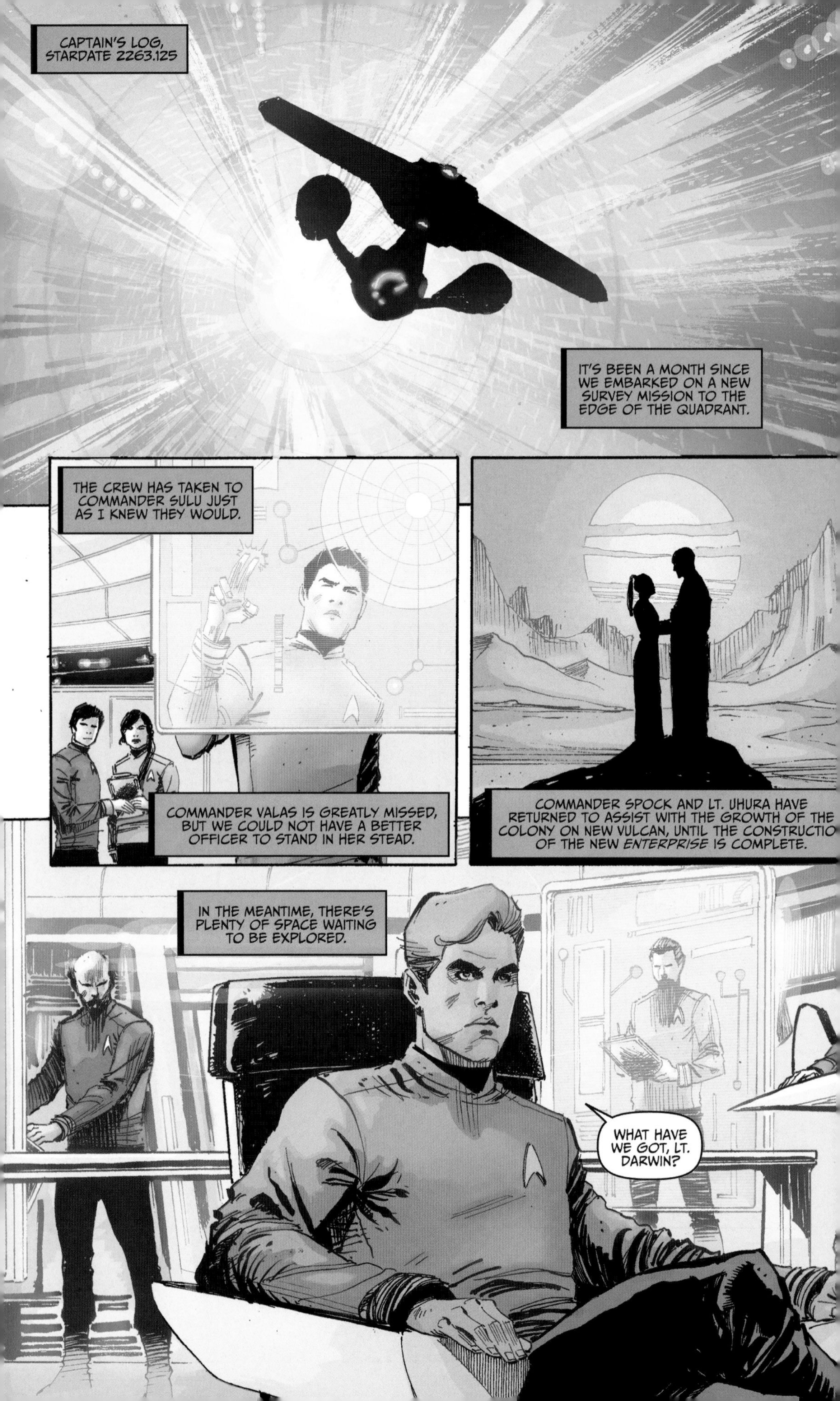
CAPTAIN'S LOG, STARDATE 2263.125
IT'S BEEN A MONTH SINCE WE EMBARKED ON A NEW SURVEY MISSION TO THE EDGE OF THE QUADRANT.
THE CREW HAS TAKEN TO COMMANDER SULU JUST AS I KNEW THEY WOULD.
COMMANDER VALAS IS GREATLY MISSED, BUT WE COULD NOT HAVE A BETTER OFFICER TO STAND IN HER STEAD.
COMMANDER SPOCK AND LT. UHURA HAVE RETURNED TO ASSIST WITH THE GROWTH OF THE COLONY ON NEW VULCAN, UNTIL THE CONSTRUCTIO OF THE NEW *ENTERPRISE* IS COMPLETE.
IN THE MEANTIME, THERE'S PLENTY OF SPACE WAITING TO BE EXPLORED.
WHAT HAVE WE GOT, LT. DARWIN?

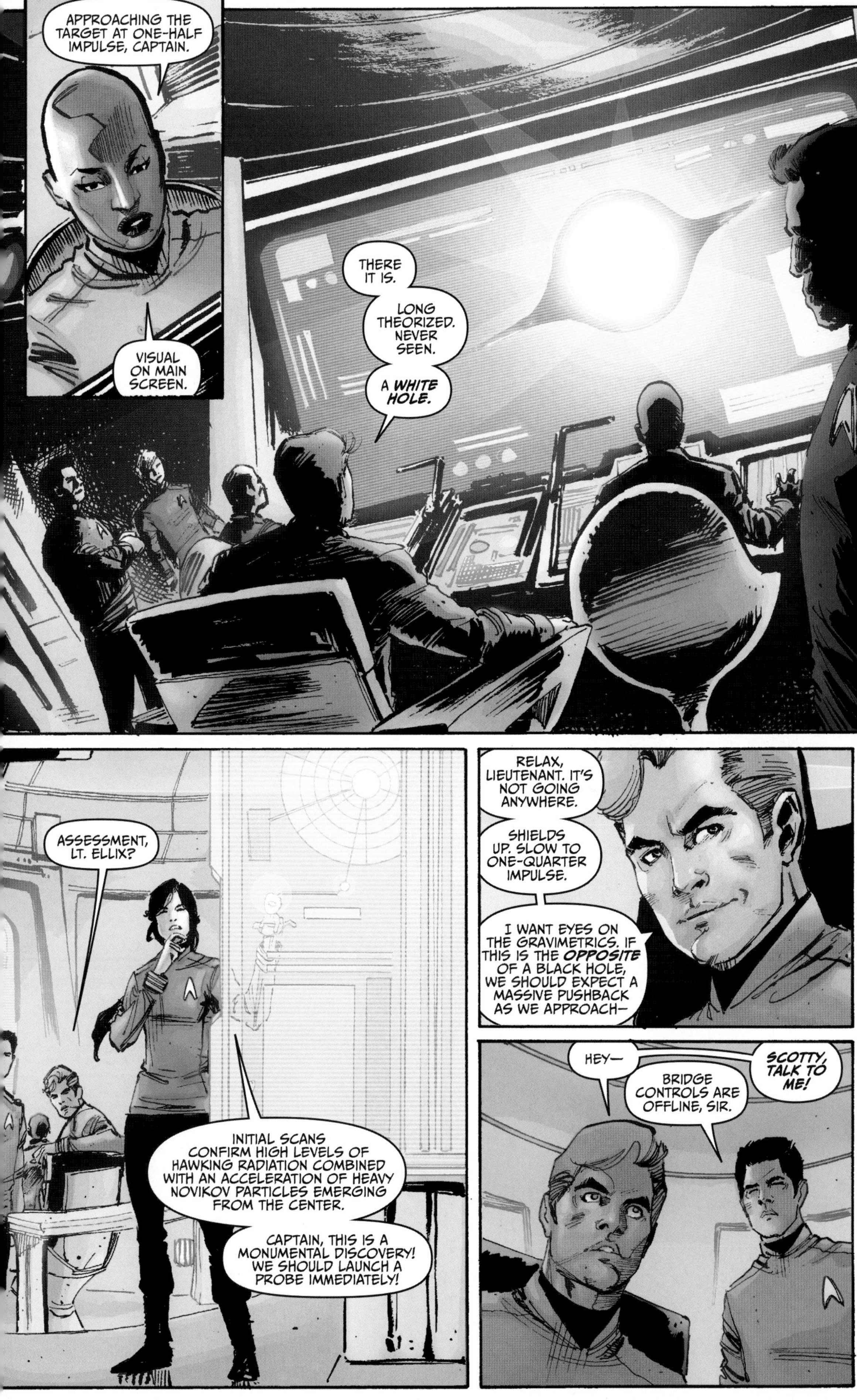
APPROACHING THE TARGET AT ONE-HALF IMPULSE, CAPTAIN.
VISUAL ON MAIN SCREEN.
THERE IT IS.
LONG THEORIZED. NEVER SEEN.
A *WHITE HOLE.*
ASSESSMENT, LT. ELLIX?
INITIAL SCANS CONFIRM HIGH LEVELS OF HAWKING RADIATION COMBINED WITH AN ACCELERATION OF HEAVY NOVIKOV PARTICLES EMERGING FROM THE CENTER.
CAPTAIN, THIS IS A MONUMENTAL DISCOVERY! WE SHOULD LAUNCH A PROBE IMMEDIATELY!
RELAX, LIEUTENANT. IT'S NOT GOING ANYWHERE.
SHIELDS UP. SLOW TO ONE-QUARTER IMPULSE.
I WANT EYES ON THE GRAVIMETRICS. IF THIS IS THE *OPPOSITE* OF A BLACK HOLE, WE SHOULD EXPECT A MASSIVE PUSHBACK AS WE APPROACH—
HEY—
SCOTTY, TALK TO ME!
BRIDGE CONTROLS ARE OFFLINE, SIR.

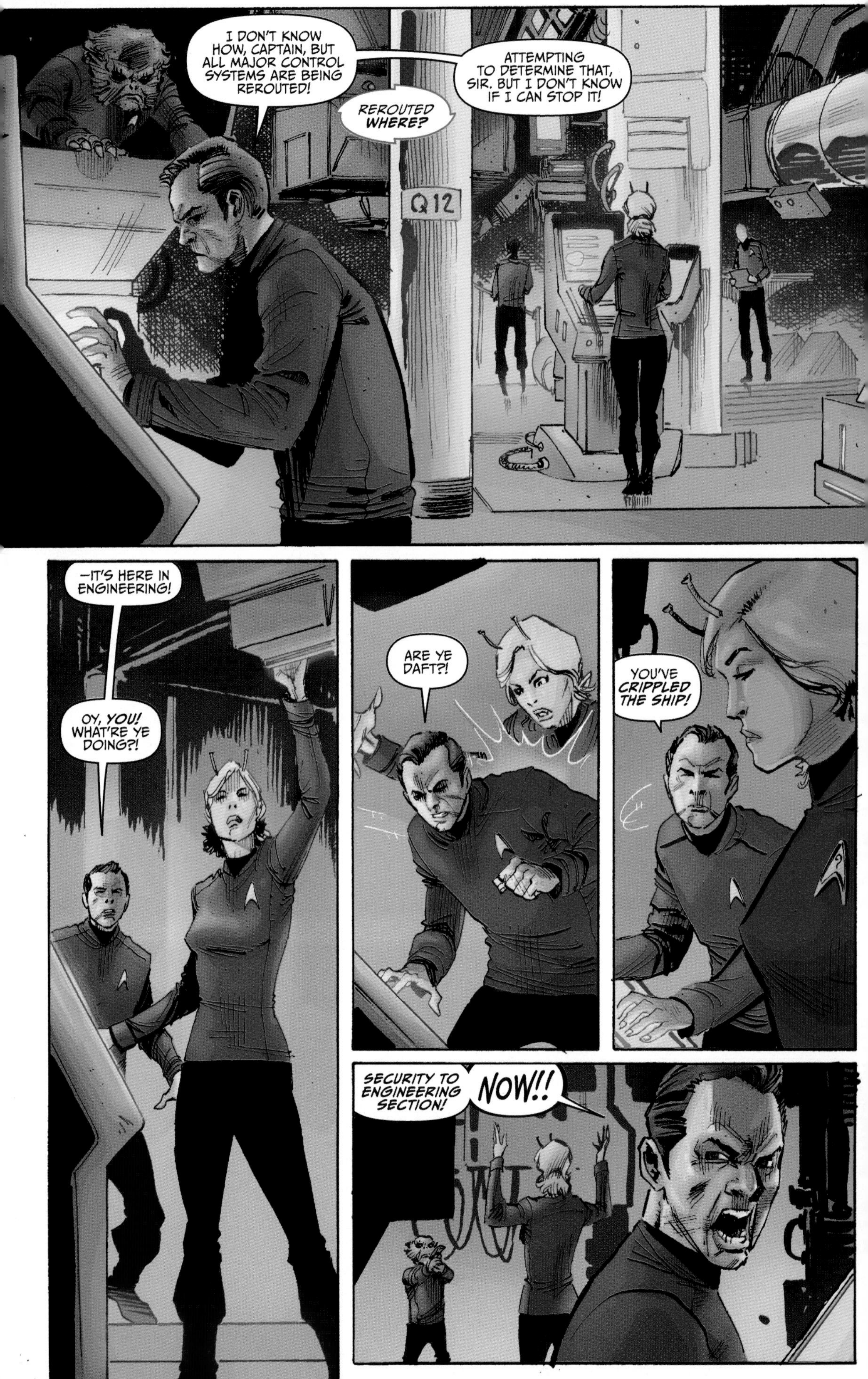
I DON'T KNOW HOW, CAPTAIN, BUT ALL MAJOR CONTROL SYSTEMS ARE BEING REROUTED!
REROUTED WHERE?
ATTEMPTING TO DETERMINE THAT, SIR. BUT I DON'T KNOW IF I CAN STOP IT!
Q12
—IT'S HERE IN ENGINEERING!
OY, YOU! WHAT'RE YE DOING?!
ARE YE DAFT?!
YOU'VE CRIPPLED THE SHIP!
SECURITY TO ENGINEERING SECTION!
NOW!!

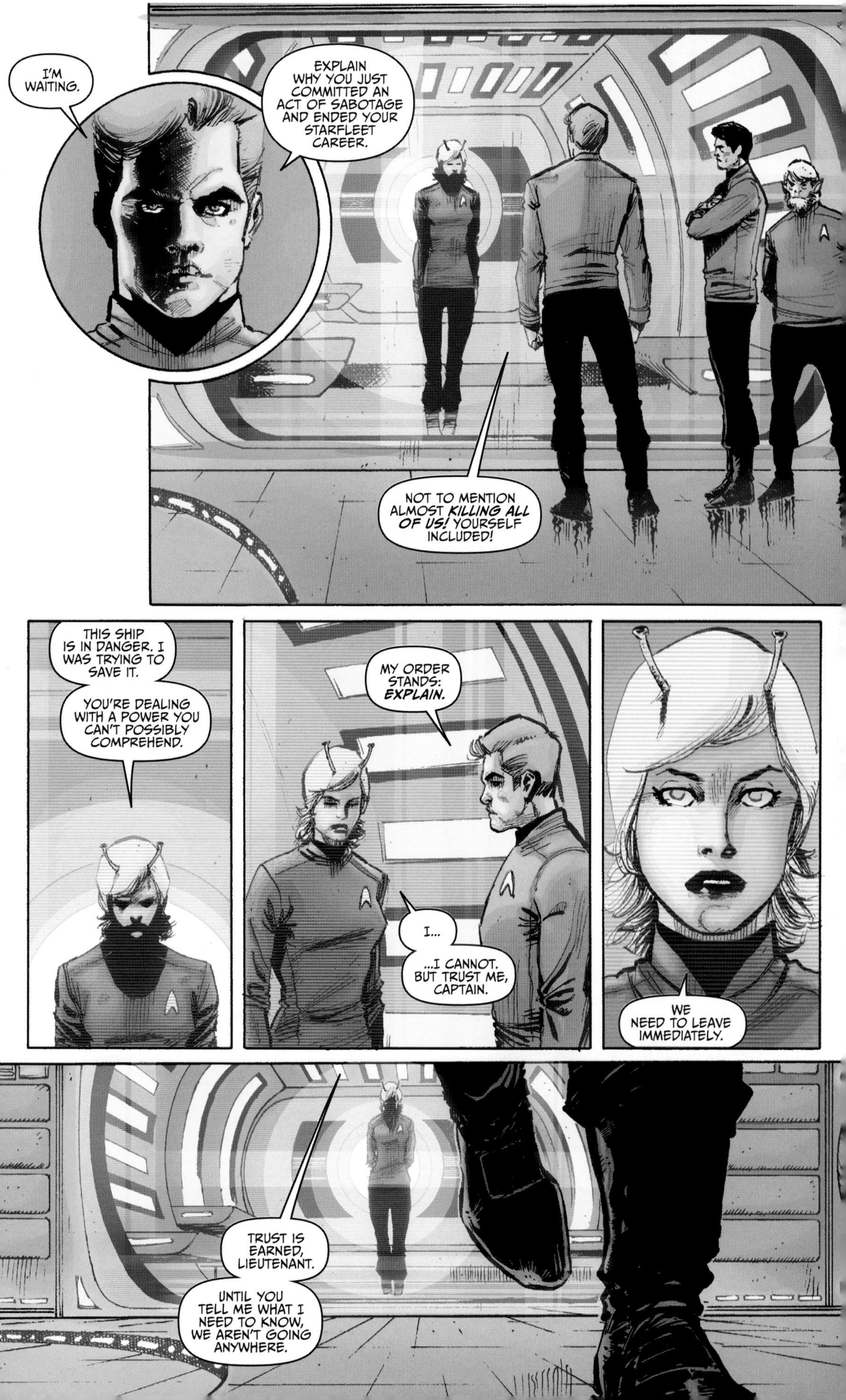
I'M WAITING.
EXPLAIN WHY YOU JUST COMMITTED AN ACT OF SABOTAGE AND ENDED YOUR STARFLEET CAREER.
NOT TO MENTION ALMOST *KILLING ALL OF US!* YOURSELF INCLUDED!
THIS SHIP IS IN DANGER. I WAS TRYING TO SAVE IT.
YOU'RE DEALING WITH A POWER YOU CAN'T POSSIBLY COMPREHEND.
MY ORDER STANDS: *EXPLAIN.*
I...
...I CANNOT. BUT TRUST ME, CAPTAIN.
WE NEED TO LEAVE IMMEDIATELY.
TRUST IS EARNED, LIEUTENANT.
UNTIL YOU TELL ME WHAT I NEED TO KNOW, WE AREN'T GOING ANYWHERE.

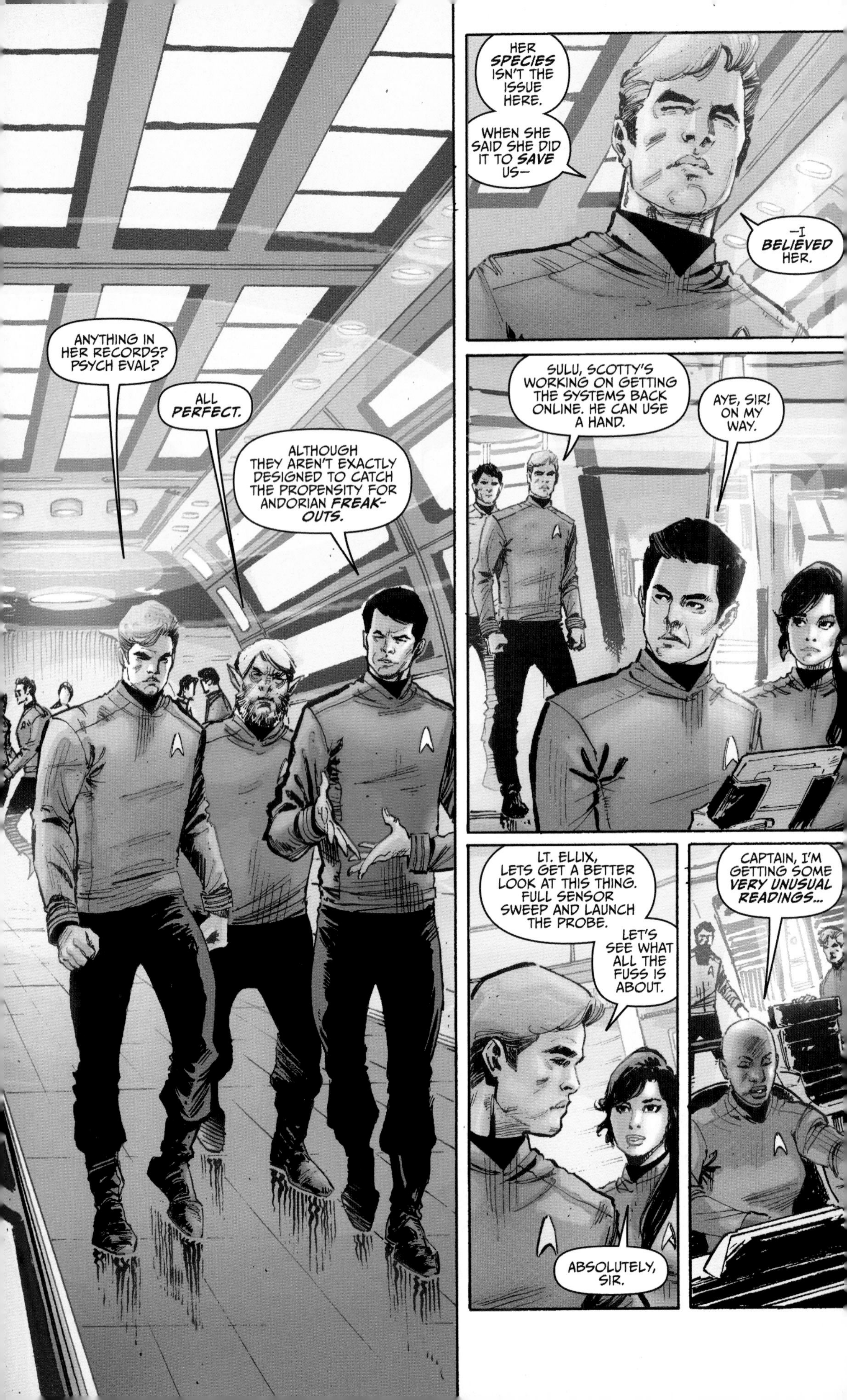
ANYTHING IN HER RECORDS? PSYCH EVAL?
ALL *PERFECT.*
ALTHOUGH THEY AREN'T EXACTLY DESIGNED TO CATCH THE PROPENSITY FOR ANDORIAN *FREAK-OUTS.*
HER *SPECIES* ISN'T THE ISSUE HERE.
WHEN SHE SAID SHE DID IT TO *SAVE* US—
—I *BELIEVED* HER.
SULU, SCOTTY'S WORKING ON GETTING THE SYSTEMS BACK ONLINE. HE CAN USE A HAND.
AYE, SIR! ON MY WAY.
LT. ELLIX, LETS GET A BETTER LOOK AT THIS THING. FULL SENSOR SWEEP AND LAUNCH THE PROBE.
LET'S SEE WHAT ALL THE FUSS IS ABOUT.
ABSOLUTELY, SIR.
CAPTAIN, I'M GETTING SOME *VERY UNUSUAL READINGS...*

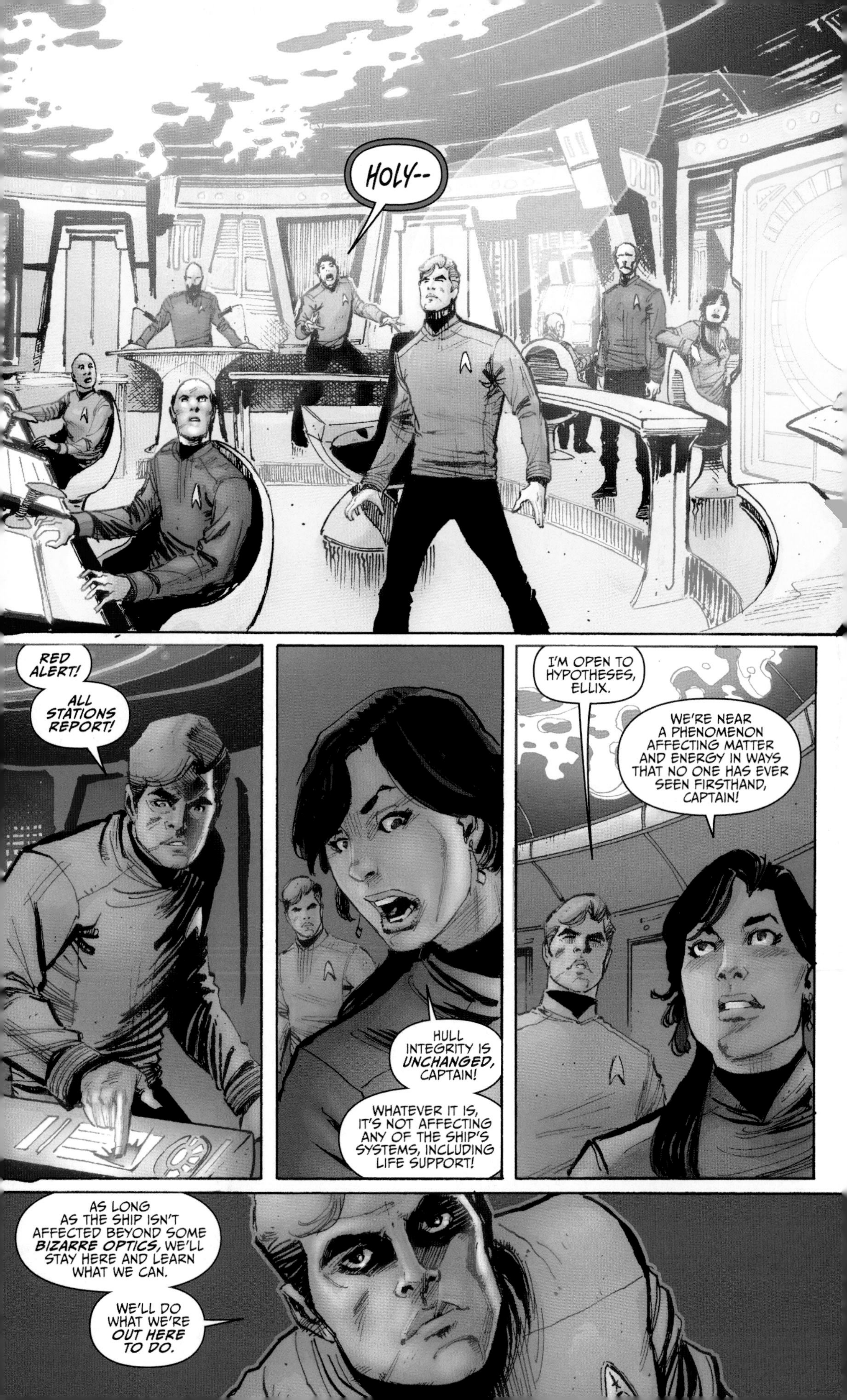
HOLY--
RED ALERT!
ALL STATIONS REPORT!
HULL INTEGRITY IS UNCHANGED, CAPTAIN!
WHATEVER IT IS, IT'S NOT AFFECTING ANY OF THE SHIP'S SYSTEMS, INCLUDING LIFE SUPPORT!
I'M OPEN TO HYPOTHESES, ELLIX.
WE'RE NEAR A PHENOMENON AFFECTING MATTER AND ENERGY IN WAYS THAT NO ONE HAS EVER SEEN FIRSTHAND, CAPTAIN!
AS LONG AS THE SHIP ISN'T AFFECTED BEYOND SOME BIZARRE OPTICS, WE'LL STAY HERE AND LEARN WHAT WE CAN.
WE'LL DO WHAT WE'RE OUT HERE TO DO.

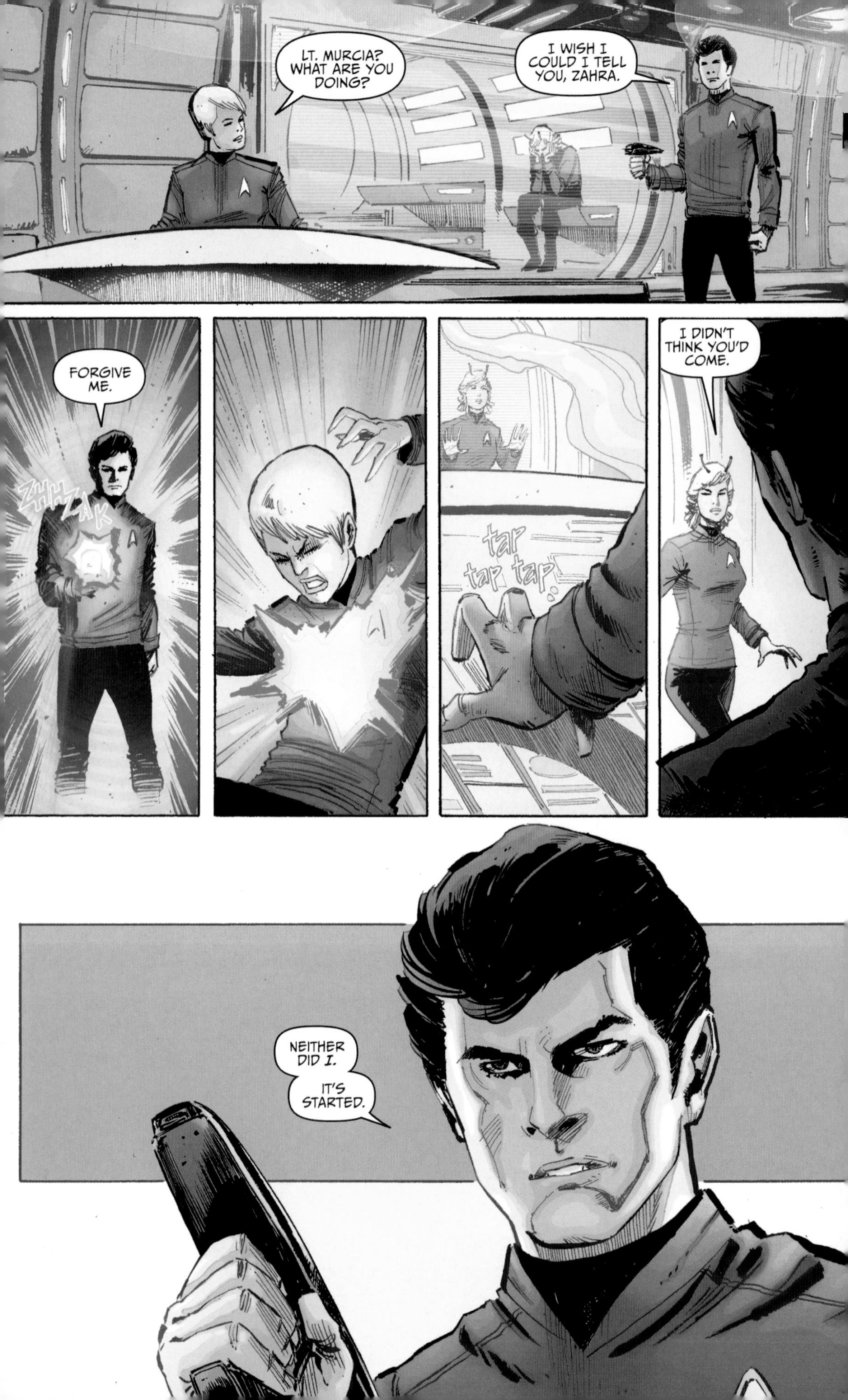
LT. MURCIA? WHAT ARE YOU DOING?
I WISH I COULD I TELL YOU, ZAHRA.
FORGIVE ME.
ZHHZAK
tap tap tap
I DIDN'T THINK YOU'D COME.
NEITHER DID I.
IT'S STARTED.

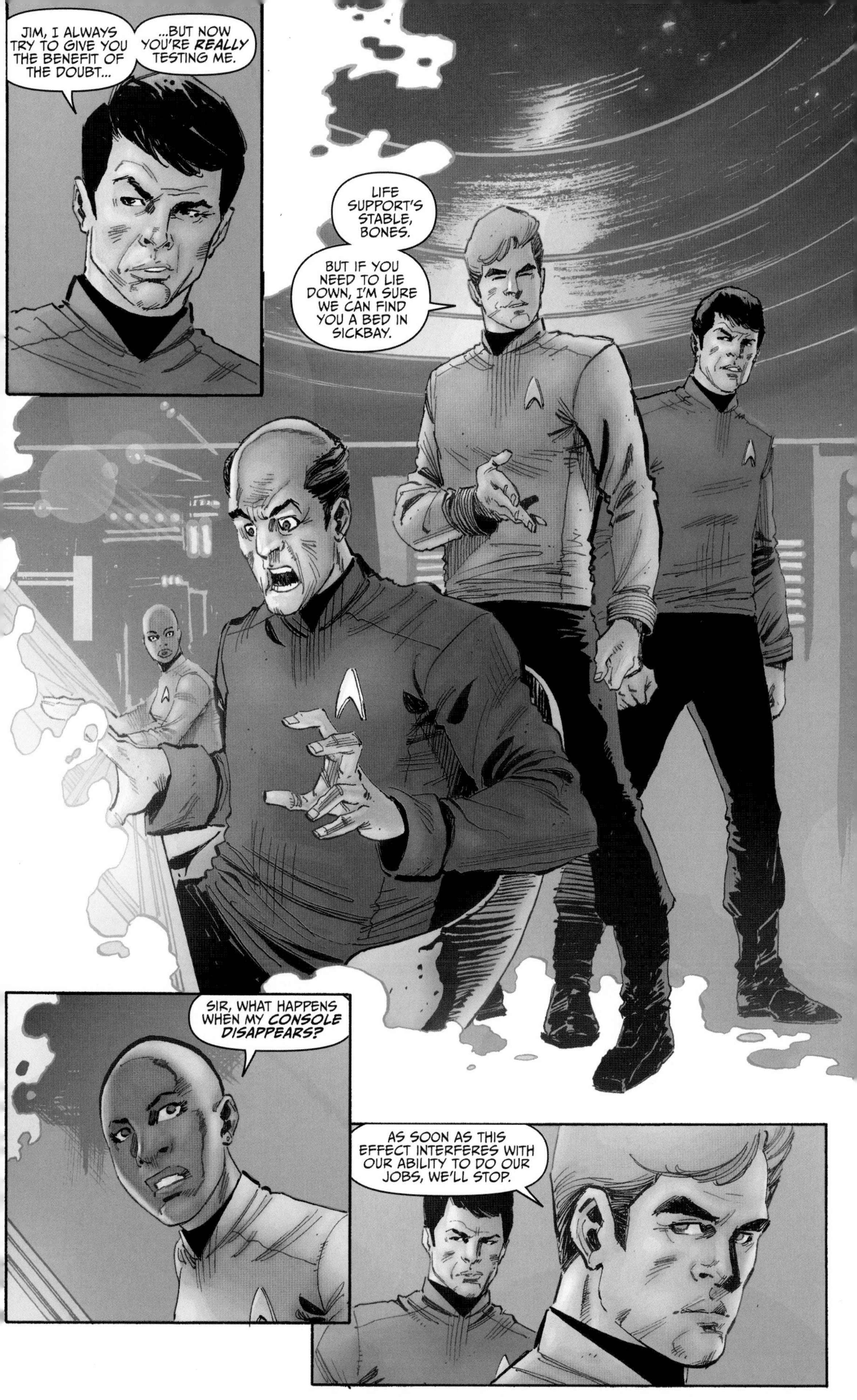
JIM, I ALWAYS TRY TO GIVE YOU THE BENEFIT OF THE DOUBT...
...BUT NOW YOU'RE *REALLY* TESTING ME.
LIFE SUPPORT'S STABLE, BONES.
BUT IF YOU NEED TO LIE DOWN, I'M SURE WE CAN FIND YOU A BED IN SICKBAY.
SIR, WHAT HAPPENS WHEN MY *CONSOLE DISAPPEARS?*
AS SOON AS THIS EFFECT INTERFERES WITH OUR ABILITY TO DO OUR JOBS, WE'LL STOP.

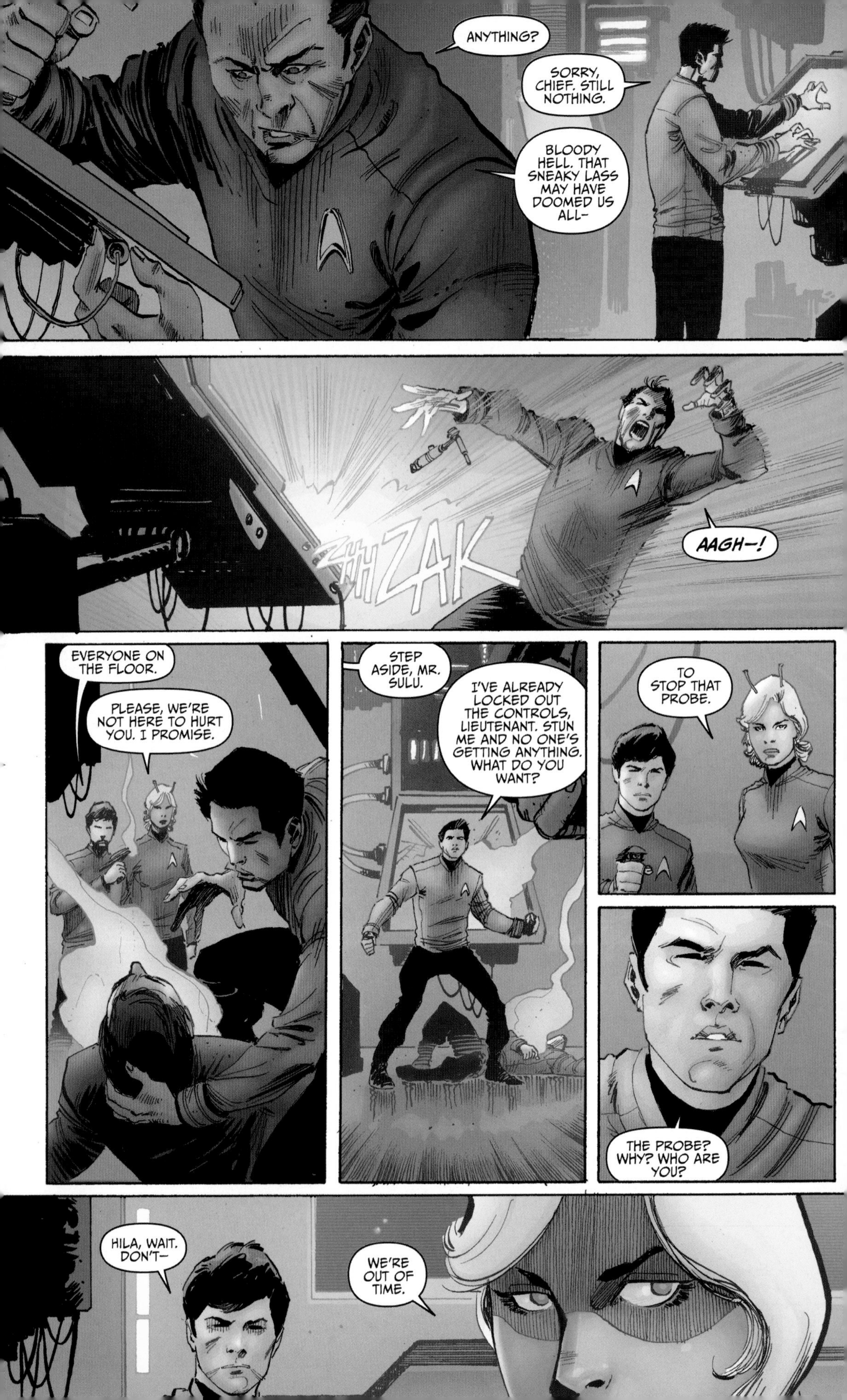
ANYTHING?
SORRY, CHIEF. STILL NOTHING.
BLOODY HELL. THAT SNEAKY LASS MAY HAVE DOOMED US ALL–
ZHHZAK
AAGH–!
EVERYONE ON THE FLOOR.
PLEASE, WE'RE NOT HERE TO HURT YOU. I PROMISE.
STEP ASIDE, MR. SULU.
I'VE ALREADY LOCKED OUT THE CONTROLS, LIEUTENANT. STUN ME AND NO ONE'S GETTING ANYTHING. WHAT DO YOU WANT?
TO STOP THAT PROBE.
THE PROBE? WHY? WHO ARE YOU?
HILA, WAIT. DON'T–
WE'RE OUT OF TIME.

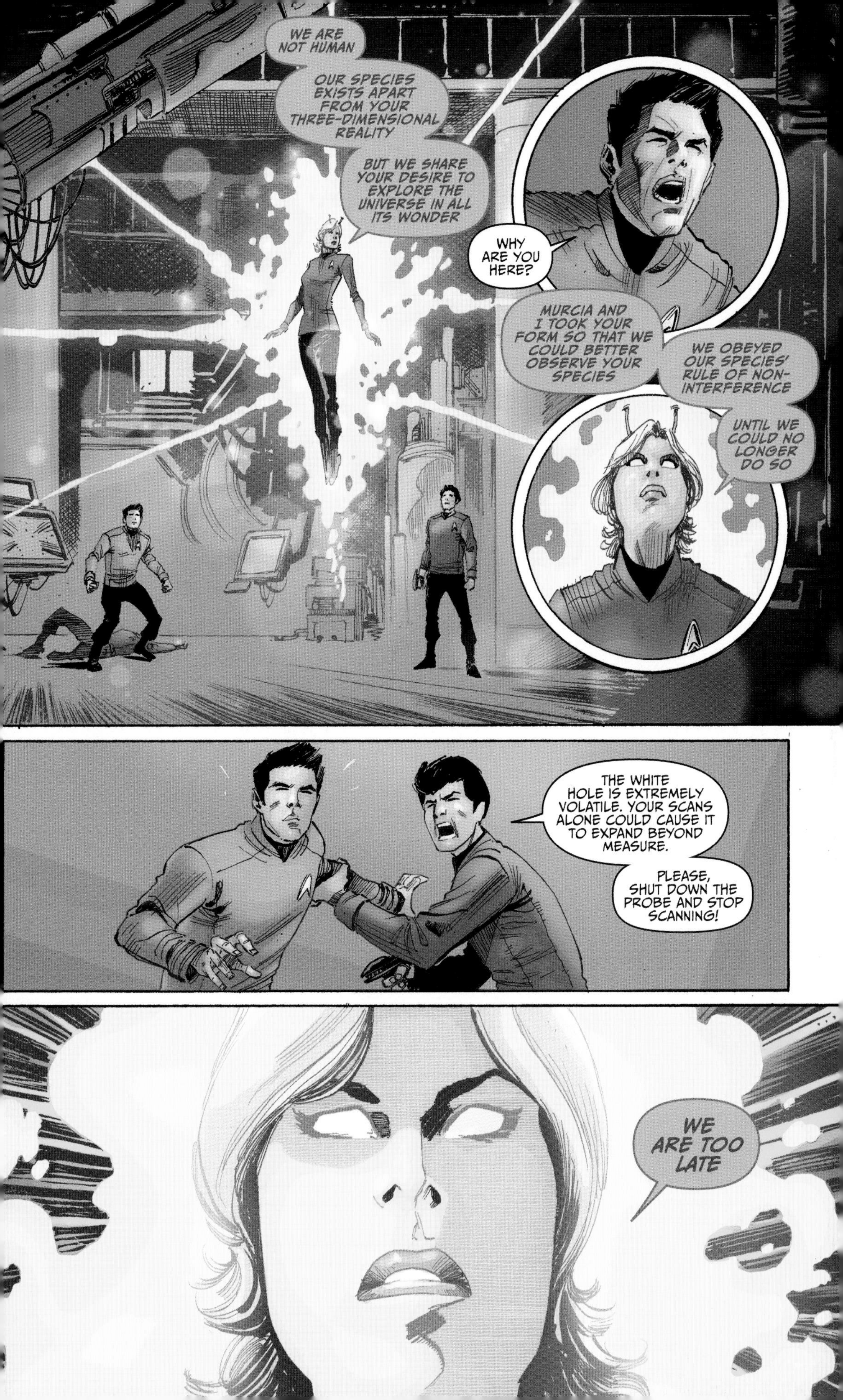

WE ARE NOT HUMAN
OUR SPECIES EXISTS APART FROM YOUR THREE-DIMENSIONAL REALITY
BUT WE SHARE YOUR DESIRE TO EXPLORE THE UNIVERSE IN ALL ITS WONDER
WHY ARE YOU HERE?
MURCIA AND I TOOK YOUR FORM SO THAT WE COULD BETTER OBSERVE YOUR SPECIES
WE OBEYED OUR SPECIES' RULE OF NON-INTERFERENCE
UNTIL WE COULD NO LONGER DO SO
THE WHITE HOLE IS EXTREMELY VOLATILE. YOUR SCANS ALONE COULD CAUSE IT TO EXPAND BEYOND MEASURE.
PLEASE, SHUT DOWN THE PROBE AND STOP SCANNING!
WE ARE TOO LATE

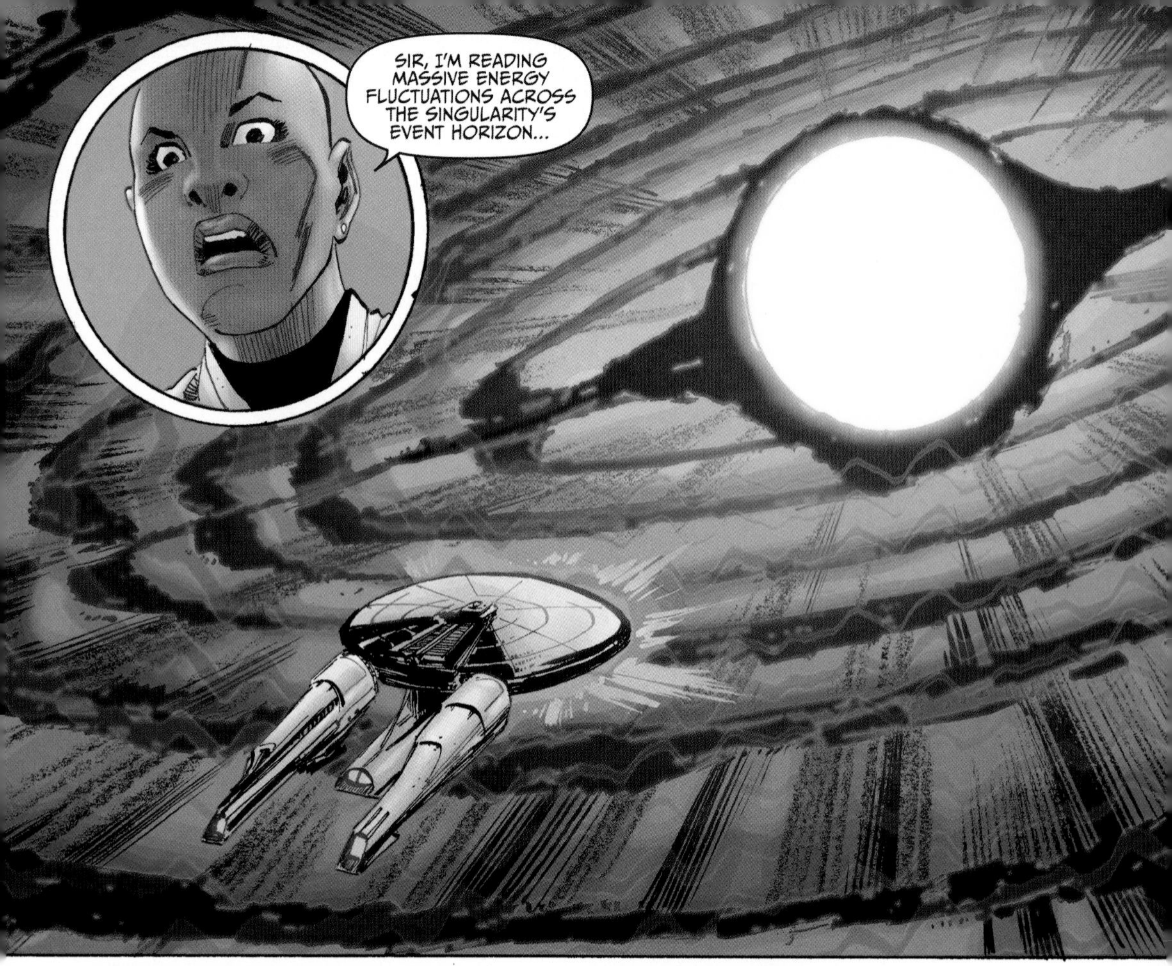
SIR, I'M READING MASSIVE ENERGY FLUCTUATIONS ACROSS THE SINGULARITY'S EVENT HORIZON...

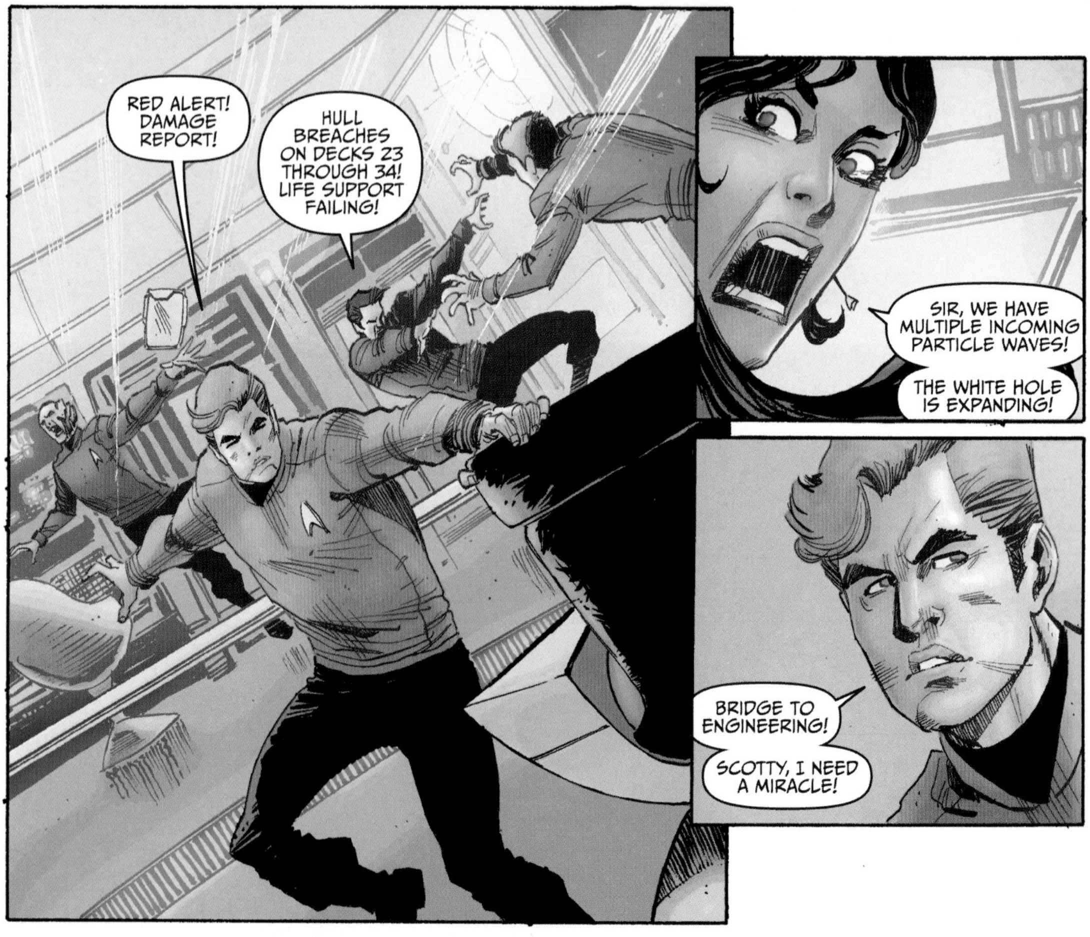
RED ALERT! DAMAGE REPORT!
HULL BREACHES ON DECKS 23 THROUGH 34! LIFE SUPPORT FAILING!
SIR, WE HAVE MULTIPLE INCOMING PARTICLE WAVES!
THE WHITE HOLE IS EXPANDING!
BRIDGE TO ENGINEERING!
SCOTTY, I NEED A MIRACLE!

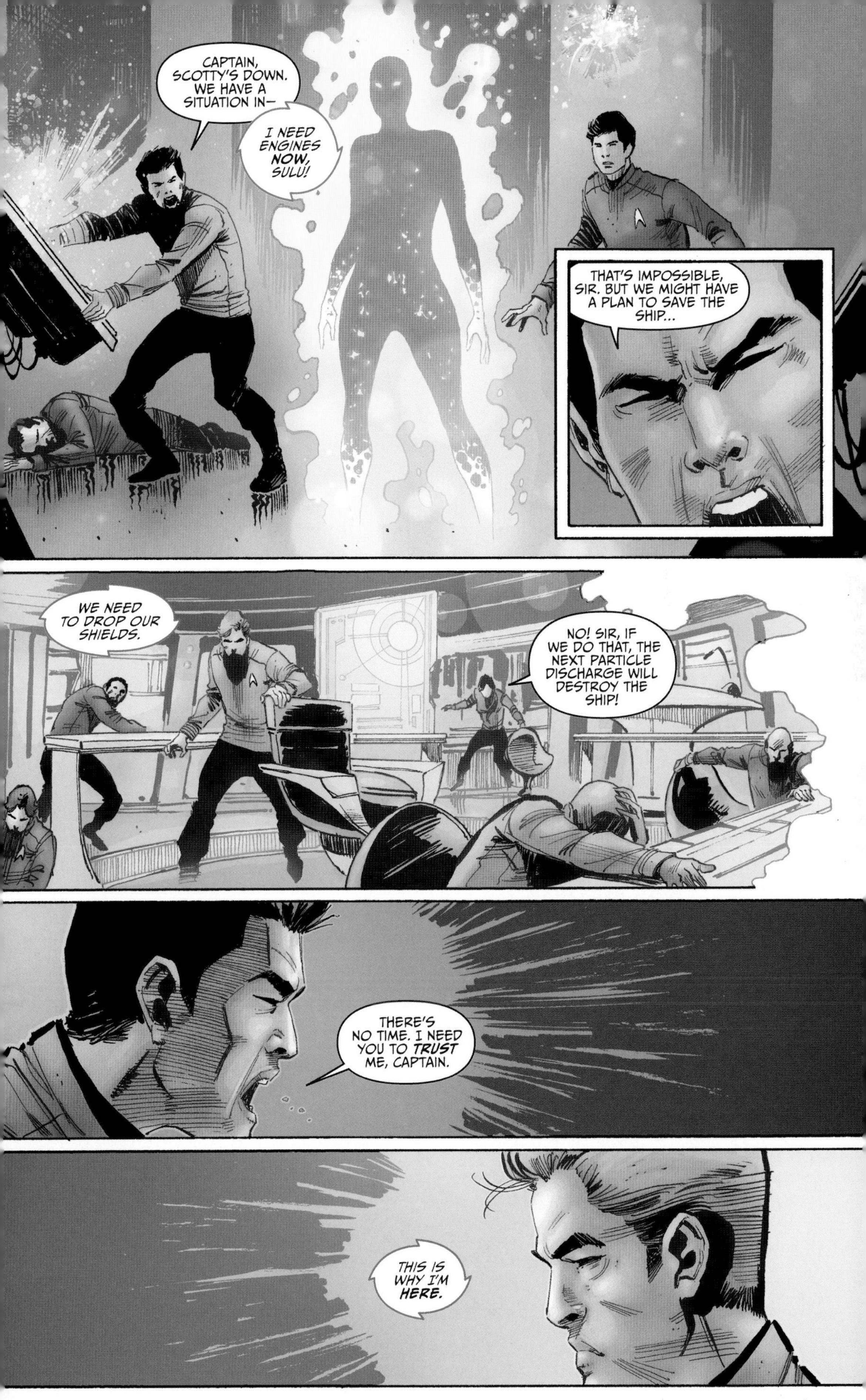
CAPTAIN, SCOTTY'S DOWN. WE HAVE A SITUATION IN—
I NEED ENGINES NOW, SULU!
THAT'S IMPOSSIBLE, SIR. BUT WE MIGHT HAVE A PLAN TO SAVE THE SHIP...
WE NEED TO DROP OUR SHIELDS.
NO! SIR, IF WE DO THAT, THE NEXT PARTICLE DISCHARGE WILL DESTROY THE SHIP!
THERE'S NO TIME. I NEED YOU TO TRUST ME, CAPTAIN.
THIS IS WHY I'M HERE.

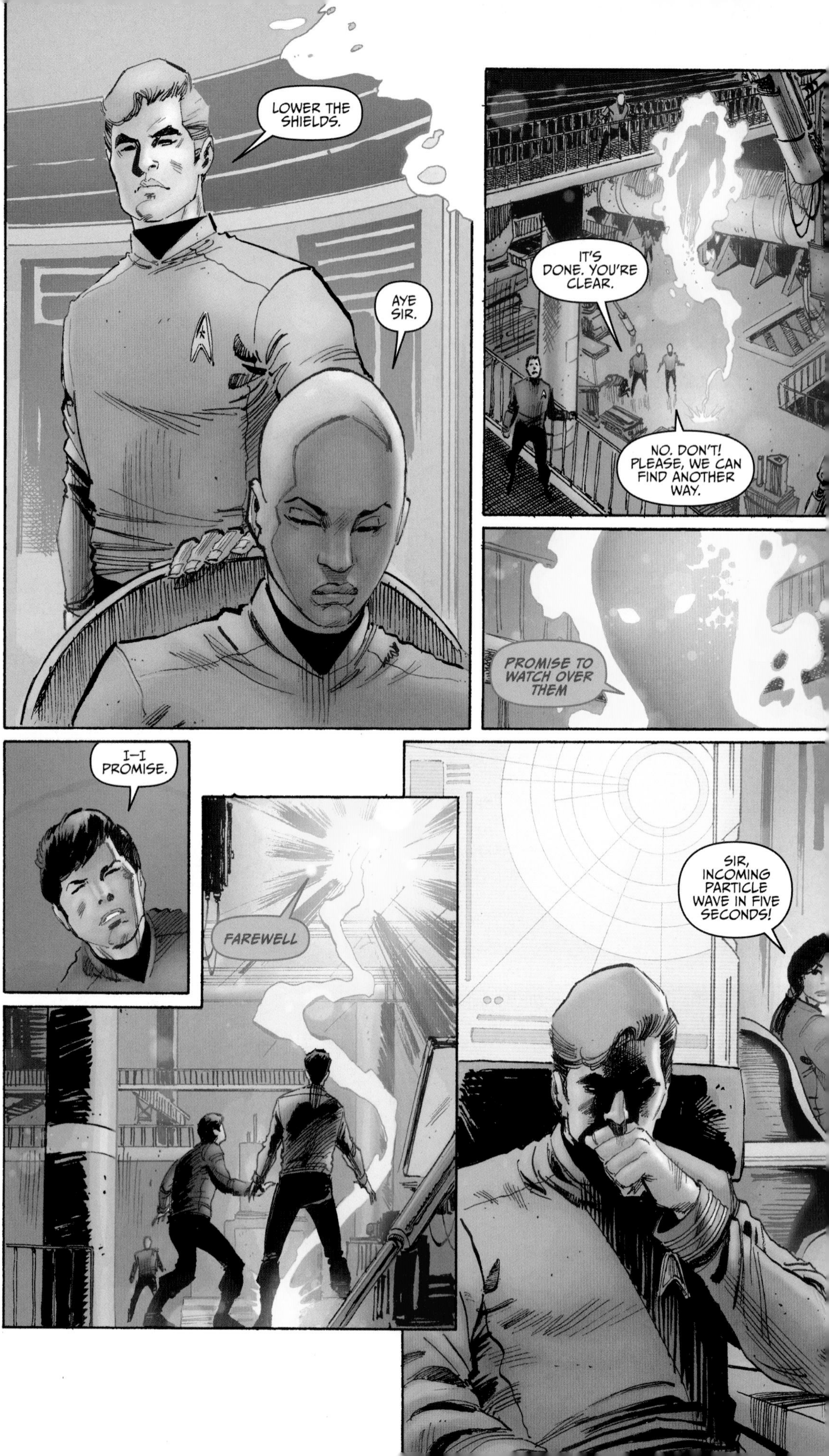
LOWER THE SHIELDS.
AYE SIR.
IT'S DONE. YOU'RE CLEAR.
NO. DON'T! PLEASE, WE CAN FIND ANOTHER WAY.
PROMISE TO WATCH OVER THEM
I—I PROMISE.
FAREWELL
SIR, INCOMING PARTICLE WAVE IN FIVE SECONDS!

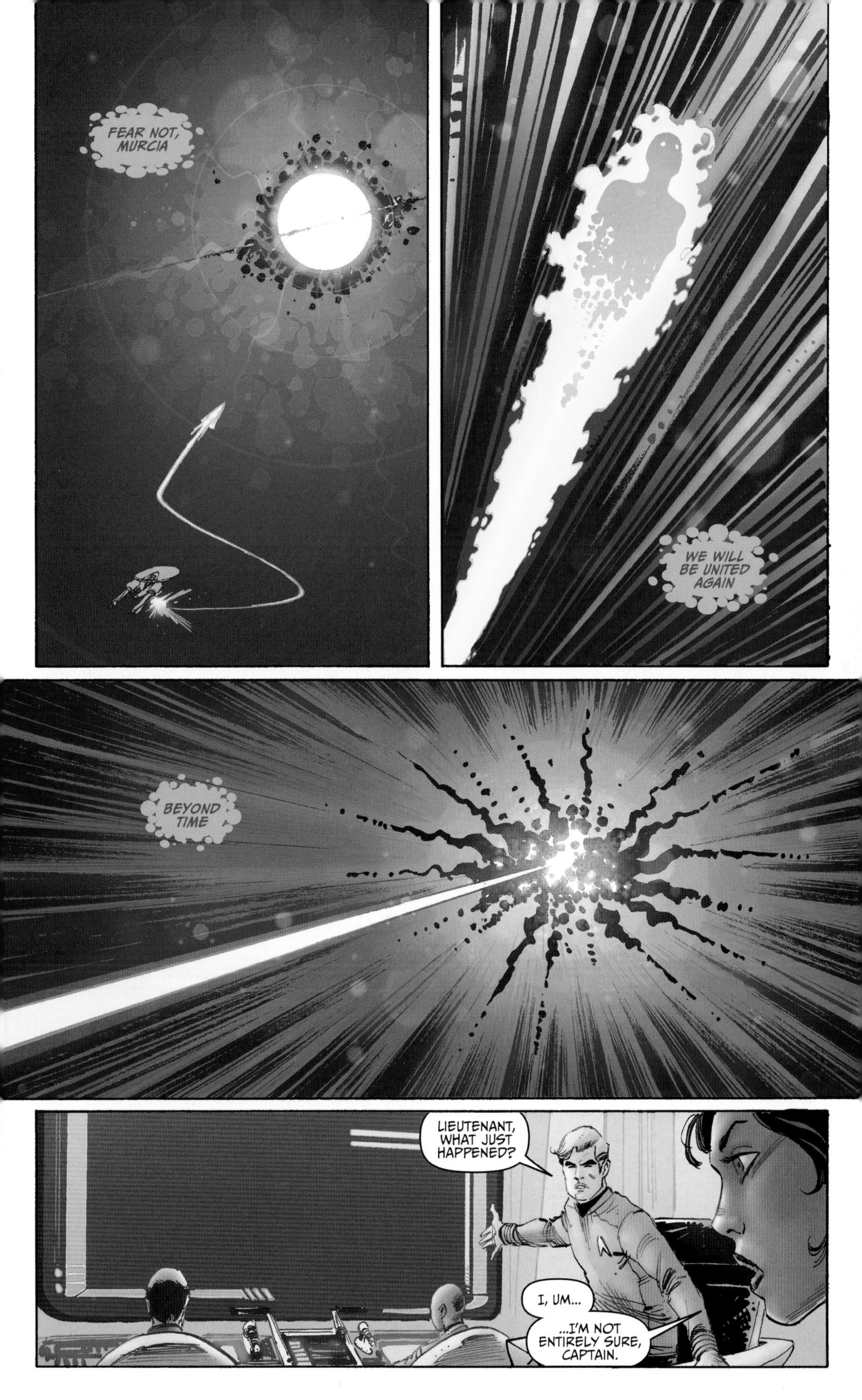
FEAR NOT, MURCIA
WE WILL BE UNITED AGAIN
BEYOND TIME
LIEUTENANT, WHAT JUST HAPPENED?
I, UM...
...I'M NOT ENTIRELY SURE, CAPTAIN.

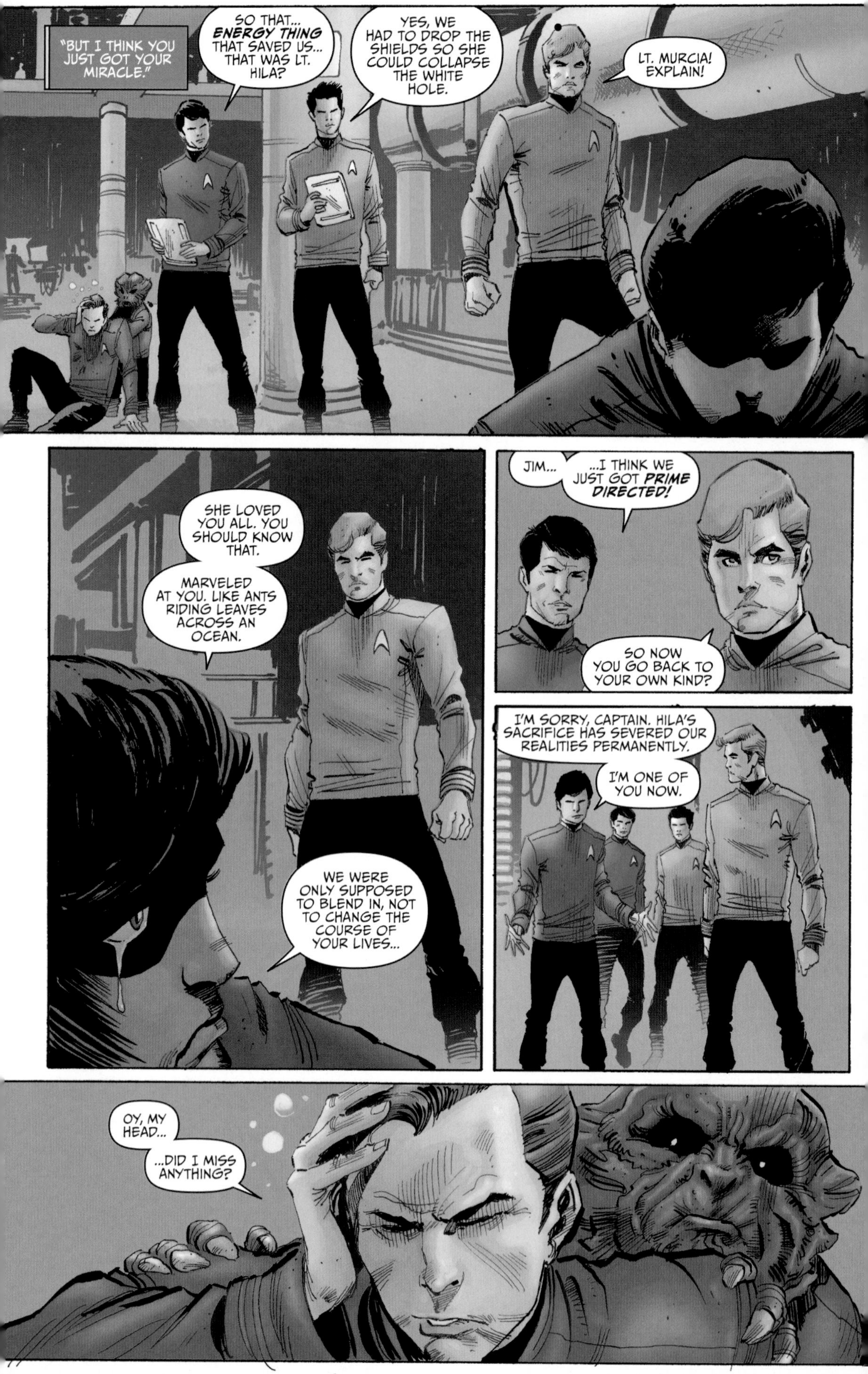
"BUT I THINK YOU JUST GOT YOUR MIRACLE."
SO THAT... **ENERGY THING** THAT SAVED US... THAT WAS LT. HILA?
YES, WE HAD TO DROP THE SHIELDS SO SHE COULD COLLAPSE THE WHITE HOLE.
LT. MURCIA! EXPLAIN!
SHE LOVED YOU ALL. YOU SHOULD KNOW THAT.
MARVELED AT YOU. LIKE ANTS RIDING LEAVES ACROSS AN OCEAN.
WE WERE ONLY SUPPOSED TO BLEND IN, NOT TO CHANGE THE COURSE OF YOUR LIVES...
JIM...
...I THINK WE JUST GOT **PRIME DIRECTED!**
SO NOW YOU GO BACK TO YOUR OWN KIND?
I'M SORRY, CAPTAIN. HILA'S SACRIFICE HAS SEVERED OUR REALITIES PERMANENTLY.
I'M ONE OF YOU NOW.
OY, MY HEAD...
...DID I MISS ANYTHING?

CAPTAIN'S LOG, SUPPLEMENTAL.

AFTER HEAVY DELIBERATION, STARFLEET HAS GRANTED LT. MURCIA'S REQUEST TO RESUME HIS DUTIES ONBOARD THE *ENDEAVOR.*

OFFICIALLY, THIS IS TO MAINTAIN CONSTANT OBSERVATION, AS WELL AS CULTIVATE RELATIONS BETWEEN OUR SPECIES.

I JUST THINK THEY DIDN'T KNOW WHAT HE'D DO IF THEY SAID "NO."

DAMNDEST THING I EVER...

IN ALL OF THE TIME I'VE BEEN OUT HERE INVESTIGATING THE UNKNOWN, I NEVER IMAGINED THAT *WE* MIGHT BE INVESTIGATED TOO, BY SPECIES MORE ADVANCED THAN OURSELVES.

FAR FROM BEING AN UNSETTLING THOUGHT, I TAKE COMFORT IN IT.

THAT THE URGE TO LEARN, THE URGE TO UNDERSTAND, CROSSES ALL BOUNDARIES...

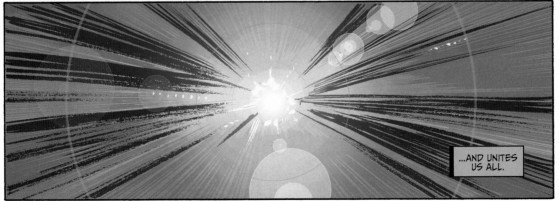

...AND UNITES US ALL.

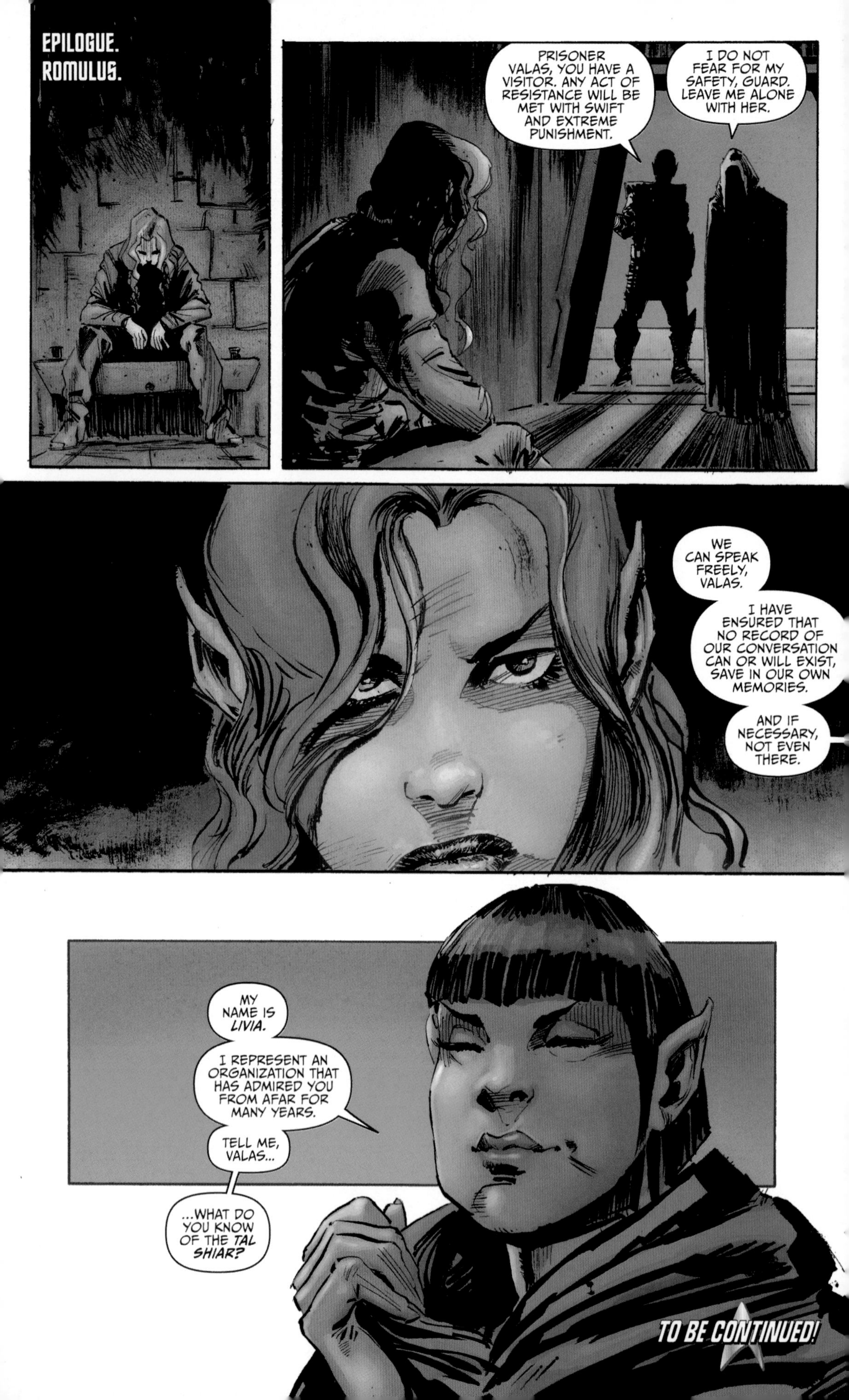
EPILOGUE. ROMULUS.
PRISONER VALAS, YOU HAVE A VISITOR. ANY ACT OF RESISTANCE WILL BE MET WITH SWIFT AND EXTREME PUNISHMENT.
I DO NOT FEAR FOR MY SAFETY, GUARD. LEAVE ME ALONE WITH HER.
WE CAN SPEAK FREELY, VALAS.
I HAVE ENSURED THAT NO RECORD OF OUR CONVERSATION CAN OR WILL EXIST, SAVE IN OUR OWN MEMORIES.
AND IF NECESSARY, NOT EVEN THERE.
MY NAME IS *LIVIA.*
I REPRESENT AN ORGANIZATION THAT HAS ADMIRED YOU FROM AFAR FOR MANY YEARS.
TELL ME, VALAS...
...WHAT DO YOU KNOW OF THE *TAL SHIAR?*
TO BE CONTINUED!

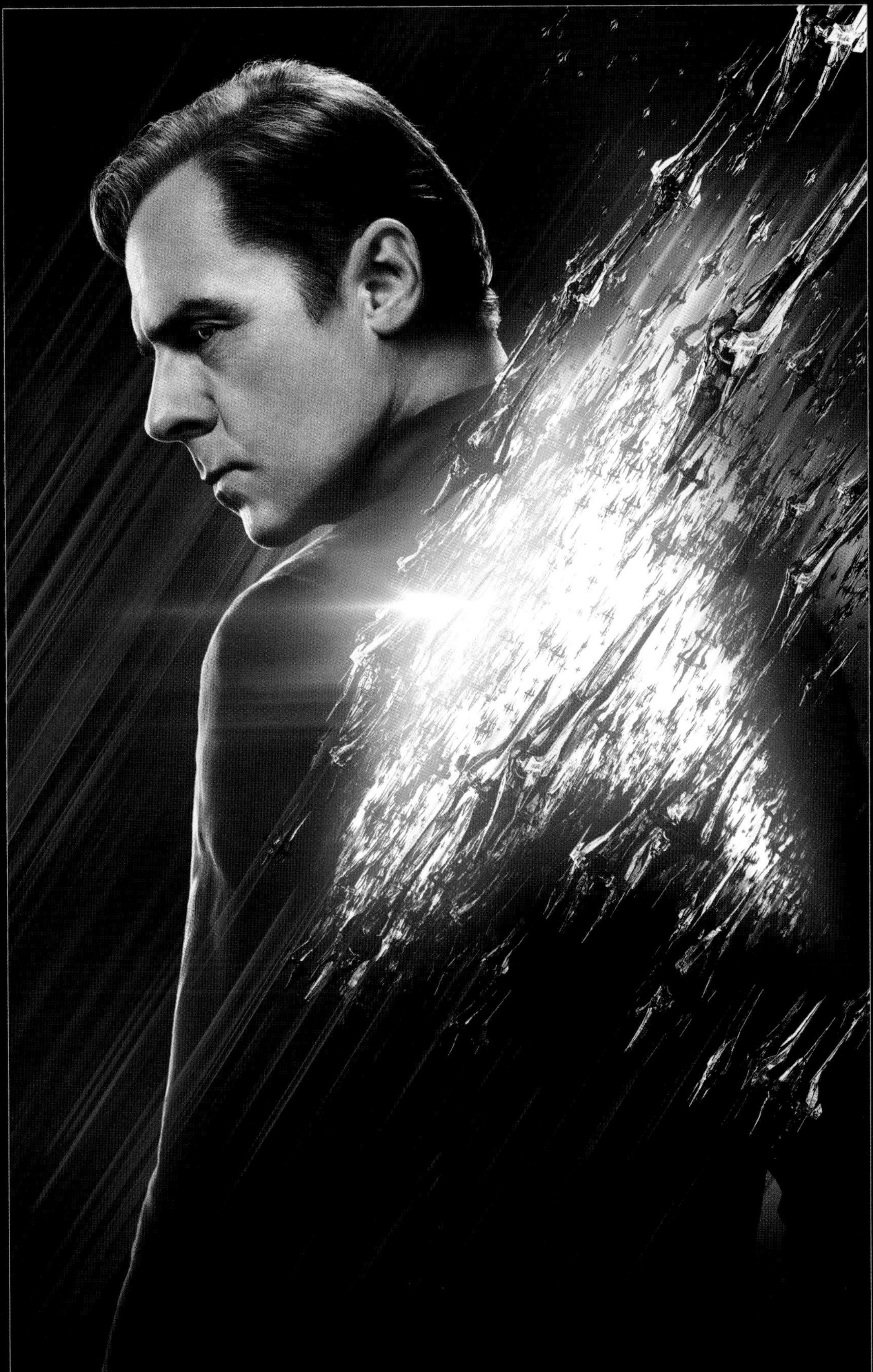

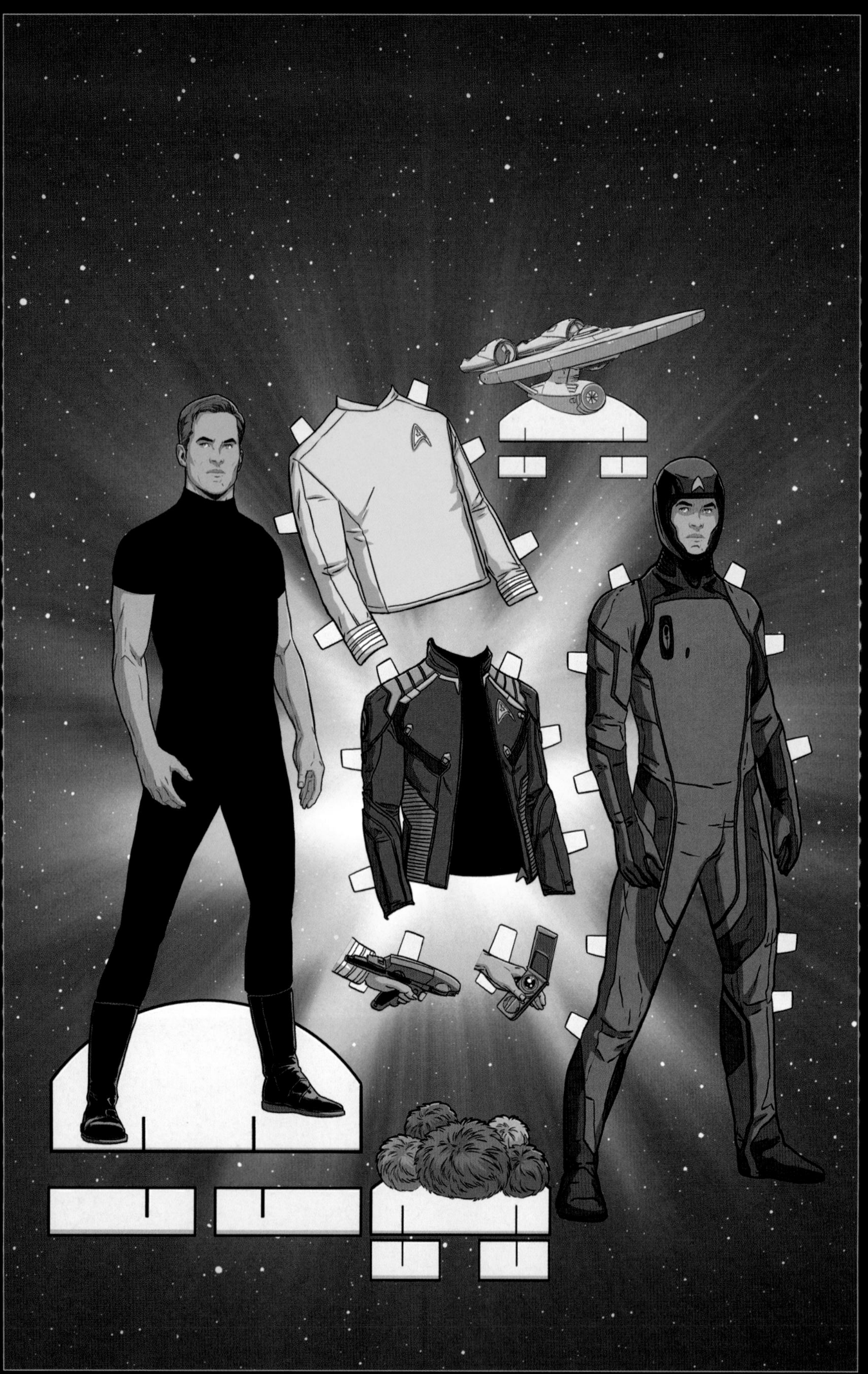

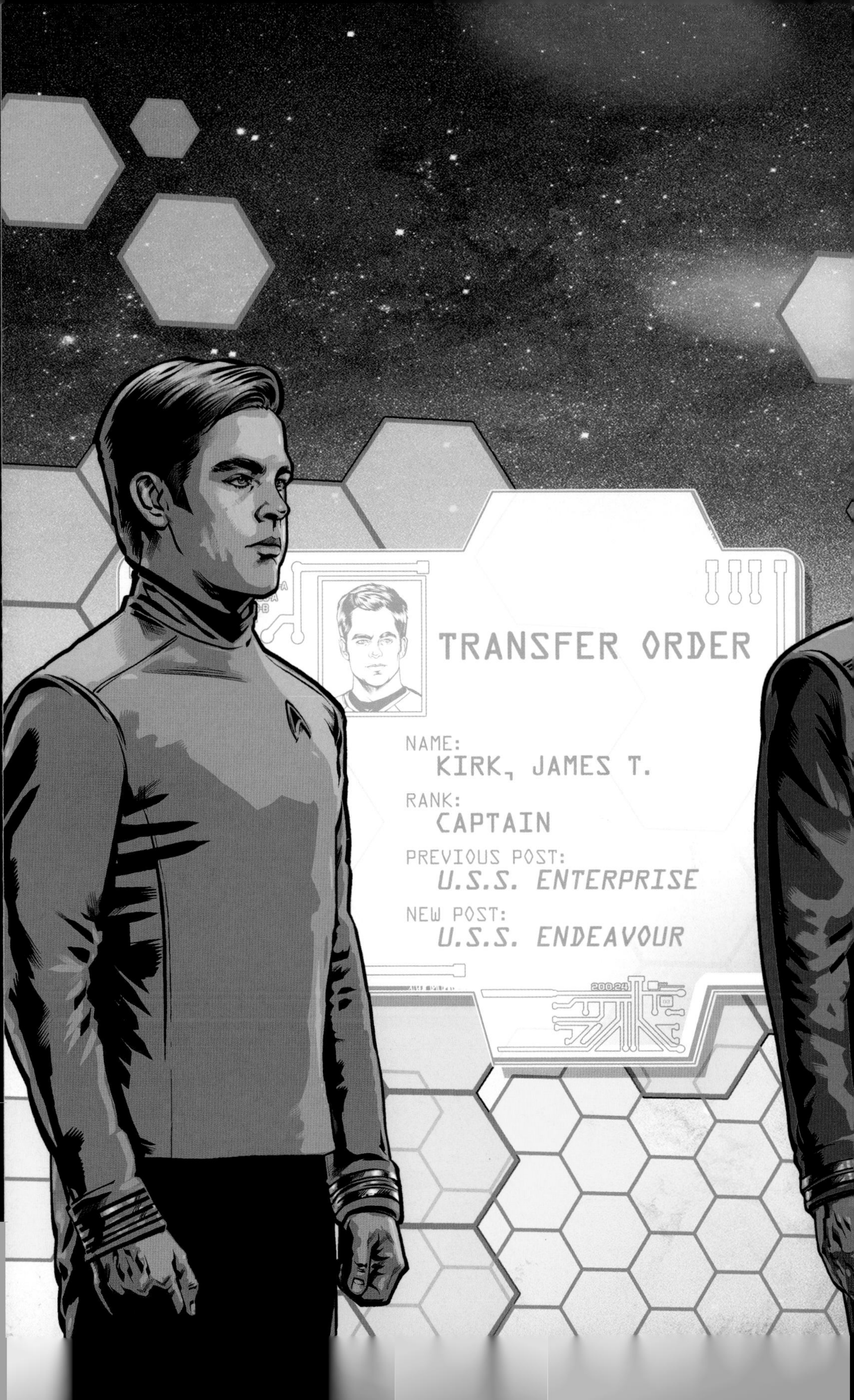
TRANSFER ORDER
NAME:
KIRK, JAMES T.
RANK:
CAPTAIN
PREVIOUS POST:
U.S.S. ENTERPRISE
NEW POST:
U.S.S. ENDEAVOUR

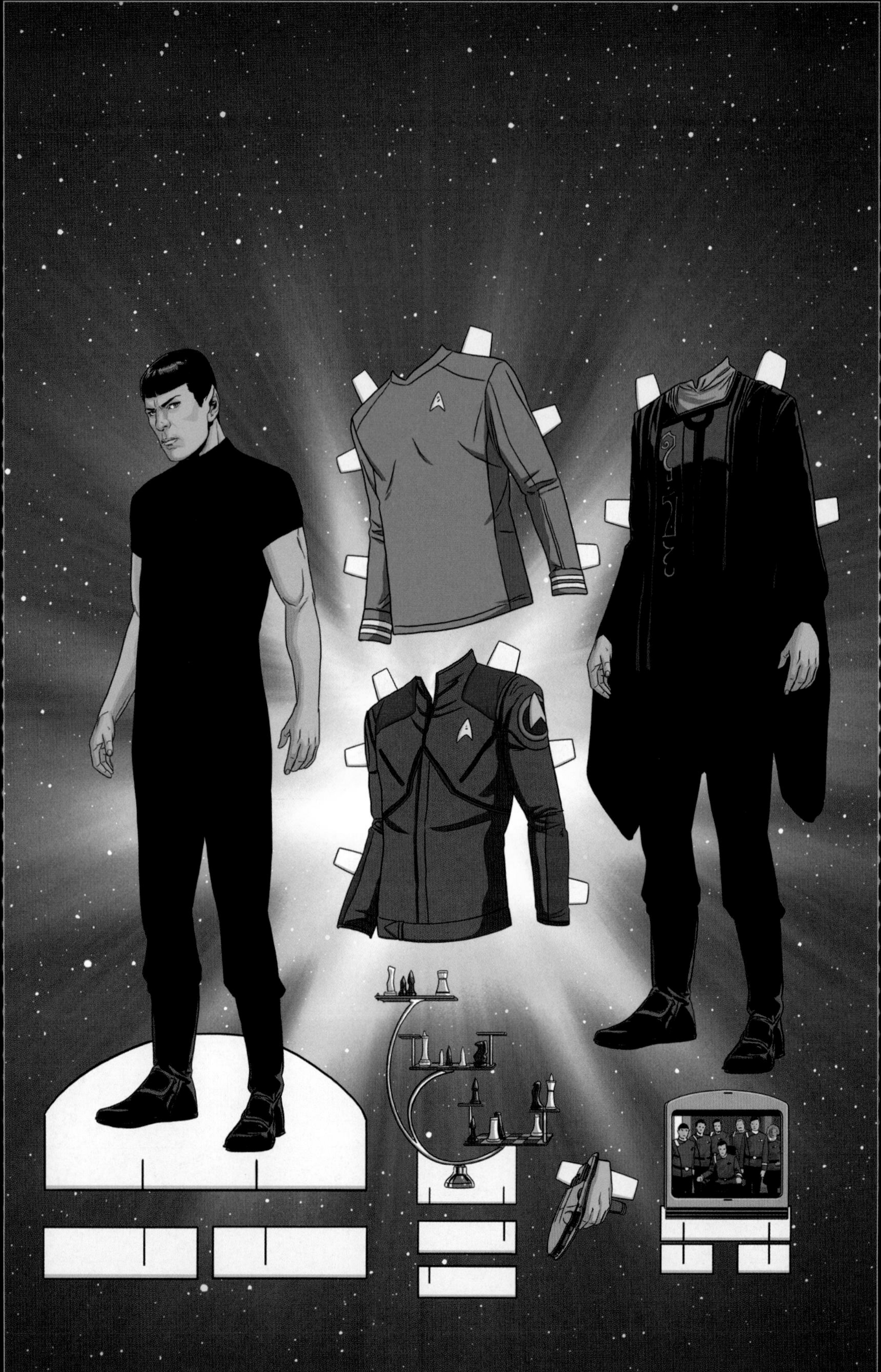

art by
Mark Laming

colors by
Mark Roberts

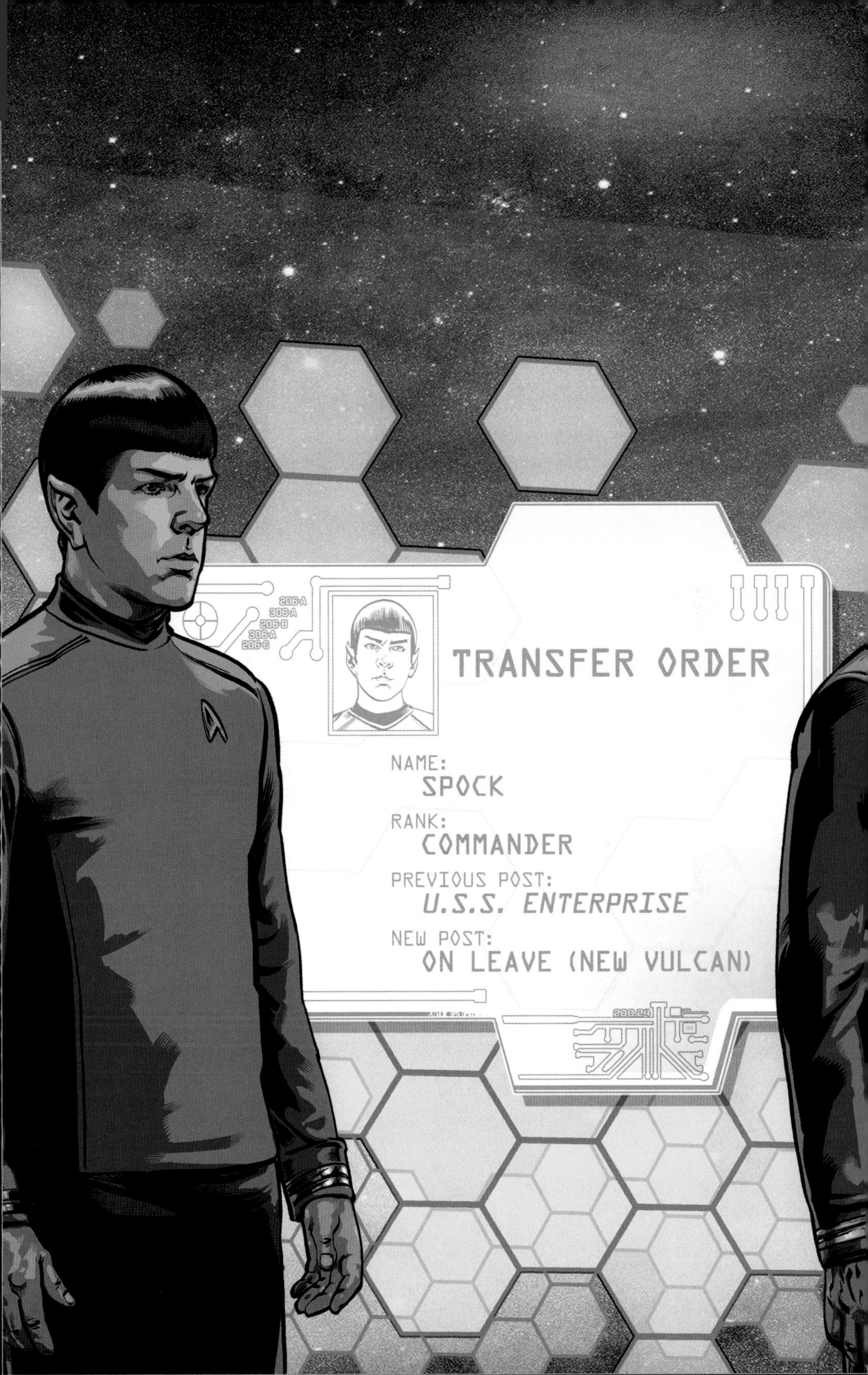
TRANSFER ORDER
NAME:
SPOCK
RANK:
COMMANDER
PREVIOUS POST:
U.S.S. ENTERPRISE
NEW POST:
ON LEAVE (NEW VULCAN)

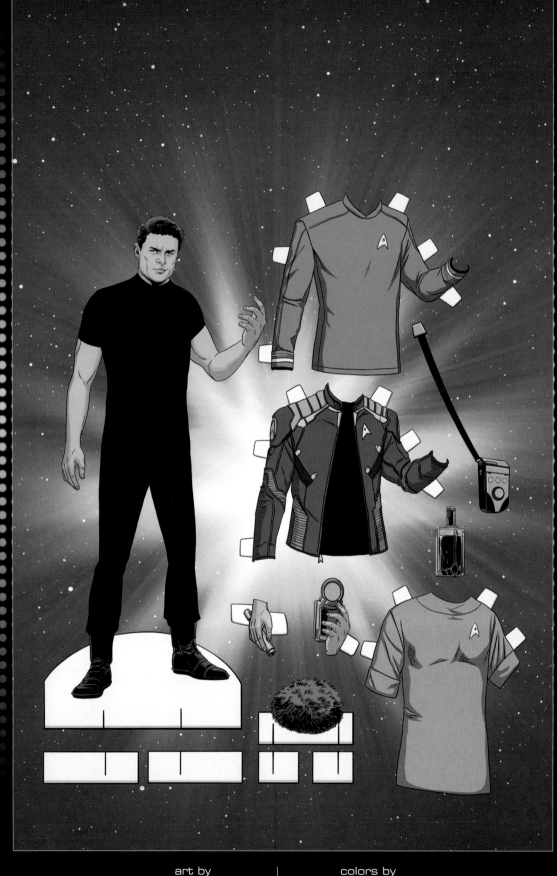

art by
Mark Laming

colors by
Mark Roberts

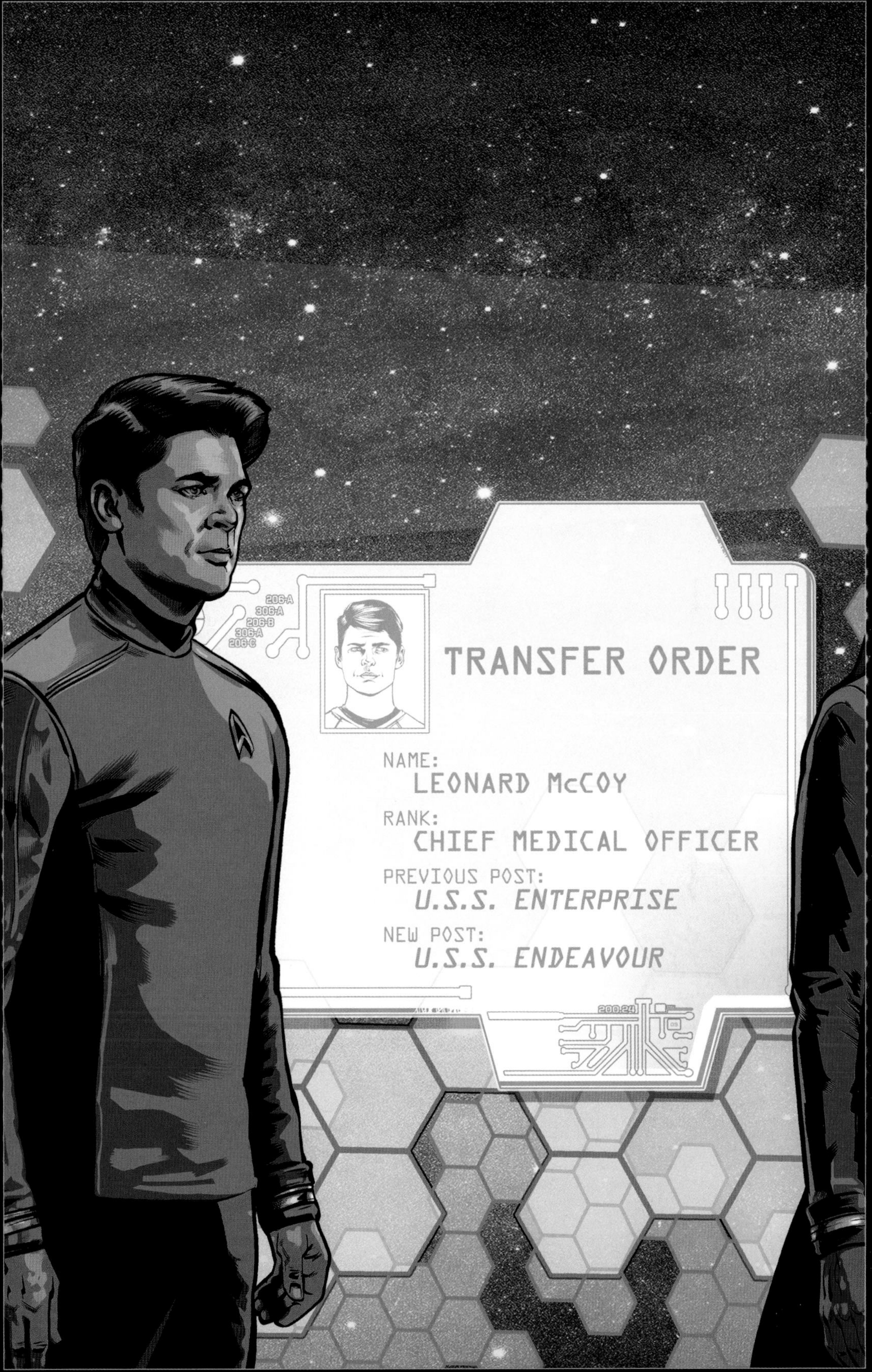
TRANSFER ORDER
NAME:
LEONARD McCOY
RANK:
CHIEF MEDICAL OFFICER
PREVIOUS POST:
U.S.S. ENTERPRISE
NEW POST:
U.S.S. ENDEAVOUR

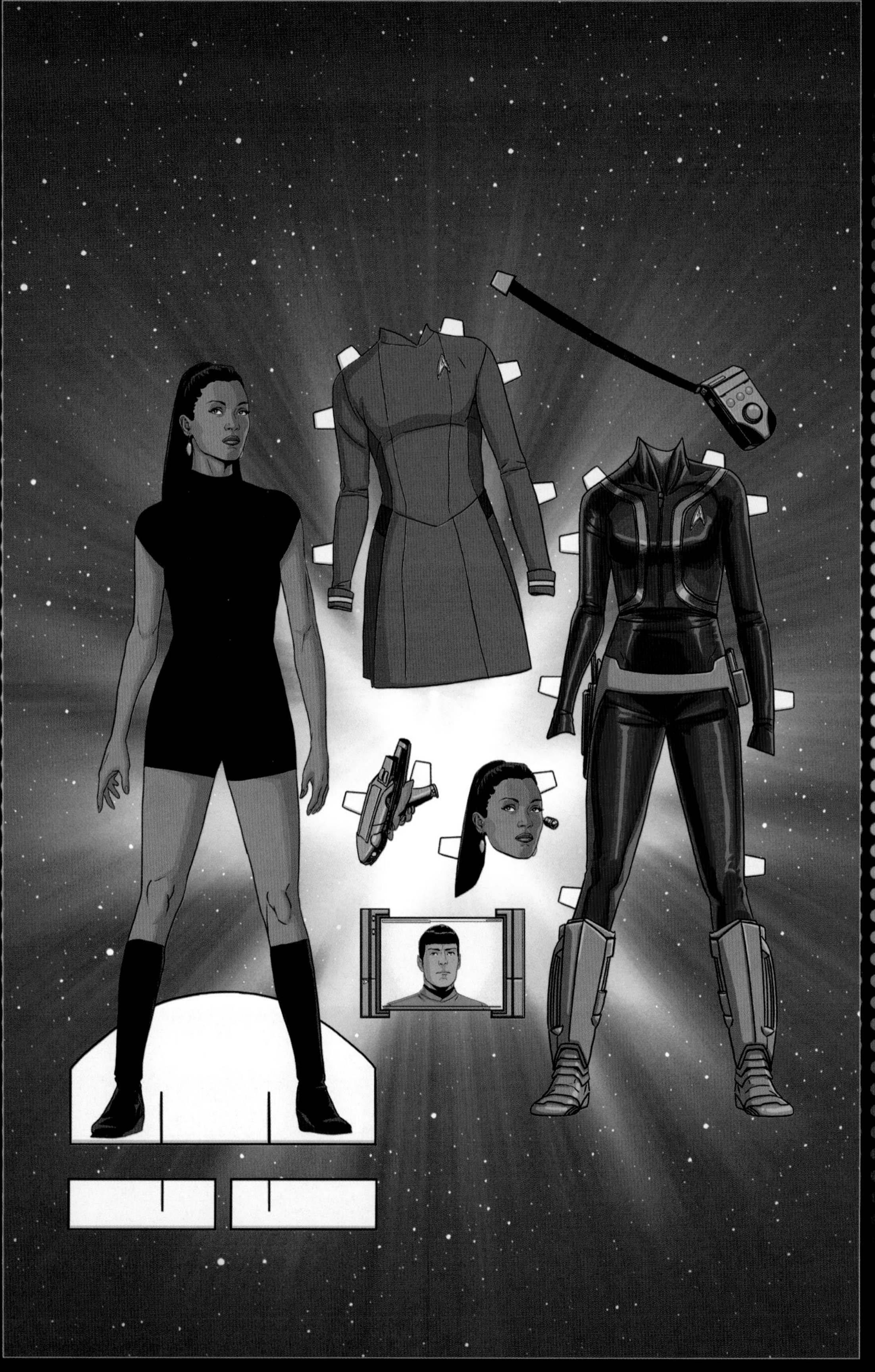

art by | colors by

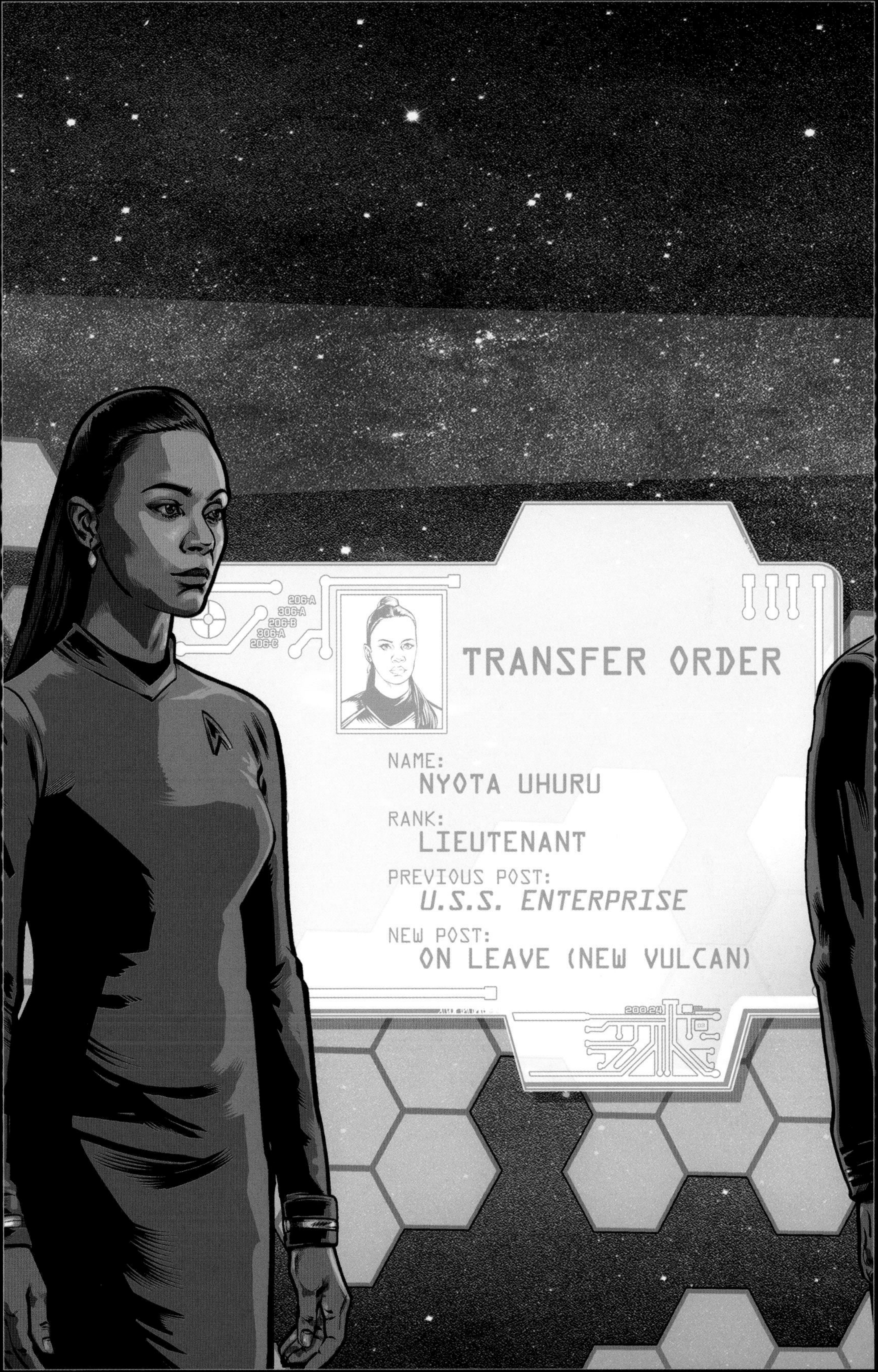
206-A
306-A
206-B
306-A
206-C
TRANSFER ORDER
NAME:
NYOTA UHURU
RANK:
LIEUTENANT
PREVIOUS POST:
U.S.S. ENTERPRISE
NEW POST:
ON LEAVE (NEW VULCAN)
200.24

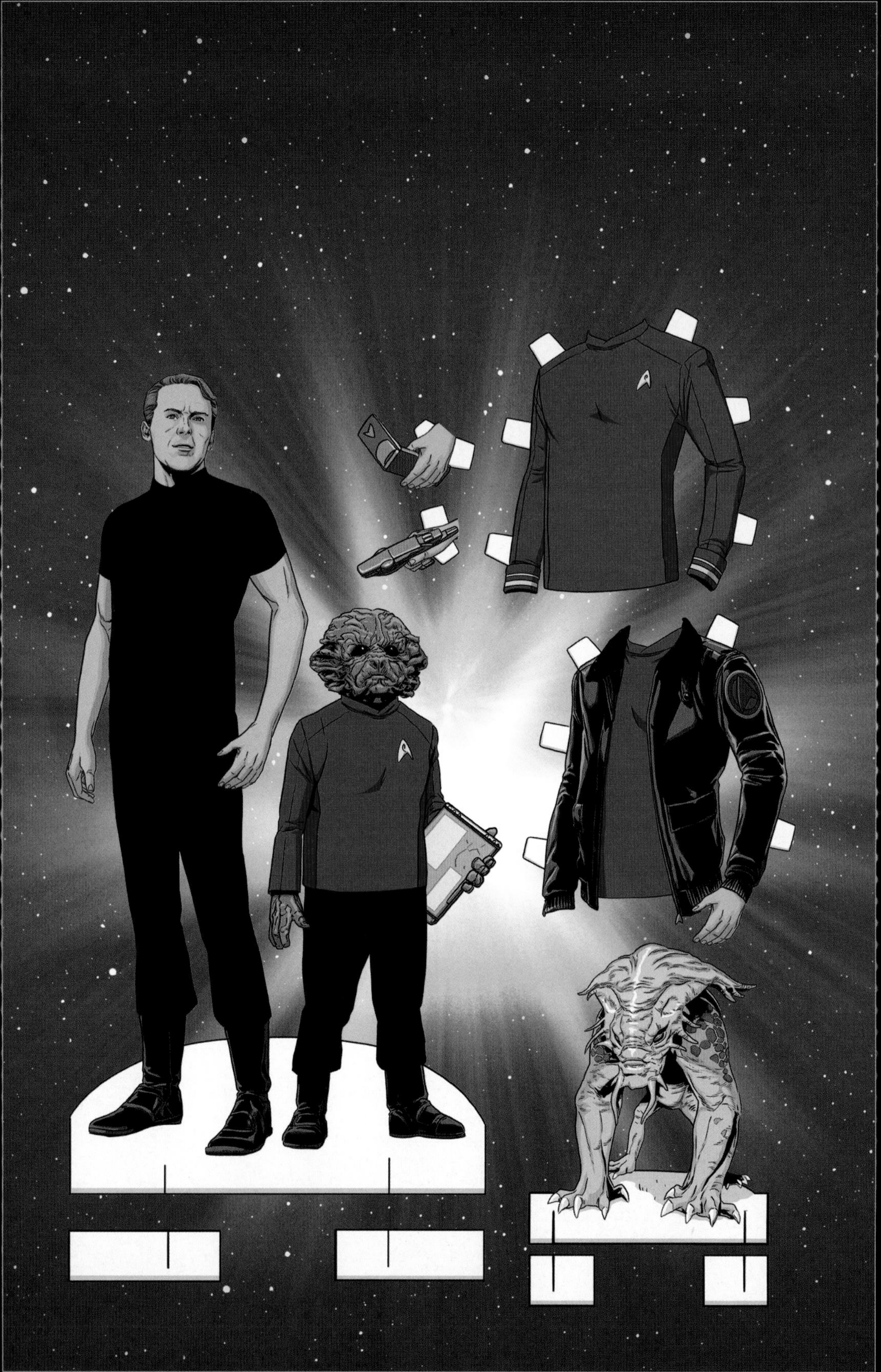

art by
Mark Laming

colors by
Mark Roberts

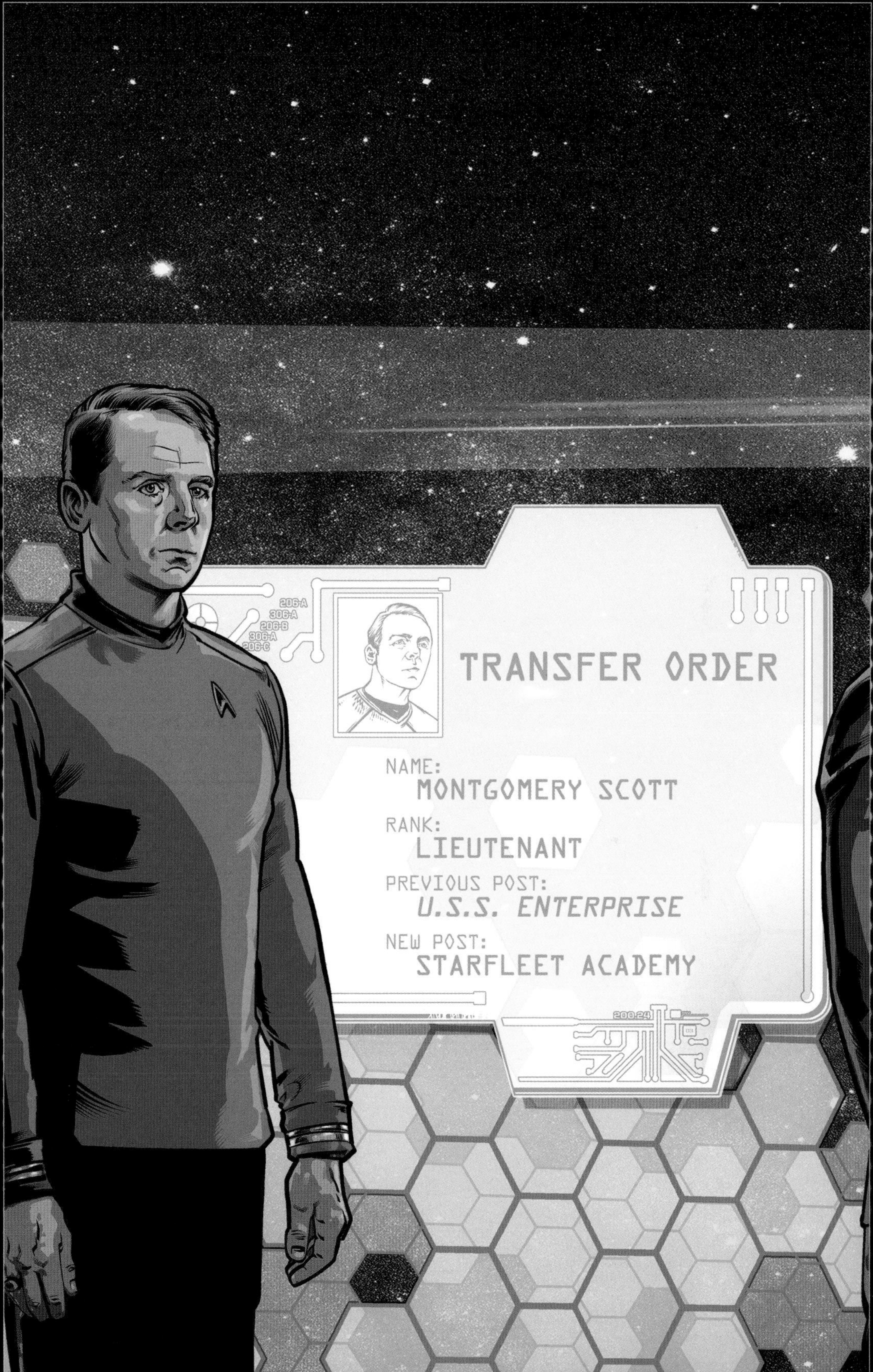
206-A
306-A
206-B
306-A
206-C
TRANSFER ORDER
NAME:
MONTGOMERY SCOTT
RANK:
LIEUTENANT
PREVIOUS POST:
U.S.S. ENTERPRISE
NEW POST:
STARFLEET ACADEMY
200.24

art by
Tony Shasteen

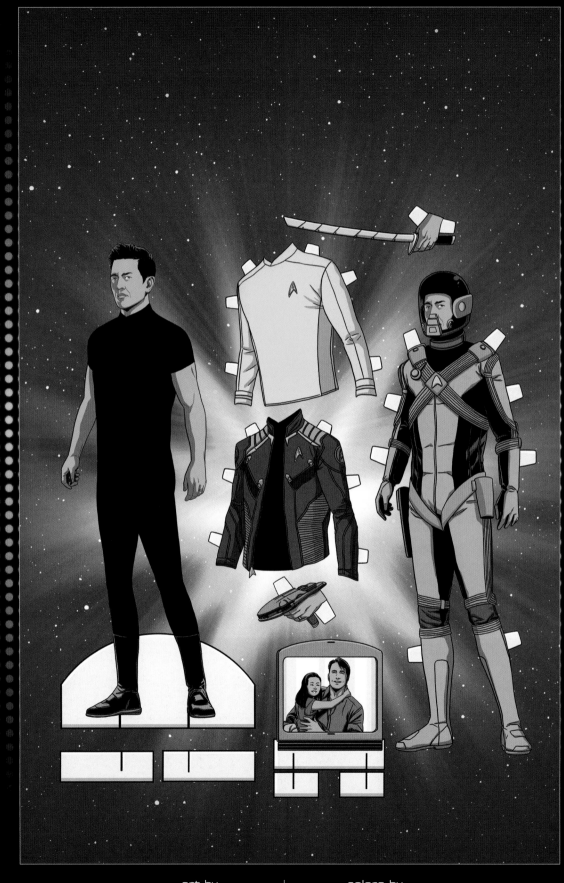

art by
Mark Laming

colors by
Mark Roberts

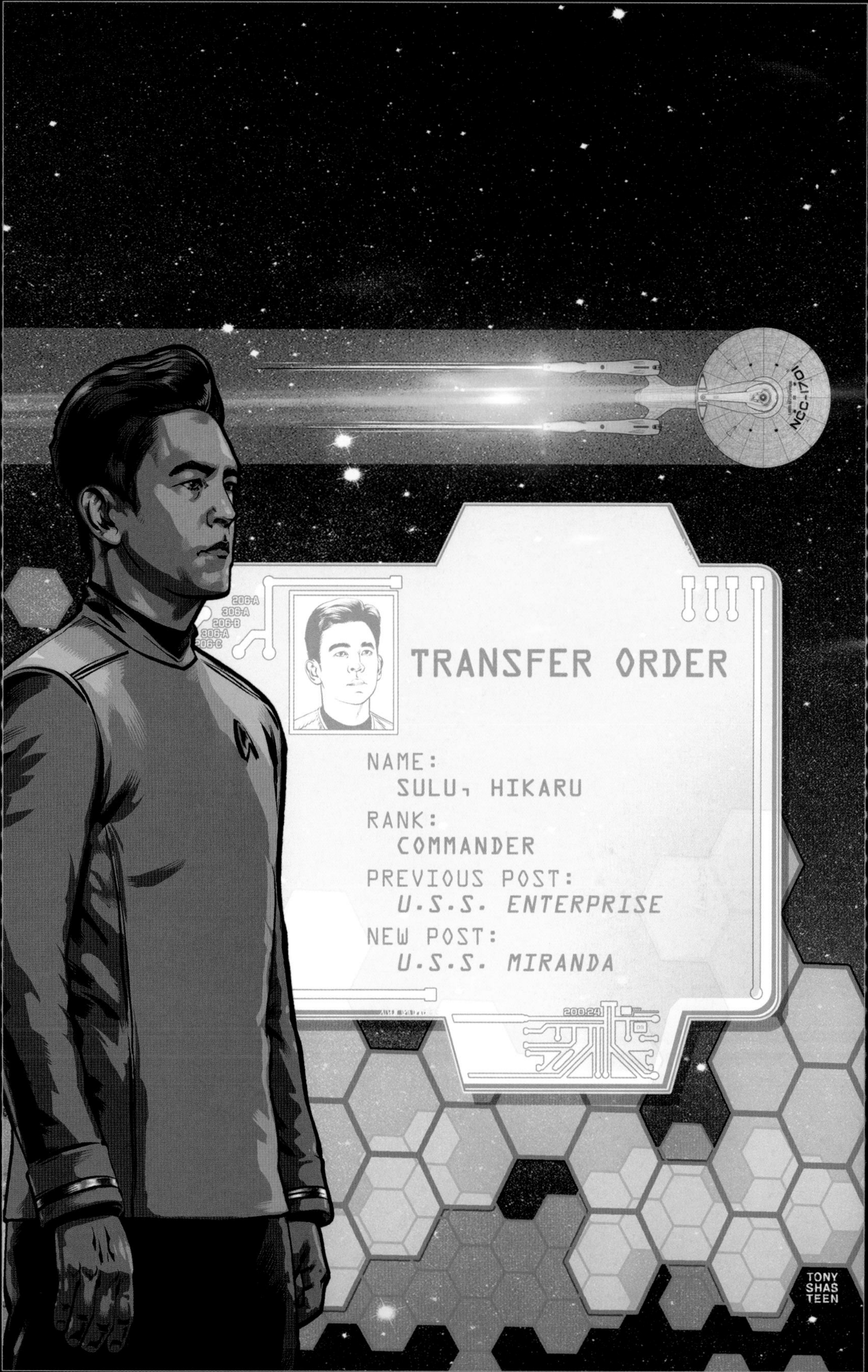
NCC-1701
206-A
306-A
206-B
306-A
206-C
TRANSFER ORDER
NAME:
SULU, HIKARU
RANK:
COMMANDER
PREVIOUS POST:
U.S.S. ENTERPRISE
NEW POST:
U.S.S. MIRANDA
200.24
TONY SHASTEEN

art by
Tony Shasteen

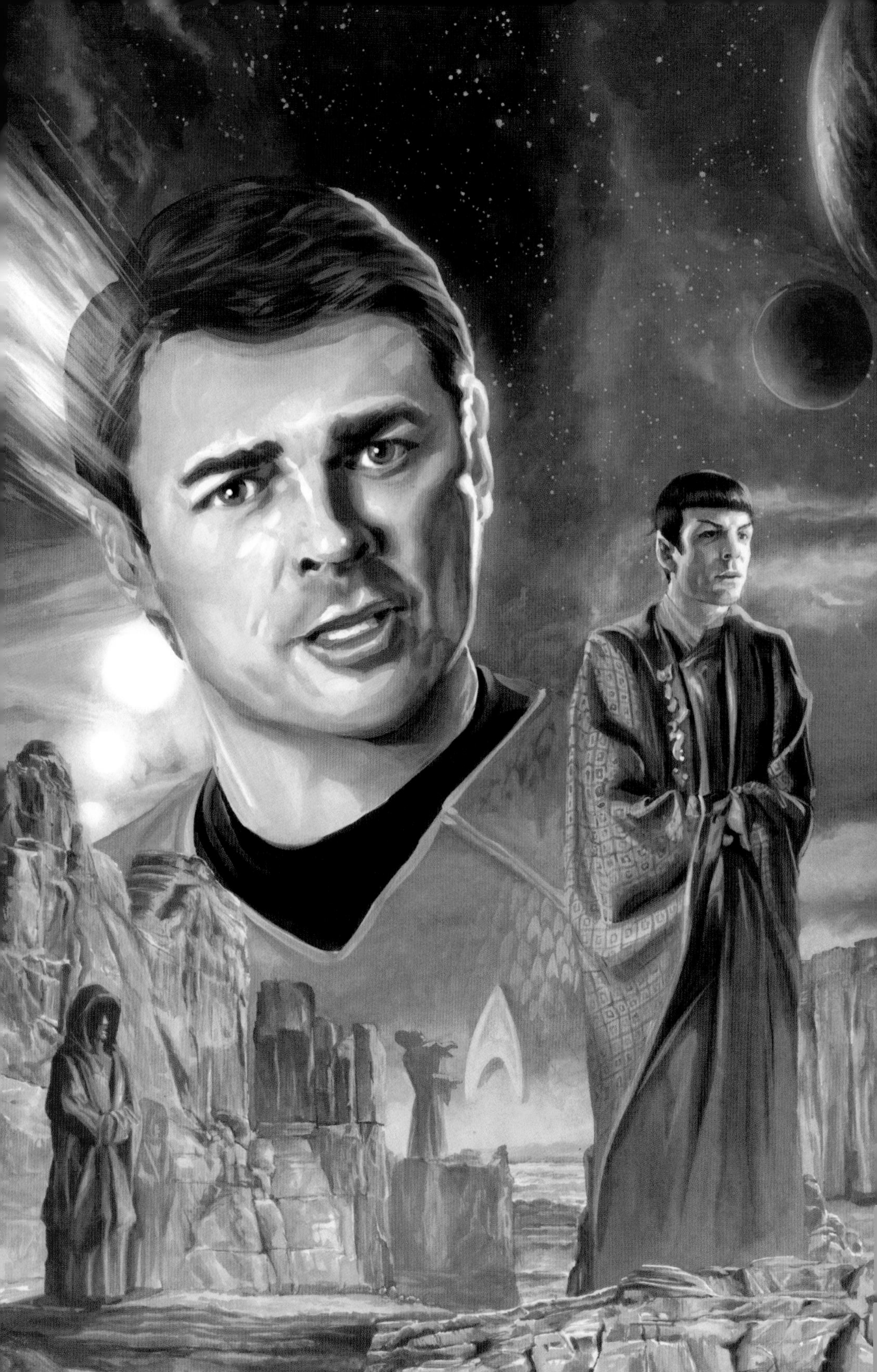

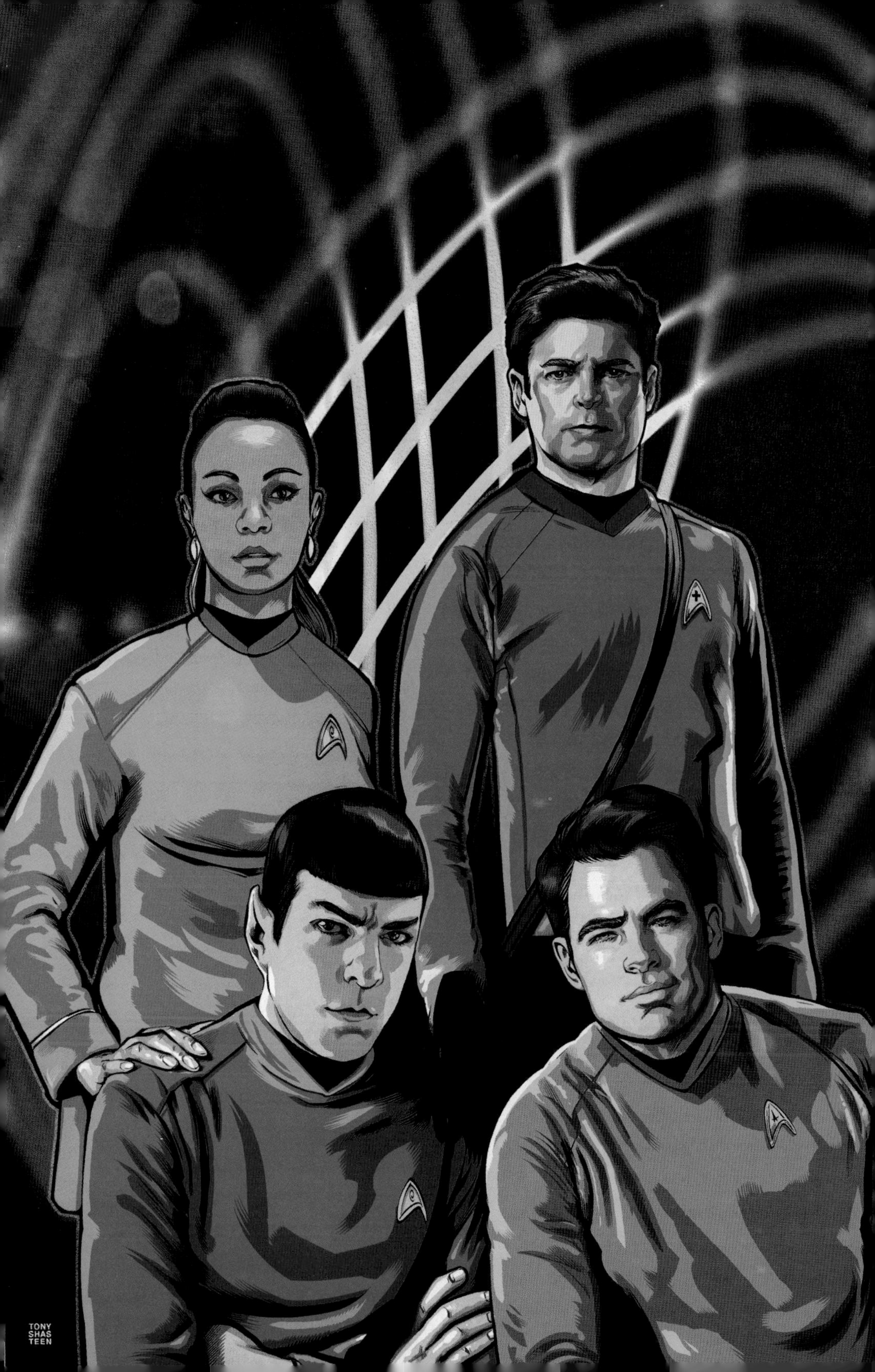
TONY
SHAS
TEEN

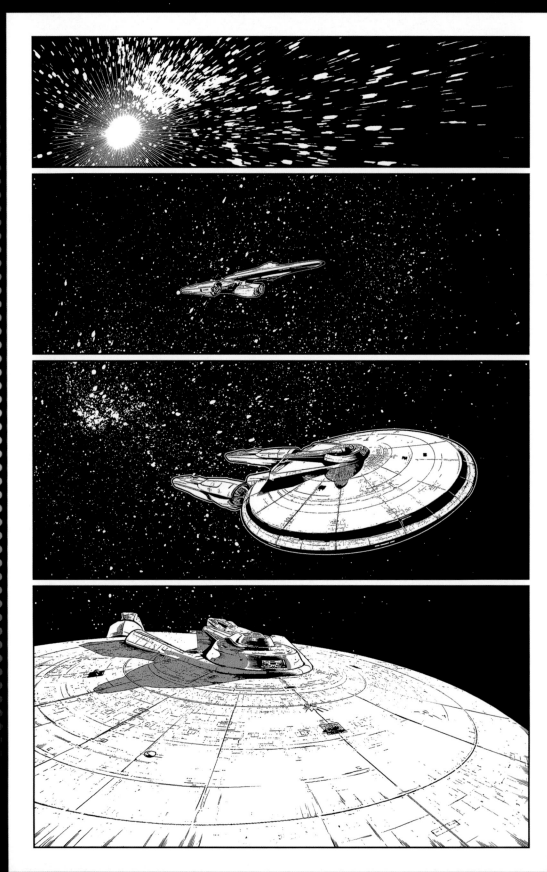

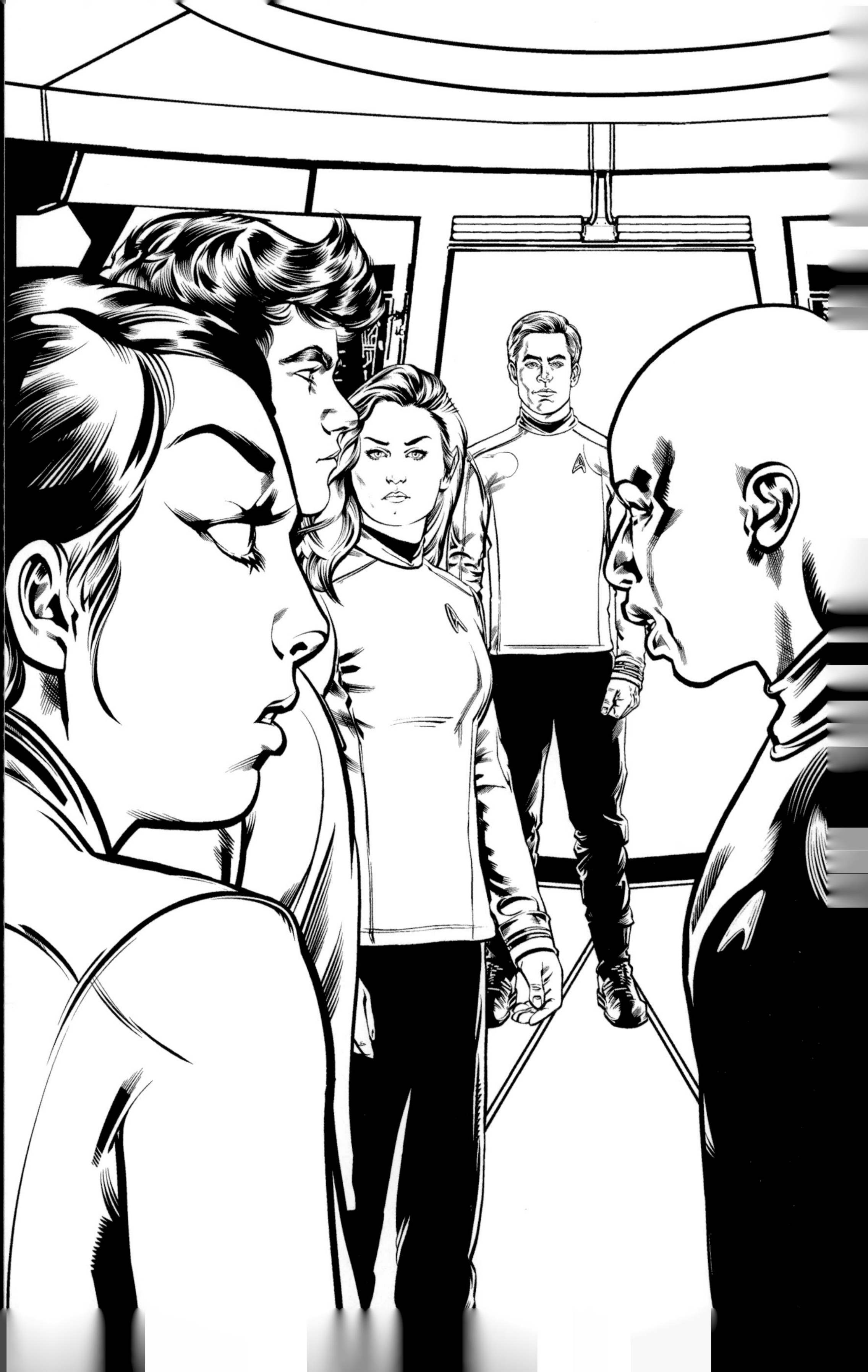

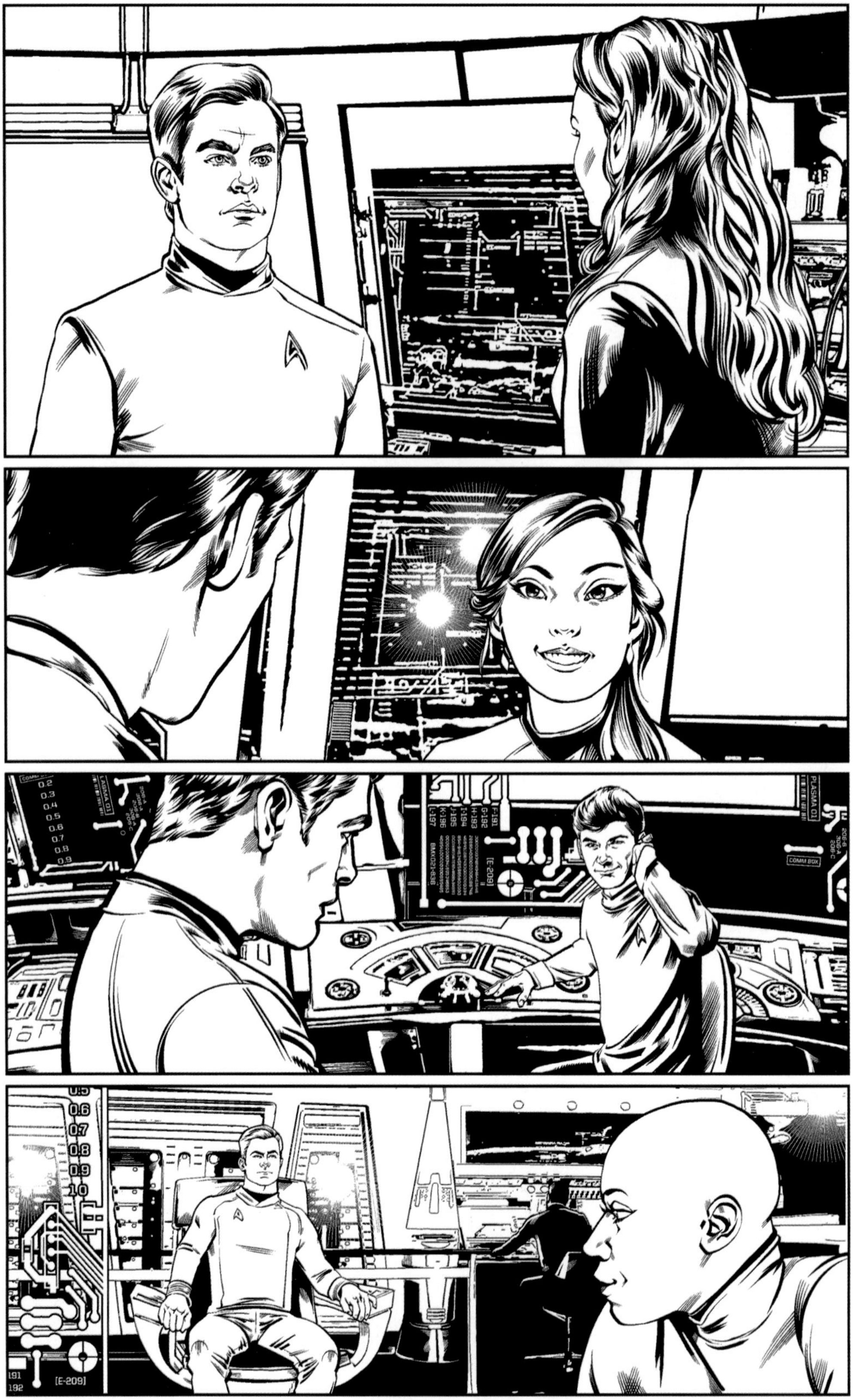
PLASMA 01
COMM BOX
[E-209]
0.6
0.7
0.8
0.9
1.0
[E-209]

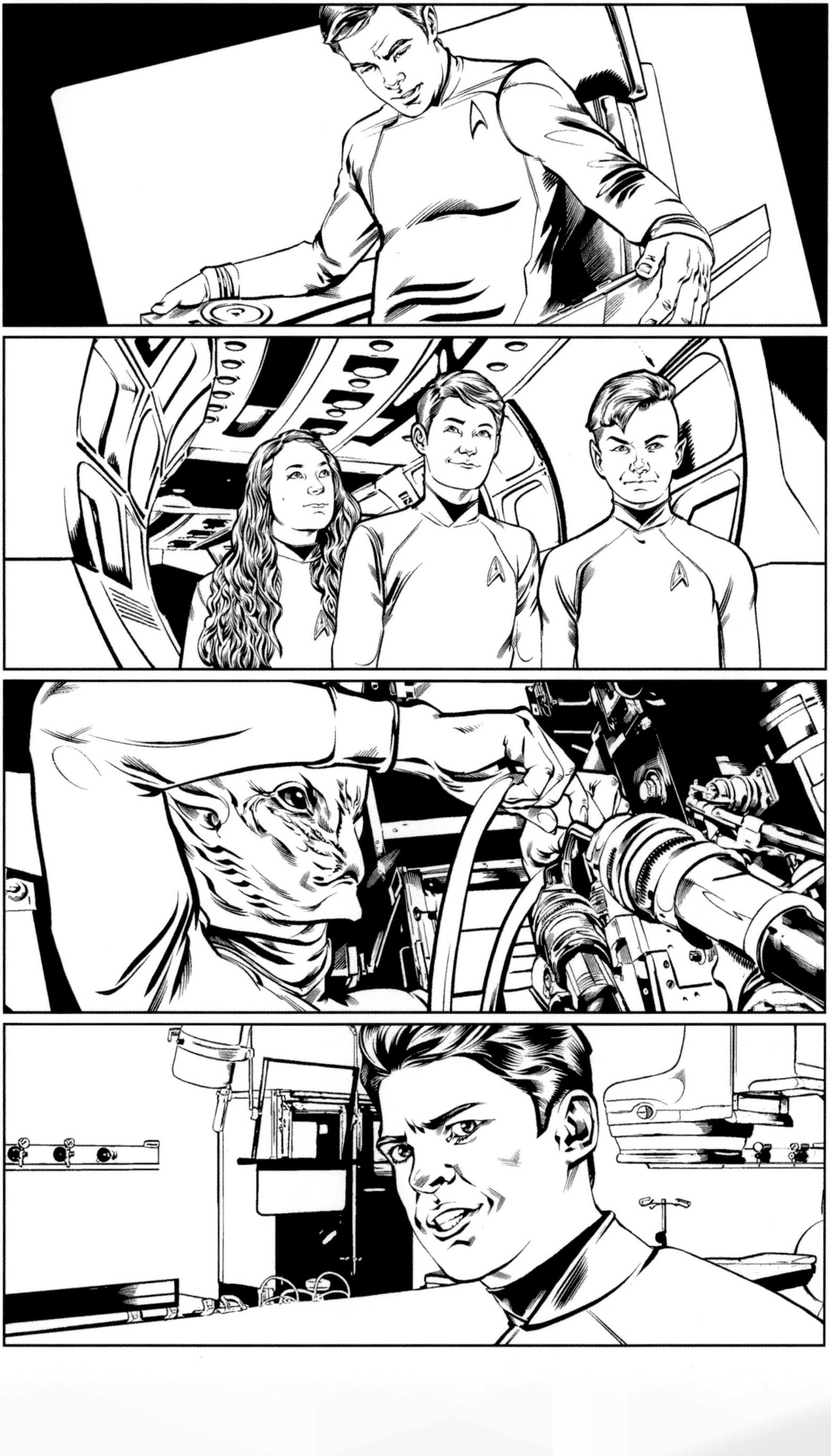

STAR TREK

BOLDLY GO